I0632729

First We Kiss

A Novel by Solange DewBerry

This book is a work of fiction. All names, places and events are fictional and are products of the author's imagination. No portion of this book may be reproduced without permission from the publisher except by a reviewer who may quote brief passages in a review.

Published in the United States by Spilled Ink Press
Newington, CT

Copyright © 2021 Tina Kane
First We Kiss

First Edition, February 2021

ISBN: 978-1-7342276-3-5

Other Books by Solange DewBerry:

You're the One for Me
Waitress in a Doughnut Shop
Meetings in Moonlight

Coming soon:
Just So You Know

Dedication

To Nesse, Red, and Ca. There's something a little magical about friendships that have lasted this long.

Appreciations

Thanks once again to my fabulous editor Liane Larocque of Edit Expert, and illustrator Sloane Moore. Special thanks to Trevann Rogers, my beta reader. Thanks for helping me see life through another's eyes.

Note to Readers:

As I've said before, it's not *out of the question* to read this as a standalone, but you might want to consider reading these in order: *You're the One for Me*, and then *A Waitress in a Doughnut Shop* and *Meetings in Moonlight* before you embark on Paul and Rhea's story *First we Kiss*. Or not, because it's such an awesome story (if I do say so myself). I leave it up to you. As long as you read them.

Best wishes,

Solange

Prologue

Berry

This is the story of how I got my third brother-in-law married off and settled into his very own happily ever after—along with his wife, of course. And let me tell you, it wasn't easy. Things, as they say, did not go according to plan.

Not that I had much of a plan.

Who am I? My name is Berry Samuels. I'm a writer of romance novels—and goodness, yes, I do love my job. I've written some fairly successful stories under my pen name, Solange DewBerry. But this isn't one of my novels. Nope—this one is a 'true story,' with just a few embellishments thrown in for when I don't know exactly what happened during the course of the actual events.

Everything I'm going to tell you is in confidence, okay? Because while the facts are pertinent to the story when Rhea (my new sister-in-law and definitely NOT her real name) first told me this stuff, she swore me to secrecy. And while I'm normally a vault when someone tells me a secret, this time it has a bearing on the story. So please, please don't repeat it. And whatever you do, don't tell Rhea I said anything. She's a dear friend in addition to being a family member, and I wouldn't hurt her for the world. And Paul, well, Paul's my brother-in-law, and very close to my husband, Moe. I'm sure you can imagine what would happen if Moe found out I was talking about him. And her. Or my involvement in fixing them up. Especially after I promised Paul I wouldn't interfere. Because I kind of swore to Moe I wouldn't.

You'd think he'd know better than to make me swear to

something like that. Or check that my fingers weren't crossed behind my back.

Okay? Are we good? Then let's go.

Twenty years ago...

"You think that was great? Watch this," Rhea crowed as she swung from bar to bar across the playscape, her grip strong and smile wide.

Paul hung upside down on another part of the structure and beamed at her achievement. "You did it," he shouted as he slipped his sneakered feet from between the rungs and dropped backward onto the spongy surface.

Rhea hooked her knee around a support bar and climbed down. "First time," she told him. Her two missing front teeth were causing her to lisp slightly. "I've been practicing and practicing."

"I knew you could do it," Paul said. "My turn. Remind me to tell you about the movie Moe let me watch last night. It was so gory..." Without a backward glance, he jumped up and began swinging himself across the length she'd just traversed in half the time it had taken her. Rhea frowned. He'd just upped the ante. Lips set with determination, she looked at her blistered palms before climbing back up and trying again, faster this time. She'd equal him, and she'd beat him if she could. Besides, she had one more thing he hadn't yet seen. She took a deep breath and kicked off.

Her arms were on fire. It seemed she wouldn't finish her second sprint across the span. She gathered the last of her strength and kicked to get herself swinging once more. She reached for the last bar, not quite touching it. She groaned and swung again, her braids with their beads clacking in her ears. This time her tingling fingertips brushed against the metal, and with a burst of determination from deep within, she managed to stretch just enough to finish her run.

She jumped down, rubbing her arms against the agony of burning muscle.

Paul nodded appreciatively. "Wow. Twice. I don't think any other girl could do that. Especially a little kid like you."

Rhea stuck out her chin. The two years he had on her grated. "Yeah, you think that was cool? Well, watch this."

Forgetting her aching arms, she clambered back up the structure until she was crouched atop it, feeling the rungs through the soles of her sneakers. She stood slowly and carefully, her arms out for balance. Rhea didn't dare look to see if Paul was suitably impressed. Taking a deep breath, she quickly moved one foot forward and then the other, sprinting across the horizontal ladder, her arms wide. Only when she had reached the other side and was holding on to a support pole for dear life did she dare look at her best friend.

Paul's face said it all. Amazement, wonder, and just the right amount of envy shown above his sunburned cheeks. "Wow," he said at last. "Didn't know you could do that. Didn't know anyone could."

Rhea scrambled down, victorious. "I've been practicing. Nana brought me here every day so I could." She quickly glanced at her nanny, sitting on a nearby bench calmly reading, her eyes looking up to scan the playground every minute or so, and smiling at her before returning to her pages.

"I'll bet I can do that, too," Paul bragged.

"It takes a lot of practice," Rhea cautioned. "I learned all about balance in my dance class. If you go to dance class, you can learn it too."

Paul made a derisive face. "Boys don't go to dance class."

3

Rhea's chin rose a notch. "There's boys there."

"I won't tell you what I think of those boys," Paul insisted.

Rhea stuck her tongue out. "They're strong boys. They have more muscles than you. They're learning to lift the girls when they run and jump at them. And they do the gigamundo leaps across the stage too. And they can balance better than you can. Ever."

"Cannot," Paul cried as he reached for the nearest bar and climbed up. "I'm not scared of anything. Just watch me."

"Hey!"

There was a shout from the sidewalk as a group of boys rolled their bikes to the playground. "Paul, why you talking to that girl?" they taunted.

Paul looked at Rhea, then back at his friends. With his pale skin, it was easy for her to see his red ears. He shrugged. "Just waiting 'till you guys got here."

She gasped. That was so unfair, but before she could say anything, Paul was standing at the top, and there wasn't anything wrong with his balance. "Hey guys, look what I can do."

"Paul, don't..." she tried to say, but the words wouldn't come. Instead, a surge of fear, envy, and hurt bubbled up, filling her, making her fingers and toes tingle uncomfortably. A tiny "You're gonna fall..." came out instead.

Paul glanced down at her and stuck out his tongue as he took another step. But then he wobbled. His left arm jerked up to try to steady himself, but he overcompensated, and he tipped in the other direction. She held her breath desperately, wishing she hadn't said what she had as she watched him flap his arms frantically. But rather than squat to hold on, he pitched over the side,

4

landing one heartbeat later in a heap on the ground.

There was a yelp as his buddies scattered. Rhea looked to Nana. She was on her phone, her calm gaze holding Rhea's with a reassuring smile. It wasn't enough. When she heard a siren in the background, Rhea unfroze and backed away from her best friend, slowly at first, before she turned and pelted away.

Ten years ago…

With his squad at his back, Paul Conrad strutted the halls of his high school. One of the guys stopped and nudged him in the ribs. "Locker, two o'clock," he mumbled.

Paul halted and looked at the girl. Despite the chaos of the school corridor, she stood quietly studying the thick textbook in her hands. Rhea, his chief rival. And no wonder—she even studied between classes. That she'd skipped two grades was no big surprise. She'd been an academic prodigy right from the start.

"I can't believe you're thinking of askin' her to the prom," Brian whispered. "Sure, she's hot, but she's so stuck up."

"Shut up," Paul replied. They'd been friends once, he and Rhea. Not that they'd spoken for years. One day she just stopped talking to him, and he'd never understood why. But he'd always noticed her, especially lately. In the last two years, she'd become a knockout.

"She'll never go," Brian persisted. "She never goes anywhere. Even if she did, she'll never put out. Ask Heather. She's a sure thing."

Paul rubbed the back of his neck. "Maybe I want more of a challenge." *Maybe I want my old friend back.*

"That's just cray, dude. Waste of your time. Besides, she's bla…"

Paul stopped his friend with a friendly fist on the collar of his tee-shirt until the smaller teen met his gaze. "Do. Not. Go. There."

Brian gulped and nodded.

The scene they were playing was as cliché as a teen movie from the 80s, making Paul want to laugh, but he had to maintain his image, so he shook his friend free with a nod.

Rhea didn't fit the mold of a brainiac any more than he did the jock that he was, with his light brown hair spiked up. Rhea was delicate. Tall and slender, her dark, ultra-curly hair reached down her back. She wore a short skirt and a white blouse. Her shoes had no heel to them, but it didn't matter as her legs were long, and the shape of them did things to his insides that he wouldn't admit to anyone.

"Man, that's not fair. No one studies between class," Brian scoffed just loud enough for anyone in the area to hear.

"Leave it," Paul said, but Brian just spouted off more nonsense. "I mean it," Paul repeated. "Leave her alone."

Brian flipped him the bird before he sauntered over to Rhea's locker and slammed it closed as he grabbed her book.

The din of the noisy hall dropped as all eyes focused on their small semicircle.

"Anyone ever tell you, you read too much?" Brian smirked as he held her book high.

"Give me that," Rhea replied under her breath as she grabbed for it.

Brian hid it behind his back. "Nu-huh. You need to go out and have some fun."

It was then Rhea looked up and saw the faces staring all around her. "Brian, give me back my book."

"I don't think so." He leaned in, his lips pursed. "Unless

you want to give me something in exchange." He puckered up and made kissy sounds.

Paul watched Rhea recoil. She tightened her fists by her sides as she took a long, deep breath. Even then, her nose wrinkled. "You're disgusting."

The other guys closed in. No one in the hall made a sound. No one made a move to stop them.

"And you're a…"

"Enough." Paul walked forward and grabbed the book from his friend and handed it back to Rhea. "Brian's a putz. Ignore him."

She took the book without meeting his gaze. "I thought you kept your posse under better control," she said breathlessly.

Paul shrugged, his fingers stroking his chin with its straggly beard. "He means well. All my boys do."

She glanced up then. Her look spoke volumes though her lips remained pressed into an unhappy line.

Paul felt his ears flame but ignored them.

"Tell your 'boys' they'd better stay away from me."

"Rhea, what I wanted to ask…" There was movement behind him, but Paul held out his hands, keeping his friends in line.

"Their trying to intimidate me won't help you win the debate next week," she said.

He shrugged again. "They mean well."

Rhea turned from him and stowed the thick book in her locker. "Yeah, right," she replied as she slammed the metal door shut and turned the lock. Their gaze met once more. "You don't believe that any more than I do."

With that, she flounced away, pushing aside the football players in her way.

Paul shoved his hands in his pockets and looked around at the ring of faces staring at him, his 'boy's, and then an outer ring of other kids, and more than one teacher.

"Move along, people. Nothing to see here," he said with his characteristic smirk—the one he'd practiced for hours. And good thing he had for it didn't match his mood at all.

Still fuming, Rhea slid into her seat. She practiced the breathing technique her yoga instructor taught her. Getting upset would just heighten an already bad mood.

"Wow, that Brian is sooo cute," her friend Cassie said as she dropped into the next seat. "I saw the whole thing. And Paul Conrad—Ohmygod, but he's so out of my league."

Rhea closed her eyes and dropped her head back. "They're both total jerks."

"Yeah, but cute jerks. I don't know how you can stand across from him during debate practice. When I just look at him, I get all gooey."

"I just do," Rhea replied. *And breathe deeply*, she added to herself. "He's just a guy."

Cassie laughed. "You're the only one in the whole school who thinks so. I don't know why you don't like Paul. He's super nice. And he's smart. If you would just get over whatever it is you…"

"I just don't like him. He's arrogant and…"

The teacher was about to close the door in anticipation of the bell when none other than Paul Conrad himself slid through the doorway. He smirked at the teacher and found his seat, book open before any more words were exchanged.

Prince Charming, he wasn't. Prince Smarmy was more like it. Rhea rubbed her hands together under her desk and then forced herself to open her trigonometry book and look down. Paul was not part of her world. Maybe he was once, but that was a long time ago. The world had changed since then. Most things, anyway.

Okay, back to the present.

So, that's their background. I snuck in that bit about Paul and the incident at school. He told me about Rhea and him in high school with their friendly competition. She never mentioned it, but I thought you should know.

Anyway, it was a long time ago. People change—I thought it important to mention that, even if they don't always change as much—or the way they think they have.

Enough from me. I'll step back—until I need to explain something else that is.

Chapter One

Rhea

Damn, it's been too long since I challenged myself this way, Rhea thought. Way too long, if her sweaty, aching body was any indication. And that was just from fifteen minutes of weight training. With the gym's trainer at her side, Rhea looked up at the Stairmaster and heaved an inward sigh. This is what she wanted, and by damned, she was going to do it. Four times a week, even if it killed her.

"I want you to do five minutes today, level two," the trainer explained. "It won't be long before you up the duration. I want you to max out around twenty minutes. You'll make up the rest of your cardio on the treadmill, elliptical, or one of the stationary bikes. Minimum of forty-five minutes total cardio, no more than an hour."

"If I live that long," she said under her breath.

The man laughed. "Everyone says that when they start. You're not in bad shape—but if you spend any more hours a day than you already do sitting on your butt, you'll start to regret it."

"I already do," she laughed.

"What do you do if you don't mind my asking?"

"I'm an attorney," she replied. "And I do sit all day when I'm not running to a meeting or to court."

"That explains why you needed such a late consult tonight."

"I put in long hours. The senior partner..." otherwise known as her mother, "...is very demanding. My caseload is sizeable. Sometimes, I have late meetings, dinner meetings, Saturday morning meetings..."

He smiled sympathetically. "I admire your dedication.

Not many women like to come here late at night."

A frisson of unease slid up her spine. She looked around. It was after ten PM. There weren't many clients at the gym, and most of them were male. "I didn't think…"

"Not to worry. The staff keeps an eye on things. We'll walk you to your car at night if you want. One of the guys here…" He jerked his chin to the lone figure working with free weights over in the corner. The man was mostly turned away from her, but she could see a full beard, hair that was long on top, pulled into a ponytail, but closely cropped in the back and on the sides. His right side, where he was working the weights, was muscular, but the left somehow seemed smaller. Probably a matter of perspective. "…is a good guy. If I or one of the other staff can't walk you out, he will."

Rhea gripped the rails of the Stairmaster. "Not necessary. I've had self-defense training, and I keep up with it."

"All good," the trainer replied. "But we take customer security seriously. I know it sucks to even think about it, but if you ever want an escort, you only have to ask. Now, let's get you started on the cardio."

Taking a deep breath, Rhea climbed the three stairs and looked around, noticing a huge structure of bars, pulleys, and weights across the vast expanse of the gym. It looked like nothing so much as an adult-sized playscape, and just as colorful as the one she used to play on. The trainer climbed on the machine next to her and explained the control panel. A moment later, Rhea began climbing the longest staircase of her life.

Within five minutes, her legs felt like jelly, and her heart was trying to burst from her chest. The trainer laughed sympathetically. "I know. I promise it'll get easier. Let's cool you down on the treadmill for about twenty minutes. I don't want you so worn out you never come back. I'm not even going to make you run—just walk at a good pace."

Breathless, Rhea nodded as she gulped from her water bottle and started on her final implement of torture for the evening.

An hour later, she let the trainer walk her to her car given she wouldn't have managed to beat off an attacker in her weakened state. Once home, Rhea stood under her shower and questioned her sanity. She still had at least an hour of work before she could turn in. Maybe, just maybe, she could bring work to the gym. If she downloaded files to her tablet, there was no reason she couldn't perch it on the treadmill's ledge. She'd seen other patrons with e-readers. She groaned as she let hot water pound her back's sore muscles. Then again, she had a pile of books by her bedside she hadn't had time to read and an even longer list on her e-reader. Maybe her gym time could be totally for her—or maybe even half the time.

No, best to focus on work and staying current with her caseload, at least for now. She'd stay away from the novels she loved, especially those with heart-wrenching emotions. Those were dangerous. Long experience taught her it was best to keep her emotions as neutral as possible.

An hour later, she fell asleep on the sofa with her latest legal brief crumpled on her chest. That was one good thing about the gym—she was so tired, for once sleep came quickly and easily.

An insistent beeping woke her at five. Rhea peeled a sheet of paper from her cheek and looked blearily around the barren living room. She never made it to bed last night. With a yawn, she pushed her hair from her face and felt around for her glasses. The beeping continued, so she stumbled across the cold wooden floor until she found her phone to shut it off.

She arrived in the office just after seven, a cup of coffee clutched in her hand along with a bag containing a whole grain muffin, her purse, computer bag, briefcase, and gym bag. The office was empty. Motion-sensitive lights flickered on as she carefully made her way down the hall to her small office. It seemed every muscle in her back and legs was aching, even those she didn't know she had. And that didn't even begin to describe the aches in her shoulders and arms.

There was a case file sitting on the desk she'd left clean the night before. "Crap, not another one," she groaned as she set her breakfast on the desk and dumped her bags behind the chair.

Rhea docked her computer and booted it up before opening the paper file. A drunk driver. A repeat offender. And the son of one of the firm's most lucrative clients. Rhea shuddered as she set it down. A perfectly horrible trifecta. She'd told her mother from day one she'd take on almost any sort of case, but she would not represent a drunk driver. Ever.

She scribbled a sticky note and set the file on the edge of her desk without reading further.

At eight o'clock, she heard activity down the hall, and Cassie, the paralegal she shared with four other lawyers, popped in with a mug of coffee she carefully set on Rhea's desk. "I thought you could use a little more java."

Rhea closed her eyes as she breathed in the rich aroma. "You are an angel here on earth. Don't let anyone tell you differently," she said before taking a careful sip. That was one thing she could say for the firm's senior partner—she insisted on good coffee for one and all.

Cass laughed. "I thought you might need it. I saw your mother drop that file here before she left last night." She glanced over her shoulder before turning back into the room. "I think she waited until she knew you were gone."

Rhea sighed. "Do me a favor and return it to her?" She took another sip of coffee. "There don't happen to be any doughnuts in the break room, are there?"

Her oldest friend laughed. "Not telling. You're the one who insisted on this health kick. If you want a doughnut, you're going to have to walk down the hall to find out on your own."

Rhea groaned. "Don't even joke about extra steps today. I nearly killed myself at that gym last night." She shook her head. "And here I was thinking I was still in pretty good shape. Nothing like watching a bunch of twenty-somethings skipping around in spandex to set me straight." And it was true. There had been other women there when she started her workout, but she was the lone woman at the end of her session. In fact, it was just her, the trainer, and that bearded guy by the time she left.

"Like you're not still a twenty-something," Cassie scoffed.

"I'm feeling like a sixty-something right now. Everything hurts."

Cassie sat in Rhea's sole guest chair. "Any cute guys there?"

Rhea shrugged. The trainer qualified as cute, but he'd sported a wedding ring and was therefore off-limits. She hadn't looked at anyone else. The bearded guy had been too far away to see. "I didn't notice any."

"You will. I'm sure you were smoking in your gym clothes, too."

Rhea laughed. "Yeah, baggy tee shirt and my old sweats. And I had my hair up. I doubt anyone looked at me twice."

"You ought to leave your hair down. It's gorgeous."

"So says the girl with stick-straight hair. I would have killed for hair like yours when we were in high school. No way was my mom going to let me get a chemical relaxer."

Cassie shook her head. "And your curls and volume are just what I was dreaming of. You leave it down and see if the guys don't come around. And I'm getting you spandex. You need to flaunt your stuff."

"I need to shape my stuff up first," Rhea shot back with a grin. "Then, we'll talk spandex."

There were footsteps in the hall, and Cassie shot to her feet. She reached for the file on the corner of Rhea's desk when an elegantly coifed older woman came to the door. There wasn't room for a third in the small office.

"Morning, Mom," Rhea said.

Cassie's grin faded. "Ma'am."

Marion squeezed her size four figure into the room as Cassie tried to ooze past her. Marion plucked the manila folder from Cassie's grip. "I see you saw the file."

Rhea closed her eyes with a deep breath before she opened them again. *Think pleasant thoughts.* "Yes." She pulled folder after folder from her briefcase. "I'm afraid that is not part of the law I am conversant on. And my caseload is already over the limit we discussed when I joined the firm. It's higher than anyone else's…"

Not taking her eyes from her daughter, Marion gave a curt smile. "Cassie, I'm certain you have other things to do."

That one scurried away, leaving Rhea to face the fire-breathing dragon all alone.

"Mom, I told you when I started, I will not represent drunks. Excuse me, alleged drunks. Thieves, wife-beaters, murderers, and rapists—yeah, maybe. Corporate criminals—our best clients. But not drunks. Never DUIs. Remember, you're the one who asked me to focus on estates and wills when I was in law school…"

"As a favor to me…"

Rhea shook her head. "You know how I feel about drunk drivers. Especially repeat offenders."

"But that was so long ago. And Brice was just over the legal limit…" She held out the file as if it were a gift. "A smart lawyer like you should be able to…"

"It wasn't his first offense. And he failed the breathalyzer."

"He was just a boy when he was first arrested," her mother said with a smile. "He's barely a man now."

"Mom, he's twenty-nine. He's got an MBA. By some miracle, he's got a wife, a house, and a fancy car. He drinks too much and doesn't want to be responsible for his actions. I'm not taking this case."

Her mother's smile faded. "Your refusing won't look good come review time."

Rhea closed her eyes. Nothing she did was going to look good come review time despite her exorbitant billable hours and high client satisfaction rating.

"I don't have anyone else who can fit this in. I'm going to have to give this case to Dougherty and Sons. I just hope our client doesn't decide to give the rest of his business to them as well."

Rhea's email pinged, and she glanced at the display. She pressed her lips together. "You could take it yourself."

Her mother specialized in looking affronted, and this moment was no exception. "Me? I haven't taken a drunk driving case in years. I wouldn't know what to do with it. You know my specialty is corporate law. I can't believe you'd even suggest such a thing."

"My apologies," Rhea said with as much sincerity as she could muster. She stood, her fingers flicking through files until she found the one she wanted. "Now, if you'll excuse me, I have clients waiting in the small conference room. She smiled, brushed past her mother, and hurried down the hall and around the corner before she stopped and blew out a relieved breath. But this wasn't the end of it, not by a long shot. The Dougherty's wouldn't want that case any more than she did.

Chapter Two

Paul

He winced as he shrugged on his shirt in the surgeon's office, not that he let her see. No one was allowed to see his pain. "So, Doc, I'm ready to go back to work, right?" He buttoned up the flannel placket and grinned at the woman. "Don't be afraid of giving me the good news. Nothin' scares me."

She shook her head. "I told you to cut back at the gym. You're pushing it, Paul. If you don't let this heal properly, you're going to be permanently sidelined. As it is, I can't see you climbing ladders with hundred pound loads ever again. There was just too much damage."

"Shit." He winced for good that time. "Sorry, Doc. Couldn't help myself."

She laughed and shook her head. "Is 'shit' the best you can do? Most guys get news like that, and I hear a heck of a lot worse."

Paul laughed. "No offense, Doc, but you look too much like my mom for me to say what I'm really thinking."

"So, she's a good looking, middle-aged woman too, is she?" The doctor gave him a broad wink. "No offense taken. I want you to cut back at the gym. Still work it, but less weight. More repetitions are okay, to a limit. But it if hurts, stop. And I mean it. You damage that shoulder again, and even I'm not good enough to fix it. You really need to go to PT instead."

He ducked his head as he pulled his sweatshirt over his shirt. "How do you know I'm working out?" he asked.

She flicked her pen at him. "Your right shoulder. Much more developed than the left—more than it was the last time I saw you. And I'm seeing strain around the scar. Not good, my friend. Don't make me call the gym and have them rescind your membership."

"No, ma'am. I'll behave." He looked over her shoulder at what she was typing into her laptop. "So, you're telling the insurance company what?"

"That I'm keeping you on disability until your next visit, which will be in one month. We'll reevaluate then."

"Another month of sitting around doing nothing."

"I didn't say that. I think you can go back to your woodshop. I think that would be good for your head as much as your shoulder. No more than two-three hours a day. And no lifting over forty pounds with that left arm, and nothing over your head."

He could feel the smile in every part of his body. "Yeah?"

She returned this smile. "Yeah. After all, how am I going to get that handmade rocker you promised me in lieu of your share of my bill?"

"Three hours a day. And you won't tell the insurance company on me?"

She made another note before she looked up with a grin. "Let's call it occupational therapy, shall we?"

"Doc, I haven't said this, but you're the best." He kissed her cheek with a noisy smack.

"The things I do to get handsome young men to kiss me." She sighed dramatically. "Now scoot. I'll see you in a month, and I want pictures of my chair at that time, hear me?"

"Loud and clear."

Ten minutes later, Paul walked into the late summer sunshine. The cool air felt good on the parts of his face that weren't covered by his beard. He'd started growing t right after the accident. It had been too hard to shave one-handed, so he grew it as a testament to his idleness. On the day he was declared once again fit, he'd treat himself to a barbershop shave and start to look like himself once again.

Pulling out his phone, he dialed his eldest brother.

Moe answered right away. "Hey Pauly, what's going on? Everything go okay with the doc?"

"Still sidelined, but she's okayed me to start working in the shop. I'm going to head over there after I grab some coffee."

"Hey, that's great. She set a limit for you?"

Paul sighed. "You had to ask."

"I need to get you healthy again. I can't keep my eye on you all the time, but I can limit how much time you spend in the shop."

"Four hours a day. Weight limits, but with what I'm doing these days, I won't need to. I'll get you or one of the other guys to help if I work on anything big."

"Let me guess. She said two hours," Moe guessed.

Paul sighed again. "Three."

"It's still great news. I'll call the guys and Mom. Berry's been wanting a reason to make a big meal, so we'll celebrate tonight. You want to bring someone?"

There was that awkward pause that always came up when Moe asked that question. "I'm, um, not seeing anyone right now."

"What? You've got dozens of numbers stashed on your phone. Call one of them. I promise we won't judge."

Paul scrubbed the back of his neck with his free hand. "I haven't been seeing much of anyone for the past few months."

Moe clucked sympathetically. "Poor baby. Not like the old days, huh?"

Paul laughed. "What can I say? I like to be on top, and

with my arm out of commission, I can't use my best moves."

"Not that I'm bragging or anything, but there's more to life than being on top," Moe reminded him.

"Oh, shut up. All you married guys, you don't know how good you have it."

Moe laughed again. "I think, little bro, that we know exactly how good we've got it. I highly recommend the institution."

"Yeah, well, easier said than done. I don't know any women I like enough to marry."

"You poor bastard," Moe laughed. "And to think I used to be jealous of you and how easy you used to pick up women. Kind of like how things stack up now a whole lot better."

Paul could practically hear his brother grin.

"I'll call Berry. She'll let Annie and Jenny know. You call Sammy and see if he wants to bring a date. Hell, maybe he's got someone to fix you up with.

"Shut up. You know Sammy's stuck on that woman from the laundromat, and she won't give him the time of day. What time you want me?"

"Six. Bring beer. We're having burgers."

It was Paul's turn to laugh. "We always have burgers."

"You're welcome." Moe hung up, but his laugher rang n Paul's ears for hours.

Berry

In my mind, this is about the time when things real y took off for Paul. For the first time since his accident, he was starting to feel good about stuff again.

The accident? I need to tell you about that.

Paul works for my husband, Moe. Conrad Brothers Construction. Paul was the foreman on a restoration of a house in our neighborhood. About six months before this story started, Paul was heading home from a job site. He'd just gotten a new truck, and it was all tricked out (his words, not mine). His ladders were in racks on the roof, and a bunch of power equipment was in the bed.

He was sitting at a red light on a road that went north-south. His light turned green, so he started across, but then WHAM, he was broadsided by a guy who claimed he couldn't see the light because the sun was blinding him. Paul got hit right in the cab. The truck and all the equipment in it was wrecked. Paul was wrecked. If not for the airbags, he'd be dead. As it was, he had whiplash, a concussion, and his shoulder was messed up to the point he needed three surgeries to fix it. This is the same shoulder he'd broken as a kid when he fell off the monkey bars.

My Moe and all the other brothers, not to mention my mother-in-law Rosemary, and my sister-in-law, Jenny, were distraught. And me—I had to stay calm for all of them, meanwhile, I was a mess inside.

That's all pretty bad, right, but that's not all. The other driver turned out to be drunk.

See, here's the thing. My husband's father was killed by a drunk driver thirty years ago. So, to come so close again, well, it really shook everyone up.

The good news is that Paul was healing. There was no question the other driver was at fault, no matter how you look at it, but he was fighting us in court—wanted us to drop the charges, so he had a clean record. And in addition to that, the guy's insurance had lapsed, so it was just Paul's company trying to sue the jackass, and he was stalling for everything he was worth. So, we were all doing what we could to support Paul in the meanwhile. He wouldn't come live with any of us, and he had no income, so we helped pay for a small apartment. We knew he'd repay us someday—that wasn't the problem. The problem was keeping his spirits up while he wasn't working so he could win this stupid court case. And in the meanwhile, the other driver was shopping around for a lawyer, so everything was taking too long. It was crazy, and trust me, I know crazy. As I've mentioned, I'm a writer, and I've needed to come up with some pretty complicated plots for my stories, not to mention some, er, interesting characters. Just ask Moe or Joey and Jenny about my characters. Or actually, maybe you shouldn't.

All I can say is, if I'd thought of this convoluted craziness as a plot of one of my stories, I don't think anyone would believe me.

And if you knew me and some of what I've experienced in the last few years, you'd find that about as comical as I do.

So, speaking of comical and characters—I was working on my latest romance. It was a two-dogs-one-bone sort of story, where the hero—a cop I was calling Sal (until I could come up with another name for him) and a lady-lawyer I had yet to name (which was giving me fits, considering how far along in the story I was), were working on opposite sides of a case. Each of them was crazy attracted to the other, but given their work relationship, they were trying to resist the inevitable. They were both proud professionals who wanted to put their careers before their private lives.

I was trying something new with this story—expanding my horizons. Like all my best heroes, Sal was loosely based on one of the Conrad brothers. In this case, it was Paul, given that he was a little more sensitive than the rest of the brothers—a good trait for a detective, I thought. And my heroine—this is where the trying something new came in—I made her a black woman. I wanted to add a note of

23

additional societal tension between them as well as their respective careers. I know, not terribly original. See, the thing is, my youngest brother-in-law has been secretly in love with an East-Asian woman for years. I thought about making my heroine the same, but then Sammy would get suspicious. And it's much too late to change that now. But I was nervous about portraying a young, professional black woman authentically, and it kept me up more than a few nights.

Anyway, I was working on the story and had just about reached the point where the two of them were going to cross the line and jump into bed with one another.

Do you have any idea how hard it is to write a love scene where one of the characters has no name? I mean, I had nothing. And none of the stand-in names I came up with was even marginally good enough. I was in trouble with this book. Big. Trouble.

Chapter Three

Rhea

The trainer was right. Within a week, she was up to ten minutes on the dreaded Stairmaster, and the treadmill wasn't quite as bad as the name would imply. And she found she could balance her tablet on both and read briefs during her cardio. The rest of her strength-training routine left her cringing at the techno music pumped into the gym.

She was beginning to recognize faces there, responding to the occasional friendly nod, but people kept to themselves, other than the guy the trainer had pointed out. He seemed to be friends with everyone, spotting guys on the bench press, chatting up the older ladies at the disinfectant stations. No matter what time of day or night she went, he was always there.

He nodded and smiled at her, but there was something about him that made her turn away. He was handsome— as much as she could see of his face. And he was fit. Climbing the tall Stairmaster one night, she got a good look at the scar on his shoulder, which explained his lopsided appearance. Despite that flaw, his body was magnificent— to the point she found it intimidating. And it was clear he was a gym rat through and through. Even if she was interested, which she emphatically told herself she was not, her mother would have a bird if Rhea were to bring someone like him home. He was clearly 'not her type.' But even not being her type didn't stop her from staring at him while he worked out.

The thing was, he was good with people. He smiled and joked and helped everyone who asked for it, and all with good cheer. She'd never in her life been that easy with people. It was a damned alluring trait, up above the fit body, the gorgeous smile, the shiny brown eyes, and thick, light brown hair…

Rhea blinked hard and returned her gaze to the tablet before her. *Focus*, she commanded herself. She had her weekly briefing the next morning, where the staff reported out on their cases to receive guidance and support from the senior attorneys on their teams. It was more like a public lashing. Signing with the firm, she never expected that being the daughter of the founding partner would open her to such scorn and criticism. But the others in the firm took their cue from Marion, and if Marion was in a derisive mood, everyone was.

She felt her heart begin to pound erratically. Rhea slowed her speed and focused on her breathing. No good ever came to her from getting emotional. That was her lot. She'd have to prove herself no matter where she worked. Her mother often reminded her that no one ever handed anyone anything that was worth much in the long run. You had to earn your own way, form your own reputation. A black woman in their profession had to work twice as hard as anyone else to be respected. Being half-black didn't mean half the disadvantages.

So, she'd prove herself. To herself, to her mother, to all those nasty, conniving, colluding…

The Stairmaster slowed to cool-off mode as she met her time target, and she had to grasp the handrails to keep from tumbling off. She glanced up as she felt someone's gaze upon her, but when she looked around, no one was looking. She pressed the stop button. A moment later, she took a long drink from her water bottle. She was feeling self-conscious as she was wearing her new, revealing workout clothes for the first time.

She took another drink and stepped off the machine

and scanned the row of treadmills for one that was in a less busy area. She started it up and set her time limit before she refocused on the case file on her tablet.

Five minutes later, someone started the machine to her right.

"Hey."

Oh crap. There was an entire row of empty treadmills that time of night. Why did he have to take the one next to hers? Rhea nodded politely and returned to her reading.

"What's so interesting?" the man asked. He had too wide a smile beneath thinning hair. "Sexy book? I hear lots of you girls like to read those while working out."

She turned to him. "Deposition. Child custody case."

"Whoa. You some kind of legal secretary then? Someone as pretty as you couldn't be a lawyer."

"I am a lawyer," she replied, not lifting her gaze from her reading. "I must have missed the memo on looks."

"It's just that you're so young," he persisted. "And pretty. I never met a pretty lawyer before."

It was on the tip of her tongue to tell him he hadn't actually met her when the treadmill on her left started. "Hey Ray. You're not bothering the other customers again, are you?"

Rhea looked up to find the bearded man to her right. His scarred shoulder was up front and scary under his tank top.

"Just making conversation," Ray replied with a friendly grin. "Not too many folks this late at night. Got to talk to someone."

"I think the lady's trying to read," the other man replied. "Hey, how about I help you with your crunches. Remember, you asked me last week?"

Ray glanced at Rhea and then looked back at the stranger as if he were thinking hard. "Yeah, sure." He smiled. "Sorry to bother you."

"No problem." She smiled. "I've got court in the morning. Need to get ready."

He frowned. "Trying to get the mother custody? It seems the mothers always win."

Rhea pressed her lips tightly. "I'm doing my best to make sure the child's interests are protected. Neither of her parents are fit, so we're doing our best to place the little girl with her grandfather."

Ray looked confused for a moment. "Oh, yeah. Okay. What's best for the kid. I get it." He stopped his machine and stepped away.

The bearded man hesitated. "Don't work too hard. You look like you're burning the candle at both ends."

Rhea met the man's steady gaze. "I really do need to prepare."

He gave her a warm smile. "No worries. Enjoy your workout. And make sure Mike or one of the other guys walks you out tonight. There were some kids hanging around when I came in. They were still looking for trouble when I checked a few minutes ago."

"I'll keep that in mind," she replied. "Thanks again."

He grinned, his eyes crinkling at the corners. So, maybe he was a little older than she thought. "Good luck with your case. I hope the kid wins."

She smiled. "Appreciate that. I do too."

He looked like he wanted to say something else, but he stopped himself, nodded, and followed Ray to the other side of the gym.

Ten minutes later, she was aware of someone looking at her again. Ray was off doing reps with his back to her, but the other man, the one with the beard, was scanning the place as if he were keeping an eye on things.

She shivered. His voice, his manner wasn't what she'd

expected. Nor his kindness. Maybe she'd been too quick to judge. It wasn't the first time. She looked up again, this time to find him looking at her. He gave her a wink before turning his attention back to Ray.

Then again, maybe she wasn't. As if she needed one more thing to be paranoid about.

Chapter Four

Paul

He whistled as he unlocked his workshop. He hadn't been back in the months since he'd been injured, and opening the doors was like getting a hug from an old friend.

Wood shavings were undisturbed. The half-built hope chest Berry asked him to make for Mattie was waiting for the lid to be fitted. He'd loved making this for his niece, imagining it as a toy box until she was old enough to think about growing up. He'd lined it with cedar for the scent as well as the bug-repelling qualities. As it was heavy—he'd need help to finish it. In the meanwhile, he picked up a broom and swept the mess he'd left six months before.

He needed to get his chops back before he attempted anything difficult. He'd need to feel confident with his equipment. Bad enough he'd have a bum shoulder the rest of his life—he couldn't afford to lose any fingers.

Emptying the dustpan in the garbage, Paul pulled a few design books off the shelf, including the notebook he'd assembled of pieces he'd seen and admired. Doc wanted a rocking chair. That would have to wait. What about a pair of candlesticks? Yeah, for that pretty woman from the gym. The lawyer. She looked familiar, but he was reluctant to make too many guesses as to her identity. It would ruin the fun of getting to know her, which he fully intended to do. He'd seen her from the first time she'd come in those doors, looking apprehensive and resolved. Over the past month, he'd psyched out her attendance pattern and matched his own to be there when she was. He didn't want to think too carefully about the reasons why. He'd never stalked a woman before in his life and didn't want to start now.

Whatever her name was, she was stunning. Her complexion was gorgeous and looked smooth as satin. But it was her eyes that captivated him. They were light brown, almost green, and almond-shaped. He could see the changes in her figure since she started working out. She was following the trainer's program religiously. He'd have to tell her to modify it, introduce some changes from time to time lest she become bored and quit, or work certain muscles to the exclusion of others.

He'd tell her if she let him. She was either painfully shy or very aloof. He didn't want to think badly of her, so he decided on the former. She'd been genuinely distressed when old Ray interrupted her. From the intensity with which she read her tablet, he gathered she was dedicated. He'd heard lawyers, particularly young ones, needed to work hard. Not that the profession was a particular favorite of his. Look at how his mother's attorney had screwed her over when his dad died. Most of the settlement money went to pay the attorney's fees. There'd been precious little left over for a widow with five small boys. He'd chosen his lawyer with a lot more care but wasn't fooling himself about any benefits he might see in the end. He just wanted to see that guy who hit him pay for his mistake. Maybe get him some help, so he'd never again get into a driver's seat when he'd been drinking.

So, that pretty lady was burning the candle at both ends. He thought for a few minutes, smiled to himself, and then began to sketch.

Rhea

She arrived in the office late the next afternoon. She'd spent most of the day at court, conferring with counsel representing each of the parents as well as a social worker and the mediator. In the end, the court had agreed that the paternal grandfather, a fairly young widower, receive sole custody of the toddler, with monitored parental visitation rights to be reviewed six months hence. The conditions required each of the parents to receive counseling to help them cope with anger, as well as to acquire job skills in the hopes that one or both might be ready for custody at some point in the future. This was the one pro bono case the firm allowed her for the year, and she was pleased with the outcome, particularly as she'd worked on it primarily on her own time.

Cassie gave her a hug when Rhea told her of the outcome, but her smile faded. "Your mother wants to see you."

Rhea contained the urge to roll her eyes. "Another new case?"

Cassie shook her head. "Same one."

Her eyes closed tightly. "I cannot, will not, take a drunk driving client. My integrity and honor may be challenged by some of my cases, but I will not do that."

"Hang in there," Cassie whispered. "She's seen you."

Rhea's shoulders sagged. "So much for my buzz," she said softly. But she straightened her shoulders and turned with a smile. "Hey, Mom. I resolved the pro bono case. The parents agreed to the terms, and the grandfather's jumping with joy to raise his granddaughter."

Marion smiled tightly. "Have Stu put it on our website. The firm needs more good-news stories to tell."

"If you have any more pro bono work..."

"You've done your good deed for the year, missy. We need to talk."

Rhea turned to Cassie. "Tell Stu I'll share the details later. I'll do the write-up, and he can post it tonight."

She turned back to her mother. "Your office or mine?"

Two hours later, Rhea was working her frustration off on the treadmill. She knew she was going too fast. Her shoulders still ached from having set the weights too high on the pull-down machine earlier that night. She'd rushed through most of her routine and was now running. Reading was beyond her as she stared at the suspended television screens before her, trying to make sense of the subtitles on four different inane programs, and succeeded with none. She thought of her conversation that afternoon, and her blood pressure spiked yet again.

Her mother's opening move had been to report the other firm wasn't going to take the case and that if theirs did not, the client would move *all* his business to another firm. Rhea had proposed to let them carry out on their bluff. Marion was not inclined to agree.

Next were threats, and when those did not work, there were promises of a promotion and a bonus regardless of the outcome of the case. Rhea politely declined and suggested another firm be asked, perhaps one with fewer scruples.

Marion, at last, let go with her broadside. She was getting tired of being the senior-most partner in the firm and was thinking of merging with another firm of similar size and reputation. It would mean more money, more prestige, more pressure—as if any of that was an inducement to Rhea to take the case.

"We need to show them how versatile we are—you are. They know you're in line for a partnership, but they don't want a partner who's been stuck in the corner doing wills and probate."

"Wills and probate are steady business," Rhea pointed out. "Not glamorous, but they pull in more and steadier income than any other part of the firm."

"But it's not sexy," her mother countered. "Boring. Don't you want to do something more exciting, more challenging?"

"If exciting and challenging means helping a drunk keep his license, then no. I get precious little enough sleep every night to want to ruin what little I do get," she countered.

Her mother's eyes glared. "It's time you started to pull your own weight. Support me in this. I don't ask much of you…"

Rhea fell into her chair. "Pull my own weight." She stared at her mother. "What's the average caseload in this office? You don't know? Okay, I'll tell you. It's about one hundred clients on average per lawyer per year. Of those, perhaps twenty are active cases of various sorts. That's the average. Most have far less. You've given me over one hundred and fifty clients, and I have at least thirty pending cases, not including the pro bono work."

Her mother's glare turned into something else. But it wasn't pity, or sorrow. It wasn't horror. It was perhaps resentment about hearing the truth, which fueled Rhea's anger all the more.

"So, given the caseload I'm carrying, the hours I'm putting in, which exceeds eighty on a slow week, even if I was inclined to endanger myself and every other driver in this city by taking on and winning this case, how exactly do you think I'd find the time to adequately represent this client?

Marion's lips pressed firmly. "I didn't know…"

Rhea took a deep breath to calm herself. "The hell you didn't. You're the one who assigned me those cases. You get the reports. And I'm doing a damned fine job. No one's complained about me—not one of them, and you know it."

"I'll redistribute your cases…"

"Give it to someone else. I will not take that case."

Marion rose from her desk chair and circled her desk. She leaned against it and folded her arms to glare down at her daughter. "You will."

"I will not. For what little conscience I still have, I will not..."

"There's no place for a conscience in this law firm," her mother snapped.

Rhea thought hard before saying, "Then maybe there's no room for me in this firm."

Her mother folded her arms. "If you walk out on me, I'm calling in your debt."

Oh, so now she was going to play dirty. "I've been paying off my college loans to you every month. I haven't missed one. You're the one who proposed to fund me, so I wouldn't have the bank's interest rates." She narrowed her eyes. "Is this why you did it? So you'd have leverage when you needed it?"

"No, of course not," Marion sputtered.

"But you threaten me with it now."

Her mother sat in the chair beside her. "That was unfair of me."

Rhea sat silently.

"I need you to take this case."

Rhea shook her head. "You know I can't, and you know the reason why."

"You haven't seen that boy in years. What would it hurt? He'd never know."

"It's not because of Paul," she said. And that wasn't all of it. She had her own principles she needed to honor. "It's just not right."

"Everyone is entitled to counsel," Marion said. "Your father believed that."

"Leave him out of this. He'd support me if he were here."

"But he's not," Marion countered. "He's lying in a hospital bed miles from here, and there he'll stay. If you won't do this for me, do this for him."

"Daddy would never…"

"You do want to continue to visit him, don't you?"

Rhea's mouth dropped open. "First you threaten me financially, now you're telling me you're going to prevent me from visiting my father?"

Marion pressed her lips closed.

"Tell me you're not saying that. I can't believe this case is that important to you or to the firm."

"If we don't take this case, the client will pull from us, and he'll take others with him. Yes, it is that important."

"Then, take the case yourself," Rhea threw back at her.

Marion shook her head. "I have too many other delicate matters to attend to. You take it, try to get the plaintiff to settle for a reasonable amount out of court. Try to talk our client's son into being practical…"

"I can't."

"Just read the file," Marion asked. "That's all I ask. Just read it. Don't tell me no until then."

Rhea closed her eyes.

"I won't call in the loans. And you can still visit your father…"

"You are going to owe me for this." The words were the fiercest she'd ever heard coming from her mouth. "You want me to sell my soul for this case, for this firm? You'd better come up with something that will make this worth my while."

"A partnership. Before you're thirty."

Rhea stood. "Not even close. If you're willing to barter away my soul, then I want something else. Something that's going to come from what's left of *yours*."

She grabbed the file, strode to the door, and slammed it

36

on her way out.

Chapter Five

Rhea

She flew into her office to grab her purse and gym bag, leaving her computer, briefcase, and the file behind. There was no way she'd read the damned thing until morning. No, she needed the afternoon off. The firm owed her being able to leave while it was still light out. Damn it, for once she should be able to go to the gym and leave at a decent enough hour that she wouldn't need an escort to get to her car.

Once there, she wiped the sweat from her brow and thought hard. Rhea promised to read the brief and refuse the case once and for all. But there was no use fooling herself. She'd have to do it. Her mother had threatened, and there was no reason to believe she wouldn't carry out her threats.

All of Rhea's money was tied up in her house. Her parents had loaned her well over a hundred thousand dollars for school, and much of it was still outstanding. If her mother called in the loan, she'd be bankrupt. And out of a job with a poor reputation for refusing to take on cases.

Worse was the threat of losing access to her father. They hadn't been close when she was growing up, but she'd been closer to him than her mother—he being a bit older and semi-retired before his stroke landed him in the nursing facility two years before. Rhea visited every weekend, spending a few hours talking to him, reading to him, or just holding his hand if he were sleeping. The thought of losing that—that had finally changed her mind.

Her face was wet, and it seemed to be more than sweat

rolling down her cheeks. She wiped at them and promptly tripped, flying off the treadmill to the floor behind.

"Ow ow ow owwie ouch," she moaned as she tried to rise from her sprawl.

"Take it easy," a deep voice said behind her.

"What? I just tripped." She scrambled to her feet, only to go down a moment later. "Crap."

There was a sympathetic chuckle behind her. "I can help you with one hand. My shoulder's not up to lifting you. Seems your ankle might have gotten the worst of it." The bearded man reached over and shut off the treadmill.

Rhea made her way to her hands and knees and then gingerly rose, favoring her left ankle. "If you could just help me over to that chair, I can rest it a while."

She looked up and saw the man. His eyes held sympathy that made her ache all the more. She nodded at his shoulder. "You know pain."

He grasped her arm and slung it around his neck, and then gathered her to him to lead her over to the small conference area. "I know pain," he affirmed.

"You shouldn't do this. I'm all sweaty and disgusting," she complained to his laugh.

"As if I'm not?" he replied. "Come on, just a few more steps. I'll take a look at your ankle. I'll bet it's not as bad as it seems."

"It feels pretty bad," she said between her teeth as he lowered her into a chair.

"If it were broken, you wouldn't be able to say that much," he countered with a grin as he pulled a chair over and sat across from her. "I'm just going to lift your leg onto my lap, okay? No sudden moves. If it hurts, just scream." He gave her a wink.

She gasped as he gingerly lifted it and lay her leg across his lap. "Okay so far?"

She gulped and nodded and chanced a look. Miraculously, it hadn't fallen off. In fact, it was hard to see anything wrong with it.

The guy untied her sneaker, prompting another whimper. His gaze met hers. "Should I stop?"

She shook her head. "I was expecting that to feel worse than it did."

"Plan for the worst, hope for the best," he said with a chuckle as he eased her sneaker off and started probing with his fingers. "This hurt?" He gave her ankle a bit of a wiggle.

"Ow, yes," she gasped.

He did something else. "And that?"

"Not so much," she admitted.

"How about this?" and he ran his finger up the sole of her foot.

She laughed. "That just tickles."

He grinned. "Good. Definitely not broken. It's starting to swell. I've got an ace bandage in my bag. Let me tape it up. I think you just need ice and rest. And if you come tomorrow, use the recumbent bike for your cardio and stay off the stairs and treadmill until the swelling is down and it feels better."

"I don't know if I want to come back," she said, biting her lip.

"After all your hard work? Don't give up now. Modify. That's what I had to do..."

He somehow managed to stand without jostling her foot and set it gently on his chair. "I'll be right back. Don't go anywhere."

"Yeah, right," she said as she bent to get a closer look at her ankle. "Of all the stupid things..."

"Accidents happen," he said over his shoulder. "Be right back."

Rhea allowed herself the pleasure of watching him walk away. His tank top fit like a second skin, leaving nothing to the imagination about his chest and belly. They were the very definition of sculpted. His rear though was a masterpiece beneath his grey sweatpants. Rhea silently wondered if a quarter would bounce on his butt should she ever get the chance.

At least I'm not so hurt I don't notice a fine man when he's in front of me. As if that would do any good. No gym rats. Not with my life right now. Though it would give Mom a stroke if I were to bring someone like him home with me. And she owes me. Don't know if I'm going to throw that favor away on something so trivial...

He was back before her thoughts had played themselves out. "Have you ever had your ankle taped before?" he asked.

Rhea shook her head.

"It's not hard. Just around and over. You want to create some support and to try to hold the swelling down, but mostly it's there to remind you not to put too much weight on it. Take it off before you shower, and then put it on again after. Sleep with it and wear it for a few days. You'll get all sorts of sympathy, have all the cute little boy lawyers do your walking for you."

"There aren't any little boy lawyers in my office," she gasped as he lifted her foot back into his lap. "I'm not sure about this."

He turned brown eyes upon her. "You take care of it now and let it heal, or it will get worse and take longer to get better. Take it from me—you don't want to mess around with this or you'll be sorry. So, let's just sit for a half hour or so, until you know you can get home on your own."

Rhea sat and watched him. "Thank you," she said as he tucked an end in—his fingers against her skin. "I really do appreciate it. I had just the weirdest day. It figures something crappy would happen."

"How about you tell me all about it? You can sit right here. I'll run next door and get us a couple of coffees?"

His smile was so guileless—Rhea didn't have the heart to turn him down. "I don't want to interrupt your workout more than I have."

He shrugged. "I was just about done. I put in a few hours in my workshop earlier, so I need to take it easy on my shoulder. So. How do you take your coffee?"

"I ought to buy…"

"Next time," he said with a kind laugh. "You need to keep that ankle up a little bit longer."

"You don't mind? I can just hobble to my car and go home. I don't need a babysitter."

"I insist. I want to check the swelling in a bit. That'll let us know if you need to see a doctor. So, let me guess, given you're a hard-bitten lawyer type, you must take your coffee black, right?"

She grinned. "I'm only up to hard-edged, working on my stubborn. It'll be a year or more before I'm in the hard-bitten territory. I take cream and one sugar."

"None of that artificial sweetener crap?"

"I think that'll come right after I turn cynical."

He laughed. "Be right back. Do. Not. Move." He looked around. "I see Ray over there. I can ask him to keep an eye on you."

Rhea laughed. "That would be the best way for me to leave. I'll be good."

"I'll bet you are," he said with another wink and loped off.

Damn, I didn't know I still knew how to flirt. She smiled to herself, testing her ability to turn her tightly bound ankle. Maybe things weren't so bad after all.

Paul

It is her. And I finally got her to look at me, Paul mused as he stood in line next door. And what the hell, he eyed the pastry case and picked out a couple of oatmeal cookies. They seemed a better choice than the chocolate chips he really wanted. She seemed like a health-conscious kind of woman, and he wasn't going to blow his chance by upsetting her. *I wonder if she recognized me?* was his next thought. *Maybe she does, and that's why she's been avoiding me, like she did all through school.* But in truth, he had no more clue as to why she had then than he had now.

He pushed through the door, holding the two coffee cups, the cookie bag snagged in his teeth. *Showtime.*

Rhea was sitting where he'd left her, pensively studying her raised ankle. A quick flush graced her cheeks when she looked up at him. *Interesting.*

"I've brought coffee and treats," he said, setting the goods on a small table next to her.

She flipped back the lid of the nearest coffee and took an appreciative sniff. "I swear it always smells better than it tastes," she said before taking a sip. "And then I drink some." She saluted him with her cup and gave him a little grin that had his insides doing backflips.

He ripped open the bag and set a cookie down on a napkin. "Hope you like oatmeal raisin."

Rhea frowned. "They're okay. Chocolate chips are better."

Paul placed a hand on his chest. "A woman after my own heart. And here I was trying to impress you."

Rhea took another sip of her coffee and nodded at her bound ankle. "I'm impressed already. You must have had some first aid training."

43

Paul pulled another chair over and sat as he picked up his coffee. "Just what I've picked up here and there. You need to know this stuff if you spend as much time working out as I do. Also on the job. I'm a carpenter and contractor—everything from concrete to finish work. The guys tend to get a lot of scrapes and bangs. It's handy to know how to deal with stuff."

Rhea grinned. "Not much call for first aid in my office. I can't remember the last time I got a paper cut. Most of what we deal with is electronic these days." She frowned. "The senior partner does like her paper though. Most of us deal with digital files. It's a lot easier to lug around a small laptop than twenty pounds of paper."

"What sort of law do you practice? Is it a large firm? I'm dealing with some legal stuff around my accident." He pointed to his shoulder. "Was T-boned. Trying to get the guy to settle up hasn't been easy."

From the corner of his eye, he saw her shift uncomfortably. "Oh, well." She fell silent. "I can't exactly provide you with any legal advice."

Paul laughed. "No need. I've got a good attorney."

"Excuse me." They both looked up to see two staff members. "Mind if we take that chair?" one of them asked.

"Oh, sorry..." Rhea made to stand, but Paul stopped her. "No problem." He shifted her foot to his lap and patted her ankle gently.

"So, what kind of law do you do anyway?" He took a bite of his cookie.

"Mostly estates. Wills. Probate. Some family law. I helped settle a custody dispute this morning."

"Right. The one Ray was keeping you from. That turned out okay?"

Her eyes shone. "It worked out for the little girl and her parents, and her grandfather. It won't be easy for any of them, but it's for the best for the child."

"That must be gratifying."

"It feels a heck of a lot better than a routine filing of papers with the court," she acknowledged. "So, you hang around the gym a lot."

Paul crumpled up his napkin and tossed it in a trashcan. "Yeah. Off and on. Since I got hurt, I cut back. My right side's okay, but it will take some time before I heal completely. The doctor wants me to take it slow to prevent more damage. Toughest thing I've ever done is holding back. Especially 'cause I can't work at the moment. Most of my jobs require more hands-on work than supervision I need to do a lot of lifting and shoving. My shoulder can't handle it right now."

"That sounds awful."

"I'd rather be here than sitting in a bar, drinking my troubles away. That's what got me into trouble in the first place." At the look on her face, he quickly added, "The other guy. Not me. He was drunk. I was stone cold sober."

Her spine relaxed against the back of her chair. "Oh, well, that's really too bad."

"Yeah. Besides, I don't have anyone to drink with anymore. One brother's still single but he doesn't like bars. The others are all married, starting families." He took another sip of his coffee. She'd only broken off bits of her cookie. On her best behavior? Or she really didn't like oatmeal raisin. "So, you work for one of those large firms, or a small one or somewhere in between?"

"Medium-sized. My parents started it. Mom still works there—the senior partner. She's looking to expand." Rhea frowned. "It's kind of an uncertain time. Lots of different sorts of cases come my way."

"And that's why you're here at odd hours. Today's the exception."

She stared into the distance for a long moment before focusing on his eyes. "Yeah, today's definitely the exception. I haven't left while it's still light out since I can't remember when. I was asked to... I needed to..." She grabbed a chunk of cookie and stuffed it in her mouth. "Let's say after the euphoria this morning, my bubble was burst. I decided I needed a little time to myself."

Paul nodded. "So, you came here to work all that off, what I assume is negative energy, and you ended up getting hurt."

She nodded, swallowing hard. "That about sums it up."

"I get it." He sat back and ran his fingers through his beard. "I come in here a lot at night, too. When I can't sleep."

"Pain?" she asked as she took a sip.

"Not so much anymore. Boredom. Distraction. I need the sense that I'm doing something. A guy can only watch so many horror movies without getting bored, you know."

She made a face. So, no scary movies. His hands ran through his hair. "I can't work. I can't play—I miss all the stuff I used to take for granted. At least when I'm here, I feel like I'm doing something for someone."

"Like helping Ray with his crunches, or me with my bandage."

He grinned at her. "And to talk to people..."

"Women?" she asked with a lifted brow.

"Busted." He laughed. "And to walk them to their cars at night so the rougher guys don't hit on them."

Rhea set her coffee down and stared at her ankle, cradled in his hands. "Like you're not hitting on me now."

"Exact..." his gaze met hers, and he felt his face flush. Maybe she couldn't see it through the beard. "Well, maybe just a little. But you have to admit I'm doing it nicely. Not too aggressive. Giving you plenty of room to maneuver."

She wiggled her foot, and he tightened his grip reflexively. "Maybe, maybe not."

He smiled again. "We're just talking. Not even flirting, hardly," he said with another grin. "Like two old friends."

She picked up her cup and stared into it. "It does feel like that. A little."

He gave her foot a gentle pat and began to knead her calf. "Told ya."

"So, you did," she agreed.

"So, since you're a lawyer and a somewhat captive audience, do you mind if I ask you something about the law. And my case?"

She stiffened and made to move. "I can't…"

"General type questions."

She settled back, though not quite as relaxed as she had been. "Okay. I'll do what I can. Too many questions and I'll have to charge you." She glanced at her watch. "I've got an hour, and then I need to get home. I have a client meeting."

"It's late!"

She shrugged. "Billable hours are billable hours. At least it'll be over the phone, so I don't need to try to get back into my heels." A furrow appeared between her brows. "And I've got a file I need to read tonight. I'm not looking forward to it."

Paul began to unwrap her ankle. "Let me take a look at this, and then I'll help you to your car. I'm done here, so I can follow you home to help you get settled…"

She withdrew her leg from his lap. "Help to the car—yes. Following me home, not so much. We don't know each other and…"

His hands went up. "I didn't mean anything by it. I'm not a stalker. You can ask any of the guys around here. Or women. But I would like to see you again. So, you can buy me that coffee you owe me." He gave her another wink.

Rhea took stock of him, and for the first time, Paul wondered what she saw. Tall. Beard down past his neck. Hair a mess—he went to the cosmetology school's monthly open house to get his hair cut cheaply and let the young men and women there experiment. It was clear she didn't recognize him.

"You could just be saying that."

"I could," he agreed. "So, I'll back off because I really would like to get to know you better. And that's not just a line. I've got a ton of time on my hands, and you seem like a very nice lady. Smart and pretty and..."

"And too busy for a relationship," she said quickly. "I appreciate the coffee and the bandage, but..."

"But I'm not the kind of guy an up and coming ambitious lawyer would date."

He glanced at her to see shame cross her face. "It's not that. I really don't have time. I work a minimum of eighty hours a week, often a hundred. And I need—I have to avoid emotional entanglements."

Paul couldn't help but cock his head. "Emotional entanglements? What about going out for a beer some Saturday night? Or maybe a movie. There's a new horror film opening in about a week."

She was so startled, she laughed.

"You know. Meet someplace. Talk. Laugh. Listen to music. Dress in jeans instead of sweats? Act like real people?"

Rhea closed her eyes, and he wondered what was going through her mind. To his surprise, she opened them and smiled. "Like real people? It seems like it's been years since I had time for that."

"So, that's a yes?" he asked.

Rhea nodded quickly, as if afraid she'd change her

mind if she thought about it too long. "Yeah, okay. Sunday?"

He grinned at her. "Sunday." He peeked at her ankle. "Looks like it's not too bad. Remember what I said? Ice it while you sit through your meeting. I'll save dancing for our second date."

"You want to take me dancing?" she asked, clearly incredulous.

He shrugged. "Sure. Why not? It's good exercise."

Rhea laughed. "Okay. Wait. I don't even know your name. Or you mine."

Paul grinned at her. "I know you."

She turned her head. "What?"

"Rhea Hansen-Chalmbers."

She stood, holding to the chair for support. "How did you know that? You didn't check my file, did you? They said it would be kept private."

Paul shook his head. "I know you from years ago."

She squinted at him. "Who exactly are you?"

"Paul. Paul Conrad."

She blanched and reached for the chair back. "Oh my God," she said under her breath. "I can't believe…I can't…"

He felt his grin turn to a frown. "You promised me, Rhea. And I know you never renege on a promise. Too much integrity. Right from the time you were five."

"Damn you, Paul Conrad. Yes, I'll see you Saturday night. But that's it." And with that, she hopped away from him, cursing under her breath.

"Call me," he yelled after her. "I'm in the book."

She kept on moving, waving her hand at him as she went. He laughed when he saw that one finger figured prominently in her gesture.

Chapter Six

Rhea

Her hands were shaking by the time she pulled into her driveway. Paul Conrad. Really? And she hadn't recognized him—how was that possible? His beard hid a lot. And while he'd been fit in high school, the last time she'd seen him, he hadn't been ripped. But the kindness was the same.

Oh crap. She couldn't see him, not even once. It would be too dangerous to her peace of mind, not to mention the equilibrium she'd fought so hard to achieve. *What if he asks me about—not, don't even think about it*, she thought viciously. She threw her gearshift into park and turned the car off. "I'll call him. I'll be civilized. I'll tell him I'm too busy. That's the truth.

"Like hell it is, girl. Coffee. That's all he wants. To talk. He's a nice guy. He won't take advantage." She groaned. "And now he's got you talking to yourself."

The keys slid into her hand, and she stared at them before closing her fingers around the fob. With a sigh that bordered on a sob, Rhea pressed her forehead against the steering wheel. "I can't do this. I can't chance it."

She took another deep breath and opened the door, then managed to get out of the car without incident. Rhea hobbled her way to the front door and opened it. She heard an engine idle, and as she looked up, saw a beat-up truck pull down the street. The sunlight was fading, but she could have sworn it was Paul. Despite her protest, he must have followed her home. "Crap," she said to her empty house as she made her way in. "And thank you," for there was no doubt in her mind he had done what he had to ensure she arrived safely. For all his faults, Paul Conrad

50

didn't strike her as a stalker, just a nice guy, which was going to make their conversation all the more difficult.

Her foot was throbbing by the time she made it to her kitchen. She opened the freezer and grabbed a bag of peas, then hopped her way to the sofa in her living room. Rhea threw herself on it and gingerly lifted her foot to the battered coffee table, the single other piece of furniture in the room. With a sigh, she plopped the peas on her ankle, hissing as the cold hit her skin. She pulled her phone from her bag and looked up his number.

Three rings later, he answered. "Hi."

"Paul, I told you not to follow me."

He laughed. "My mom would kill me if I hadn't. Nice digs. A little lowbrow from what I expected for you, lawyer lady."

She rolled her eyes. "It's what I can afford. Student loans..."

"Yeah, yeah, I get it. You're about three blocks from Moe and his wife, Berry. You remember him? Joey and Jenny are across town. They're building a place he designed..."

"Paul—the reason I'm calling..."

"You're not reneging, are you?"

She bit her lip. "I'm not sure I can do this."

"Are you still mad about that stunt Brian pulled in high school? I still give him hell for it every time I see him for messing up my plans to ask you..."

"No, not that." She sighed. "It's just that I'm really busy. My caseload—I've got this new one that I agreed to take on, and it's giving me fits."

Paul was silent. "You're still mad at me."

"No. I know it was that bonehead who tried to sabotage me, not you. I still won the debate."

He laughed. "You slaughtered me." In the background,

she could hear him turn the engine off. "It's just coffee, okay? Two old friends catching up? A movie every once in a while."

"That's it? Just talk? Not a date. And no horror movies."

His warm laughter filled her ear. "My days of asking you on a date are over. A man's ego can only take so much battering."

She felt herself smile in spite of herself. "Okay. Coffee and talk, and you forget you know where I live. We meet one time and then become nodding acquaintances at the gym. Not friends on social media…"

"I get it," Paul managed to say. "Boy, you lawyer types really like to spell things out, don't you."

It was her turn to laugh. "My most difficult cases are where the law is ambiguous. I don't want to leave anything open to misinterpretation."

"Am I going to have to sign a contract before I pick you up?"

Rhea laughed. "I'll have one ready, just in case."

"Fine. So, let's say we meet at The Sweet Shop for coffee Sunday morning?"

"That doughnut place on Elm? I've never been there."

"What! Come on. How can you have lived here all your life and never once set food into The Sweet Shop? My brother Joey's wife, Jenny, runs their catering business. That's how they met when she was a waitress. All my brothers meet there for breakfast once a week."

"You guys are all still close?" Even she could hear the wistfulness of her question.

"Yeah. Sammy still works for Moe. Once my shoulder's back up to strength, and I have my settlement money, I'm going to set up shop myself. Hey, know any good lawyers who could help me set up a business?"

"You're going to compete with your brother?"

"No—I'd never do that. I like the fine carpentry end of things, fancy woodwork. We don't get a lot of call for that from Moe's customers. I'm usually a site manager on jobs, but I want to start making custom furniture and cabinets. I was all ready to begin when I got hit. Because the idiot who hit me's insurance lapsed, he's been dragging his feet about settling. My company covered me, but not for everything I'm due. I've had to use all my savings just to keep body and soul together. I'm counting on that money to start over. I'll still work for Moe until things get moving, but I hope with a few spec pieces, I can get some word of mouth, so I can start to get customers."

"You always did like shop, but you were so smart..."

Paul laughed. "Yeah. No one could quite find a place to categorize me. Jock. Smart. Likes to work with his hands. I got my degree in business admin with an emphasis on building trades. Hey, you wouldn't happen to know of anyone who might be interested in some finely crafted pieces, would you? I have a few I built for spec. When we meet, I'll show you some pictures."

Rhea sighed as she looked around her nearly empty house and thought about her student loans. "I'd love some handcrafted furniture, but cash is kind of hard to come by these days. Maybe in five years..."

"I can see I won't get rich off of you this week. Okay, so you need to ice your ankle, and I've got to get myself some dinner. We'll meet Sunday, Oneish? You know where The Sweet Shop is, right?"

"Yeah. Speaking of dinner, I guess I'm going to microwave the peas that are on my ankle. Can't put them back in the freezer. By the way, my ankle feels better. I'll give you back your ace bandage when I see you."

"It's a date—I mean, it's a plan," Paul laughed. "See you then."

Rhea set her phone down and smiled to herself. All those years of not talking to him, convincing herself he was a jerk, and he was a nice guy all the while. And ambitious. She squinted, trying to remember some of his pieces from the annual art show put on by the school district. He'd made some impressive things—a finely worked end table and a breadbox. Nothing like the bookends most of the other students had offered. "Good for him," she mused as she lifted the limp plastic bag from her ankle. "And not too shabby at first aid either."

Berry

"Hey Ber, is Moe around?"

"I'm fine, thanks, and how are you?" I replied to Paul over the phone.

Okay—here's an aside for you. If I was really writing this down as a book, my editor would call me out on inserting an information dump, but since I'm not... Okay, it's like this: not that I don't love Paul as much as I do my other brothers-in-law, and certainly more than I love my own brother, sad as that is for me to admit, but there's always been something a little aloof about him. I mean, he's a smart, sweet guy and just as good looking as the rest of the brothers. But he's not like Joey, who's always been a bit edgy. Or like Pete, who's a bit of a dreamer. Sammy's just the goofy youngest brother. Moe—my Moe, is the strong one—the eldest of the bunch. Not that he's not funny and loving, and of course, I love my husband more than just about anything. But Paul—he's been more stand-offish than the rest of them. And yes, he knows about my 'talent.'

If I were a betting woman, I'd guess he might be the most unnerved about my ability to bring characters to life—

such as I do. Well, yeah, I guess it is kind of weird and spooky. Oh, right, I haven't said much about that so far. I will—just give me a chance.

Anyway, Paul's made it clear on more than one occasion he doesn't want me getting involved in his love life. And I pretty much promised him I wouldn't interfere (unless he asked me to, or someone else asked me to, or if I just couldn't help myself because he was making a mess of a good thing, but of course, I never said any of that out loud). But that's all beside the point. Aside over.

Paul laughed. "I'm glad to hear it. I should have asked. And how's Mattie and Thing Number Two?"

"Mattie never stops talking, which is making me hope baby number two turns out to be the strong, silent type." t was true. My daughter started talking at twenty months and has never looked back. She even talks in her sleep, which is pretty darned adorable.

Paul chuckled. "Takes after me, in other words."

I laughed. "Moe's on his way home. Did you try his cell?"

"I did. He didn't pick up."

"He hasn't gotten the hang of the Blue Tooth yet. I'll have him call when he gets here." I thought a moment. "Anything in particular I should tell him? He's going to ask, and you know your reply will affect how soon he returns the call."

"So, it's not just you being nosy?" he asked.

I didn't get mad because I could hear the smile in his voice. "That's only part of it." I took a breath. "Is it about a woman?" I knew it wasn't anything new about his shoulder, as he'd just been here a few days before, and that was all he could talk about."

I heard him pause—the silence was fraught with

potential. "Well, kinda." He paused again. "Someone I used to know. A long time ago. I guess you could say she's unfinished business."

Okay, you can't dangle something like that in front of me and expect me to remain silent. "Oh?" Yes, I can probe discretely when necessary.

He laughed again. "Yes. From high school, Miss Nosy."

"That's Mrs. Nosy to you," I muttered because Mattie had just wandered into the room, and anything I said within her hearing was fodder to be questioned and repeated *ad nauseum* for the rest of the day, into the evening, and again on the morrow. Plus, I made him laugh again. Paul's got a wonderful laugh. "Maybe you want to come for dinner? I've got turkey meatloaf and mashed potatoes and peas ready to go."

"Peas?" he asked, and I swear I'd never before heard him sound so excited about a vegetable.

"Peas," I confirmed. "In butter sauce."

"I'll be there in five minutes."

So, Paul arrived a few minutes after Moe. We ate with Mattie entertaining us from her place of honor in her high chair. After bath time, Uncle Paul had the honor of reading her bedtime stories, and he succumbed to the Mattster's wheedling 'just one more' about fifteen times. We were listening in on the baby monitor with our feet up, laughing the whole time.

When Paul finally staggered down the stairs and collapsed onto my sofa, Moe pressed a commiseratory beer into his hand.

"You go through that every night?" he asked after a long pull from the bottle.

Moe slapped his little brother's knee with a grin before he sat back and wrapped an arm around me. "We finesse it and don't get suckered into reading more than seven stories a night." He saluted Paul with his own bottle. "Much obliged to you for taking her on. I didn't think Berry and I would get any alone time tonight." He gave me a big noisy kiss and dropped his arm to my hip—no easy feat given I was seven months pregnant.

"You mean, you two just—eww. I don't need to know that stuff," Paul said, turning away, his cheeks flaming above his beard.

I laughed and pushed my husband. "Don't tell him stuff like that, Moe." I smiled at my brother-in-law. "He's just teasing you. We were just talking." I turned back to my husband. "Tell him, Moe."

My husband just smiled and waggled his eyebrows. "Yeah, you like to call it 'talking.' When you don't call it 'communicating,'" he repeated with a snort and exaggerated air quotes.

"Cripes, you guys, give a guy a break, will you?" Paul said. "It's not like you're newlyweds anymore."

Moe hugged me tighter. "Nope. Better than that, little brother. But you don't want to hear about our sex life…"

"Moe…" Paul and I groaned at the same time.

"…I think you came over here to tell us about yours." He laughed as the two of us groaned again.

"Not exactly. It's just that I met a girl…"

"Is she under eighteen?" I asked with a lifted brow. "Your mother won't approve."

Paul ducked his head. "Woman. I met a woman, okay? Moe, you remember little Rhea that I used to play with?"

"The jungle-gym girl?" he asked. "She had about a hundred braids and had you beat six ways to Sunday on the monkey bars." One corner of his mouth lifted in a smirk. "Turned you down for prom as I recall."

Paul ducked his head. "Yeah, her. All grown up. I ran into her at the gym a few weeks ago, and I finally had a

57

chance to talk to her when she fell off the treadmill..."

"You didn't push her, did you?" my husband asked.

I gave Moe a shove. "Paul wouldn't do that. Would you?"

He looked hurt before he laughed. "Of course not. She fell off on her own. I bandaged her ankle, bought her a coffee and a cookie."

Moe's left brow rose. "And made a date with her?"

Paul sat back, smugly. "Yeah. You should see her. She's so beautiful. She's a lawyer now. I had to do a lot of fancy talking to make her agree to see me. Told her it was just coffee, not a date. I'm meeting her at The Sweet Shop Sunday."

"You hound, you," Moe said, leaning forward and smacked his brother's knee again. "Good for you. It's about time you started chasing women again." He looked at me. "No offense, sweetie."

I patted his arm. "None taken." I looked back at Paul. "So, you like her?"

He looked at the bottle in his hands, smiling dreamily, and nodded.

Moe squeezed my hands. "He had a crush on her forever. She wouldn't give him the time of day in high school."

It was my turn to lower my brows. "Paul, what did you do to that poor girl?"

"Woman," he said smugly.

"She was a girl then—and don't quibble with me. What did you do?"

He laughed, but his smile quickly faded, and he shrugged. "I don't actually know. We used to hang out at the playground in the park, just being kids and goofing off. And one day, she just ran away and wouldn't play with me anymore."

I looked at him hard. "There must have been something."

He looked at me innocently. "I broke my clavicle. She took off. Mom said it was her nanny who called the ambulance. Rhea was nowhere in sight."

"It's true," Moe added. "I remember walking him over there all the time. The nanny would watch both of 'em, then walk him home. But one day, Rhea stopped going. Broke his heart."

"And in high school, she snubbed me. We were on the debate team together, had all the same AP classes, but she wouldn't give me the time of day."

"Your friend was a jackass," Moe added.

Paul nodded. "He was. But only because she snubbed me. He was trying to…"

"Be a jerk," Moe said.

Paul sighed. "Yeah. But I put a stop to it." He turned to me. "I wanted to ask her to the prom. I couldn't get her to look at me long enough to ask."

"So, who did you go with?"

His gaze went to his boots. "I, uh, well, I asked one of her friends."

It was my turn to sigh and shake my head. "Nice going, Romeo."

"If it's any consolation, we had a miserable time."

"Oh yeah, I'm sure that makes it all better. So, who d d Rhea go with?"

Paul mumbled something.

"Huh?"

"She went with her other girlfriends."

"Did you at least ask her to dance?"

Paul covered his face with his hands. "Do we have to talk about this now? It's ancient history."

"Paul Conrad, you can bet anything she remembers it

like it was yesterday."

He sank into the cushions, his hands still on his face. "Why is it you females have to have photographic memories about every awful thing a guy ever did?"

"Because... because..." I glanced at my husband who looked back at me with an innocent inquiry, ruined only by the mischievous glint in his eyes. "Because we are female, and that's what we do," I managed to sputter. "So, deal with it."

They both laughed, and in the end, so did I. "She must have liked you a bit if she agreed to meet you for coffee," I said once I wiped the tears from my eyes.

"Yeah," he agreed. "Of course, I had to lie and tell her it wasn't a date. It was just coffee."

Moe high-fived his brother. I frowned at them.

"I sure hope you plan to be a little more adult when you meet her," I groused as I rubbed my belly. It seemed the baby was trying to get in on the action with his father and uncle.

Paul's grin faded. "Berry, you have to promise you won't interfere."

Moe turned to me at the same time with a pointed look. "She won't."

I spread my arms wide. "Who me? I haven't even met the woman, and I never mean to interfere. It just happens."

Moe dipped his chin. "Really, Ber?"

I lifted a shoulder. "Okay, well, maybe I encouraged things with Jenny and Joey..."

Another sardonic look from my husband made me smile. "And you know I never intended all that hullabaloo in the first place when you and I met, Moe," I cried. "If you remember, if Trista hadn't called you, you and I never would have gotten together in the first place."

Okay, reader. Time for another quick aside to fill you in. I've mentioned to you that I write romance novels, right? I've had a bit of success with it in the past few years and was able to quit my day job, so I could write full-time in addition to being a full-time mommy.

But here's the thing. When I'm writing, you see, I have this... well, let's call it an ability to make some of my characters come to life. Yes, you read that right.

Most of the time, it's been temporary. They've all gone back into their respective books and live out their happily ever afters between the pages, paper or electronic. The exception was, well, unexpected, but it all turned out okay in the end.

This isn't something I brag about. Other than one friend of mine, only the family—the Conrad family—knows about it. I don't dare tell my parents or brother. And I have no idea how it works. It seems to happen primarily when one or another of the Conrad brothers is embroiled in a romance. The first time was when Moe and I met, and subsequently with the other brothers. And it hasn't always been easy for me or for them. So, you can imagine that Paul was a bit gun-shy at the thought I'd 'interfere.' But I didn't want to and truly had no intention of it. I mean, I was seven months pregnant with a two-year-old and trying to finish my latest manuscript and find a name for my heroine before I delivered. There was no way I needed the complication of loosening fictional characters into the real world on top of everything else. So, what I said before about helping Paul with any romance—that was in the form of moral support and not supernatural aid. Truly, I couldn't conjure someone up if I tried. It only seems to happen when I least expect it. Enough of this aside and back to this story.

Moe's gaze softened. "Okay, I get it. But you leave Paul and Rhea alone."

I nodded. "I promise I won't go out of my way to do anything. If you want to bring her here to meet us, I'll be friendly and supportive." I held up my hand the way I did when I was a girl scout. "I promise."

Of course, the best-laid plans and promises never go exactly as you expect. What would be the fun in that?

And my ankles were crossed. I was too pregnant to cross my legs.

Chapter Seven

Rhea

The only easy thing about getting ready for coffee with Paul was knowing she had to wear flats. Her ankle was better, but no matter the temptation, she wasn't going to wear heels. They were too dressy. And smacked too much of 'date.' Plus, they made her ankle hurt.

So, she donned a pair of skinny jeans that were a smaller size than she'd worn before she started working out, and a loose top that screamed 'lazy Sunday I'm not dressing up for anyone,' other than a starburst of bling that caught the bright autumn sunlight. And hoop earrings, because really, she was a woman who had to wear conservative diamond or pearl posts throughout the workweek, and she needed to strut her stuff sometime. Oh, and a touch of makeup along with her loose hair. Just 'cause.

But she made sure she was late. She wanted Paul to feel a touch anxious about whether or not she would show. And she didn't want to be the first one there and have to peer out the window every few seconds to look for him as if she were the one who was anxious.

When she arrived a fashionable ten minutes after the hour, Paul was waiting outside, casually sunning himself. He gave her a bright grin when she walked up to him. "Hey. You look great. I'm allowed to say that, right?"

Rhea grinned back. "Compliments are always welcome, so long as they're not gratuitous."

"Oh, lady, you keep tossing those big words at me, and my head's going to spin."

She cocked her head to one side. "Yeah? I don't think so. I Googled you. I know you're no dummy. First in your graduating class at the university. Full scholarship. Tons of offers out of state, and you're still here?"

He took her elbow to lead her inside with a shrug. "I like it here. Other than the odd car crash, that is."

She winced. "It must have been terrible."

He held the door open. "It wasn't a picnic. Still waiting for the other guy to settle. He's being a jackass. He's trying to do this out of court because he knows he'll lose his reputation. We could have been done months ago, but he's being stubbornly stupid. He wants me to forgive and forget and agree that he owes me nothing. I can't believe the courts have allowed this to go on."

A shiver ran down Rhea's back. "That's a shame. I wish I could help, but you know how things are."

Paul shrugged. "We don't have to talk about it. I'm just glad you're here. It crossed my mind you might stand me up."

Rhea laughed. "And let you humiliate me? Not likely. I just got in the habit of going to that gym. If I hadn't come today, I wouldn't be able to show my face there again."

He touched her hand with one finger. "I'm glad you did. Really glad."

She met his gaze and found herself smiling into his eyes. "Me too." She looked down at the menu. "What's good? If I'm going to blow all my hard work on sweet, fatty food, I want to make sure it's worth my while."

He pushed her menu down and smiled into her eyes. "Just on the record, I'm not one of those guys who thinks skinny women are all that. Nothing wrong with having a few curves."

She snort-laughed. "You say that obviously having never been a woman whom others judge by their size and shape, not to mention the color of their skin, quality and texture of their hair, clarity of their complexion or designer labels on their backs. Or the size of their butts."

He nodded. "Thank goodness. I know that's all true. I might've been a jerk about stuff like some of what you said once upon a time. I like to think I've matured a bit." He looked down at his menu before he gazed at her once more. "Other than big butts. I still like those." He winked.

She took his measure, her face carefully neutral before her grin broke through. "Yeah?"

He laughed. "Sorry, but yeah. Other than that, I'm the poster child for maturity."

"Hmmm."

He met her gaze, his clear and earnest. "I think so."

She turned back to her menu. "Time will tell. Not that I have a lot of it. I told you I can only stay an hour. I've got to work later."

Paul sighed. "Yeah, okay. But if in this hour I act like a jerk, you have permission to call me on it."

It was Rhea's turn to set down her menu. "You mean it?"

His brown eyes were open, clear, and compelling. "How else am I going to know?"

"Know what?"

"That I'm forgiven for whatever I did all those years ago to make you stop talking to me."

Rhea felt herself blanch. Her fingers tingled, and she dropped the menu to wring them under the table. "I don't know what you're talking about."

Paul shook his head slightly. "Okay. No worries. But you can still tell me if I'm being a jerk—unless I'm being one on purpose to tease you, okay?"

Her tension ebbed. "And I'm to know the difference, how?"

He gave her a wink. "Let's just say I'll make sure you do." He winked again. "It's my way of flirting."

Rhea stared at him until she caught his meaning, and then her open mouth swirled into a grin. "Deal." She glanced back at her menu. "But Paul?"

"Yeah?"

She felt his gaze upon her, but she refused to lift her eyes to him. "That bit about being open and honest about jerky behavior—that only goes one way."

Rhea glanced at him quickly to see raised eyebrows, but his surprise was quickly replaced with a laugh. "Ooh, I still love a challenge," he said and rubbed his hands together.

Monday morning, Rhea blinked back her fatigue as she reached for her coffee. The hour she'd allotted Paul had turned into three, filled with good conversation, laughter, and more. What exactly that 'more' consisted of, she wasn't quite certain, but she hadn't felt that good in years. Maybe it was the fact that it was the first time in forever she'd had three hours straight where she hadn't thought about work. Or perhaps it was just that she'd been in the company of a charming man who hadn't exactly put the moves on her but expressed his interest nevertheless.

It hadn't hurt that every one of his brothers happened to stop by in that three-hour span. Rhea had liked all of them and their wives and children as well. Even the youngest, Sammy, had a charm all his own despite his affecting a cowboy hat and the requisite teasing that followed.

After, she'd driven over to the nursing home still grinning to herself, and spent an hour with her father by singing to him. "Maybe I could do a relationship someday," she muttered as she drove home. And then she'd had a glass of wine and ignoring her briefcase, pulled out a book, though she'd hardly read more than a page, given that Paul's face swam before her mind's eye, replacing the words on the page. "I could really fall for him," she mused aloud before refocusing on her story. "But I can't let that happen. I can't." She'd fallen asleep dreaming of running across the monkey bars, Paul chasing her, and the two of them laughing their fool heads off.

But the timeout from her life was over. Monday morning, she opened her laptop and scanned her emails. The office coffee tasted nothing like the smooth blend from The Sweet Shop. And her whole wheat and oatmeal bagel was the next best thing to disgusting. She tossed it in the trash rather than take another bite. *Paul would never eat garbage like that. No. Stop thinking about him. Nothing is ever going to go anywhere with him. Stop. Thinking. About. Him.* She closed her eyes and went inward for a moment to find her calm center. *You can do this. You didn't make any plans with him. You'll see him at the gym. That's all. Casual friends.* She took a deep breath. *Better*, she thought.

Her phone rang. It was too early for the receptionist. And regardless, this was coming in directly to her extension. "Chalmbers, Hansen and Associates, this is Rhea Hansen-Chalmbers. May I help you?"

"Is this a good time to talk?"

Her heart started to hammer. "Paul? Is everything okay?"

"Yeah. I know you get an early start, and I wanted to catch you before your meetings begin."

"I..."

He cleared his throat. "I just wanted to tell you how great it was to see you yesterday. Totally made my day. I'm still not hitting on you—just to be transparent."

Rhea laughed. "Yeah?"

"Yeah. It's nice to reconnect with you. And I won't even tell you how nice it would have been if we'd been friends all the time instead of just now."

"Paul, if we'd been friends in high school, there'd be no way we would still be friends. And neither of us would have been as good at debating as we were. Something would have happened…"

"Okay, okay, you made your point." She could hear a smile in his voice. "The important thing is we're friends again. And since I know you probably won't want to go to the gym until your ankle is better, I thought maybe we could catch lunch today. Just as friends."

She quickly glanced at her calendar, but there was an afternoon meeting tentatively booked that she didn't recall being scheduled when she left on Friday. "Today's not good. I'm not free at lunch until Thursday."

"I guess asking you out for drinks after work is out of the question then?"

A quick glance confirmed her evening wasn't her own. "Nope. Someone blocked off my time. Must be a firm thing that came up."

"Okay," he sighed. "How about we compromise and meet for a drink after work on Thursday instead? That way, you won't have to rush back."

"Paul…"

"I know—I know. You work killer hours. But one drink. One hour…"

"Like coffee was only going to be one hour?" she teased.

"Yeah, like that," he laughed.

"Okay. I'm marking the time off on my calendar now," she said and tapped on her keyboard. "Now, I have to go. I have a ton of things to do today."

"Okay lawyer lady. I'll see you Thursday. I'll text you

where. It's a great place just around the corner from me. We can both walk there."

"I'll see you then, Paul."

She hung up, staring into space until she caught her reflection wearing a goofy grin on the glass of her diploma hanging opposite her desk. Rhea forced it from her face as she focused on her computer, trying oh-so-hard to not think of him.

Two hours later, there was a tap at her door. She looked up to see her mother holding a file in her arms. "Good morning, Darling," Marion said with a toothy smile.

"Mom," Rhea replied with a nod of her head.

"Did you have a nice weekend? I'm sure your time off was well spent."

Rhea nodded. "I went to the gym and sprained my ankle." *I also reconnected with a really great guy, but I'm not going to tell you about him.*

Her mother's brows creased in concern. "You're okay?"

Rhea flicked her hand in the air. "It's fine. I'm keeping it bandaged. No heels for a few weeks."

"But darling, everyone knows your suits look so much better in heels..."

"Mom," Rhea breathed. "I'm not going to permanently damage my ankle just to look good."

"Oh, fine," Marion huffed. "You'll just need to greet your client sitting behind a desk for the next few days." She tapped the folder against the palm of her hand. Speaking of which, I spoke with our clients over the weekend. I can't tell you how happy they are you agreed to take on this case. They expressed confidence in your abilities to see it through to a successful conclusion."

Rhea reached for the file without standing. "And they promised to be cooperative for mediation?" she asked.

Marion laughed. "Oh, you know how they are. They'll

cooperate in their own way."

The first throb of a headache scurried across Rhea's forehead. She closed her eyes and prayed there was at least one doughnut left in the break room. Preferably crème filled. With chocolate frosting. "Mom, you were supposed to tell them…"

"I did, I did," Marion soothed. "It's just that the whole family is so upset about this turn of events. It's not as if Brice wanted to hit that other driver. Things happen. They want it to all go away."

At least I had fun yesterday. And I'll see Paul again. Strictly as friends. Or more. I don't know, but I want to. "I'm sure they do," Rhea replied. "But do they realize…"

"I filled them in on the law," her mother replied. "And so will you when you meet with them this afternoon. I've booked the largest conference room for one o'clock. Cassie will clear your calendar." She reached over and tapped the file Rhea had been ignoring. "Best read up now, darling. You need to be on top of this before they arrive. They're expecting great things from you." She looked down at her shoes. "From us."

Mother and daughter's gazes met. "You're seeing this case through to a successful conclusion will put us in a positive position when it comes time to merger talks with Vinder and Associates. I plan to insist you be made partner as part of my negotiations. You know what that means."

More hours. More compromises. The complete and utter destruction of what remains of my integrity. "Tell me, Mom, do you mean that as a condition or as a bargaining chip?"

Marion's mouth became a thin, straight line. "Whatever do you mean?"

Rhea closed her eyes as another throb of pain passed across her forehead. "I think you understand the question,

70

but in case you don't, let me put it in the vernacular. What's in it for me?"

Her mother shuddered slightly. "I will have your best interest at heart, Rhea. I always have. I always will." Marion turned and strode away before Rhea could comment further.

With a sigh, she turned the file over and opened it. The legal forms were familiar to her, and she began to scan it carefully for pertinent information. She stopped at the first line. Brice Post vs. Paul Conrad." Her hand slammed the file shut.

"Mom," she called. "Mother!" but Marion had left the floor.

"Oh shit. I should have known," Rhea muttered. She reopened the file and began to read the police report. A half-hour later, she shut the file and shivered. The accident report and photos were gruesome. Paul's injuries were far worse than he'd let on, and the material damage to his vehicle and equipment was substantial. Full mention was made of her client's prior DUI and lapsed insurance. "Why is this even being contested?" she asked her empty office.

Rhea re-read the contents. In the back was a cutting from a newspaper. The client's father apparently had an interest in running for state office. Ah. Of course. Having a convicted drunk driver for a son would be a blot on his name. *Why not admit there's a problem and run on a platform of getting help for people like him? Oh, never mind, it's too damned obvious*, she concluded.

"But Paul—he doesn't have the resources to go up against this firm—or the family." She looked up and stared out her small window. *And my being friends with him— that's a major conflict of interest. It's enough to recuse myself. Not that we talked about it, but we did some. And I expressed sympathy, as a friend.*

Rhea reached for her phone and pressed the button for her mother's office. One ring and Marion answered.

"Mom, I can't take this case."

"Darling, we've been through this. You have to."

"It will be a conflict of interest. You knew it before you gave me this file. It's Paul Conrad. He's a friend of mine. You knew that."

"Darling, that was years ago. You and he haven't spoken since."

"Mom, I met him for coffee yesterday."

There was silence on the other end of the phone. "You're not sleeping with him?"

"No," Rhea confirmed. "We're friends. We go to the same gym."

"But you're not personally involved?"

Even if I wanted to be, I couldn't now. "No. It's casual."

"But, if you were, you might be able to influence..."

"Mother! If you're suggesting what I think you are, that is as unethical as..."

"Oh darling, I was just thinking out loud, not suggesting anything. If you're not dating him, which of course you wouldn't, given his circumstances in life, there's no conflict. Just don't see him anymore. Join another gym. The firm will pick up the tab. In fact, we'll offer gym memberships for all our staff. Won't that be a nice new benefit for everyone? So it doesn't look in the least like..."

"The timing would be suspect."

"Oh, details," her mother laughed. "It's not going to come to that. Simply work with Paul's attorney. Get him to see the light and settle this thing. One week, maybe two, and it's all over."

"It's not that easy," Rhea argued.

"It's just that simple. Darling, you need to trust me on this. Oh, and by the way, tonight we're having dinner with

72

the Vinders. I want you to meet Tony—Antony and his son AJ—Junior." There was another pause. "Tony tells me Junior's very interested in meeting you. Imagine what it would be like if the two of you formed an attachment—how great that would be for the future of our combined firm."

"Tell me you're not matchmaking," Rhea groaned.

"Of course not, Rhea. He's engaged. I was just daydreaming. At any rate, I know you two will hit it off—the future senior partners must form a strong relationship. It's essential for the continued success of the firm. Now, I simply have to prepare for my own client meeting. I'll see you tonight. We're dining at La Fluer. Seven o'clock for drinks. Do not be late. And for goodness sakes, if you can't wear heels, at least take off that dreadful bandage."

The phone clicked off.

Rhea stared at the receiver in her hand a full minute before she set it gently in its cradle. "Okay world, things have hit rock bottom. They can't possibly get any worse." She closed her eyes. *Oh, right. I have to break my date with Paul for Thursday. I have to let him know.* "Shit," she said out loud as she rubbed her fingers together.

She got up in search of the elusive doughnut. The way she was feeling, she'd settle for a stale jelly stick.

Chapter Eight

Paul

He slipped his phone into his shirt pocket and gave it a pat. "Rhea, you are really something," he said to himself as he got out of his truck and made his way into the workshop. "You don't know it yet. It'll take some time, but I'm yours, and you are mine, and that is that."

"Hey, what are you so happy about? And why are you here so early?" Moe asked as Paul came through the door.

"I have a few hours to do some woodworking," Paul replied, sounding a hell of a lot cheerier than he had in months. "Thought I'd do it while the light's good."

Moe squinted against the huge open door. "The sun's barely up," he complained.

"So, what are you doing up and around instead of lollygagging in bed with your bride?" Paul teased. "She let you up for air for once?"

With a scowl, Moe turned back to the open tool chest he was organizing. "Yeah, well, when a woman's kind of late in her pregnancy, she kinda sometimes doesn't want to see the perpetrator of her condition, even if she loves him dearly."

Paul snorted. "She told you to get lost."

Moe smiled sheepishly. "Well, yeah, maybe." He rubbed the back of his neck. "It might have had to do with my not waking up when Mattie wet her bed last night. And for the record, I feel horrible about it. So, as soon as the florist opens, I'm calling in a huge bouquet of roses for her. With a box of chocolates. And I'm going to stop at the jewelry store on my way home."

"I am so not getting married," Paul muttered.

"You say that now. As soon as you meet the right woman—and that Rhea sure looks a lot better than you said…"

"So much for the liberated male. It's her mind that interests me," Paul announced.

Moe snorted again. "Yeah, right."

"She's brilliant. And funny…"

"She's a ten, little brother."

Paul folded his arms high upon his chest. "And yes, she happens to be good looking."

"You like her." His big brother grinned. "You really like her. You always have."

Paul felt a blush start at the base of his neck. "Yeah, so what?"

"Pauly's got a girlfriend, Pauly's got a girlfriend," Moe chanted as their youngest brother strolled in. "You hear that, Sammy? Paul's got a girlfriend."

Sammy slapped Paul's good shoulder. "That c-chick you were with on Sunday? Way to go, bro. She's g-gorgeous."

"She's not a chick, you moron. And she's not mine. Not yet. We only went out the one time."

"If I know you, you've got s-something else planned. When you g-gonna introduce her to Ma? You know she doesn't like it if we hold out on her. And Berry or Jenny or Annie's b-bound to mention her," Sammy stated.

Paul squinted at his younger brother. "You sure you want to be the only single Conrad brother left? Think about the pressure."

Moe laughed as he snatched the cowboy hat off Sammy's head. "He thinks he's going to be the hold out. That the love bug won't ever touch him."

Sammy grabbed the hat and stuck it on his head with a

75

scowl. "I can wait my turn, but s-seems like it w-won't be long now."

"Come on, you guys. I haven't even kissed her yet. Crap, did I really just say that?" Paul ran his hands through his hair distractedly, wincing when his shoulder moved the wrong way. "Let me think. I don't want Ma scaring her away."

The three of them laughed. Rosemary could be formidable.

"You always said you're not scared of anything," Moe teased. "Not even Ma?"

Paul scowled. "Not even Ma. I'm not seeing Rhee 'til Thursday after work. I figure I can date her a few more times before I reintroduce them. Ma knew her when we were kids."

"Don't wait too long," Moe cautioned. "I think Ma will like her. She's mellowed out since three of us got married, and now she's got grandkids. And counting"

Sammy shuddered. "You know her. It w-won't be enough. She w-wants at least two from each of us."

Moe shook his head. "I've done my part. I don't dare ask Berry to have a third. I don't care how many bedrooms my house's got." He gave his younger brothers a stern look. "And no snickering. I don't see either of you taking up the slack."

Sammy laughed and went to the small office to find his task list for the day. "Don't l-look at me. I've got p-plenty of time."

Moe turned his eyes to Paul. "So, he thinks. But if I'm right, you're next to take a trip down the aisle. And brother, you'll be happy you did. No matter what you're thinking right now."

Paul shrugged. "I don't know what the hell's going to happen. I just know what I want is to win the lawsuit and win that woman. And before that can happen, I want both of you out of here so I can concentrate and get started."

Rhea

"Cassie, come on a coffee run with me."

"What?" the para asked. "I've got a ton of work…"

"I have a question. A legal question. And I think better when I walk," Rhea said through her teeth. "I'm buying."

Cassie grabbed her purse. "Why didn't you say so?"

They walked to a coffee shop on the far corner. It was an ordinary place the senior staff would never frequent, given the high-end patisserie on the opposite corner.

"What's going on?" Cassie asked as they were seated by the window sipping their skinny lattes.

"I have an ethical question. Strictly off the record."

"Does it involve a man?" Cassie asked with raised brows. "A client or potential partner?" She took a delicate sip. "And for the record, I know you already know the answer but want me to confirm it for you."

Rhea hung her head. "Not exactly, no, and yes." She glanced around and out the window. "I met someone. A guy I used to know. We've hit it off."

Cassie's eyes sparkled. "You really like him."

Rhea's cold fingers warmed as she rubbed them against the corrugated paper cup shield. She sighed. "I guess I do." She lifted her lids. "As a friend."

"A friend. Got it." Cassie winked. "So, if he's a client—or a potential client, you give his business to one of the other attorneys."

"Not a client." Rhea studied the foam on her coffee. "He's suing one of our clients."

Cassie winced. "Oooh. Not good." She blinked hard as she thought. "And you really like him? Willing to give him up until the lawsuit is finished kind of like-him?"

"The lawsuit has already taken six months, and little's been done. It could take a very long time." Her brow furrowed. "The case is ugly. My client's best hope is that we drag it on so long the other guy will give up due to the expense. At least that's been the strategy so far, and for the life of me, I can't think of a better one. He's guilty as hell—not to mention a truly despicable person. At least according to his file."

"And you're not getting any younger."

Rhea smiled wryly. "Thanks for the reminder."

Her friend shrugged. "So—at least you can give the case to someone else."

Rhea shook her head. "Not. This is the new case my mother forced me to take."

"The accident? Oh, Rhea honey, I'm so sorry. That's got crap written all over it in capital letters. You have to drop him or quit. There's no other way."

Rhea dropped her head. "I'm not sure how long it would take me to find another job."

Cassie reached out and tapped her hand. "You really like him that much? You've never gone for a guy like that."

"That's the thing," Rhea sighed. "We're just friends. And I want to stay just friends."

Cassie blinked at her and then blinked again. "Sure, you do."

Rhea's fingers clenched under the table. "I'm not ready to get emotionally involved with any…"

"Girlfriend, you already are," her friend corrected.

Rhea hung her head. "You're right. What am I going to do? I can't quit my job for some guy I've only had coffee with."

Cassie laughed. "You're stronger than you think. You're smarter than anyone else I know. You can do anything you want, anything you need. And I've got your back." She smiled. "Remember, there's other guys out there, every bit as good as the one you like," Cassie added gently.

Rhea shook her head without looking up. "I know all that stuff you said. But this one... he's special." She glanced at her watch. "Oh, sugar. I'm running late. I've got to meet with the dreaded client in ten minutes." She grabbed the bag containing the apple-and-coffee cake muffin she'd yet to try. The bag hit the coffee cup, and it began to spin on its stiff paper bottom. Both women gasped as Rhea reached for it. Miraculously, it righted itself just as she grabbed it. Rhea looked at the cup in her hand and shuddered. "I have to give him up," she said quietly.

"Maybe until after the case is settled," Cassie agreed. "So, what you really need to do is settle it. Quickly." She paused a moment and gently shoved her friend. "I read that file. OMG, it's Paul. From high school. I can't believe this. You? Him? After all this time?"

They walked out the door. "Yeah. And if I win the case against Paul, he's going to hate me forever," Rhea explained. "And if Paul wins, I don't know if he could forgive me for arguing a case against him. And if I lose the case, my mother would then hate me and probably fire me, and then who would hire me?"

They were at the door to the firm. Rhea was about to open it when Cassie stopped her. "There's one other option. You can see that it gets settled fairly, so everyone is happy."

Rhea stared at her friend. "And when, for as long as you've worked here, has my mother ever been satisfied with a compromise? Those are as good as losses to her."

Cassie looked at her, stricken. "Oh. Right. Well, my friend, you are officially up shit's creek."

Three hours later, Rhea wanted to crawl under her desk, but to maintain her dignity, she walked back to her office on a swollen ankle that ached. It hurt almost worse than it did when she'd first injured it. *That's what stress is doing to you.*

The client meeting had truly been hell. Her client, accompanied by his father and wife, had demanded she insist that the charges against him be dropped. The accident, he claimed, was due to the sun being in his eyes and nothing to do with his blood alcohol level. He said he regularly drove after a few drinks and never had any problem. It was just the sun that time, that was all. The fact that the weather report claimed the weather to be cloudy was an error, he claimed. As was his blood alcohol level. The lapsed insurance he didn't want to talk about.

The father sat silently at the end of the table, watching her, watching his son. The son's wife sat by her husband's side, her hand clenched in his, her face pale.

"You do realize that the projected legal costs to defend you, and may I add that I think your case is not defendable, will be more than what the plaintiff is asking for in damages. I recommend you voluntarily check yourself into a detox facility, and as soon as possible. Then, if you just..."

"No!" her client roared. "I'm not a drunk. I refuse to have anyone write down I'm an alcoholic. If I'm convicted, they'll take away my license. How am I supposed to support my family if I can't drive? It's not right. It's not fair!"

Rhea sat silently as he fumed and frothed as he paced around the conference room. When he lifted a decorative vase as if to throw it, she, his father, and his wife all came to their feet.

"I suggest you set that down, Mr. Post," she said in her sternest voice. "I will not represent you if you act like a spoiled child. Now, sit down, and let's discuss this like adults."

The man looked to his father, who shrugged as he glanced at the phone in his hand. His wife held out his chair.

They'd gotten nowhere and agreed to meet the next day to try again. Her client refused to shake her hand upon departing, muttering he wanted a new lawyer. A male layer—a white one. His wife looked at Rhea helplessly and followed silently. Rhea could not recall the woman saying a word in all the hours they'd been closeted.

"I'll talk to him," the father said as he left, taking her hand in both of his. "I can see why your mother wanted you to take this case."

"Why do you want to pursue it?" she asked. He was, after all, the one footing the bill. "It makes no sense, and doesn't help your political aspirations."

"It's my son's choice," he replied. She could read nothing in his eyes.

Rhea had just dragged her visitor's chair closer so she could rest her foot on it when her mother popped into her office. "How did things go?"

Rhea shook her head. "The son's a spoiled brat. He won't see reason and seems to think money is no object. This case doesn't have a chance in hell of going his way…"

"That's not very optimistic of you," her mother said. "I thought you said you could…"

"Mom," Rhea said patiently. "I never made any promises I could win this. I'm less sure of it than ever. I have no faith the client would stand up to cross-examination. He's got a hair-trigger temper and no common sense. A mediator would laugh him out of their office."

"You'll get him to see reason," her mother assured her.

"I'm recommending he settle. That he seeks treatment for alcohol addiction, that he admits he did wrong, pays up, and then moves on. Showing remorse is the best way for a judge or jury to show any mercy."

Marion's face tightened with every word. "That is not..."

"That is the best course for the client and for the firm. It's the sensible thing, the *right* thing to do."

"I promised his father we'd get the charges dismissed."

Well, that was just plain absurd, she thought. Rhea shook her head. "You should know better than to promise that, especially if you're not personally representing the client."

Her mother shook her head. "You don't understand."

Rhea stared at her mother. "Then explain it to me."

Marion glanced over her shoulder into the hall, then stepped into her daughter's small office and closed the door. "We have to win this case. For the firm."

"What?"

Her mother closed her eyes, and a tear leaked out of one. "We're not doing as well as we claim. Revenues went down after your father took ill. In recent years, they're down even more. We had some unfortunate losses. Our investment portfolio hasn't performed. I'm not looking to merge with the Vinders for the fun of it. It's a matter of survival. For me to leave you something."

Rhea stared at her mother. "And you're only telling me this now because..."

"I didn't want to worry you. Or have you say something untoward at the wrong time. We need as many billable hours as we can get, and you're the only one I can ask. The Posts can afford this, and he wants to see how his son behaves under pressure before he runs for office. If we win this—he's promised to send clients our way." Her mother closed her eyes and leaned back against the wall. "There's a judge—we're trying to get in his jurisdiction. I think I can persuade him to see things our way…"

"That's so wrong," Rhea hissed. "I can't believe I'm hearing you say this."

Marion's eyes snapped open, and she lasered a look at her daughter. "When you've been at this game as long as I have, you learn to play by your own rules. If you want to succeed, you have to do what's right by your clients, no matter the cost."

"I can't practice this kind of law," Rhea said in a small voice. "I've worked hundred-hour weeks for you, taken your abuse—I cannot do this too."

"You have to. For your father."

"My father would never have expected this from me," she shot back.

"Oh, your precious father. He was no goody-two-shoes. He'd have done it. I know he did worse in his time. To make a buck, to make his reputation."

"The risk—what sort of reputation would we have if this came out?"

"One exactly like every other firm in this city, in this state," her mother lashed out. "We're no different, other than the color of our skin."

"Don't you see, Mother? If it comes out, it'll mean they'll come down all the harder on you than anyone else. You have to be extra scrupulous."

"You can't eat scruples in the poor house, missy. I don't plan to be there. And you will take this case, and you will do everything you can to draw out the hours and bring cash into this firm. And you will win this, one way or another." Marion whipped around and opened the door. "We're meeting Tony and Junior at seven. You will be ready, your face made up, your clothes fresh, and you will be wearing high heels. The son's quite a player. I want him to notice you."

"You'd sell me out?" Rhea cried.

"No, my precious daughter. But he doesn't need to know that, now does he?"

She was gone before Rhea could formulate a reply.

Chapter Nine

Rhea

Later that night, Rhea left the restaurant with her head spinning. The hour was late, and she'd consumed one too many glasses of wine. Her mother had laughed and schmoozed to her heart's content. No one would ever know she was desperate. Even Rhea. Wouldn't a review of the firm's books illustrate how dire the situation was?

The talk of the evening revolved around everything but a possible merger of their firms. Rhea smiled gamely but had little to contribute to the conversation, unlike her counterpart. He was a man about her age, but he'd made partner two years out of law school. It was clear he hadn t started at the bottom as she had. It was also clear he had far more ambition than skill. Once or twice she heard talk about possible judgeships for the father. Well, that was a clue.

The dinner had finally drawn to a close. Rhea excused herself to go to the ladies' room as the others were leaving. When she stepped outside, she found a huge puddle on the sidewalk outside the awning. Rhea looked left and right. No one was around. She closed her eyes to focus and then leapt over the puddle, landing on her good ankle. There was a gasp, and her eyes spun to see her mother talking with the two men across the street. *Please please please don't let them have seen that.*

She settled herself and pasted a smile on her face. "Gentlemen. Mother. I thought you had already left."

Her mother's eyes looked frantic above a plastic smile. "We were waiting for you, darling. AJ was just saying he'd like to work with you on the Post case. Wouldn't that be interesting?"

Rhea turned to the young man and met his smirk. "Have you handled many drunk driving cases? I'll admit this is my first."

He gave her a wink. "I've had my share. Call me in the morning. I just want to be the fly on the wall to see how you handle yourself." He widened his smirk and pressed a card into her hand. "Just between friends. And then sometime you can see me in action too."

Rhea suppressed her shudder and redoubled her smile. "I look forward to it." She linked her arm with her mother's. "Mom, can I walk you to your car?"

"Certainly, darling. Gentlemen, it's been a pleasure. One I expect we will repeat many times in the future."

The men smiled and nodded their heads before they drifted off to identical large, black SUVs. Rhea tugged her mother's arm back to the parking lot.

"I cannot believe you did that. In front of them. Thank heavens they were facing away. Isn't it time to end that nonsense?" Marion whispered furiously as Rhea pulled away.

Rhea shrugged. "You know I can't exactly help it. I never could."

Her mother shook her head. "I know no such thing. All I know is that you were a difficult child, and you delight in tormenting me. Why couldn't you be more like me? Why?"

"I don't know, Mother. It would have been simpler if I was."

Marion released her arm and pulled her keys from her bag. "You will call Tony at the crack of eight tomorrow. I'll have you moved into the large office next to mine before The Posts arrive. Do you hear me?" Marion jerked open her car door and slid inside. "No questions. Have the

86

secretaries help you. And as far as anyone is concerned, you've been there for the past year. We'll say your nameplate fell off and is being repaired."

Rhea stood there, bemusement dueling with a headache. "Yes, Mother," she said far more docilely than she felt. "And if I'm lucky, Junior will take the case so I can get back to doing what I do best."

Marion gave her a furious look and slammed the door shut. She roared out of the parking lot without another word.

"I should only be so lucky," Rhea muttered to herself. "Oh, Paul," she moaned as she slid into her own car.

Paul

On Friday night, Paul glanced at his phone for the seventeenth time. He was early, and he already knew Rhea wasn't inclined to be on time for their date—their meetings. Shit. No, their—their whatever she wanted to call them. He knew her life was far from easy, and the woman had no downtime to call her own. But he'd do his damnedest to keep her out past her curfew if he could. It was Friday, after all. She'd had to cancel the night before due to work. He supposed he'd need to get used to that sort of thing happening.

He tucked the phone away, and absently rubbed his shoulder through his broadcloth shirt. It felt strange to be dressed up. It had been months since he'd worn anything as formal as a button-down shirt unless it was flannel. He'd even dusted off his iron to press a sharp crease into his chinos.

He glanced out the window again, seeing his reflection as the daylight faded and turned the glass into a mirror. He'd taken scissors to tidy his beard and also scraped the long hair on the top of his head into an elastic. No man-bun for him, but there was nothing wrong with cleaning up.

A car door slammed, and he peered through the glass to see Rhea hurrying across the sidewalk.

She looked beautiful. Her hair was in loose curls about her shoulders. She wore a suit, the jacket open so he could see a form-hugging blouse beneath. Her skirt wasn't short, but it was tight enough to show off her rounded hips. He smiled at her flat soled-shoes. Nothing wrong with those legs.

She breezed in the door, glistening with the light drizzle that was falling outside. "Sorry, I'm late. I rushed over. I had a call that..."

Heart thumping, he rose and took her in his arms and kissed her forehead. "No worries. You're not late. And I would have waited if you were."

She looked up at him. He wasn't certain if she was stunned or just trying to catch her breath. "You really shouldn't be that nice to me," she said as she wiped the moisture from her cheeks. "I'm—I'm..."

Paul linked his arm with hers and drew her into the restaurant's bar. They stopped behind another couple at the hostess desk. "Don't you dare talk yourself down when I'm around," he threatened with a false growl. "My mother worked far too hard to teach us guys to be gentlemen. Besides, nothing negative you say could possibly be true."

She leaned into him and breathed deeply. He could see her hands clench on the strap of her shoulder bag. He noted how the neon blue light from the bar shone on them oddly. She took another breath and stood upright. "Okay. Okay, thank you. It's just that it's been a hard week, and—and..."

"And we're here now. To have a glass of wine. Maybe some appetizers. You can decompress all you want. We're just here to talk, remember?"

He smiled. He couldn't help it. She looked so distressed and so lovely. Her fingers flexed and found new purchase on the leather strap. When the corner of her lips turned up, his heart started to pound.

"You're right. I shouldn't bring the office with me."

The hostess brought them to a tall bistro table. Rhea grimaced as she placed her bag on the edge. "I hate these," she said as she hiked herself up. "They weren't designed for short women wearing tight skirts."

Paul laughed in appreciation as he shifted a hip onto his tall stool. "I can give you a boost with my good arm," he offered.

She laughed. "Nope. I've got it. Reminds me I need to start some routines on those adult monkey bars at the gym next week."

"You can do that arm over arm, no problem," he told her.

"You know I can," she said as she glanced up from the wine list.

"Not so sure I could still walk across the top like I used to," he said.

He wasn't certain, but even in the dim light, she seemed to blanch. "I wonder what's good," she said, changing the topic. "I missed lunch, so I'd better eat, or I won't be responsible for what comes out of my mouth. And I want to leave you with a good impression." She met his gaze above the menu. "Paul, this is the last time we can see each other."

Paul felt a stabbing sensation somewhere in the vicinity of his gut. "I don't mind your talking about work, but no talking about ending our—our friendship," he said with as much levity as he could muster.

She gave him a sad smile. "Something came up—I can't see you after tonight."

He closed his eyes briefly but forced them open at the same time he painted on a smile. "You've met a new trainer," he said. "Someone with bulging biceps—a matching set. Or superior quads, and gargantuan glutes."

Rhea laughed. "No, not that—I mean, we can still say hello at the gym like regular people, but I'm—I've got this difficult case, and I'm—I'm going to be really busy. There's a merger at the firm, and my dad's got pneumonia—it's just crazy." He watched her clench her fists and rub them on the edge of the table. "I need to stay focused."

What wasn't she saying? "So, after a few months, when your case is over, we can, you know, meet for lunch, or drinks, or coffee."

She looked down at her lap. "I'm not sure," she replied so low he had to lean forward to hear. "You may—may have moved on by then. Or not like me anymore."

Oh. Crap. Paul's heart started to race. He stood and moved his stool closer as he waved the waitress away. He sat and wrapped his good arm around her. "I don't know what the hell you're talking about, Rhee." She'd shed her jacket, and her arm was warm and soft, her defined musculature not reducing her utter femininity.

She took a deep breath and shook off his arm with a bright smile that didn't quite extend to her eyes. "Let's not talk about it right now, okay? We're here to have a good time."

Paul leaned back. "Whatever you want, boss," he said. "I'm thinking I want to order something special. I don't usually drink the hard stuff, but I think a single malt scotch sounds good."

She drew in a deep breath. "Make mine a bourbon," she said with a smile. "We'll toast an old friendship regained."

"Now you're talking. And I think some bacon-stuffed

potato skins and those blinis. I've never had them, and they sound fancy. And stuffed radicchio. That sounds like something you would order—what with it being green and all. Sound good?"

Rhea seemed to be holding in a smile as she nodded. "That sounds excellent. Except radicchio is red."

Paul chuckled as he waved the waitress over. "We're ready now."

Two hours later, Rhea's face hurt from smiling. She pressed a glass of ice water to her cheeks to cool them. "I can't believe you want to ride in a hot air balloon," she said with a shake of her head. "Do you have a death wish?"

"Just think about how beautiful it would be to see the fall foliage from the air. I hear it's like floating on a cloud. You don't feel the wind, just drift along on the breeze."

She could just see him, gazing out with those intense brown eyes at the landscape all around them. His face would be wreathed in an excited, adrenalin-fueled smile. "With flame above, a wicker basket below. No, thank you. Just think of a bumpy landing. Bad enough taking off and landing in a plane. At least then, you have an aluminum shell around you."

"I'd bring my camera and take pictures of the journey of a lifetime."

Oh, to see him. To know she'd be there with him that far into the future. "I'd be huddled in the corner, trying to keep from spewing my breakfast," she laughed.

His grin turned maniacal. "So, I'd snap a picture of you looking green and hold it as ransom over you to get what I want."

"As if you'd dare!" she laughed. "You'd have to drug me to get me into one of those things in the first place." She closed her eyes, the bourbon making her dreamy and relaxed. "Nope. For me, the perfect day is spent on a

91

sunny beach, on a blanket with calm, warm water in front of me, a beach chair on the sand below, and a pitcher of margaritas on one side and a pile of good books on the other."

"Boring," he crowed.

She lifted her chin. "So, we really aren't compatible after all. I knew it."

"Hey, I'm all about compromise. What if we were to do the balloon ride in the morning and then hop on a plane and go to the tropics in the afternoon? That sounds do-able. Maybe they have balloon rides in the Islands..."

Rhea giggled. "I don't think so." She slid her credit card into her purse, having just won the right to pay for their meal.

"I'm looking it up," he said as he pulled out his phone."

She tipped it down to look at the time. Her heart started racing. "Oh Jeeze. It's late. I have to go."

"Don't tell me you need to do more work. It's after ten."

"I need to put in another three hours," she replied.

He laid a rough-skinned hand on her arm, his touch gentle. She wanted more of him, so much so, she tried to pull away from the agony of knowing what could never be. "It can't wait until the morning?"

She closed her eyes. The image of her recalcitrant client and then her future partner swam before her mind's eye, and she shook her head. "No—I—I can't explain, but I do have to go. I've got this client—and a future partner— and it's all so complicated." She slid off her stool and winced as she landed on her weak ankle. "I need to make a good showing tomorrow. I need to prep..."

Paul stood and took her arm. "Okay, I get it. Sorry to keep you out so late. But we were having so much fun."

She put her hand on his arm, and the shock of their physical connection—small as it was—nearly undid her.

She slid it off and fumbled for her purse. "I know. It's not your fault. I should have been paying attention to the time."

She shrugged on her jacket.

"We'll do this on the weekend the next time." He took her elbow and guided her through the crowded room.

Rhea pulled back. "I told you—there can't be a next time."

Paul's smile faded. "You don't mean that. I get that you're busy. Let's say we make a date—not a date-date, but just set up time to meet. In a month. You'll be doing better in a month, won't you?"

She bit her lip. "This case, I think it could take a while—into the new year. I can't get my clients—I can't even tell you that much. Oh, Paul."

They stepped out into the fresh night air. "Rhea…"

She dared not look at him. "Don't make this more difficult than it already is," she asked softly.

"I know I'm not dreaming when I say there's something between us. There always was. I think there always will be," he replied, all trace of humor gone.

It was true, but she couldn't give in to something that could never be. Rhea shook her head. "You have to believe me when I tell you I can't. It's not for me—it's for you."

"For a smart lady, you're not making any sense. I m trying to understand, but all I can think about is that I want to kiss you. Really kiss you." He leaned his forehead down to lightly touch hers. "And I'm thinking too, that maybe you want to kiss me just as much as I do you."

She clenched her trembling hands and wanted to step away, but her traitorous feet would not move.

His hands were on her shoulders, rubbing them gently until they moved upward to cradle her face. She lifted her lids to stare into his eyes. "Oh Paul…"

"Shhhh," he said and brushed his lips against hers as softly as a breeze. "Tell me it's okay to kiss you. Please. I want to so badly."

"Paul, I..."

He must have taken it as consent, for his lips met hers again, gently pressing, nibbling before they parted. Of their own volition, she turned up her face to meet his lips again, and this time the kiss was deepened, but if it were he or she who started it, Rhea did not know. All she knew was that his hands were warm as they lit upon her cheeks. He was gentle and kind and put so much into that chaste kiss that she could not stand it, for before she knew it, Rhea was on her toes, her arms around him, her face turned to slant her lips across his. Her mouth opened, and he explored it with his tongue, darting inside as if uncertain of his welcome.

She made a sound of pleasure unlike any she'd ever made before, and he heard it, answered it with a groan of his own.

"Rhea," he breathed as he broke their lips apart and held her tightly. "Don't tell me we can't see each other again. I lost you for so long. I can't bear to again. You can't tell me that whatever this is between us doesn't feel right."

She pulled away and pressed her forehead to his sternum, shaking it slightly. "Paul—there are things about me—things I can't tell you."

"Work?"

She shook her head, then nodded. "Work, life..."

"You can tell me anything," he breathed.

"That's just it." She pulled away, tugged her hands free of him. "I can't. As much as I want to, I cannot."

"Rhea..."

She shook her head and stepped back. "I wish—oh how I wish things were different." She looked around wildly. "I have to go."

"I'll call you."

She shook her head, turned, and walked away.

"I mean it," Paul called to her as her steps carried her across the street.

Rhea took a ragged breath, turned her face as she continued to walk. "Don't," she managed, before she turned again, to her life, to her agonizing cases. "Please don't," she whispered again as she got into her car, slammed the door, unable to look at him once more.

Chapter Ten

Berry

"...and then she drove off."

Paul shoved his chair away from my kitchen table, stood, and walked around and around until he threw himself into another chair. "What kind of woman would kiss me like that—like she meant it, wanted it, wanted me, and then just leave?" He ran his hands through his hair, wincing as his left shoulder moved too fast. "I don't get it."

I held the table still when he pushed away a second time. My peppermint tea had sloshed but not spilled the first time he did it, but with each word, my poor brother-in-law grew more frustrated. I was glad Moe was upstairs giving Mattie a bath while Paul poured his heart out to me. Moe is a charming guy, and I love him with all my heart, but his sensitivity meter can't always be trusted, especially where his brothers' hearts are concerned.

"It sounds like there's something she can't tell you," I offered.

"But we're friends. She can tell me anything," he cried out. Well, not cried. To be honest, he sort of whined but I'm trying to make him out to be heroic. Given that it's my job, I hope you understand.

"You're friends now, but you and she haven't spoken in years," I reminded him. "And she's a lawyer. She has to be careful who she trusts, especially with sensitive stuff. Attorney-client privilege and all."

"I guess," he said, slumped with his hands clasped between his knees, his shoulders hunched. If I had to describe a dejected hero in one of my novels, it would be exactly how Paul was sitting at that moment.

"I guess you really like her," I said under my breath.

He nodded, not lifting his head. "It's crazy how much I do." He looked at me then, and I swear his eyes were pooling with tears. "I can't believe it happened so fast. Like I've been waiting for her all these years. Ber, I think I love her…"

"Paul, that's crazy. You just reconnected." I tried to stand for emphasis, but the baby I was carrying kind of anchored me to my seat. It's hard to make grand, dramatic gestures when you're in your seventh month. I needed to work on my vocal cues.

"I was in love with her when I was seven," he replied. "As much in love as a little kid could be. She was always special. Smart, cute, sassy. She skipped two grades, Ber, she was that smart. She was fearless…"

"Oh, come on," I interrupted.

"No. You should have seen her flying across those monkey bars, trying new stunts." He pressed his hands over his eyes. "I used to copy everything she did." He dropped his hands, and then his head. "Like a jerk, I used to brag I was first, but it was always her. That's when I first broke my collarbone. Trying to copy her. I was showing off. To impress her. She ran to get help…" He closed his eyes to remember. "Damn, that was when we stopped being friends. Just like that." Paul looked at me again, his eyes glittering still. "Just like last night. Sudden. No explanation. She just decides it's time to go, and boom, she's gone. I got no say…"

I must have tsked or something as he looked at me sharply.

"What?" he accused.

I thought a long moment before I replied. I didn't want him angry with me, but I thought he deserved a different point of view. "From what you described, unless it's work-related, or family pressure, maybe she's not all that stable. I mean, if she's doing this to get your attention or to lead you on…" I couldn't finish my thought.

"You're wrong, Berry." Paul's voice was gentle but firm. "You don't know her, you don't understand. She's the most stable, grounded person in the world. There has to be something else. You're right. It's probably work or her family. I know her dad's in a nursing home, and her mother has always been kind of distant. I never met her. Rhea always had a nanny. Her folks never went to school things—even award ceremonies. I think the only time I ever saw them was at graduation."

He sat back, his face once again resembling the good-natured brother-in-law I knew and loved. "As if we're anyone to talk, what with all your 'woo-woo' stuff."

Upstairs we could hear Mattie shrieking gaily amid sounds of splashing and Moe's chuckles. I winced, thinking of the puddles on the floor. It was truly a miracle we didn't have water stains on the downstairs ceilings. Yet.

"Speaking of woo-woo stuff, the Mattser isn't showing any signs of being able to…" and he gestured vaguely.

I shook my head definitively. "None. And we don't talk about it in front of her. Annie's her only connection to that world. And it's not like I ever exhibited anything like that until I was older…" Kind of. I seem to remember some weird stuff when I was a kid… but never mind that. I pressed my lips together. I didn't need to tell him Moe and I were always on the lookout for any 'special' qualities in our daughter. Thank goodness there was nothing. So far. "I don't know what I'd do if she had any sort of, well, you know."

He nodded. "Yeah, that would be a nightmare." He played with the water glass before him. "So—what do you think I should do?"

"I think you need to respect her request and leave her alone."

He pressed his lips together. "I was afraid you'd say that."

"I don't want you arrested for stalking her," I said, hoping for some levity.

Fortunately, he smiled. "Yeah. I couldn't believe she kissed me back. I mean it was totally spontaneous. I just wanted to spend time with her, like a buddy. Not that I didn't hope, of course."

I grinned and told him, "You'd make the perfect hero for a story of mine. Are you sure you don't want my help…"

He shook his head. "That might of worked for Moe, Joey, and Petey. You know Sammy's gonna need all the help he can get. But not me. I don't want to have anything to do with that stuff."

I sighed and rubbed my belly as my son tried to do a summersault. He was pretty much out of room for gymnastics. "I respect that. Besides, I'm too far along in my story. There's no way I want to get side-tracked by having to corral any heroines out in the real world for you right now."

He lifted his glass as if in a toast. "Good thing, and thank you. When I get my girl—and I will get her one way or another, even if I have to wait years, it's going to be based on my own hard work, good planning, and my innate charm. I wish you could get to know her. You, Jen, and Annie—even Ma would love her. She'd be the perfect addition to the family…"

"You want to marry her?" I asked carefully. Of all the brothers, Paul was the most adamant about never wanting to formalize a relationship. Even Sammy had acknowledged he knew he'd eventually succumb.

He sighed and leaned closer. "Don't you dare tell Moe

or the other guys, but yeah."

"Well, damn," I said under my breath. Inside I was all grins knowing something my husband didn't. I'd have bet even my mother-in-law Rosemary didn't have a clue. "You're secret's safe with me," I assured him. Which wasn't saying much. Truthfully, some secrets weren't all that safe in my hands other than about the 'woo-woo' stuff, and in this family I married into—a secret that lasted twenty-four hours was a rarity indeed. Unless it was something one of my sisters-in-law told me. Those were sacrosanct.

"You have to give her space," I cautioned him. "You said she's still going to the gym. You have to be respectful but chat her up there. Maybe you can find out more of what's going on. Be there for her when whatever it is gets resolved. If she's got something to hide, she's probably got a good reason for it."

He nodded and then sighed the longest, saddest sigh I'd ever heard.

"And don't pry. And whatever you do, watch out for red flags. I'm not going to tell you she's nuts. I've only met her one time, and we didn't really talk. But you can't tell her about..." I gestured around myself, "...you know what. That's only for family members, and then only once we know they won't rat us out to the authorities."

I'll admit it. I was afraid if anyone found out about my abilities, I'd be taken away in a white van to some secret location where humorless men in white coats would run experiments on me, and I'd never get to see my dear husband and children or assorted family members ever again. I loved my career, but I was fierce in my desire to maintain our privacy, especially since Pete and Annie now had a little baby of their own—an entirely human, ethereal and calm, beautiful six-month-old little girl. Oh and Jenny and Joey'd had a robust little boy about a week before that.

One more person, Mrs. Mc G, er, McGillicuddy knew about me. She's a, um, friend who has some rather unusual abilities in her capacity as a professional matchmaker. I'll explain about her some other time except to say I've been helping her chronicle the romances she's promoted and hoped to publish them as fiction sometime.

No, this woo-woo stuff wasn't entirely bad. In fact, at times it was downright good. If unnerving even for those who were accustomed to it.

Regardless, our conversation came to an end when Moe came down, hauling a fresh, clean, and still somewhat slippery Mattie over his shoulder. It made me long for the early days when he was afraid to pick her up for fear he'd hurt her. Now I worried how he'd treat his soon-to-be baby son—would he forget about delicate necks and soft spots on the top of his head?

He plopped our daughter down on what remained of my lap, and I was treated to a warm cuddle from my first baby. I dressed her in her pajamas, and a moment later, she leapt from my lap into her uncle's arms. He was soon zooming her around the kitchen to her delighted squeals.

Moe helped himself to a glass of water from the fridge and sat down to look on cheerfully as his daughter's life was casually threatened with tosses into the air and near crashes of made-up airplanes.

"So, how's things?" he asked Paul. "See any more of that Thia? I liked her."

I glanced at Paul. He hadn't hesitated as he flew Mattie beneath the ceiling fan, but his put-put-put noises diminished in volume and enthusiasm. "It's Rhea. And we're, uh, taking a break," he said. "A short break." Paul threw a meaningful look my way that my husband certainly caught but wisely didn't comment on. "She's really busy right now. Big case or something."

"You sure she didn't just decide she'd had enough of you?" Moe asked with a yawn. "You are kind of shallow, you know."

Paul grunted as he brought Mattie down for a bumpy landing—her favorite part. She ended up back in my arms, where I pretended she was a delicate little flower for the two seconds it took before she squirmed away and went to play in the corner with her blocks—all irregular angles and smooth, rounded edges thanks to Uncle Paul's workshop.

"Just because I don't share all my deepest thoughts..."

"Yeah. Right. Deep," Moe snorted.

Paul shot him a look of brotherly disgust as he threw himself back into his chair. "...deep thoughts with you doesn't mean I don't have any. Rhea likes me just fine."

"So, how long is this time-out going to last?" Moe asked, wading into deeper waters than he knew.

Paul shrugged. "A few weeks. She's got to put in a lot of hours preparing for some big case. I'll see her at the gym. Now that I can put in a few hours in the workshop each day, I'll adjust my workouts to when she can go." He glanced quickly at me and back at his brother with his chin up. "I'm not letting her out of my life."

Moe nodded as he glanced over to see Mattie building a tower slowly and carefully, stopping after each addition to see if it would teeter. She topped it off with a pink plastic teacup and saucer.

"Well, in the meanwhile, I mean, while you're waiting for her, why not let Berry introduce you to one of her single friends? Or Jenny or Annie? They all know a lot of babes." Moe shot me a guilty glance. "I mean eligible young women."

"I don't think I'd like any of Berry's women," Paul muttered. "No offense," he added with a quick look my way.

"None taken. Besides, my circle of unmarried babes has been shrinking lately," I said. "Remember, we went to about six weddings last year."

He grinned at me. "Yeah. I remember. I think I knocked you up right after the third one."

That's my Moe. Heart of gold. Manners—not so much.

"I don't need help finding women," Paul said, just the teensiest bit defensively. "I've always been a chick magnet." He gave me another guilty sideline glance. "Sorry, Ber."

I threw my hands up. "I give up on you two. For tonight. You can be sure this son of mine is going to have a lot more manners than either of you."

"Within your hearing," Paul and Moe said at the same time.

"Well, that's better than either of you," I shot back to their laughter. Which, of course, made Mattie's tower tip over, sending the teacup sliding across the floor and under the cast iron radiator where I'd never be able to reach t until after this baby was born. She let out a howl of delight at the destruction around her. And to think my mother wants to give her a real china tea set.

"You two help her put those away. I'm not doing any bending over for the next three months," I reminded them. "And Paul, you can read her three bedtime stories. Moe and I will be on the couch in the parlor."

He made a face. "You two aren't going to be fooling around while I read, are you?"

Moe smiled and waggled his eyebrows before winking at me. I glared at my husband, all in good fun. "I don't think so."

"Rats," Moe chimed in, right on cue.

Paul

It took an hour before he tucked his sleeping niece into her bed and replaced the railing, said good night to his brother and sister-in-law, and climbed into his beater. He took a long route home, driving past Rhea's to see a light on in the back of the house, in what he assumed was her kitchen. It was a tidy little cape. Nothing special. It struck him as odd, given that she'd grown up in luxury. Why did she buy an ordinary little house instead of a high-end condo? Hers was a neighborhood of contrasts. Some houses had swing sets in the back yard, while others had wheelchair ramps. The driveways were full of everything from economy cars and trucks to high-end SUVs. Then again, Rhea was a study in contrasts, so it would make sense she'd buy someplace that was not all one thing or another.

He pulled over to the curb and put the truck in park for a moment while he stared at her home. He could see himself living there with her, helping her fix the place up, making custom furniture or built-ins. He'd get Pete to help with the landscaping. Joey could design a new façade and maybe a bump-out in the back, or a dormer upstairs. Moe and Sammy would help make the changes. Or they could sell it and buy something they could both love...

Paul shook himself from his daydream. He still didn't know how he'd get Rhea back on track in their relationship—if they even had one. But he'd still be friendly at the gym. And attentive. He'd let her know he was waiting for her.

Shallow? Maybe once upon a time. Faithful was more like it. It was the Conrad code. He'd never cheated on a girlfriend in his life. Which wasn't to say he hadn't given women an easy excuse to leave once or twice. He'd made an off-color joke or say something to piss them off, but he'd never cheated, not so much as thought about it. So far, there hadn't been a woman that he'd regretted letting get away.

Except for Rhea. Now that he knew she was the woman he wanted to spend the rest of his life with, he'd spend as much time as he needed to win her over. He almost snorted a laugh, thinking about her saying he'd move on to another woman. Like hell. He'd been there, done that, all the while waiting for her when he didn't even know that's what he was about. And he wanted her to stay, no excuses or exceptions.

Providing she didn't learn about the family secrets— okay, Berry's secret. Or Annie's for that matter. Or if she heard about some of their so-called friends from years ago. Any one of those things would undoubtedly make Rhea jump in her car and drive as far away from him as she possibly could go. Nope. It was going to be a good, long while before he revealed any of that to her.

It should have made him sad. There were so many things wrong in his life, so much unsettled, but he didn't despair. Perhaps that was the benefit of being shallow. Things didn't get to him. He still had hope.

With a snort of derision, he put his truck in drive and made his way home. He'd get her back. Just as soon as he figured out how.

Rhea

Her skin prickled. It took a moment before she realized she was rubbing her arms, but once she was, there was no going back to studying the file until she figured out what was going on.

She left her kitchen and a cup of chamomile tea on the table and made her way gingerly through the dark house to the front window. Her ankle was still sore. That flying leap the other night hadn't been the smartest thing she'd ever done, but there were times she just could not help herself.

Moving her curtain a fraction, Rhea glanced out her picture window to see a truck idling out front. She squinted to see the driver's profile, and her hand flew to her mouth when she realized who it was.

Heart pounding, she dropped the curtain, only to flick it back again. He wasn't getting out. He wasn't even looking in her direction. He seemed instead—lonely.

God knew she was lonely too.

Rhea closed her eyes and imagined herself sitting next to him. Her fingertips were pressed to the cool glass, and in her mind's eye, she saw their vehicles parked side by side in the driveway, the two of them on the sofa, or laying in the bed, holding hands, asleep.

She flashed them open to see movement outside. In the lamplight, she imagined she saw him nod her way, smile, and drive slowly off.

"Godspeed," she whispered. "And good luck. We're both going to need it."

Chapter Eleven

Paul

His mother's voice rang out over the flagstones on his brother Pete's backyard patio, "Paul."

"Damn," he whispered under his breath before he turned and smiled at her. "Hey, Mom. I didn't know you were coming today." He bent to kiss her cheek.

"Sure, you didn't." She gave him a playful swat on his good shoulder. "Pete and Annie didn't tell you I was on my way to see my grandbaby?" She hooked her arm through his, effectively turning him back into the house.

"They might have mentioned it," he replied. 'I remember thinking you wanted to fuss over the little princess. You can see me any old time."

She gave him a squeeze. "You're still one of my babies," she said in her take no prisoners voice. "And you're still hurting. Of course, I wanted to see you. Besides, the baby's sleeping. Can't do much except admire her."

They went in the back door. "I told Pete to take Anne out for a cup of coffee. Poor thing hasn't been out without the baby in weeks. She needed to get some fresh air and a little attention from her husband. I told him to rent a hotel room."

"Ma," Paul groaned. 'Why is it I have to hear about my brothers' sex lives, whether or not I want to?"

She gave him a light dope slap. "Sex! No. So, they could take a nap." She looked at him sideways. "Why? You afraid of a little sex talk? I thought you weren't scared of anything."

Paul rubbed his head. "No. And why are you so

concerned about everyone's sleep patterns? The baby, Pete, and Annie..."

"When you have one of your own, you'll understand," Rosemary replied. "Now sit. I'll make some coffee, and you can tell me how the case is coming."

"My lawyer said the idiot finally got someone to represent him. She says his lawyer is good, reasonable and thinks we should finally be able to settle through mediation. If I'm lucky, we might be done in a month."

Rosemary's face brightened. "They've sure been taking their time for something that shoulda been done months ago. And your brother tells me you're going back to work?"

He shrugged. "I'm not ready to work for Moe. I see the doc again in a few weeks. I'm at the woodshop for a few hours a week. Making a little something here and there. Keeping busy."

"And Moe tells me there's a girl...?"

"Moe's been telling you a lot of stuff," he complained. "There is no girl. I met up with someone I used to know. You remember Rhea from when I was a kid?"

"Skinny little thing with the beautiful eyes? Had all those beaded braids? I used to love playing with those."

He smiled. "Yeah. That was her. All grown up now."

"Pretty?" Rosemary asked.

"That doesn't even begin to cover it." He grinned. "Still the smartest person in the room. She's a lawyer, just like her parents. She works too hard."

His mother frowned. "That makes dating a challenge."

"Which is why we're not dating. She's got a big case... we're taking it easy. We'll pick things up in a few months."

Rosemary frowned. "I don't like the sounds of that. Maybe Berry or one of the others has a woman they can introduce you to."

Paul rolled his eyes. "Ma..." he warned.

Rhea

"I want a report on how the case is shaping up."

Rhea jumped at the interruption and ripped the envelope she'd been slitting open with her father's gold plated letter opener. Her new office was carpeted, something the old one lacked, so the clatter of her mother's high-heeled footsteps no longer broadcast her impending presence.

She set down the implement on the corner of her desk and faced her mother. "It's going as well as can be expected," she replied. "It didn't help having Junior at the last meeting. Our client kept looking at him for answers rather than me. It was disconcerting and more than a little intrusi…"

"But are you making progress? AJ said you were pressing for a settlement. He felt he needed to step in to keep the case on track."

"I *am* pressing for a settlement," Rhea replied. "It is in everyone's best interest."

"Well, Junior wasn't very impressed with you."

Rhea sat back and rested her hands behind her head. "And did it occur to you that he might think it in his selfish best interest to talk me down in front of you? More for him when you and his father retire."

Marion inspected her manicure. "I'm certain that's not the case."

Rhea stared at her mother. "And I'm certain it is. But if you want to give him the case, I'll be more than happy to hand it off. Get back to doing what I do best and helping people with real work." *Though Paul would suffer if I did.*

Her mother tsked. "You could be so good at this if you just set your mind to it."

"I don't want to be good at that sort of law."

Marion tsked. "You really are spoiled despite my best

efforts. Do you think I had the opportunity to turn cases down when I was just starting out? Of course not. I took what I was given, and I did my best for each of my clients. I didn't have any personal feelings about them. If I'd ventured an opinion, the partners would have laughed me out the door."

Rhea looked at her desk and took a deep breath. "Maybe I'm not cut out for this firm after all. You make it sound as if you had no choice, but the truth is, you chose to stay. You were smart, and I'm not saying it would have been easy, but you could have gone to another firm. You could have hung out your own shingle. You didn't have to take cases you didn't want."

"I did what I had to do to succeed," Marion replied. "And so will you." She went to the window. "Tony tells me AJ asked you to dinner and that you said no."

Rhea thought back to the cryptic text message she'd received the day before. "He asked if I wanted to get together some time." She picked up her cellphone and scrolled to find it. "He wanted to hang out." She held the phone out to her mother. "See. No mention of dinner."

Her mother took the device. "You have to read between the lines, darling."

Rhea took the phone back. "I did. This is code for a hook up. He's engaged. I told him if he wanted to make plans to discuss the case, to let me know. I haven't heard back from him."

"Nor did you make plans with him." Marion gracefully sat in one of the two chairs opposite Rhea's new desk.

Rhea blew a curl out of her eyes. "Really, Mother?"

"You could have been more receptive."

"I don't have time for this," Rhea stated. "I'm working day and night trying to find out how to salvage this shit-storm of a case, keep up with my other work, and now I'm to blame because your potential partner's son doesn't have the balls to ask me out on his own, so he has to talk to his father, who has to talk to you, and I get blamed for rejecting him? Truly? Is this what my life's come to?"

"You needn't take it out on me." Her mother pouted as she stood. "And here I am, just trying to be cupid's messenger."

"Cupid?" Rhea caught the letter opener before it skittered across the desk. "Cupid?" Her voice was rising. "Are you going to tell me next I have to marry that sorry excuse of a lawyer for the sake of the firm? Because in case you forgot, he's already got a fiancée, and I will not be a willing participant to bigamy. So, if you are, you can assume this is the last time I will come in to work in this office."

"Oh, calm down. You always were so excitable. The next thing I know, you'll be shooting green sparks out of your fingers."

Rhea set the implement down in the middle of her desk. "For your information, I've never once shot green sparks. They've always been gold, or silver—blue on rare occasions. And none since high school. I've at least put that behind me."

"No, these days, you just jump over monster puddles when people are looking. If you have to be a freak of nature, the least you can do is to hide it." Marion stood and headed for the door. "I'll tell Junior to stop being a distraction. But he wants to be kept abreast of the case as much as I do."

"I don't understand any of this, Rhea admitted. "Nothing adds up."

"That's for me to worry about, darling," her mother said as she made her way through the door and down the carpeted hallway. "Don't forget, I want a status report tomorrow following your next meeting. Ta-ta." And she closed the door behind her.

Rhea groaned and rested her head on her desk. "How the hell did I get myself into this mess?" she moaned. Moments later, she heard a twang and thud. She looked up to find the letter opener imbedded the back of the wooden door.

"Crap," she said and rested her head once more. After taking a deep breath, she rose, strode to the door, and pulled the knife out of the wood. She ran her finger over the gash in the door, healing it. "I'd better work off this energy. Fast."

She leaned against the wooden panel and closed her eyes. "To whatever spirits are listening, help me make this right."

Paul

He knew the instant Rhea walked through the gym's door. There was a change in the air pressure, or perhaps the last of the afternoon sun shone a little brighter through the plate glass windows. Whatever it was, his head turned to see her swipe her membership card through the reader. Their eyes met, and she acknowledged him with a slow, subtle nod before she looked away.

Had it only been ten days since they'd seen each other? She looked drawn, more exhausted than ever. Her face was thinner with stress lines around her mouth. Maybe she missed him as much as he'd been missing her. Maybe, his new, more sensitive conscience told him, there was something more than the neglect of his heart going on.

He returned his attention to helping a friend perfect his form when curling hand weights. He needed to give Rhea time to work out whatever it was she needed to expunge, and then they'd talk.

Ninety minutes later, after she'd gone through her workout at the weight and toning machines and spent time on her cardio routine, she was at the water fountain refilling her water bottle. He approached her.

"Hey," he said as casually as he could.

"Hey, yourself," Rhea replied, taking a long sip. That gave him time to admire the curve of her throat and to watch the muscles work beneath her skin as she drank. A bead of perspiration trailed down her throat, making him want to lick it away.

He looked away as she lowered the bottle. "Things okay?" he asked gently.

Rhea shook her head. "Actually, No. Things are not very good at all."

"Want to talk about it?"

She nodded, her eyes bright, and he wondered if she was blinking back tears.

"There's that coffee shop next door. We can order tea, seeing it's late."

"I need the coffee to stay awake," she replied. "I have work when I get home. I shouldn't have even come tonight."

"Get your stuff. Another ten minutes won't hurt," he urged.

Rhea sighed and nodded, but she didn't move. "Yeah I don't think I'm good for much right now." She looked up and met his gaze. "I was hoping you'd be here tonight. I— there's something I need to tell you."

"Let's go," he said as gently as he could. His hand went to her shoulder, and he turned her toward the locker room. "I'll be in the lobby."

She hung her head. "Yeah. Okay."

He watched her walk away. Gone was her jaunty

step—her toes were practically dragging, and his gut tightened. Whatever it was she needed to tell him, he had a feeling he wasn't going to like it.

Rhea

Feeling as if she were underwater, Rhea dragged an oversized sweatshirt over her gym clothes and shoved her things in her bag. She pulled her purse from its depths and slung it over her shoulder, and sat on the bench. She closed her eyes. *How am I going to tell him? How can I ease the blow?*

She straightened her shoulders. *Just tell him. Don't be a coward—just say it.*

Paul was waiting by the front door, leaning on the counter and kidding around with the staff, but straightened as soon as he saw her, and his playful grin melted into concern as his eyebrows tented. "See you guys tomorrow," he said to the man and woman behind the counter. "You ready?" he asked Rhea.

She nodded. "Yeah. Let's get this over with."

Paul frowned as he opened the doors with his bad side, wincing slightly. "I get the feeling I'm not going to like what you're about to tell me."

She was silent, so he tried again. "So, you're married and have twin daughters you've kept secret from me. Or you're an alien abductee with superpowers and are about to return to planet Zybxx, and you have to erase all memory of you from my mind."

She snorted a reply—she simply could not help herself. "You're closer than you may think," she replied. "I think this is going to need something stronger than coffee and cookies. Do they stock vodka next door?"

He laughed. "I asked but, no go. We could go someplace else, but the only bars that wouldn't turn their noses up at us right now are the kinds of places I would never take you."

She looked down at her clothes. "Yeah, I guess. But a dive bar would suit my mood. Better than this place." She pointed her chin at the brightly lit coffee shop. "It's too damned cheerful."

Paul chuckled. "We could go to my place, but that's closer to a dive bar than I like to admit."

"We can't go to mine." Her voice sounded flat to her own ears. "This will have to do."

She pushed open the door and held it for Paul. They got on the short line, retrieved their drinks, and moments later found a small table.

"So, tell me how and why the world is coming to an end," Paul asked, one side of his mouth turning up. "I can't make it better until I know what the problem is."

Rhea set her cup down carefully and pressed her fingers over her eyes. "I wish I could joke about this, but I can't." She dropped her hands. "It's like this. The case I've taken on, the one that's giving me fits…"

He covered her hand with his. "Do I need to beat someone up for you?" he teased. "Pay off a judge?"

She drew in a deep breath and withdrew from his touch, then tucked her hands into her lap. "I'm representing Brice Post."

"You're representing…" She watched him take a gulp of air. "You're not serious."

"I wish."

"How… I mean what… why…" His sputtering ended quickly, and he rubbed his bad shoulder distractedly. "I don't understand."

Rhea ducked her head. "There's client-attorney privilege."

"But why did you agree to take this on?"

She shook her head. "There are reasons," she said slowly. "I'm not at liberty to discuss them with you. But you were bound to find out. I wanted to at least give you the courtesy of telling you myself."

"Thank you," he replied, though it was clear he didn't mean it as he stared into his cup.

"In a perfect world, I would be able to tell you how sorry I am..." she began.

"Save it," he replied curtly.

She nodded and pushed her cookie in his direction. "I can't eat this."

"I don't want it," he replied in a diminished voice.

"I can hardly eat anything anymore," she said, though it was hard to tell if he was listening.

"Why?" he asked.

"Why tell you?"

"Why are you representing that...that..."

"Everyone is entitled to representation," Rhea replied softly.

"Maybe I should ask, how could you? There are other lawyers," he said bitterly.

"Ah. Well. That's the million-dollar question, isn't it?" She was silent. "That's the part I can't talk about."

"Is that son of a bitch paying you a million dollars to keep his ass out of jail? Because giving me what's my due would be a hell of a lot cheaper."

"Paul, I can't..."

"Can't or won't?" he asked, shoving back his chair.

People began to stare.

She looked him in the eye as steadily as she could, ignoring the rage within. She clenched her fists and breathed deeply. "I cannot. Not now. Not until it's over. Not even then. Client-attorney privilege."

She looked up at him—his arms crossed over his chest.

"I don't understand. I thought we were friends. I thought—thought we could be so much more," he said.

She winced. More heads turned. "I... I thought so too.'

The background chatter seemed to die away.

"And you're willing to throw that all away, throw away your own life and happiness for a case? Against me?"

She bowed her head. "It seems that way."

"Goodbye, Rhea."

Her head popped up. "Paul..."

But all she could see was his back, storming through the small crowd, slammed open the door and headed and out into the darkness.

She felt the gaze of strangers swivel from Paul's angry departure back to her, and she ducked her head. There was sound again, people talking in hushed voices. She focused on her coffee and felt heat creep up her neck and cheeks. She grabbed her cup lest it slide away from her and be hurled against the wall.

The front door whooshed open again. She lifted her head to see Paul charging in. Her mouth opened in surprise, but before she could say a word, he scooped her into his arms and kissed her. Kissed her with fury and rage. Kissed her with regret and tears. He kissed her long and hard as if he loved her. He kissed her until it felt like goodbye.

And then, once more, he was gone.

Chapter Twelve

Berry

Now, I don't normally mind my home being a place of refuge for my extended family. I'm actually flattered my brothers-in-law think of me as a big sister they can confide in. I know it's because I'm married to their eldest brother, but when their hearts are aching, it's me they come to, not Moe.

I don't mind. Normally. But it was late—okay, late for pregnant-old-me, and I'd put in a full day of being mommy and writer not to mention all the wifeing (is that a real word? Well, it is now) I'd done, and I was just about to get into bed when I heard pounding on the back door. Moe was out. I was going to ignore it, but when I saw Paul's truck in our driveway, I knew I'd better let him in. I hurried (well, hurried for *me*) and threw open the door. "Is everything okay?"

He brushed past me. "Moe home?"

"No." I shut the door behind him. "He's at the contractors' meeting. He won't be home until close to eleven." I looked at him again and at the kitchen table. It was quieter in the kitchen, and he was less likely to wake Mattie. "Something's wrong."

He sank into a chair.

Now you have to understand something. Paul's a big guy. Tall like the rest of his brothers. And despite his injury, he's still strong, especially on the right. He's got a loving, sunny disposition—remember I told you he can be kind of shallow? A fun guy. Lots of friends. Women love him. He's muscular without an ounce of fat on him (that I could see, and given my status as sister-in-law, I didn't look *that*

118

hard), but that night he just seemed to curl in on himself until he was small as a baby. Okay, I'm exaggerating. Small as a child. He looked so beaten down. I wanted to take him into my arms to comfort him. Given my state I settled for rubbing his arm.

"Berry," he sighed. "She's gone over to the dark side."

I did not laugh. I swear it. I wanted to, but the look on his face—his whole posture kept me from bursting out in unseemly guffaws. He hadn't even looked this dispirited after the accident.

"Do you want coffee?" I asked.

He shook his head. "Got any bourbon? No, that's what she drinks. I want something strong."

I rummaged in the liquor cabinet over the sink, up on my tiptoes, which was no easy feat. "We have vodka, and I think there's tequila. I can't reach either."

He came up behind me, and I stepped aside as he reached for a bottle. "I'll get you a glass," I said hurriedly. The last thing I wanted was for him to take it from the bottle. The Conrad brothers aren't big drinkers. They all claimed they could hold their liquor. I'd never seen one of them drunk, but I didn't want to test that theory.

"Thanks." He set the tequila on the counter and returned to his seat. Of course, he wanted me to serve him, but given the circumstances, I was happy to play bartender. I poured a stiff shot and handed it to him as I recapped the bottle and shoved it halfway behind my flour canister when his back was turned.

I sat across from him and waited until he took a sip. He winced and then downed it, sucking air through his teeth like a cowboy in an old western.

"What happened?" I asked after he'd taken a breath and wiped the tear from his eye.

Paul told me. Not that there was much to tell—just a

few sentences about what Rhea said and how he'd reacted. He wasn't going to tell me about the kiss, but I think it slipped out of its own accord. And *that* told me more than the rest of it combined.

In a word, the situation sucked.

We sat in silence as he checked his glass for any remaining drops, then pushed it away. He didn't ask for a second shot or look for the bottle, just stared at the table.

I sighed, and he looked up.

"Any words of wisdom?" he asked wryly.

I took a deep breath. "I'm thinking." Which I was, furiously. Unfortunately, fatigue and hormones were working against me that night. A moment later, I shook my head. "Sorry. Not a one."

"How about if you put on your Solange hat?"

It's not that I have a split personality in the classical sense, but I like to think that my powers to bring characters to life originate with my alter ego rather than plain old Berry Samuels Conrad. "I thought you didn't like Solange?" I replied with a bit of a smile.

"At this point, I'm ready to take any advice I can get." He scrubbed his face with his hands before he looked straight at me. "I've never—I've never had my heart broken before."

"Oh, Paul." I reached for his hand.

Which was, of course, when Moe walked in the kitchen door. His brows lifted in surprise, but he's a sharp guy. I saw him scan the kitchen counters, and I knew he had a good idea of what was going on when they lit on the bottle and then on his brother. I nodded, and he nodded, and that was that.

"You makin' moves on my wife, little brother?" Moe asked jovially as he sat down beside me and slung an arm around my shoulders. He pressed in for a kiss. "I have to

120

tell you, she's the best there is, but if you want her, you're going to have to go through me to get her."

Paul grunted. That one shot was obviously enough to do the trick.

Moe leaned closer to whisper, "Is the guest room ready?" I nodded, and he kissed my cheek again. "I'll make sure he gets upstairs." He leaned back. "Ber, you look exhausted. Why don't you go on up? Paul and I'll do some talking. You want another belt?" he asked, nodding at the bottle while snagging Paul's keys off the table.

Paul shook his head. "That stuff is awful. I thought you kept better hooch."

Moe walked me to the kitchen door. "I keep the good stuff hidden from you and the other guys. Don't want you coming over here all the time, making free with my booze."

Paul gave a snort-laugh as Moe kissed me again and shooed me up the stairs. Did I mention what a good guy my husband is?

He told me all about their conversation the next morning while Paul slept off his hangover. It turns out the poor man really couldn't hold his liquor after all.

This is pretty much what Moe conveyed, but given my writing proclivities, I'll tell it to you my way.

"So, she's the opposition. Doesn't mean much," Moe stated.

Paul looked at him, incredulously. "She's the smartest woman out there. My case, the one I thought was air-tight—she's gonna rip it to shreds. That woman never gives an inch."

Moe shook his head. "She's smart, all right. And smart lawyers try to find compromises. Maybe this is a good thing. Since she likes you and all."

"I don't know about that. She chose that case over me."

"Maybe she'll throw it for you?" Moe asked, hopefully.

"Not if she wants to keep her job," Paul replied. "I feel like she punched me in the gut."

"That's the tequila."

Paul grimaced. "No. Felt that way before I drank your cheap shit." He hung his head. "Lawyers. They're all scum."

Moe sat back and rubbed his chin. "The lawyer who represented Ma sure was, and should have been declared incompetent or disbarred. But this is different. We're all over your case. And you have an excellent lawyer. We checked her out good before you hired her. She thinks she can win it."

Paul nodded. "I know. But Rhea's on the other side, and know she sided with them over me… it hurts, man. It really hurts."

"Yeah, that sucks," Moe agreed. "But maybe there's more to this. Have you talked to your lawyer yet?"

"I don't like to call after hours. She bills me double."

"Call her in the morning. Tell her that you and the opposing lawyer have a relationship of sorts. Maybe that will be enough to force Rhea off the case. Or make it easier for your lawyer to work with her. This might not mean anything. Or it might be the best thing that could have happened."

Paul nodded as he stared into space. "But what's this mean about Rhea and me—our relationship?"

There was a long silence when Moe started to wish he had a drink in his hand. "I don't know, Pauly."

"Here's the thing. I want to hate her. I really, really do. But I can't."

"Give it time, bro," Moe replied.

[Okay—aside to reader: this was not my husband's

122

finest moment, and trust me, I gave him hell for it. Aside over.]

"No. I don't want to hate her. I think Berry's right. There's other shit going on. She doesn't want this case. I can tell. She said as much…"

"Paul, don't go feeling sorry for her—no, that's not what I mean. Don't give up on your case because she's on the other side of it. You're in the right. That ass-wipe hit you, totaled your truck, and all your equipment. Nearly killed you. And was uninsured. To top it all off, he's stonewalled with your insurance company and with you, so you've gotten next to squat. He needs to pay for the damage he caused. Not to mention all the pain and suffering he's put you through while delaying this case."

Paul's eyes practically glowed when they turned on Moe. At least that's what I imagined. "I am not throwing in the towel, and I'm going to fight as hard as ever for what's due me. It's just gotten a hell of a lot harder."

"You can't let her distract you." Moe paused. "You don't think this is all a big plan to derail the…"

Paul reached across the table and grabbed Moe's shirt front, lifting him. "Don't say it. Do not say it. This is no conspiracy. She's not devious. You should have seen her, Moe. She was practically crying when she told me. She didn't have to. She could have kept seeing me, working on me to drop the case, and she didn't. She could have called or texted me instead. Hell, she could have let me find out through my lawyer or when we got to court. But she didn't. She met me and told me face to face."

Paul let Moe go. Moe straightened his shirt and sat down, smiling at his brother. "Good. You have your head on straight now."

"So, why do I still feel like I got the shit kicked out of

me?"

"Bad booze and the fact is, you did. The rest of it's going to take some time, but at least you know what's what. Separate the case from the woman. That's the only way you're going to survive this. When it's over, see if there's anything to salvage between you two. But you have to get through it."

"It sucks," Paul pouted. "The whole thing sucks."

"Welcome to the world of adulting," Moe replied. "Lots of it sucks. But the good parts are really, really good. Focus on that. Getting your shit together, getting your body back in shape, your ass back to work, and your money in court. Your love life's going to have to take a backseat until then."

Paul stood up and stretched. "You're right." He hung his head. "I have to figure out how."

"You've done okay so far," Moe reminded him.

"Yea, but that was before I knew I was in love," Paul said sadly.

Moe, to his everlasting credit, didn't say a word, just slapped his brother on the back, and showed him up to the guest room.

Which, of course, was all great. But the problem was, the problem still remained.

Chapter Thirteen

Rhea

First, it was a broken fingernail—not just a chip but a ragged tear down to the quick. And since she kept her nails short, to begin with, there wasn't much to file off. Naturally, the snagged nylon followed. But when the heel of her favorite shoes broke in a crack on her front walk, Rhea knew it was a sign from above she shouldn't go out.

But she didn't have Junior's cell phone number, so calling to cancel was out of the question. Asking her mother for the number was even more out of the question, so Rhea went back into her closet for damage control. And she did have a nail file, a second pair of stockings, and damn it all, another pair of shoes that went with her dress.

"Maybe I'll just get drunk. On his dime," she muttered as she got in her car. "Or better, let him get drunk and reveal all his secrets, so I'll have something to hold over his head."

She checked her teeth in the rearview mirror and gave an evil smile to make herself feel better. "Nice going, Rhea. Real adult." She laughed to herself. "What's that phrase? When you're going through hell, keep going."

She gripped the wheel and backed out of her driveway.

Twenty minutes later, she arrived at the restaurant.

In his designer jacket and slicked-back hair, Junior was sitting at the bar, a nearly empty tumbler of amber liquid between his hands. He didn't stand, but his smarmy grin had her gritting her teeth in a semblance of a return greeting. Rhea imagined some women would find his artifice attractive—his fiancée, for example. But she didn't see it. There was nothing about him that could compare to

Paul's ready smile and casual good looks.

"Fashionably late?" he asked with a carefully raised brow.

She laughed as carelessly as she could manage. "Cascading wardrobe malfunctions. But I'm here now."

He looked her over and then turned the stool next to his so she could sit. "So, you are. And looking hot, I might add."

She slid a hip to the stool and placed her bag on the bar. "I was going for sophisticated. I guess I'll have to work on that."

"I think hot's better," he said and signaled the bartender for another drink. "What's your poison?"

Rhea ordered her favorite bourbon to his raised brows. "Expensive taste, I see. I didn't expect that of you. I figured you as a mojito or cosmopolitan sort of girl."

Rhea bared her teeth at him as she shrugged. "My parents have expensive tastes. I suppose I'm like them in some regard."

"So, what was it like, growing up a mixed girl?" he asked as he swallowed the last of his first drink and began on the next.

She swallowed her astonishment. "I'm not sure how to answer that. Maybe you can tell me what it was like growing up with two white parents, steeped in white privilege, and I can tell you what was different about my life."

"Ooooh, feisty. I like that," he said and swallowed a gulp of his drink as she sipped hers. "So, I'll bet I'm the first white guy you've dated, huh?"

Rhea set her drink down and took a deep breath. She turned to him and smiled as gently as rage would allow. "Let's get some things straight right from the start. You need to be respectful to me. First of all, calling me a girl

126

when I'm twenty-seven, graduated first in my class, and am living independently is demeaning. And if by some chance you're calling me a girl because my skin is brown, that's downright insulting. And if you did it deliberately to rile me, I'm leaving now."

He spread his arms wide, manufactured innocence on his face. "Hey, I'm just making conversation. I didn't mean anything..."

She reflected his smile right back at him. "For your information, your 'conversation' lacks a certain moral sensitivity. And if you tell me you only said it because you're kidding around, or because you've had one too many, then I'm telling you right now that I don't like your sense of humor or the fact that you're plastered before we've even spent ten minutes together." She waited a beat. "And please, whatever you do, don't tell me *I* don't have a sense of humor because we both know it's not true, and you're just being a boor and want to cover it up by blaming me for overreacting. So, do us both a favor—if you can't or won't behave tonight, let's bring this farce to an end right now."

She sipped her drink, not letting go of his gaze.

Junior ducked his head and stared into his drink. "Yeah, yeah, sure. I get it."

"So, to answer your question, you are the first white *boy* I've ever had drinks with. I wouldn't say we're dating. But if you meant to ask have I ever been romantically involved with a *man* with pale skin, then the answer is yes, I have. As I have with men of dark skin. And if you're interested in the politics of my dating history, I was seeing a man of Japanese ancestry for some time, and one who was born in southeast Asia—oh, his skin was lighter than mine but darker than yours, since that seems to be what you want to know. They were all in law school with me, or accountants, doctors, or other professionals. And no, I don't plan on telling you the sizes of their dicks or their prowess in bed, so spare us both and don't ask. Okay?" She gripped her glass before it could slide across the bar and dump its contents in his lap. That would have been a shameful waste of a good drink.

From the corner of her eye, she saw the female bartender wink and give her a thumbs up.

Rhea batted her eyelashes at Junior as his jaw dropped. "So, what's it going to be? Still want dinner?" she asked coyly.

"Uh, yeah?" he replied.

"Then maybe you should ask the host at the front desk if our table is ready. I think you've made enough of a spectacle in the bar."

Junior stumbled to his feet and grabbed his drink, looking wildly around until Rhea turned him by the shoulders and pointed him in the right direction."

The bartender came up to her. "Sister, you nailed it."

Rhea pressed her hands together and bowed her head. "Thanks. Wish me strength to get through the rest of the evening without killing him." *Literally*, she added silently.

Dinner was interminable. Rhea didn't know if he was still drunk, shook up, or just plain stupid, but Junior put his foot in his mouth more often than he did food. And when he managed to get to a topic that didn't have to do with ethnicity, he was bragging about his new car, his condo, or the vacations he took.

She had only one bad moment when the busboy clearing a nearby table had trouble keeping the plates and silverware in this bucket. They had an alarming tendency to spin out, almost as if they were trying to fly across the room. Rhea took a calming breath and closed her eyes. So much for friends telling her she's grown up spoiled because she always had the latest computer or cell phone model. The only thing she and Junior had in common was a direct lack of parental involvement in their lives. At least she'd had Nana. The idiot across from her didn't seem to have had anyone who put the breaks on his overactive sense of importance.

"So," he said when dinner was at last over, "Your mom, my dad…" He waggled his eyebrows.

Rhea's eyebrows hit her hairline. "I beg your pardon?"

He snorted his laughter. "You mean, you don't know? My dad's doing your mom. That's why they want the merger."

"Doing? Did you just say *doing*?" Rhea asked w th deadly calm.

He didn't seem to notice. "Yeah. It's been going on for months. I can tell you my Mom's livid. I mean, Dad's been fooling around for years, but this is the first time he's doing it with a black chick—I mean woman."

She felt the blood drain from her face.

He laughed. "You mean you didn't know? That's rich. I mean, the two of them are all over each other when no one else's around. I suppose you could say she's doing him if you wanted to." Junior doubled over laughing.

"My mother still happens to be married to my father."

He flipped his hand away impatiently. "Yeah? So? Technically, my parents are still married too." He looked at her closer. "You didn't know." He bent over laughing. "Oooh, so uppity before, and you didn't know this shit. Damn, that's funny."

Rhea clenched her bag shut, lest her cell phone fly out, and bean him between the eyes. "I guess the joke's on me, isn't it," she said. "Ha. Ha. So funny."

He sobered for a moment before he burst out laughing again. "This is a riot. I can't wait to tell dad how naïve you are. I mean, really, Rhee, what did you expect? Fidelity?"

She pressed her lips together. "As a matter of fact, I did."

He goggled at her for a moment before he burst out laughing again. "I can't believe this. No wonder you want to mediate that case rather than milk it. Oh man, you're never going to make partner if you're that naïve. How the hell do you expect to make any money?"

She breathed through her nose with her eyes closed. One. Two, Three... all the way to ten before she opened her eyes. She reached behind herself for her purse strap before she stood. "Well, you've certainly been a fount of information. I can't say I've ever had such an... informative evening."

"You're leaving?"

"I have work to do," she replied. "Files to read. Deposition in the morning, you know, lawyerly activities. I'm sure you're familiar with the concept of billable hours."

He scoffed. "I have people do that for me."

"I'm sure your clients appreciate that," she replied with a smirk she just couldn't keep from her face. "Now, if you'll excuse me..." She turned to go, and it took every bit of self-control she possessed to walk and not run.

He stopped her with a hand on her shoulder. "I thought..."

She whirled on him and took a long look at that hand before it recoiled as if she'd burned him. "You thought? Really?" she said through clenched teeth. "Shall we take out an ad in the paper?"

"I thought we could get a nightcap. And you know, fool around."

Rhea couldn't help the harsh sound that escaped. "Seriously?"

"Uh, yeah?" he swallowed audibly. "I mean, if Dad and

your mom can…"

She closed her eyes briefly, and when she opened them, she wondered if she could possibly be convicted if she incinerated him on the spot, not that she'd ever tried that before. The idea had merit. "Your father and my mother are adults. They make their own choices. I am also an adult. I choose to go home. Alone." She glared at him. "Do I make myself clear?"

"Uh, well, Dad said…"

Rhea once again counted to ten. She then counted again before straightening her spine. "I really don't want to know what your father said." She shook her head. "I was right about you."

He straightened his back and smiled. "What about?"

"You are a boy."

His smile faded. "What are you talking about?"

"You can't think for yourself. Your father said this or your father said that… so what? I'm not cheap. Screw that. I'm not for sale. You want to sleep with someone, find a woman who's willing. Preferably one who's too drunk to realize what a moron you are." She did a facepalm. "Oh, wait. I thought you were engaged. You're cheating on your fiancée?"

"Hey…"

He was offended? Her grin felt feral. "You can tell your father I said that. No, wait. I'll tell him to his face if you don't get the story straight." She pulled her phone from her purse. "As a matter of fact, I've been recording our entire conversation. Not admissible, I'll grant you since our firms are not courts of law, and I didn't get your permission ahead of time. Our offices, however, can be considered courts of public opinion. You want your mother to hear all the things you said to me tonight?" She raised a brow. "Or your fiancée? I have no problem sharing."

"Damn, you don't play fair."

What smile she had left faded. "I'm a lawyer, bub. Get used to it. I'm leaving now. I suggest you call someone because, in my expert opinion, you've had too much to drink to get yourself home without damaging someone's health or property. I'm being forced to represent one drunk driver, and hell will freeze over before I agree to represent another or am accused of being an accessory."

Rhea tapped the maitre'd in the foyer. "Sir, I believe this gentleman has had too much to drink to drive safely." She handed him her card. "Unless you want this establishment to be sued for allowing a drunk patron to get in a car and possibly cause property or bodily injury, or death, I suggest you call him a cab."

Junior was sputtering as the man soothingly asked him to hand over his keys. She walked away at a steady pace and got into her car. She glanced behind to see if there was any traffic coming. At the all-clear, she took off, gripping the wheel so hard, she was afraid she'd pull it from the stem.

"Damn, that felt good. Worth every second of the hell Mom's going to put me through tomorrow." Her smile faded. "And she's got a few things to answer to, herself."

Chapter Fourteen

Rhea

She walked into her mother's office the next morning.

"I'm busy," Marion said as she glanced up and then down to the open file on her desk, effectively dismissing her daughter.

Rhea came in and shut the door. She took a seat across from the large desk. "Junior says you're sleeping with his father."

Marion's head jerked up.

Rhea forced a smile, though she had no doubt it was grim. "He said, and I quote, 'My dad's doing your mom. That's why they want the merger.'"

"What?"

"Don't make me say it again," Rhea said. "Is it true?"

"It's a lie," Marion said softly. "I'm not sleeping with Tony or anyone else."

"He was quite insistent. Said his mother is livid."

Marion rose and looked out the windows behind her desk. "I have gone out to dinner with him. To discuss the merger."

Rhea waited silently.

"He made the suggestion..." Marion added. She turned swiftly. "I turned him down. You have to believe me."

"I'm not sure my believing you is relevant. But if you want to pursue this merger with a man who would speak about you that way—to a man who would blatantly cheat on his wife..."

Marion sat, her shoulders slumped. "Tony and his wife are estranged. They have been for years. Yes, it's true he's had relationships outside his marriage. But I—I have not. I have never cheated on your father. I'm still his wife, and I respect the vows I made to him."

"Junior was quite insistent. Which was when he propositioned me."

Marion hung her head in her hands. "That rat bastard," she said under her breath. "I warned his father I wouldn't tolerate that kind of behavior." She lifted her head. "You didn't sleep with him, did you?"

Rhea scoffed. "You have to ask?"

Marion dialed her desk phone and put it on speaker. "This is Tony. Leave a message at the beep."

"Tony, your son is being a jerk to my daughter, and I won't stand for it. Call me." Marion pressed a button and ended the call. "It won't happen again. This merger is going to go through, and I won't stand for that."

"You really want to condemn me to work with that jackass from now into the future?" Rhea asked her mother. "And I'm surprised you haven't heard from him yet." She explained about preventing Junior from driving himself home the night before.

"No. No, no, no. Tony's trying to get him married off."

"From what I can tell, that won't stop him—look at the example his parents have set."

Marion shook her head. "I'll talk to him."

"I want an apology," Rhea told her mother. "I'm working this shitty case and putting up with that douche looking over my shoulder. I have my limit. There's a hearing coming up this week, and he wants to be there. I want him to stay far, far away."

"I'll do what I can," Marion replied.

"You have to do better than that," Rhea said as she stood.

"I said I'll do what I can," Marion replied testily. "But you're the one who has to figure out how to get along with him. Now, don't you have work to do?"

"Always," Rhea replied in the same tone. She tugged on the strap of her bag and willed the silver sparks to stay put. "More than I have time for."

Berry

"Why is he here?" Paul asked his lawyer. "I thought it was just us, the mediator, and Rhea."

"He's observing," Rachel replied. "Until he gives us a reason to request he leave, we have to allow it. We don't want to seem contentious from the get-go." She glanced at the mediator. "In other words, it'll make us look like jerks if we get too demanding."

She looked at me over Paul's shoulder. "And you did ask your sister-in-law to come today."

Yes, I asked Paul if I could come with him. For some reason, Rhea's client was not present.

Paul shrugged. "That's because she wanted to see this procedure, in case she ever needs to write a scene for one of her novels. And she promised to sit quietly."

It's true, I did. And I would, even if it killed me. Unless I went into early labor, that is. I thought (though I didn't say anything to anyone), if things started to go downhill, I could fake labor pains.

Paul's lawyer shrugged. "She and Rhea are certainly chatting it up over there."

Paul glanced over his shoulder. Rhea and I *were* talking. There was no reason not to be pleasant to her, at least not yet. I really liked her. Under any other circumstances, I'd be asking her over for tea, or shopping, or help her plan a wedding. Mattie's told me more than once she wants to be a flower girl, though that's not the only reason.

I was also keeping an eye on whoever that other lawyer

was. He hadn't exactly said what his role was, and as I had promised to not ask too many questions, I couldn't make a fuss. I didn't intend to write any scenes involving court stuff in my book, but the family felt Paul needed moral support. The brothers were all working. We were afraid Rosemary would be a distraction—Joey thought she might try to intervene. Besides, it was one of those rare days my parents were able to spend with Mattie. That doesn't happen often, and I didn't want to hover over them. But I was also nervous. My daughter doesn't always take well to people she doesn't know well. And being the only grandchild on my side of the family, I was fully prepared for my mother to spoil my daughter rotten in the space of two hours.

I didn't want to ask Rhea about that jerk. She didn't look very happy to have him there. I had the distinct impression she was talking to me so she wouldn't have to talk to him. Interesting.

"Shall we get started?" The mediator asked. He was a kindly, older gentleman. He introduced himself, shaking everyone's hands, and mentioned he had several grandchildren when he asked about my gigantic pregnant belly. As we were talking, a court reporter entered the room and sat quietly in the corner.

And so it began.

Paul's attorney explained what happened, citing the police report, Paul's injuries and the doctor's reports, the insurance company's evaluation and recommendation for settlement, as well as the opponent's initial request to settle outside the normal channels and later demand to drop all charges.

Rhea spoke next, citing her client's request that the accident be stricken from the record as the sun was in his eyes, and it wasn't the fault of his blood alcohol level at all.

He didn't want to pay for damages, and in fact, wanted the whole thing dismissed.

Now, don't get me wrong. I knew the son-of-a-gun who hit Paul was guilty as hell and deserved to be punished, but the way Rhea laid it out, I almost believed her version of events. What I didn't like was the way her partner sat in the back, smirking. That irked me to no end. And when I say irk, I mean bothered. Really bothered. To the point of anger. I'm not a violent person, but trust me, if I thought I could get away with it, I would have smacked him. Hard.

The mediator listened to both sides, silently. He looked at Paul, and me, and Paul's lawyer; at Rhea and her—whatever he was. He shuffled the papers in the file in front of him and made a few notes. "I see." He rose and shook hands all around. "I'll need to think about what we've discussed here."

"I think it's clear to all of us that the charges should be dropped," Rhea's shadow said to the mediator with another slimy smile. Actually, it was a good smile. The man was too good looking for his own good. And he dressed nicely. But his cologne bothered my nose—you know how sensitive a woman's sense of smell can get when she's pregnant. Truthfully, it made me want to retch. I delight in my profession, for it allows me to use words like retch with aplomb. And aplomb—that's another good word. I'll have to work it into a story one of these days.

But back to the jerk. The mediator looked at him and smiled as one would smile at a child who was being fresh and deserved to miss dessert because he'd been flinging peas with his spoon when he thought the adults weren't looking. "Well, young man, I guess that's for me to decide, now isn't it?" He gave a warm, kindly chuckle that I only wish I could describe for you. It implied good humor and a 'not on your life, buster' vibe all at the same time. Too bad the jackass was too wrapped up in himself to notice how flat he'd fallen.

Paul helped me up. I watched him tense as he looked at Rhea. The slick guy had his hand on her back. I could tell she wanted to move away, but there was nowhere for her to go, what with the table in front of her, the chair beside her, and Slick Willy blocking her exit. There was something about her—a strong emotion she was hiding, something I can only describe as 'contained.' I needed to think about it a bit more. I glanced at Paul. If we'd been cartoon characters, there would have been steam coming out of his nose and ears. I squeezed his hand hard, and he jumped.

Paul's lawyer made her way out of the meeting room. We followed, and I glanced back to see Rhea shake that man's hand from her. She looked daggers at him. I only hoped Paul could see her reaction, but he had been careful not to really look at her in the time we'd been in the room. The two of them hadn't exchanged even one word.

I sighed, glad I wasn't writing their love story. I had no idea how to resolve their impasse. I just wanted to get home before my daughter was spoiled past the point of a good afternoon nap.

Rhea

"What the hell were you trying to pull in there?" Rhea yelled when she and Junior were alone in the parking lot. "You ruined everything, you smarmy son of a bitch." She pulled her keys from her purse and pressed the fob. "If I'd wanted to derail my own case, I'd have brought my client with me. But no. You had to come to do the honors. And despite your promising me you'd keep your mouth shut, you had to go and open your pie hole."

Bad enough she and Paul had been in the same room,

on opposite sides of the table. No amount of groundwork had prepared her for the torture of looking at him. And then that idiot had to open his mouth. Rhea threw her hands up in disgust. "I'm so angry I could..." She opened the car door with more force than was necessary and threw her briefcase in the backseat. He directly slammed it closed and cornered her.

"What are you gonna do. Go cry to your mommy?" he asked.

"What the hell..."

"She's lying, you know. She and Dad are doing it. She didn't want to lose face in front of you. But you know what you are? You're a crybaby. Can't handle things on your own, so you have to cry to your momma. Well, I can tell you once I'm in charge of this firm, I won't put up with that shit. And once your mother retires, there'll be no one for you to go crying to. I'll force you out so fast—you won't know what hit you."

Rhea swore under her breath. "That's got nothing to do with this. You're a liar. I know it, and you know it. And that mediator knows it. You have zero integrity."

He laughed. "Integrity. Who needs it? I've got a family name and the family firm."

She folded her arms. "You won't last long. You're not as smart as you think you are. Your clients are going to run if they can't trust you to see to their best interest. It's clear you're only in this for the money. And don't think I'll be shy about pointing that out."

For the first time, he looked astonished. "You'd stab your partner in the back?"

She stepped closer, and he moved back as if she were a repelling magnet. If it hadn't been so serious, she would have laughed. "No. I'm saying it to your face right now."

He backed away from her. "You're crazy."

Rhea smiled and took another step forward. "Maybe I am, maybe I'm not. You really want to find out?"

Junior looked left, and he looked right. "I'm getting out of here."

"You interfere with my case again, and I'll make sure you're sorry." She took another step just to see him back away from her. Satisfied, she turned and got in her car, watching with no small amount of glee as he ran to the other side of the parking lot, his phone pressed to his ear.

She looked over her shoulder to find Paul was talking to his lawyer before the courthouse. His gaze met hers, and she felt a shudder run through her. "Damn," she whispered to herself.

Berry

I sat in the passenger seat of Paul's truck, staring across the lot as he and Rachel spoke about the hearing. I watched Rhea and that guy come out; saw her hollering at him and throw her stuff in her car. I couldn't hear them, but boy were there fireworks. I don't think either of them noticed, but I would swear there were sparks shooting from Rhea's fingertips by the time they were through. And I mean that literally.

Things were certainly getting interesting.

At long last, Paul finished his conversation and slid into the cab. "Everything all right?" I asked.

He nodded as he buckled his seatbelt and started the engine. "We were both kind of worried when Rhea was talking. She was watching Mr. Finders when Rhee was talking, and he seemed to be buying it."

"Oh?" I asked.

He nodded silently as he looked left and right before pulling into the street. "Yeah, but as soon as that jackass opened his mouth, Rachel knew we'd be okay." Paul gave a very Conrad-brother snort. "What a jerk, making the assumption that just because they're both men he'd automatically listen to him instead of Rachel. The mediator has three daughters, all lawyers. He's not about to fall for that crap."

"So, that's good?"

"It's a good sign. We won't know until the mediator makes his decision. If we don't like it, we still have options. But I don't know how long it will take."

We were silent for a few minutes as he drove me home. "Rhea looked tired," he said out of the blue. "Tired, but beautiful."

"Um hmm," I agreed. "I noticed you didn't talk to her much. Or look at her."

He shrugged. "It's too hard. And with that guy putting his hands on her. I wanted to… to…"

"It would have gone badly if you'd reacted. I wouldn't be surprised if the guy was goading you," I told him.

Paul looked grim. "That's what I was thinking, but damn, that was hard."

He fiddled with the radio, and we listened for a block or two.

"Paul?"

"Yeah?"

"Did you ever notice anything, er, unusual about Rhea?"

"What do you mean?" he replied in a careful voice. I waited a moment to gather my thoughts, but before I could, he burst out, "No. No, don't go there. I know you're pregnant and all. And I love you like the sister I never had, but don't go thinking there's anything woo-woo about her. Because there's not. She's as normal as you—okay, maybe not you, but as normal as I am."

I thought about her unusual self-possession, and I

remembered those sparks. Maybe it had been my imagination. Maybe not.

"Okay—I guess I was thinking along the lines of, oh, she dresses nicer than most lawyers." Not a great fib, but I didn't have a lot of time. And there was something special about her—special as in I could see how much he was in love with her, and I knew with certainty she was in love with him. But there was another something about her I didn't have a name for it. At the rate they were going, I wasn't certain I would ever be able to put my finger on it.

We came to a stop sign. I felt Paul look hard at me, but I refused to meet his eyes. "Berry."

"It's my hormones, okay?"

The car started to move. "Yeah. And that's *all* it better be," Paul said through clenched teeth.

Rhea

She fumed all the way to the office. "Thinks I'm a crybaby, does he? I'll show him. I'll wipe his ass with that crybaby stuff." She grabbed her things and hurried into the office. *I'll bet he called his father to complain about me. Time for damage control.* She ran up to the second floor and dashed to her mother's office in time to see her mother place the phone back in its cradle.

"What the hell happened?" Marion asked.

Rhea narrowed her eyes. "Why don't you tell me what you heard happened."

She rose and walked around her desk and folded her arms. "I've had enough of this foolishness."

"I made my case to the mediator. I did a damned fine job of it. And then *he* had to open his mouth to play the good-old-boy card. Ruined everything. I called him on it in the parking lot."

"That's not what Tony said. He said you botched the

142

case, and Junior had to save you."

Rhea laughed. "I'm not surprised. But here's the thing. That jackass apparently forgot there was a court reporter in the room. There's an audio recording to back it all up. What I don't have is a recording of what he said to me in the parking lot afterward. He means to gut this practice after you retire. He's going to rip its heart out, all the work you and Dad put into it. He's out to fleece his clients and not look back."

Marion sagged. "I can't believe that. His father is so... so..."

"He also repeated the charge you two are sleeping together."

As Rhea watched, her mother sank into a nearby chair. She moaned softly. "This isn't how this was supposed to go. It was all supposed to be so easy." Marion looked up. "I was doing this for you, baby. I was preserving it for you. All that your father and I worked for, I wanted you to have it. That's all I ever wanted."

Rhea set her bags down and knelt next to her mother. "It's not what I want—none of it. I want a good life. I don't want to be worked to the bone."

"You don't understand. As a black woman in a white man's world..."

"I get that," Rhea said sharply. "I get that truly and fully. I live it every single day. But I want to choose my own battles, and having to live with a law partner who will scorn me day in and day out is not how I want to live the rest of my life. Do not doom me to that fate."

"What else is there for you?" her mother moaned.

"I don't know, but I sure as hell don't want to be indentured to this firm, unable to leave when things go bad. I want to live my own life, do good as I see fit. Take clients I can support and help instead of trying to help rich

143

crybabies avoid responsibility for their actions."

Silence seeped into the room.

"Mom, if you're sleeping with him, just admit it."

Marion hid her face in her hands. "I don't want you to hate me," she said softly. "You can't possibly understand my loneliness..." Her words trailed off.

Rhea fought hard to find her equilibrium before she spoke. "You really don't know me very well, do you?" she said after a long silence. "Not if that's what you think."

"What? My own daughter?" Marion cried. "Of course, I do. First in her class in high school at sixteen, first in your undergraduate class with a double major of Poli-sci and history. Editor of the law review in college, and salutatorian. You missed being first by a quarter of a percentage point, and that's only because you missed a few classes due to the flu your second year. Of course, I know you."

Rhea felt the rage push up, but she tamped it down. "You know the facts. What about my heart? Do you remember my favorite book when I was little? No—oh, that's right. It was Nana who read it to me. You didn't allow me to attend any sleepovers, or have friends over at our house, no birthday parties..."

"Can you imagine a Hansen-Chalmbers at a bowling party?" her mother shuddered.

"What about the name of the first boy I wanted to kiss but couldn't? How about the fact I cried myself to sleep after my prom because I didn't have a date because none of the boys who asked met your approval. Speaking of which, do you know the names of the friends I did go with?"

"But..."

Rhea could not stop. "Did you know I toyed with the idea of being a lesbian my junior year in college but realized it was only to try to shock you? What about my boyfriends? Remember meeting any of them? Oh, that's right, you couldn't come to school for parent's weekend because you and Dad had to go to Brussels my freshman year, Paris in my sophomore. I think I didn't bother telling you about it the last two. Why bother? So, don't tell me about loneliness. I've been lonely all my life, not that you noticed."

"But, darling, I was busy building your future," her mother sputtered.

"You could have been present in my life instead. That would have meant a hell of a lot more than money."

"I'm sure you're exaggerating," her mother tried. "I was there."

"Were you?" Rhea asked. "Were you really? For a dance recital? Choir concert? Award ceremony?"

For the first time ever, Marion looked abashed. "I may have missed one or two events. My career has been very demanding."

"Name one," Rhea challenged.

"I can't when you put me on the spot. And this thing with Tony wasn't about you. It was about me and my needs," her mother countered.

"Oh, forgive me." Rhea couldn't keep the sarcasm from her voice. "Of course, it's about you. So, tell me, why lie? Why not just tell me you're in a relationship with him? Don't you think I'm old enough to understand?"

"I—I didn't want you to think badly of me," her mother replied in a small voice.

"And chance my learning about it the way I did was because that was so much easier."

"It's not what you think. We're in love."

"Love?" Rhea threw up her hands. "All the more reason to be upfront about it. So maybe I could celebrate that with you? But no, instead, I had to learn about it from that jackass you want to be my law partner. Nice going, Mom. This is really so much better—for you."

"I knew you'd take it badly," her mother tried.

Rhea grabbed her bags. "I'm taking the rest of the day off."

"But darling, you need to…"

She whirled, and the look on her face must have stayed whatever her mother planned to say.

"Maybe that's a good idea. I'll call and ask for those transcripts. Perhaps I'll suggest Tony exert a little more control over AJ until he learns some sense."

"Tell him to say out of my way, or he's going to get mowed down," Rhea said as she left. "And I want to see the merger documents. I'm still a specialist in that arena. Don't you dare sign anything until I've had a chance to go through them."

"I've only signed the intent documents, darling."

"Keep it that way. Have Cassie send me the link to the rest. I'll go through them tonight. And for your information, we are going to mediate this drunk driving case, and our client is going to pay what he owes in damages, pain, and suffering. And I'll be damned if he gets off with anything less than community service and mandatory attendance for alcohol abuse counseling in addition to paying for damages and emotional distress. And that will be the victory we can be proud of. I'll see you in the morning."

She slammed the door on her way out.

Chapter Fifteen

Rhea

She didn't want to go home. She was too tense for the gym, afraid she'd pull something if she tried to work out, so she went furniture shopping instead. Facing her empty house night after night had become just too depressing. So, she'd go a little deeper in debt. At that point, what did it matter? Win or lose the DUI case, she was due some money. But she couldn't find anything she liked.

Hours later, she walked into a coffee shop for a late lunch. Recognition dawned as she realized she'd come to The Sweet Shop, the place she and Paul had met for breakfast a few weeks before. The yeasty scent of freshly baked bread and cookies overwhelmed her senses.

She was about to turn around and walk out when the hostess greeted her. "I remember you. A friend of Paul C's, right?"

Rhea nodded. "Yes. Are you still serving? I can go elsewhere if you're closing."

"Anything for a friend of Paul's—or any of the Conracs. I'm Hero, by the way. I own this place."

"Rhea Hansen-Chalmbers." They shook hands.

"I'm down a few items, but my baker and I have been experimenting today, so I can bring you a few things to taste if you don't mind flour, butter, and sugar."

Rhea grinned. "That sounds like heaven."

"Sit down in the corner booth, and I'll be back in a few minutes. Help yourself to coffee. I'm short-handed this afternoon. And don't worry, all the regulars do. I'll be back in a flash. Free wi-fi if you're interested. The password s sweetbutter. One word."

The kind woman walked away. Rhea slid behind the counter and poured coffee from a full pot, finding cream in a small pitcher nearby. She slid into her booth and closed her eyes to savor the rich brew.

The bell tinkled, announcing a new customer. Rhea kept her eyes shut, but something inside her went very still. Footsteps neared and then stopped. She opened her eyes as she felt a presence before her. "Mind if I join you?" Paul asked as she blinked again.

Rhea pulled her purse off the table. He took that as assent and slipped in across from her.

"Hero said to help myself to coffee. I assume that extends to you too."

He grinned. "Hero and I are practically family. My brother Joey's married to her niece. We all spend a lot of time here." His smile faded. "Hero offered me a job as a short-order cook until I get my settlement. If I can't go back to construction, or to—well, let's just say I've thought about it. Except I can't cook."

"I'm kind of surprised you're still talking to me."

He sighed. "It's not like you called *me* a liar. I think that judge…"

"Mediator," she corrected. "He's a retired judge."

"That guy," he said pointedly, "knew what he was about. Until your partner opened his trap, I was actually getting kind of worried."

It took everything she had to keep from rolling her eyes. "I can't discuss the case with you. I probably shouldn't even be talking to you now."

"Do you want me to go?" he asked.

She shook her head and slowly spun her coffee cup between her hands. "No. I've missed you." She hung her head. "I know I'm breaking the rules by saying this, but you don't know how sorry I am to be representing my client. If I had any choice…" she said in a low breath.

Paul covered her hand. She felt a jolt and fisted her hand lest a stray spark make itself known. "I know, Rhee. I don't understand it in here," and he covered his heart with his free hand. He then pointed to his forehead. "But in here, I get it."

She nodded, not losing sight of his gaze.

He pulled back and greeted Hero with a kiss on the cheek as she set a large plate of pastries between them. "I had no idea you were here. I'd have brought more."

Rhea laughed. "You didn't expect me to eat all of these, did you?"

Hero grinned. "I expected you to taste all of them and let me know what you think. Since I'm trying out new recipes, they're on the house. Just take notes on what you like and why, and what you don't." She reached for the coffee pot and topped off Rhea's cup, snagging one for Paul along the way. "I'm locking up in a few minutes, but you sit as long as you want. I'll be in and out for a bit while I clean and get ready for tomorrow." She bustled away and began to draw the shades on the large plate glass windows.

Paul gave Rhea a one-sided smile. "I kind of feel like I'm on my first date without a chaperone," he said wryly.

She laughed. "No dates. Today was a big step in getting your case resolved, but I'm not holding my breath. Anything can still happen."

Paul sighed again. "You'd think I'd be used to waiting, but my whole life is on hold until this is settled."

"To be purely selfish, I'm trying to speed things along," Rhea confided. "That goes against what they want me to do to increase billable hours. I have too many people looking over my shoulder and second-guessing me—t's really put me on my mettle. I'm doing the best I can under the circumstances."

"What about that clown you work with?"

Rhea couldn't suppress an eye roll. "You can tell your lawyer I'm doing what I can to get him removed from any further proceedings. He's a..." She paused. "I can't talk about what he is. But I want him away from me."

"So, you're not seeing him?"

Rhea shuddered. "No."

"My lawyer said that there's talk of a merger and that you and that nimrod are dating."

Rhea laughed. "I went out to dinner with him once, for the sake of the firm. He was a jerk. I am not seeing him again." She took a deep breath. "I know I shouldn't say this, but he's the kind of guy a woman doesn't like to be alone with."

"If he tried anything..." Paul said, rising.

Rhea laughed. "Down boy. I can handle myself."

"I don't like the idea of anyone giving you a hard time." He stared at the uneaten pastries between them. "I don't like the idea of any man spending time with you, for work, or for..."

This time she laid her hand on his. "Paul, I'm not dating anyone. I have less time than I did when we first reconnected." She felt her brows lift. "What about you?"

He shook his head. "Moe wanted Berry to fix me up with a friend of hers, but I said no."

Their gazes locked. "Good," they both said and smiled.

"This case won't last forever," Rhea said in a low voice. "But we can't chance seeing each other again until it's over. No matter what the verdict, I don't want anyone to ever think the outcome was in any way tainted."

He pulled away. "Okay. No problem."

She caught his arm and leaned forward. "Paul, don't settle for less than you have coming to you. You've waited this long. I'm going to work as long and hard for my client as I can, but don't you dare agree to less than you deserve just so we can see each other again sooner. We don't know what will happen between us. You're worth more than that."

He smiled at her, the first sunny-happy-go-lucky smile she'd seen in weeks. "Oh, I don't intend to. But I do intend that whatever happens between us, whenever it happens, will be worth the wait. Make no mistake about that." He frowned. "Once it's over, there's no reason to keep us apart, is there?"

She shook her head. "No legal reason," she replied.

"Good. He slid from the booth, drinking his coffee as he went. He snatched two pastries and, with a wink, sauntered down the aisle and into the kitchen where he said his farewells. He must have exited through the back, for he didn't reappear.

Rhea smiled into her coffee and took a nibble at the closest confection. It was buttery and flaky and came apart in her mouth with a burst of sweet marzipan. Heaven. With another sip of her coffee, she realized talking to Paul had fixed whatever it was that ailed her. The sparks that had been zipping up and down her nerves all day were finally calm.

A week passed. Rhea focused on her other cases as she waited for the Mediator's report. She went to the gym almost every night, nodding at Paul across the way if he happened to be there, and swallowed her disappointment if he didn't appear.

She read the contract that had been drafted for the merging of the two firms. Rhea met with her mother and Tony and pointed out changes she felt should be made to ensure a more equitable distribution of responsibilities and profit. Tony argued with her, but to Rhea's surprise, her mother defended her recommendations. It was agreed that the combined firm would maintain two separate locations, given that neither had the space for the entire staff. Discussions on a physical merger were put off for the future. But Junior set up an office on the first floor of her building, much to Rhea's dismay. She did everything she could to avoid running into him, including locking her door when she was working late and called for another lawyer to walk her to her car if it was dark when she left.

She was going over a file with Cassie late one afternoon when a knock on her open door drew Rhea's attention to Junior. "Got a minute?" he asked as he walked into her office.

She glanced at the time and then her calendar. "We have a client meeting in five."

"I don't need that long." He waved a sheaf of papers before his face. "These just came in. They were sent to me. The Mediator's reached a conclusion. He finds for the defense."

Rhea held her breath. "Let me see those." She scanned them, her heart racing, and then speared her gaze at him. "How did they manage to get your address instead of mine?"

Cassie let loose a snigger.

He shuffled his feet. "Uh, I might have..." He let his words trail off.

"You really are a son of a bitch," she said under her breath.

"Listen, I know I was wrong. I want to make it up to you. I'll get the correction made. You can check it before I hit the send button."

"Exactly why should I trust you for that?" she asked.

His cheeks formed splotchy red patches. "Because

we're going to be working together and need to trust one another. I know I said some really stupid things. I want to start making it up to you now. Show you that you can trust me."

"I don't trust you to not screw this up," she said boldy. Her phone buzzed. The receptionist's voice announced her clients. "We'll be right down."

Rhea glared at Junior. "I'll deal with this later. You get that email address correction made, stat. That'll be the first thing you need to do."

He smiled. "Sure, Rhee, no problem."

"My name is Rhea," she said pointedly. "R-H-E-A. You don't have my permission to call me Rhee. That's reserved from my friends."

"Yeah, okay. I get it." He hung his head. "I'll have Cassie set up the call with your clients to see if they'll accept the terms. Okay?"

Cassie nodded with an undisguised look of disgust.

"Yeah, fine. Don't do anything else." She left the papers on her desk and brushed past him.

Paul

He sat on the examining table. "So, Doc. What's the verdict?"

She frowned. "The chair is lovely. Better than I expected. I hope you didn't lift it yourself."

"Nope. Got my brothers to load it into the truck. Over my limit."

She nodded. "You're looking much better. Another month of taking it easy should do it. You can increase your activity, though. Add another ten pounds to your weight limit, and you can work up to four hours a day I think. If it starts to get sore, slow down. You know the drill. We'll re-evaluate it then."

"Can't make it another twenty?" he asked as he pulled his tee-shirt over his head.

The doctor looked at him over the tops of her half-moon glasses. "Fifteen. Every other day," she agreed with a wink. "But no over doing it. You hear me? Don't make me call your mother."

"What about sex?" he asked.

"I'm married," she said with a straight face.

Paul laughed. "Um…"

Her brows rose. "You mean you haven't had sex since this happened?"

"I know, hard to believe," Paul replied.

"As long as you don't strain your shoulder, go ahead. I don't know your preference but at least for a while, may I suggest you let your partner be on top?"

He grinned at her. "Yeah, you can suggest all you want. And I go for women. Exclusively."

"No pushup positions," the doctor warned. "And don't let her tie you up too tightly. Other than that, you're good to go." She gave him another wink and handed him a slip of paper. "I'll see you back here in a month."

He turned his phone on as he headed out to his car, and it beeped immediately with a text notification from his lawyer.

> Tried to call but your phone was off. Case settled. We got everything we asked for. The other side will deposit the full settlement amount into my escrow account tomorrow morning. I'll deduct my fee and send you the rest. Call me later.

Paul nearly dropped the phone. "You're shitting me," he said aloud. "Oh, excuse me," he said to an older woman who passed him with a scowl.

He quickly texted his mother, brothers, and sisters-in-law. Case settled, party at my place.

I (as you could have guessed, this is Berry interrupting), of course, texted everyone right back.

Paul's place is a dump. Burgers and beer here tonight. Everyone welcome.

I followed it up with one to Paul alone:

Bring Rhea. No excuses accepted.

I wanted to show off my new baby to her.

Chapter Sixteen

Berry

I suspect Rhea wasn't certain what was about to hit her. Or more to the point, embrace her. The only thing she knew was Paul called to tell her he was picking her up at her place at six and to be ready. She hadn't expected to be driven three blocks to my house and certainly didn't think the rest of his family would be there to celebrate Paul's victory. There was more than enough food (mostly hamburgers—it's a long story) with all the fixings, beer, wine, salad, chocolate cake, and French pastries. I'm happy to report that my mother-in-law and sisters-in-law, along with Moe and his other brothers, did all the cleaning and prep work as I sat back and nursed little Maximillian.

Of course, we were all thrilled to have Rhea there. I at least knew how much Paul liked her, and I told my sisters-and-mother-in-law that if Paul wasn't going to hold a grudge, we shouldn't either. Rosemary was a little stiff at first, but she eventually warmed up, especially once I put my baby in Rhea's arms and the colicky little darling fell asleep as she rocked and crooned to him under her breath.

And Paul— I've never seen him so happy. Sure, the money was a big deal, but the moral victory was what stood out for all of us. The Conrad brother's father had been killed by a drunk driver when Sammy, the youngest brother, was a baby. Rosemary saw hardly a penny in settlement. It all went to lawyer fees. She struggled to raise her family without any help (and she did an excellent job of it). So, Paul's victory was all the sweeter.

And the way he looked at Rhea—well, if he hadn't told

me he was in love with her, it wouldn't have taken me long to figure it out. And she was looking back at him with just the same longing, and (please don't think I'm exaggerating) a bit of trepidation. Maybe a bit more than a tad, come to think of it. I wasn't certain why I thought that, but I consider myself a fairly good judge of character and a professional people-watcher, so I'm sticking by my observation. And of course, I turned out to be correct, but that's getting too far ahead in this story.

As the evening wore on, Sammy begged off early as he had plans with friends. Those of us with little kids (namely the three married brothers) needed to get our little darlings into bed. And Rosemary toddled off on her own, claiming she and her friends were heading out on an adventure the next day, and she needed her beauty rest.

I shooed Paul and Rhea off, so Moe and I could fall into bed for the two hours before our little bruiser would awaken for his next feeding...you know the new baby drill. I don't have to spell it out for you.

I'll share what they told me later, and I'll let my rather formidable imagination take over with what went unsaid...

Rhea

She gently touched Paul's hand on the steering wheel. "Paul, I don't know what to say—except thank you for inviting me tonight. That should have been awkward."

He gave her a quick glance, then focused on the road, but she saw his smile. "You had a good time? I know my family can be a bit... er... boisterous."

She sighed happily. "I loved every minute of it. I was always so jealous of you with all your brothers. I would have killed to have just one. Or a sister. Your sisters-in-law are so nice. I think Berry knew I was uncomfortable, so she gave me something to do."

"Yeah, hold a crying baby," he laughed.

"He was a sweetheart once he stopped." She closed her eyes, recalling his soft little body in her arms and his sweet smell. "And it didn't take too long."

"You must have the magic touch." Paul laughed again. "He screams his head off when anyone else holds him, even my mother. I think Ma's offended that one of her precious grandchildren doesn't quiet down for her."

Rhea grinned at him and wiggled her fingers. "Maybe he just recognized a kindred soul."

"So," Paul said, "do I take you home? It's not too late. And tomorrow's Saturday. I hope you don't have to get up early to work."

"I can sleep in a bit," she mused. "Did you have something in mind?"

"Do you want to grab a drink?"

"Not really. I had two glasses of wine. That's my limit."

He nodded. "Same here—or beers." He scratched his head. "There's a coffeehouse with acoustic jazz I've been meaning to check out. It's not far. We could get a table in the back and maybe talk some."

She couldn't help but smile. "I'd like that."

Paul hit the blinker and put the car in gear.

A half-hour later, he looked across the small table to see Rhea entranced by the music. Her eyes were half-closed, and she swayed as the mellow tones of a tenor sax filled the basement room. Her hands were wrapped around a mug of cocoa that she'd seemed to have forgotten as the music took hold. The original piece came to an end, and she opened her eyes to applaud. "I want to see if he's selling CDs or if he has anything to download," she said as the musician left the stage.

Paul covered her hand with his. "I know he does. Guy's a carpenter. Works for Moe sometimes. He usually plays with a quartet or trios. I've seen him a few times, and it blows me away every time. I can't believe someone that good has to work a day job too. Sammy's the same way. Plays guitar and sings, but won't go for the big time."

Rhea shook her head. "I've got a friend with a degree in fine arts. Wonderful painter. But she went to law school so she could afford to pay off her school loans. Not that she's a bad lawyer, but her heart isn't in it."

He covered her hands with his. "There are so many great artists and artisans who do what they have to, to survive." Their gazes met. "What about you?"

She bit her bottom lip. "Me? I don't have any talents."

"No? I seem to remember you did some dancing once upon a time."

She couldn't stop her smile. "That was a long time ago. I miss it, but I never thought I could do it professionally."

"You could do it unprofessionally," he said, making her laugh. "You don't have to master a subject to love and practice it. Nothing wrong with being a dedicated amateur."

Rhea laughed. "I never thought about it that way. Instead of going to the gym, I could take ballet classes."

"I'd miss you if you did, but we'll see each other outside the gym."

She blinked hard as her eyes grew misty. "Really, Paul?"

His fingers tightened over hers. "Rhee. I've been patient." He leaned closer and brushed his lips over hers. "But don't you think…"

She pulled away, frowning. "I don't know what to think."

Paul smiled again and kissed her lightly. "I thought by your coming out with me tonight that you were thinking the same thing I was."

She moved closer. "What exactly are you thinking?"

"That you," and his lips brushed hers once more, "And

I..." Another soft kiss. "Were meant to be."

She felt his smile with hers. "Were we?" she asked.

"We still are," he replied and lifted her fingers to his lips. "You taste like chocolate and marshmallows."

"And you taste like ginger spice," she countered as she moved to kiss him.

"So, you agree?"

Rhea sat back, still holding his hands. "I... well, I..."

"I'm not taking no for an answer. If that makes me sound like a caveman, so be it."

"And here I thought you were so civilized," Rhea said with a grin.

He shrugged and gave her a wink. "Don't believe what you see. It's all a veneer."

"I know you better than that."

"And I want us to get to know each other even better."

She saw a flicker of indecision cross her face, reflected in his eyes.

"Not that. I'd never press you to have sex if that's worrying you. My caveman instincts aren't that pronounced. I mean, maybe we talk more. And kiss some more. And then I'll take you home and say goodnight after we make plans to go to dinner tomorrow night."

She laughed. "You're not planning on burning through all your award money, are you?"

Paul shook his head. "I have other plans for it. A pizza won't break me. I'm going to replace my truck for one thing. And all the equipment that was destroyed. I've got bills that have been waiting to be paid."

"I didn't really think..."

He squeezed her fingers again. "I know you didn't. I don't think I can go back to work for my brother. The doc thinks my shoulder won't ever be strong enough to do what I once did no matter how careful I am. So, I'm going to try to make a go at my carpentry business. Furniture, cabinets, that sort of thing. Smaller pieces too. I'll get someone to help with the larger stuff and the installations. I'm going to need capital to keep me going until I get customers. But with Moe pushing business my way, and Joey, with his architecture firm doing the same, I think within a year I'll be solvent. I'll keep living at my dumpy little apartment until then."

"And pizza doesn't cost much," she said with a smile. "If you want the occasional shrimp scampi dinner, maybe I can treat."

"You mean it, Rhee? You're not just being nice to me tonight to make up for representing that jackass, are you?"

"I'm not just saying that to make you feel better. But Paul, it's been a while since I've been involved with anyone. I'm kind of out of practice."

The look in his eyes turned tender. "That makes two of us."

"I meant about dating. I'm still really busy, what with the merger." She bit her lip. "My mother's asking me to do more than ever…"

"You have to learn to say no. Burning the candle at both ends—not such a good idea. You deserve a life of your own." His smile grew, and he gave a small laugh. "You deserve me."

Her grin expanded. "Do I?"

He nodded emphatically. "Without question." His smile faded, but the look in his eyes did not.

"Paul, I want this. I want you, and me, and to see what we can make of a relationship, but you're going to have to let me go at my own pace."

"I'm not going anywhere, Rhee. There's never been anyone else I've felt this way about. I'm not a kid anymore, and I'm not going to hare off on you. I'll wait as long as you

161

need me to."

"You have to promise, Paul. Promise me you won't get scared off by… by things."

He laughed and kissed her cheek. "If by things you mean your work schedule, or your scary mother, or that jackass who thinks he's all that, then the answer is no. I can handle it. I'll be there to rub your shoulders when you've been working too hard. I'll make you dinner when you're too tired to cook yourself, as long as you don't mind frozen dinners. I happen to be excellent at ordering takeout."

She laughed and pressed her forehead to his. "Yes, that's what I mean by stuff—and maybe other stuff too."

"There's no 'stuff' I can't handle. Remember, I'm not scared of anything."

She laughed, and Paul pulled her in closer. "Then we have a deal?" he whispered.

She looked at him and nodded. "As long as we keep on feeling the way we do right now."

"Lady, the way I'm feeling, I don't think it's ever going to end. And I don't want it to."

Rhea closed her eyes as tears pooled. "I hope you mean that, Conrad. Because if you break my heart, I'm going to sue your ass, and I'm going to win."

Chapter Seventeen

Rhea

"Do you like museums?" Rhea asked the next afternoon when Paul called to confirm their pizza date.

"Are you talking don't touch that statue or they'll arrest you kind of museums, or natural history museums with dioramas of ancient civilizations, or the kooky collections of two-headed snakes in someone's garage kind?" he countered.

She laughed. "All of the above."

"I like them all just fine. And since we're on the subject, what's your opinion on wine tastings?" he asked in return.

"I'm all for it as long as it's good wine," she told him.

"Well, we won't know until we try it. How about country fairs?"

She sighed happily. "I love country fairs as long as there's deep-fried food. And there's this antique extravaganza that happens about an hour from here...I've been meaning to go for a while. And seeing as you have a truck..." Rhea laughed again. She just couldn't help herself. "There's so many things I've been wanting to do for so long."

"And you're talking to someone who won't mind doing all of them right along with you. But I get to pick stuff, too. I mean, what if I want to go to a monster truck show?"

Rhea paused for a long moment. "Are you serious?"

Paul made a strangled sound on the other end of the phone.

"Would it be a deal-breaker? I mean, wouldn't you rather go someplace like that with one of your brothers?"

"Rhea..."

She heaved a massive sigh. "Okay. I'd go with you, but would it be okay if I brought a book? Or wore earplugs and a face mask?"

"So no one would know you were with me?" he asked.

"No. Fumes."

"As long as you brought one for me too. And no, I don't like that stuff. I was testing you."

She blew out a relieved breath. "How would you feel if I asked you to go shoe shopping with me?"

"If they were for some killer heels? No problem."

"Too bad I only wear ballet flats most of the time," she replied.

"Damn, woman, don't tease me like that."

She laughed. "I have about three hours of work. Do you want me to meet you?"

"I want to pick you up. I bought my new—well, new used truck today. I got a sweet deal."

She smiled. All of Junior's comments about Paul running through his money were obviously sour grapes. "I can't wait to see it."

"And I can't wait to show it to you. So, about seven? Does that give you enough time? And, can I keep you out late tonight?"

"Seven is fine. And you can keep me out sort of late. I have something I need to do tomorrow."

"You're not working again, are you?" he asked in disbelief.

"No. I've got a standing date..."

"Rhee, you said you weren't seeing anyone."

She smiled to herself, seeing his pout in her mind's eye. "With my father. I try to go every Sunday. I missed last week and don't want to again."

"Oh, jeeze," he said. "I'm sorry. I should have known."

"Don't be. I like when you act all jealous."

164

"I hate feeling jealous," he admitted. "Makes me feel like I'm eight again."

"Paul, if this thing between us…"

"No ifs about it, Rhee."

She couldn't help but grin. "Whatever—what I want you to know is I would never knowingly make you jealous. I—I don't like to play those kind of games."

"Oh, darlin', you don't have to worry about me."

"What? You were the biggest player in high school," she squawked.

"Oh, that," he said dismissively. "That was an earlier, less refined version of me. One who was trying to get your attention any way I could."

"You had one hell of a reputation," she accused him.

Paul chuckled. "I know, and man, did I love that. But that was mostly talk. I didn't have time to fool around like people thought I did. Remember, I was taking the same honors classes as you, plus I was working construction part-time with Moe and the guys. I'd'a been dead if I did all that and messed around with all the girls who wanted to sleep with me."

"Really?" She threw just the right amount of doubt in her voice.

"Really. You remember me ever having a steady girlfriend?"

"I wasn't paying that much attention," she sniffed.

He laughed again. "Okay, Miss Snooty. Well, I didn't. My dad, my brothers, and me, we're the loyal type. One-woman men, every one of us. I don't know if you remember, but my brother Joey had that awful girlfriend…"

"Berry and Jenny were telling me and Annie about her the other day."

"Right. He couldn't shake her."

"Why didn't he break up with her then?"

She could almost hear Paul shaking his head. "I told you. He—we don't roll that way. It would take some extremely extraordinary circumstances, and yes, I know that's redundant. You're on notice. If you want to get rid of me, you're the one who's gonna have to do the breaking up. As far as I'm concerned, you're it. Period. Finito."

Rhea gasped. "That's a hell of an expectation, Paul. You could warn a girl."

"I believe I just did," he replied smugly. "Anyway, you're not the only one who's got stuff to do. I'll see you in four hours." He gave what sounded like a kiss and then was gone.

"I'll have to break up with you?" she asked the silent phone. "No, I don't think I want to do that, ever. But once you find out about me, that might all change, Mr. Conrad. You might very well break your streak."

Paul

From the corner of his eye, Paul watched Moe walked into his woodshop and stopped to listen. He waited until Paul turned down the radio before saying, "I can't remember the last time I heard you whistle."

Paul responded with a smirk. "It's been a while since I wanted to. Take a look at this." He set down the stained cloth he was using and held up his latest creation.

"Nice. What the heck is it?" Moe asked.

"I made Rhea a candlestick."

"That's the craziest looking candlestick I've ever seen." Moe sauntered further into the woodshop and set down his toolbox before taking the candlestick from his brother. He turned it over and on its side. "I don't get it. Where do you put the candle?"

Paul took it back and set it on the worktable. "Observe," he said with a flourish and took a multi-colored U-shaped candle from a box. "I saw Wanda a month ago at a craft fair. Remember her? I described what I wanted, and she was able to make this for me." He set it in the copper-lined cradle and snapped a small metal strap over the middle to hold it in place.

"When Rhea and I first reconnected, and I found out how hard she works, I told her she was burning the candle at both ends. I thought about it and came up with this design. As soon as the doc gave me the go-ahead to work again, I roughed it out. I couldn't stand to work on it while I was waiting for the case to settle, but once it did, and Rhea and I started talking again, I finished it. Wanda brought the candles over this morning."

It was Moe's turn to give a whistle of appreciation. "Very nice. And clever. Think she'll get it? Hell, if you and Wanda wanted to keep collaborating, you could make a bunch of these for sale. She goes to craft fairs all the time. I'll bet she could get some commissions for you."

Paul nodded. "I've been pricing it out in my head as I stained it. I'm going to give it to Rhea tonight."

"Whoo-hoo. You're seeing her two nights in a row?"

Paul gave his brother a tolerant stare. "And when you first met Berry, didn't you spend every free minute with her?"

"Well, now, things were a little different then," Moe said, rubbing his chin. "There were certain extenuating circumstances that kept me from doing that."

"But if you could have..." Paul said.

Moe gave his brother a slow grin. "I would have moved in with her right after our first date."

Paul smirked. "Rhee and I are going for pizza tonight."

Moe slapped him on the back. "You go, son. We're gonna get you hitched before you know it."

For the first time in memory, Paul didn't shy away from

the thought. "Yeah, that's kind of what I'm thinking too."

"You tell Ma yet?" Moe asked. "Not that I'm telling you what to do or anything, but she figures she's got us all on a roll. Poor Sammy's sweating bullets, 'cause he knows as soon as you put a ring on some girl's finger, he's next in line."

Paul's grin faded. "First of all, Rhea's not some girl. She's a woman. A hell of a woman."

Moe held up his hands. "I didn't mean anything by it. I call Berry a girl all the time just to get her worked up."

"Well, maybe you ought to find another way to tease your wife. Rhea hasn't had the easiest life…"

"What? She grew up rich," Moe exclaimed.

"And lonely. Her parents… And you don't know what she's suffered. Having money's no barrier to having a crappy life," Paul said heatedly. "It's not like she's militant about it," he continued, his eyes squinting. "She's got the strongest character in the world. But I don't want you or any of the other guys giving her any shit about anything. You got me?"

Moe backed up a step. "I'll watch what I say."

"Better you watch what you're thinking," Paul shot back.

"Damn, you have it bad," Moe said, shaking his head. "I get it. I'll tell Joey and Pete. The girls—I mean, Berry, Annie, and Jenny won't be a problem."

"That leaves Sammy," Paul moaned.

"The baby," they said at the same time and smiled at each other.

"He gets away with shit," Moe said. "Always has."

Paul paused a moment. "Well, maybe we should let him run off his mouth and see how Rhea reacts. Should be educational."

"And entertaining," Moe added with a cackle.

Paul looked at his phone. "Crap. I've got to pick her up

in an hour. I still have to get home, shower, wrap this…"

"And Berry's gonna kill me. I told her I would only be out for an hour, and it's been three," Moe said as he ducked his head. "Don't you dare say anything to her, but I swear, running that buzz saw gives me less of a headache than listening to the baby cry."

Paul chuckled as he slipped the candlestick into a bag. "Yeah, and who exactly is the one who rushed his wife to have another kid? Maybe you ought to bring the little guy over here and let him run some of the equipment. Before long, Sammy's gonna leave the family business too. You'll have to change the name from Conrad Brothers to Conrad and Son."

Moe slapped his brother on the shoulder as they headed for the door. "The way Mattie's going, it'll be Conrad and Daughter. Or just Miss Mattie Conrad, Bossypants."

Paul laughed. "Remind me when I get Rhea to agree to marry me that we won't have kids."

"Oh no, little brother. If I can, so can you. In fact, I insist. And if I didn't, you'd still have to answer to Ma," Moe added, giving the fourth Conrad brother a noogie as they walked to their trucks.

Chapter Eighteen

Rhea

She dropped the living room curtain and rubbed her tingling hands down her pant legs. *This is crazy. Why am I so nervous? It's not like I don't know the guy. Or don't like him. Maybe I like him too much, and that's what's scaring the hell out of me.*

She heard a truck pull into her driveway and the engine shut off.

Calm down. Breathe. It's just Paul.

"Yeah, right," she said out loud with a laugh.

The doorbell rang, and she made herself walk slowly to her small foyer. "Hey."

He stood on her front step, a goofy grin on his face and a bag in his hand. He leaned forward and kissed her. It was awkward, and a bit wet, and very, very sweet. But his feet stayed firmly planted on her welcome mat.

Rhea opened the door wider. "You can come in, you know."

His grin grew bigger. "I didn't want to assume. I gave my brother hell earlier today for, well, for being my brother, so I figured I'd best practice what I preach."

She laughed and closed the door behind him. "Do I want to know the details?"

"No one suffered bodily harm, and we parted still brothers and friends." He held out the gift bag to her. "For you."

Her heart started racing all over again. "What's this?"

"Our first official date?" he asked. "I mean, I know we've been out, but this is starting fresh. And last night didn't count as it was spur of the moment. Besides, it was Berry who'd pretty much forced me to bring you last night. I don't know what she'd'a done to me if you'd'a said no. Talking about bodily harm and all…"

Rhea laughed again. "Should I open it?"

"You'd better, or I'm gonna die worried about whether or not you like it."

She looked up at him. "That dire, huh?"

"No, but I do want to know what you think."

She carried the bag to her sofa in the middle of the room. With one hand, she cleared a stack of files and set the bag down on the small coffee table. With careful fingers, she parted the tissue paper and pulled out his gift. She felt him watching as she turned it over and around. She turned to him. "Paul…"

His brows lifted. "Tell me you don't hate it," he said in a low voice.

"I don't hate it," she said, setting it down and throwing her arms around him. "It's the most beautiful, thoughtful, silly, wonderful thing anyone's ever given me," she whispered. Rhea pulled back just enough to kiss him. "Thank you. I adore it."

"You wouldn't have rather had flowers? Or chocolate? Or a new car?"

She ran her finger over the smooth wooden frame and then the candle while she shook her head. "You made this?"

"I was inspired," he told her.

She laughed again. "It's the perfect gift. And yes, I get the point. I never want to burn this candle because it's so beautiful."

He sat back and grinned, his arms spread on the back of the couch. "You really like it?"

"I can't think if I want to keep it here or at the office and show it off there."

"I want you to keep it where it'll remind you that you have a life to live that's your very own. One I intend to be a big part of." He thought for a moment. "Come to think of it, let's call this the prototype. I'll make you one for every room in the house and another for your office."

She curled in next to him and rested her hand on his chest, her head on his shoulder. "I really do love it. Thank you." She reached up and kissed him again, getting mostly beard. "Ugh. That wasn't pleasant."

He curled his arm around her and ran his free hand over his chin. "I guess it's time for me to lose this. I promised myself I would once I was done with this business."

Rhea curled her fingers through it. "I like it, but it's not good for kissing."

He smiled and tightened his arm around her. "As if I needed a better excuse."

"Wait—what? You don't have to shave for me."

"Rhea, who else would I do it for?"

"But Paul..."

"But Rhee..." he mimicked, and she laughed. "It's not a big deal. And trust me, if you don't like how I look without it, I'll grow it back the next day."

"Paul, things are... this is... it's so much, so fast."

He kissed her forehead. "I know, and I'm sorry. I'll slow down. I won't shave until next week, okay?"

She giggled. She couldn't remember the last time she had. "What am I going to do with you?"

He pressed his lips together as the light in his eyes danced.

She sighed. "Just say it."

"You're gonna have to keep me," he said softly.

She nudged the candlestick with her toe. "You keep being sweet and thoughtful, and I won't be able to do anything else."

They sat together, arms around each other in a comforting silence until her stomach rumbled. "You re hungry. Me too," he said. "Want to get going?"

Rhea opened her eyes, not even being aware they'd closed. "I haven't been this relaxed in years."

Paul's laugh was a rumble under her ear. "If this is relaxing, imagine how you'll feel once we…"

She pressed her fingers to his lips. "We're not going to talk about that yet," she said.

"Huh?"

"Soon," she told him. "Just not yet."

He settled in and held her a bit tighter. "You're the boss. Just tell me when and where, and I'll make sure I m ready."

I am in such trouble, she said to herself.

Paul

"You have the last piece. I'm stuffed," Paul said as he pushed the pizza pedestal toward Rhea.

"I'd say," she replied with a wink. "You ate three-quarters of it."

"I was hungry. You think carving wood all day and being this charming is easy?"

She laughed as she cut the remaining piece into two neat wedges and slid the smaller on her plate. "If I eat it all, I'll be back in my baggy sweats at the gym."

He took the piece with a sigh. "The sacrifices I make. ."

Rhea bit into her piece and then took a sip of wine. There was something about watching her throat as she swallowed that made Paul crazy. Not that he imagined they'd be sleeping together that night, but it didn't mean he didn't want to.

"More wine?" he asked.

She shook her head, and her tight curls bounced around her face. He was glad she'd worn her hair down. Not that she wasn't beautiful when her hair was captured in a bun at the base of her neck, but something about her loose curls made her seem happier. Or maybe it was being with him that made her that way. He couldn't help but hope that was true.

"Me neither."

Rhea leaned in closer. "You've never driven drunk?"

He shook his head. "Never been sloppy-falling-down-can't-remember-what-I-was-doing drunk. As soon as Moe understood what happened to our dad, he made a vow that he would never drive drunk—and as each of us got old enough to understand, he made us swear we wouldn't either. It wasn't the usual pinky-swear stuff. He made us cut ourselves on the finger and do a blood-swear."

She shook her head. "That must have made you that much angrier—the guy who hit you."

He nodded. "I notice you don't call him your client."

"I never wanted to represent him." She shivered. "That was the worst thing I've had to do since passing the bar. Even before I knew you were involved."

"Can I ask what leverage your mother used to convince you?"

Rhea bit her lip, and the sparkle went out of her eyes. "I'd rather not talk about it."

Paul reached out and covered her hand with his. "Families can be the best part of your life and the worst," he said.

He could almost see her ears perk up. "Even yours?"

Paul grinned. "You want to know what it's like having four brothers—all of whom are my size, gang up on me when they want me to do something I don't want to do? Just imagine a line of them standing in front of you with

174

their arms folded." He illustrated, his arms across his chest, biceps bulging.

Rhea's eyes widened. "What did you do to deserve that?"

"Stupid stuff. Like when I asked out a girl they didn't like. Or said I didn't want to go to college." He rubbed his hands through is hair. "We tend to not disagree too ofter." He finger-combed his beard. "Which isn't to say I haven't been in that line when one of the other guys is being a jerk. Like when Moe broke up with Berry over… well, it doesn't matter over what."

"He did? I thought you said…"

Paul felt his cheeks heat. "Extenuating circumstances. And it was all kind of, well, surreal. I can't really tell you about it. Sworn to secrecy and all that…"

She reached over and tugged his arm. "Now I really want to know…"

He looked around, hoping for a distraction. "Oh, crap. Look who just walked in."

Rhea turned to see Junior and a woman. Paul assumed it was his fiancée. "Double crap. Don't be scared. Just act natural," she whispered.

He laughed. "You know nothing scares me. I don't think I could do anything else." He could feel his smile fade. "You're not going to be in trouble for seeing me, are you?'

"Not legal trouble," she said under her breath. "Damn t. He's coming over here. Let me… Oh, hi, Junior."

Paul looked at the man and his beautiful, blond fiancée. He slid out of the booth and stood.

His brows high, Junior gave a smarmy smile, his hard still on the woman's back. "Rhea. Mr. Conrad. What a surprise to find you here."

"You're out of your normal stomping grounds, aren't you?" Rhea commented politely.

"Won't you introduce us?" Paul asked. Junior was eyeing Rhea with a calculating look he didn't care for.

"Oh, sure. This is my fiancée, Christine. Rhea Hansen-Chalmbers and her mother just joined the firm…"

Rhea held out her hand with a broad smile. Paul sensed the effort it took her to paste it on and keep it. "My parent's firm and Junior's just merged. And this is my friend, Paul Conrad. Before Junior tells you, I just helped settle a case for a client. Paul was the plaintiff. We've known each other for years—since we were children."

Christine held out her hand. "He mentioned the case to me. He helped you with it, didn't he?"

The woman turned and held out her hand to Paul. He glanced at Rhea. She held her composure in a remarkable way. "He sat in on a few meetings to observe, as part of the merger, but the case was mine."

"But he said…"

"Oh, that's old business, darling," Junior said. Paul noticed Christine winced as his hand tightened.

Christine shot Junior a pained look before she turned to Paul. "It must have been so hard on you two while working against one another."

Paul'd had enough. He turned to her with his best grin. "Well, we were about to start seeing each other when the case came up. Rhea said it would be a conflict of interest, so I had to cool my heels. Now that the case is settled, I don't have to wait anymore. This is our first 'official' date." He took Rhea's hand and kissed it.

"That's so romantic," Christine sighed. "Don't you think so, hon?"

Junior smirked. "Oh, you know I'm not romantic."

Paul thought he heard Rhea snort, but when he turned to look at her, she wore the same stiff smile she'd had since the couple had walked over. "Don't let us keep you from your dinner," she said.

"I'd have thought with all that money Mr. Conrad just received you'd be celebrating with champagne and caviar."

"Oh, I'm more of a pizza and burgers kinda guy," Paul said. "I might make it a gourmet burger, though." He winked broadly at Christine. "I've got lots of other things to spend my money on. Like flowers and candy for Rhea."

"Oh, I prefer champagne and caviar," Christine said. "I wanted seafood tonight, but Junior insisted we come here."

"Did he?" Rhea turned to her future partner. "That's interesting. Well, don't let us keep you. We were about to ask for the check."

His hand was still holding hers. Rhea twisted her fingers and tugged Paul down next to her. "I'll see you bright and early on Monday. It's my turn to observe you, remember? For that divorce you're handling. Where there's an allegation that you've been—rather that the case has been taking an unusually long time to settle?" She smiled sweetly. "I've handled divorces of that size many times. And child custody cases. Lots of happy outcomes—well, as happy as a divorce can be. And I write prenups." She winked at Christine. "We can chat over coffee sometime. I'll tell you all about them."

Paul watched Junior's smirk faded. "Well, don't let us keep you. Come on, darling. Our table is ready."

Paul wrapped an arm around Rhea and kissed her cheek as the other couple walked off. "Anyone ever tell you you're devious?" he asked.

Rhea fluttered her eyelids at him. "Why, Mr. Conrad, that's the nicest compliment you could ever have paid me."

He laughed. "I thought that guy was a shithead the first time I met him. Why in the world did your firms merge?"

Rhea drained her wineglass. "Beats the hell out of me." She looked around and then leaned in close. "I'm doing everything I can to make sure my exit strategy is in place before my mother and his father retire. I do not want to work with that man one day longer than I have to. I wrote it into the merger documents—shocked me neither of them contested it. Sometimes it pays to be underestimated, and you can be sure I'm going to use it to my advantage. And what I said about sitting in on his case—his client is accusing him of dragging his feet to rack up the bill. Knowing what a player he is, I'm not surprised. Junior's father already asked me to take the case over. Junior doesn't know."

"Babe, that's going to mean a lot of hours, isn't it?"

"I'm not scared of the hours. I'm afraid it's going to get ugly before it gets better."

Paul kissed her lightly. "Just so you know, I've got your back."

Rhea's eyes softened, and she caressed his face, beard and all. "And that's why I plan on keeping you around."

Chapter Nineteen

Rhea

"Daddy, I have to tell you about this guy I met."

Rhea stroked her father's hand. He was awake and looking at her. She squeezed his fingers and, for a moment, thought there was a gentle pressure back.

"His name is Paul Conrad. I haven't told mom about him yet. I mean, there really isn't much to tell."

She stopped, and there was that sensation once again.

"I knew him when I was little. We played together at the playground. Nana used to take me. I stopped—I stopped playing with him when I made him fall off the monkey bars."

She paused and took a deep breath. "I didn't push him, not really. It's more I thought him off. You know."

Her father's eyes never left hers. He heaved a sigh.

"Yeah, I know. That was one of the first times *it* happened. He broke his shoulder. Nana called the ambulance." She hung her head. "I was so scared. I ran home. By myself. It's a wonder I didn't get killed. I don't remember stopping for traffic lights. Maybe whatever it was that made me—you know—protected me."

Rhea bit her lip. "I never told Mom. She always got so mad when *that* sort of thing happened. And I didn't want to hurt him. I really didn't. I was just so mad at him for leaving me for his other friends."

She rose and walked about the room. "Nana talked to me after that. She said whatever it was I had—my superpower—that I would have to learn to control it until it was ready to go away on its own. She promised me it would, one day. When I was older."

Rhea wandered back to her chair and sank into it,

179

taking his hand once more. "The problem—and I still can't talk to Mom about this—is that my superpower is still with me. At twenty-seven. Yeah. I know. I can hardly believe it myself, except I live with it every single day. And I can't tell you it's one hundred percent under my control."

There was another meaningful breath from him, and she took his hand once more. "I don't want you to worry about me. I didn't mean to tell you about that. I *do* have it ninety-nine and ninety-nine one-hundredths under control. I squeeze my hands when they start to tingle. And when I can't stop it from happening, I can at least direct it, so it's not destructive. And I try to avoid situations that would set me off. Emotional situations."

She laughed. "Yes, that includes Mom at work. Not the easiest thing, but each day I get stronger."

His hand moved again—she could have sworn it did. "You want to know more about Paul. Right." She felt a smile wash over her face. "He's tall. His hair is brown, and he wears it long but sometimes ties it up. It's so soft and silky...and his smile..." She took a breath and collected herself. "He has a beard, or he did last night. He was going to shave it after the trial—yes, that's another long story that I'll save for another time. But that's settled, and he has his money. He's got plans for it. He works construction—a family business. Yes, I'm dating a man who does physical labor, but now he's more of a craftsman—an artisan." She smiled off into the distance. "He's very creative. He makes handmade furniture, one of a kind pieces, the kinds of things you see in magazines. He's starting his own business with what he got from the settlement. He showed me his business plan last night. Very prudent. He's not wasting a penny."

She frowned. "Mom's not going to like this. I don't know how to tell her. Did she tell you she's approved a merger? I don't like it, but there's not a lot I can do. The paperwork is all in order. Tony senior isn't so bad, but his son is awful. He propositioned me. And he's engaged."

Rhea squeezed her father's hand. "He just happened to run into Paul and me at the pizzeria last night. I'm sure it wasn't an accident. My fingers were tingling so badly, I thought I'd shoot off sparks. I don't know what he's up to, but I'm nervous about it. He doesn't like that I turned him down. He's also one of those sugar-covered bigots who hides their disdain with a smile. He's a spiteful man-baby. Last night he almost dared me to tell his fiancée he'd propositioned me. Of course, he told her he was the brains behind my case." She bit her lip. "I took the high road. Mostly. I want to bide my time to make sure if I need to come out fighting, I have all my ducks in a row." She laughed. "And yes, that's a terrible mixed metaphor, and yes, I do know better."

Her father blinked. Right. He wanted to know more about Paul. "Paul is great. He's someone I can talk to, to tell anything. He knows how hard I work. Said he has my back."

There was a little more pressure. Rhea sighed and squeezed her father's hand. "Okay, not everything. I haven't told him about my superpowers."

She lowered her head and rested her forehead against his hand. "Daddy, I don't know how to tell him. He's the first guy I've known that I can see myself with long term. I don't want to scare him." She straightened with a sniff. "You know I love you and Mom, but I've been alone for so long. I know you did your best, but things weren't always easy. This is the first time I'm letting myself dream of having my own family. Daddy, he's got four brothers and a mother. Three of his brothers are married, and they all have babies. They welcomed me. They liked me, even though I argued a case against him.

"There was no weird stuff about the color of my skin. It was all so—so natural to be there. They accepted me. I mean, that alone is a huge inducement, but it's Paul I'm attracted to. It's Paul who makes me feel good about myself—as a part of a pair. It would be so hard to walk away from that. If I can just control it a little longer—until he and I have been seeing each other for a while. I want to wait until we love each other." She felt her cheeks heat. "He's already told me he wants me for the long term, Daddy. Do you know how good that felt? Do you know what it's like to be wanted? For me. Not what I can bring him, not for bragging rights. I want to bring him to see you. He said he wants to visit."

His finger did move that time. "Daddy?" He closed his eyes, and his finger moved once more. "Daddy, move your finger if you want me to bring him here." There was a gentle pressure. "I will. As soon as I can. I will. Oh, Daddy, thank you." She leaned over and wrapped her arms around her father's frail shoulders, and held him. "I know you'll like him."

She rose and looked into her father's familiar blue eyes. There were tears. "Maybe I'll make you a grandfather yet. And I *will* tell him about—you know. I will. I just have to wait for the right time." She grabbed a tissue and wiped his eyes carefully, clutching the paper in her fist.

He heaved another sigh. "I love you, Daddy," she whispered. "I have to go now. I need to work today. Paul and I are going to a movie tonight. Yes, I'm finally getting out and doing things. Not just the gym where I read briefs as I work out." She wiped her own cheek and laughed. "I'm starting to live. I want you to be happy for me. I love you, and I'll see you next week."

She kissed him again and gave him one more hug

before she left.

Rhea hurried from the room, wiping her tears as she turned to go. Coming toward her was a man holding a woman's elbow. They looked vaguely familiar—he graying at the temples, tall and broad-shouldered. The woman was about her height, well-coifed. "Is that Hugh Chalmbers' room?" the woman asked. "Is he okay?"

Rhea's feet felt frozen to the ground. "Yes, and he's fine—you are..."

The man tsked, too busy to be bothered, but the woman eyed Rhea nervously. "Are you Rhea?"

Her back stiffened, and she clenched her hands. "Yes."

The two strangers looked at one another. The man sighed. "I was afraid this would happen."

"It's for the best," the woman said before she held out her hand, none-to-steadily. "I'm Debra, and this is my bro—oh crap, this is our brother, Milo."

The sparks that had been lying dormant wanted to fly. Green gold, silver, red, violet. She took a deep, shattered breath, and then another. With great effort, Rhea unclenched her fingers and took the woman's hand. "I'm... I'm speechless."

Debra pulled Rhea into her arms. "I know. I'm sorry for this being so awkward." She let her go. "I'm sorry, I just had to do that. I've been wanting to meet you for years."

Rhea stepped back and looked at her siblings. "Awkward doesn't really cover it."

Her brother held out his hand. "I won't force you into a hug like Deb did. But I am happy to meet you. With every year, it grew more difficult to reach out until it was easier to pretend... or keep pretending... you know what I mean."

"I—I suppose I do," Rhea sputtered. "Daddy's fine. We just had a long talk—rather one-sided," she said with a small laugh. "I don't know if you've visited him before?"

They shook their heads. "We've been dreading it. We last saw him just before his stroke. Our mother... she was angry about the divorce all these years. It was simpler for us to sneak visits with him when she wasn't paying attention, and she was always paying attention. She died a few months ago. There were no more barriers. We just needed to get up the courage and find the time," Debra said. "I know how bad that sounds."

"He can't speak, but if you hold his hand, he can press it a little," Rhea told them. "He's alert. The doctors can't say how much he understands, but I think he does. Just speak slowly. One at a time. Seeing you..." she looked from one to another. "It might be a shock."

"We won't stay long," Milo said.

"I was in there for an hour, so he may be tired. Don't expect too much."

"You visit him? Milo asked.

"I try to come every week," Rhea told him.

The two looked at each other, but whatever silent communication they shared was lost on her. "Listen, this is hard for all of us. I'm used to him being this way." She dug into her purse. "If you want to talk, here's my card. I'd be happy to see you somewhere other than this corridor."

Debra clutched the card. "You mean that?"

Rhea shrugged. "Let's figure this out. I mean, it's not easy for any of us, but we're all adults."

Milo pocketed his copy of the card and took his sister's elbow once more. "I'll leave it up to you two," he said curtly. "Now, if you'll excuse us?"

Rhea shrugged. "You know where to find me. I never knew where to find you," she said simply.

Debra winced. "I will call. With or without my—I mean, our brother. We'll have coffee, and you can meet our kids and my husband and..." Her brother elbowed her sharply.

"Well, let's take it one step at a time."

Rhea gave them a small smile and stepped aside. "Don't stay too long. I'll tell the nurse to stop by in five minutes. I don't want the shock to kill him."

Paul

"So, let me tell you what I did today, "Paul said as he unpacked a bag of Thai food onto Rhea's kitchen table. "Sammy helped set up the new equipment, and we tested it out. Moe brought Mattie and the baby to give Berry a break, and the little guy actually stopped crying when we turned the router on." He laughed. "We finally found something louder than him. We had a bunch of scrap lumber from a recent job, so we got to play with all of it. Pine, oak, spruce, even some cherry. It was great to see how the machines worked with the different wood."

Rhea looked up at him, her eyes shining. "Yeah?"

He nodded. "Then they had to go—and I knew you'd be a few hours, so I just stayed and doodled some. Joey gave me his old drafting table. Much easier on my arm. I started putting some table designs together. I'm thinking reclaimed or live edge boards if I can find them." He pulled some sheets from a tube. "I thought this one could go over by the staircase. And this one could go by the sofa. You don't mind being the guinea pig for my new designs, do you?"

He glanced over her shoulder as she looked at his drawings. "These are great. But I don't think they'd be here long. You start showing your work, and these will get snapped up so fast you won't be able to make new ones fast enough."

"Well, that's why I called the local veteran's action line and left a message. I told them I wanted to know if any of their guys might be interested in some part-time work that could go full-time if things pick up. Told them I can't pay much, but I'm willing to train. I need guys who can be on their feet, lift stuff, move around, and aren't afraid to use the machines."

Rhea's gaze met his. "Paul, that's such an awesome idea."

He shrugged. "Moe's gotten a few guys that way. I thought I'd do the same. Not that I'm expecting just guys. If any female vet wants to learn woodworking, I'd take her on."

Rhea turned and hugged him, hard. "You are so special," she whispered.

"Hey, now." His arms went around her. "I wasn't telling you just to remind you how lucky you are to have me."

She gave a watery laugh. "Sure you weren't."

He held her closer. "Yeah, you got me. I was. I'm doing everything I can to make myself irresistible. How'm I doing?"

"You're at about nine point nine," she laughed and pulled away.

"On a scale of twenty?" he asked with a wink.

"Not telling. Now, do we eat this stuff with a fork or chopsticks?"

"Babe, you can eat it with your fingers if you want," he assured her. "I won't tell."

Rhea set out plates while Paul hunted for silverware. He glanced around the kitchen. It was, in a word, utilitarian. The house must have been fifty years old, and the kitchen looked like it had never been updated. "Thought about some new paint?" he asked as mildly as he could.

"I make it a rule to not think about paint," she said with a pained look. "New paint means scraping old paint, and primer, and drop cloths and hair rags and brushes and rollers and fumes. Not to mention hours of work and scrubbing paint from under my fingernails."

"Or you could hire someone."

Rhea pulled out a chair and sat, pulling a carton close, and smelled the contents. "Can't afford that. I've got too many loans."

Paul sat across from her and opened another carton, then dug in with a spoon. "Not to sound too crass, but I thought your folks were loaded. And don't tell me you're not making good money."

He must have been mistaken, for it sounded as if Rhea snorted. "My parents did make good money, but it's theirs. I had to pay for school. Undergrad and grad. Because they had money and insisted on claiming me as a dependent, it was hard to get need-based scholarships. My mom said I'd appreciate my education more if I had to pay for it."

She sighed and looked up. "I did get academic scholarships, but it wasn't enough. I worked through college. Then I had to pay for law school—more loans. I was paying too much in rent. My old nanny left me some money. I used that for a down payment on this place.

"And before you ask, the car was a gift from my mother when I graduated law school. But insurance isn't cheap on a Lexus. Or taxes."

"So, if people think I'm after you for your money, it's actually the other way around," he joked.

"You've got a lot more collateral than me," she told him. "But, it's your ego that I find most attractive."

He chuckled and dug into his dinner.

"This is good," she said around a mouthful. "Spicy."

"Warms you up on a cold winter day," he agreed.

"But it's fall," she commented.

Paul laughed. "It'll be winter soon enough. So, how was your visit with your dad?"

Her eyes sparkled. "He wants to meet you."

Paul blew the steam off his next bite. "Whenever you say."

187

She set her fork down. "Today's visit was actually kind of interesting."

He lifted his brows. "Interesting how?"

"I ran into my brother and sister."

"Why don't you all go together?" he paused, and his eyes narrowed. "Wait. What? I didn't know you had a brother and sister."

"From my dad's first marriage. It was the first time I met them."

"Holy sh..." He set his own fork down. "Excuse me. What? How can you be so—say that so calmly?"

She gave him a wry grin. "Lots of practice."

"Must be a law school kind of thing. Except, you were always pretty hard to rile up back at school. But how..."

"My dad was married to their mother when he and my mother met. My parents told me he divorced his first wife before they started seeing each other. I always believed that, and it's not something I'm going to question now. But Debra and Milo were never part of my life. I always knew of them, but Mom and Dad never wanted to talk about them. I asked if they could come play with me, but I was told they were too grown up. They must have been in their late teens or early twenties when I was born—I really don't know."

"No pictures or anything?"

Rhea shook her head. "If my dad had any, he didn't keep them anywhere I could find them. As siblings, they were purely theoretical. If my dad saw them, it wasn't at our house. I have no idea if he went to their weddings. I know at least my sister has children..."

"Oh, honey." Paul rose and went around to her chair. He slid her out and lifted her, then sat and pulled her onto his lap. "My poor Rhea. That must have been a shock."

She laid her head on his shoulder. "I don't know who

was more surprised. I gave them my card and asked them to call me if they wanted to get together."

"Why don't you call them?"

She met his gaze. "They didn't give me their numbers. I don't even know my sister's last name—if she changed it when she got married. Or if my brother is married or gay or anything. I just don't know. I've resisted Googling them. I don't know if I'm scared or nervous, but I kind of want them to show some interest in getting to know me."

"Sweetheart." He held her close and rubbed her back. "You should have told me right away. Here I was blathering on about hanging out with my brothers this afternoon…"

She sat up and placed her finger on his lips. "I like hearing about them. A real family. I don't want you to stop playing with them or their kids. You're so lucky to have them—I can't even begin to tell you. Seeing mine… it made it all so clear to me."

He pressed her head gently back to his chest. "You have me, and you can have my brothers if you want 'em. If your sister calls, invite her over for a barbeque. We'll have them over, and my family too, to sort of loosen things up, not to mention, overwhelm them with numbers. We'll fire up the grill…"

"I don't have a grill."

He snorted. "We'll get you one. We can make Moe cook. He loves playing with fire, and it'll keep him out of trouble. Unlike the rest of us, he can actually flip burgers, so long as someone else makes them." I'll make us a picnic table and…"

Rhea laughed. "Slow down, bucko. You're getting ahead of yourself."

He shrugged, pulling his sore shoulder just a little. "Just making plans."

"Um, maybe you can let me up so I can finish eating?"

she suggested.

Paul snaked his arms around her hips. "I kinda like having you here. Let me enjoy it for a minute. If I can't sleep with you, this is the closest I'm gonna get until you change your mind."

She laughed again. "Good thing you're cute because subtlety's not your forte."

He couldn't have stopped his grin for all the money in the world. "You think I'm cute? I thought you liked me just 'cause I'm so brave."

"Let me go. Cute and egotistical. It's a wonderful combination. I mean it, Paul. Let me up. I'm hungry, and I'm not above stabbing you with my fork."

He laughed and released her. "Since I'm so comfy here, I'll just move your plate and mine." He switched them as she grumbled with a smile and sat.

He watched her take a bite of her dinner. "So, about our sleeping together," he said. Her eyes flashed as she choked back a laugh. "When exactly do you think we'll get around to talking about it?"

She chewed hard and swallowed. "What I just said about your not being very subtle? I'm giving you double points for being devious."

"Hey, I'm crazy about you. I don't mind us spending all our time together out of bed, but I want to know when we'll get to spend time together in bed, too," he said as if it were the most reasonable thing in the world.

"I thought maybe once we were done with dinner?" she said rhetorically. "I find it kind of hard to talk about when I'm busy trying new food."

"Did you ever think about trying new food while in bed?"

She wrinkled her nose at him. "Really, Paul? Really?"

He shrugged again and winked. "I may not be able to cook, but I do know how to make a bed and wash sheets."

Rhea laughed again. "I'm going to have my hands full with you, aren't I?"

"I'd say so," he replied with a waggle of his eyebrows.

"I'll add incorrigible to the list. I'll bet your mother used to tell you that all the time."

He let out a laugh. "If my mother knew it, she would have said it. She used other words instead. Idiot. Dunce. Blockhead. Knucklebrain. Sweetheart. Or maybe that was for my brothers. It was sometimes hard to tell."

"It must have been a zoo at your house."

"A circus," he said quickly. "We weren't in cages, but we would have swung from the chandelier if we'd had one."

"I would have loved to have seen that."

He chuckled. "I say give it a year at my brother's house when the baby is walking, and Joey and Pete's kids are too. Mattie will be the ringmaster—I mean ring leader. Then you'll know what it was like."

She set her fork down. "I hope so. I really hope I get to see that."

Paul reached across the table. "You will. I promise. And if you want one of ours to be one of the barking seals, just say the word."

He watched her face as it went from tender to outrage to disbelief. "Did you just say what I thought I heard you say?"

"What did I say?"

"You implied an alleged child of mine would be a barking seal."

"Ooooh, alleged child. You're getting all lawyer-y on me. That's hot."

"Paul..."

"Okay. Our *alleged* child might prefer to be an acrobat. Or a lion who jumps through rings of fire. Or be the ring of fire. We'll just have to wait for him to state his preference. Or hers. Or maybe one of each flavor of *alleged* children, so we can have more than one act."

She sputtered. "I am not going to get through this meal."

"What? Too much cuteness? I can dial it back if I must," he said with a straight face.

"I'm not sure what I'd call it, but cuteness wasn't the word I was looking for."

"How about alleged cuteness? That way, you don't have to commit to it until you're ready."

"I'll be committing myself to something," she muttered as he laughed.

"Bedlam, or to me. Your choice."

"Paul..."

He ducked his head with a grin. "I know, I know. I can't stop the hilarity, but I'll tone it down, at least what I say out loud."

She waved her finger at him. "That's one thing I'll never ask you to do. Keep me laughing—please."

He nodded and returned to his dinner, satisfied he'd gotten what he came for.

Chapter Twenty

Rhea

"So, is tonight the night?" Paul asked Rhea the following Saturday. They were walking out of the coffee house where they'd heard an acoustic trio.

"For what?" she asked.

"For you know what," he said with his usual eyebrow wiggle. "I mean, making out on the couch is great and all, but one of these days I'm gonna cream my pants, and that would be plain old humiliating."

Rhea laughed as she glanced over her shoulder to see if anyone was listening to him.

She'd actually spent a lot of time thinking about it—at times other than when resolving the mess her new 'partner' had made of a simple divorce. The couple had a prenup, which should have made everything simple had Junior acknowledge it's presence in the case file.

She'd thought about Paul during lunch, and while she was driving to and from her office, considered inviting him up to her bed. When she was working out at the gym, she thought about the two of them getting naked, especially when Paul was across the place, and she could see his firm body shown off to perfection. She'd thought about it when she should have been reading briefs at night. She even dreamed about their making love and had been confused and disappointed to wake up alone and found it had all been the product of wishful nighttime thinking.

She'd thought and thought and wondered and worried. If she waited too long, the suspense was going to be the death of her emotionally. That was a sure recipe for disaster. She hadn't yet found a way to tell Paul about her peculiarity, and his playful banter, mixed with soulful conversations about things that mattered most to them, hadn't left an opening to tell him that his new-found girlfriend wasn't exactly normal.

"Paul, I…"

She stopped suddenly when she saw her brother driving by in a late model European sedan.

"That was my brother," she said, pointing at the black car.

"Have you heard from him or your sister?"

She shook her head. "No. I called the nursing home. Dad slept through their visit. I don't know if he was aware they were there. I don't know if he'll remember our conversation."

"I'm going with you," he told her. "No matter what your answer is tonight. Maybe I ought to wait until after I meet him to stay over."

She scoffed and gave him a small push. "You're not going to ask him for permission to sleep with me, are you?"

He got in the passenger seat of her car with a silent smile.

She followed and started the car, pulling into traffic only to stop at a red light. "Well?" she asked.

"What? Of course not," he replied, clearly affronted. "I'm going to ask his permission to marry you. When we're ready, of course. I know how you like to plan things in advance."

"What the…"

"The light turned green," he said. "So, you'll drop me off at your place, and I'll drive home. I'll come back tomorrow, and we'll go from there, okay?"

"No." Her reply was out of her mouth before she knew what she was going to say. "Not okay."

He looked crestfallen. "You changed your mind about

my visiting?"

Rhea shook her head. "No. I want you to visit. What I mean is, I want you to, you know, stay with me. Before we visit him."

She could see the teasing glint in his eye in the light of the streetlight. "So, you want me to come over early, and we'll spend time together before we drive to the nursing home?"

"Paul, I'm trying to be serious here."

"Then you'd best speak clearly."

"I want you to spend the night…"

"On your sofa."

She looked heavenward. "Not on my sofa."

"I'm not sleeping on the floor. You don't have a rug in your living room."

"Not in the living room."

"You don't have a rug in your spare bedroom either," he quipped. "Or a bed. Boxes are out of the question. I'm not a cat."

"Paul, I'm about to change my mind."

"Bathtub?" he asked, hopefully.

"No."

"You have mice in your kitchen. I'm not sleeping with mice, even if you let me stay on the table."

"I have mice? The realtor said…"

He held her hand. "I'm teasing. No mice."

She took a deep breath. "I've given this a lot of thought, and I want you to spend the night. With me. In my bed."

She could see him try to hold back his smile. "Just so I'm clear, do you mean sleeping in your bed?"

"We might sleep. Some," she acknowledged.

Paul rolled down the window. "Oh, so you mean you want to have sex with me tonight."

"Paul!" she cried as those walking by looked in at them.

She hit the gas and banged her finger hard on the button to roll up his window.

He laughed. "You make it sound like it's such a big deal."

Rhea gripped the steering wheel. "Me? A big deal? When that's all you've wanted to talk about for the past month almost?"

"It's what I've wanted to do since I first saw you again," he said with a laugh. "I didn't start talking about it until I thought I had a chance."

Her fingers tightened on the wheel. Thank goodness her directional signal masked the sparks leaping from her fingertips. "You'd better not be spending all this time with me just to sleep with me and run off tomorrow."

"Rhea, sweetheart, please calm down. Of course, I want to sleep with you. It's part of my wanting to be with you. Always wanting to be with you. It's like the last hurdle of the unknown. And it is a big deal. I just don't want to make it *too* big a deal—not that I'm not saying there's nothing big about it…"

"Would you get to the point?" she asked through gritted teeth.

He sighed, and it was a happy sound. "Okay. I'm nervous. I didn't want you to know."

He turned to her in the dark interior. "I haven't been with a woman in over a year. I have no idea how my shoulder is going to hold up. I don't know what you like, and as much as I hate to admit it, you can be kind of formidable. I want to please you. A lot. Because I want to sleep with you. A lot. For the rest of our lives. I kid around when I'm nervous because it's part of the guy code. Which I just broke big time. Never admit fear to a woman." He turned to look out his window.

"You mean it?" she asked.

She sensed his nod rather than saw it.

"Because I haven't been with anyone in a long time either," she admitted. "And when I was, it wasn't all that good. Because I always get nervous and worried that I won't be good enough. Or that I'm with the guy for the wrong reason. Or that I'm just not cut out for good sex because I am too uptight, or there's this thing about me you ought to know…"

He placed his hand on hers. "Rhea, we'll get through this. We're both a little uptight. And it's supposed to be fun."

She turned into her driveway, pulled up the parking brake, and shut off the car before resting her head on the steering wheel. "Fun. Right."

He rubbed her back. "Last I remember."

She let out a harsh laugh. "Right. Okay. Let's do this."

She yanked her door open and got out, marching up the walk to her door. As she reached for her housekey, she realized he wasn't with her. "Paul?"

He grinned from inside the car. She walked back to the driveway. "What?" she demanded.

He said something, but she couldn't hear him, so she opened his door. "What?"

He gave her a quizzical smile. "I said I think we're off to the wrong start."

She turned to the front door, her arm wide. "But I…"

"How about we try again?" He patted the driver's seat. "Come back. Let's start over."

She was about to argue, but her mouth snapped shut. She rounded the car as his door shut again, and returned to her former position with her arms folded and stared straight at her garage door. "Okay. Now what?"

He pulled at her shoulder. "Now, you kiss me. And then I kiss you. And we kiss a few more times."

Her shoulders sagged as she laid her head on the seat rest. "I told you I was terrible at this."

"That remains to be seen. All I know is that you're tense about this. I can fix that."

"Backrub?" she asked, hopefully.

He grinned at her. "That can be part of it. Later. First, we kiss."

She took a deep breath. "Kissing is good."

Paul tugged one of her hands and turned it over, pressing his lips to her palm. "When done right, kissing is better than good. Kissing is one of my favorite things."

"In the driveway?" she asked skeptically.

"Anywhere." He pressed another kiss to her hand. "We can kiss in public, and no one needs to know how intimate we are. We can kiss in private and that can be foreplay all by itself." He stopped. "You do know about foreplay, right?"

She laughed, and her other hand loosened its grip. "I've heard of it."

He grinned, and his hands moved to cradle her face. "Then let me kiss you, Rhea, my dear, wonderful, worried woman."

He pressed his lips to hers, persuading her to open a moment later. He delved in lightly, teasing his way about her mouth as she chased him, and she felt her body loosen along with the laughter.

Paul grew more insistent. His hands moved to her shoulders, rubbing and kneading. It felt so good she wanted to groan. His lips parted from hers. "You okay?" he asked softly.

She nodded. "Oh, yeah."

She felt his smile as his lips took hers once more. His arms slid around her, tightening as they went, his hands seeking her skin between her top and her jeans. His fingertips were warm and just rough enough without

198

scratching.

Paul deepened the kiss, and Rhea heard herself moan in response. It was the oddest thing, being so deeply involved with her body, his body, yet floating above watching the goings-on as a not exactly uninterested bystander. *Stop thinking so much,* she commanded herself, and she felt as if she were zipped back into her core, one single individual intimately involved with the man in her arms.

He pressed her again, and her elbow hit the emergency blinker, startling them both. Paul sat up, hauling her with him. "I think," he said, breathing hard, "It might be time to bring these proceedings into the house." He pressed the button, and the blinkers clicked off.

She rested her forehead against his and nodded, trying to catch her own breath. "Okay."

She did not move, other than her hands, which ran through his hair.

"Um, Rhee?" Paul said after a long moment.

"Ummm?"

"Kinda cramped here," Paul said with a chuckle.

She sat up, feeling her cheeks burn. "Yeah, right. In the house."

He caught her face in his hands. "It's not snowing. The wind isn't bitterly cold. So no rushing this time," he said with a light kiss. "No marching off. We go in together like lovers do."

She gave him a smile.

He undid his seatbelt, holding her hand all the while. "Let's meet at the hood of the car."

She felt her smile grow.

In the dim light, she saw his smile turn mischievous. "Unless you want to race to see who can get to the front door first."

"Nope."

One brow rose.

"You have an unfair advantage, being closer. And not wearing heels," she said.

"I can see I'm going to have to work hard to sneak anything by you."

It was her turn to raise a brow. "You did say you liked smart women."

"Woman. One. You." He kissed her nose and opened his door.

She darted out of the car, and his arms were ready for her as they met in the small space between the garage door and the bumper. "This is better," Paul said as he bent her over his arm.

She kissed him then and began to walk him to her front door. "I don't know about you, but these public displays of affection aren't doing the job. Let's get inside."

His arms went around her, and he turned, so they walked side by side. "I like the way you think."

She opened the door, and they spilled inside. Rhea closed the door, and a moment later, he had her back pressed to it. "I think I want to kiss you, right here, right now," he murmured as he began to do just that. "And while we're at it, we'll take our clothes off, real slow. And make each other crazy with lust."

Rhea shivered as his lips traveled to her neck. His hands were once again sliding under her shirt, inching higher and higher. She could feel the drag of her tee-shirt along the way, but could not summon a single iota of complaint or dissent. Her hands framed his face, and he turned to kiss her wrist, her hand, taking each in his own.

Palms touching palms, fingers entwined, Paul leaned in and kissed her lips, deepening it as she sighed. "You still okay?" he asked softly. Her reply was to find his mouth with hers.

"More," she whispered.

His lips traveled to her neck and down the vee of her soft top. Their fingers still entwined, he pushed her jacket off before he caught the hem of her shirt and lifted it until he could kiss the warm, smooth skin of her belly. "Rhea," he breathed. "Take this off."

She didn't need to be asked twice as she crossed her arms and, in a swift movement, flung it toward the living room.

His hands loosened hers as he ran his fingertips over her skin and kissed each visible inch.

Emboldened, Rhea tugged at his down vest and taut shirt until he looked up and smiled. With a flourish, they were gone.

He rose and brought his arms around her, flesh to flesh. "Much better," he crooned into her ear before his kisses traveled along her neck and made her shiver.

"Are we ready to go upstairs?" she whispered.

He shook his head as he hooked a finger in her bra and tugged down a cup, only to open his mouth on her breast and tease the tip with his tongue. "I want you boneless before I carry you to your bed," he said before applying himself to her other breast.

"I don't know if I can stand much longer," she moaned as desire shot from her breast to her center and back again.

Paul grinned again and wrapped her arms around his neck. "Up you go," he said and hoisted her so her legs went around his hips, and he held her bottom with his hands. "Better?" he asked as he leaned against the door to free up his hands. "Hold on. Whatever you do, don't let go."

She shook her head and gasped as his mouth returned to tantalize her once more. She pressed her head back, her eyes closed. "Paul, we have to go…"

His hands came back to cup her bottom. "I did this in the wrong order," he said with a soft laugh. "I need to get you naked."

"I can be naked in the bedroom."

He shook his head. "In my fantasy, I have you naked right here. I make you come—screaming right here at your front door." He pressed her back to that wooden panel.

She gulped. "I don't know if I can."

He laughed as he slid her until her feet reached the floor. "I do, and that's all that matters."

He reached behind her and unclasped her bra. It slid down her arms, and he stood, staring at her breasts. "You are more beautiful than I ever dreamed," he said reverently before he pressed a kiss to one and then the other.

With a quick jerk, he loosened his belt and the fly of his jeans and toed off his shoes. They dropped to his ankles, and he kicked them away, leaving himself clad only in knit boxers that revealed more than they covered.

"Your turn," he coaxed, and Rhea fumbled with the clasp of her jeans before shimmying them down her legs. She kicked them away and looked down to find her panties half off. The appreciation in Paul's eyes was all she needed to peel them off the rest of the way. He reached for his boxers, and then the two of them stood there, equally naked, looking their fill at the other.

She reached out and touched the scar on his shoulder. "Is this going to be okay?" she asked.

He turned his head and kissed her hand where it lay on his skin. "I'm going to make it be okay," he told her. "You don't need to worry about a thing." He leaned in to kiss her again, and this time, there was no mistaking his arousal as it pressed against her belly, hard and warm and throbbing. She stiffened, and his hands came up to soothe her arms and back. "Don't worry about this, Rhee. We'll make it work. We're doing great so far, aren't we?"

She looked into his eyes. There was love there, along with a fair amount of lust. And concern. She nodded. "I'm working on it."

"Stop working," he murmured and kissed her eyelids closed. "Just enjoy."

With that, he began to kiss his way down her body, taking his time, soothing her, pressing his lips and tongue where it seemed she most needed and wanted them. Until he came down to her mons. His hands stopped, and he glanced up at her.

She waited a moment because she suddenly knew she had the power to do so, and then nodded. Paul smiled, a smile unlike any other he'd gifted her with, and then closed his eyes and continued his path of kisses.

It seemed the most natural thing to lean back against her door as he lifted her leg and draped it over his right shoulder. His hands caught hers then as he pressed his nose deep between her legs. He kissed her then, right there where she'd never been kissed before. Rhea hissed her approval and thrust her hips out for more.

With a groan, Paul loosened her hands and spread her wide, his tongue following along its natural path to taste her deeply.

"God above," Rhea crooned and pressed closer for more of what he was giving her.

He kissed her again, and then some more, his tongue darting in and out, sucking and tasting. She hardly noticed when he inserted a finger and added it to the party that was going on down below.

"You are delicious," he muttered, pressing in for more kisses. "I could do this all night."

She could not help but laugh. "So could I."

He deepened his penetration. "This is better than I ever dreamed it would be."

"Paul, I..." she ground her hips around.

"You're close." It was a statement, and he redoubled his efforts, his tongue pressing hard right where she needed it. Somehow his fingers inside curled around and pressed, heightening the sensation until she thought she would be pulled apart. And a moment later, she was. Her body convulsed around her core, and the sound she made was one she had no idea she was capable of. "OhGodohGodohGodohGod," she cried out, and but for his hands holding her up, she would have sunk to her knees.

Paul kissed her once more, his fingers still within her as he came to his feet. He kissed her hard, and for the first time in her life, she tasted her own salty essence. He slipped his fingers out slowly and slid his hand around to her bottom to rub gently.

"I don't think we have anything we need to worry about, do you?" he chuckled as he tugged her away from the door and into his arms. "Darlin, you came so hard, I could've sworn you were shooting off golden sparks. The next time you come, I'm keeping my eyes open."

Which was when Rhea chose to faint for the very first time in her life.

Chapter Twenty-One

Paul

Terrified, he watched Rhea as she came out of her faint. He'd held her tightly on his lap until she came to.

"Now, I'm not going to lie to you, he said slowly. "I've been with a few women in my life. Don't ask me how many. I never kept count—and they don't matter now that we're together." He gulped in a breath. "But I never had one faint from coming before. Damn, woman. Don't tell anyone, but you just took ten years off my life."

He wasn't kidding. He knew she'd come hard. She was supposed to, and then he planned to make her come again and again, if he could stand it before they repaired to the bedroom. But then Rhea's eyes had rolled up in her head, and she began to collapse. It had been all he could do to get his good shoulder under her middle and ease her down gently.

It took everything he had to lift her and carry her to the only furnished bedroom in the house while he was shaking like a leaf. He sat them both as gently as he could on the mattress on the floor and then rubbed her hands until she stirred. It couldn't have been more than a minute, but it felt like a lifetime. And his erection had wilted. Good thing. He'd needed all the blood his brain could handle.

"I fainted?" she asked, then looked down at herself and him. "I'm so embarrassed." She crawled out of his lap and curled into a ball.

He lay beside her and held her tightly. "You're not sick, are you? We'll have to use a bed—I suppose I could get used to it, but hell, Rhee, you could warn a guy."

She curled tighter. "I've never fainted in my life," she

said in a little voice. "I never came so hard before," she added a moment later.

"Well now, that's what I deserve then," he said and couldn't keep a modicum of pride from his voice.

"I don't think it was my coming that did it," she said.

He sat up and looked down at her. Brown curls hid her face, and he brushed them aside. "Then what did?"

"Maybe because it's been so long?"

Paul lay back. "Whew. Well, then I guess I'll have to make sure we do this at least once a day, so we don't have that to worry about again."

"Rhea rubbed her hands over her face before she turned to look at him. "Every day?"

"At least once," he said with a wink.

"How in the world will I ever get anything done?" she asked. "I feel so wrung out."

Paul grinned as his hand snaked over the covers to hold hers. "Maybe that's a good thing. For you to do a little less, I mean."

Her hand loosened his. "Maybe it is." She turned on her side and her fingers began to explore his chest. "Well, let's hope that's a story we'll laugh about…"

"You mean I can't tell the grandkids?"

She snorted and pulled away. "How can you even joke about it?"

"Hey, stuff comes to mind, I just gotta say it," he replied. He pulled her hand back where it was. "Now, as long as you're okay, I think there was something else we intended to do before we were interrupted." His hand nudged hers a little lower. "Poor guy got scared and lost all his enthusiasm. You might want to do a little something to encourage him back in the mood."

Rhea laughed, but her hand wandered down, exploring his body slowly and thoroughly before reaching down between his legs. "Is this what you mean?" she asked as she clasped her hands around him.

Paul had the wherewithal to flex his belly muscles in return. "Yeah, that's the stuff," he managed to gasp.

It didn't take long before he was restored to his former robust strength. Paul was about to roll over to nestle between her legs when he realized his pants and condoms were downstairs. "Uh, Houston, we have a small problem."

Rhea's hand stopped. "Oh?"

"I left something in your foyer. Protection."

She laughed and rolled to her nightstand. "No worries. I bought these. I hope they're the right kind." She placed a box on the pillow between them.

She'd gone all out and gotten a deluxe brand he'd never used before.

"You like to be prepared." He opened the box and placed a few packets under the pillow before tossing the closed box over the side of the bed.

She grinned. "It's my training. Expect the unexpected. Or guide things to your way of thinking."

"All right then." He looked into her eyes as he propped himself up on his elbows. "You want to do the honors, or should I?"

Not losing his gaze, she ripped a package open and pulled out the latex disk. She unrolled the condom onto his now aching erection.

Rhea sat back and appraised him. Her slow sweep of his body made his so hard, he was afraid he would explode too soon. "Like what you see?" he asked through clenched teeth.

"Um hum." Her smile grew slowly. "Very nice."

"Works for me," he said as he lay back on the bed and crossed his arms under his head. "Care to start out on top?"

She smiled and pulled her leg over his lap. "I thought you'd never ask." She positioned herself on him and put a finger to her mouth. "Remind me. How does this work again?"

He laughed and levered up to kiss her. "I think you'll remember. Just take your time."

Rhea flashed him another smile, brighter than before. "Yeah, I think it's starting to come back to me now." She began to move over him, teasing him gently.

"I knew you'd remember," he said through gritted teeth. "Now, let's see if I live to tell the story."

She laughed, and that was the last coherent thing either of them said or thought for quite a while.

And to set the record straight, the last thing Paul could do was keep his eyes open when he and Rhea came together, so if there were any more sparks, it was a mystery to them both.

Rhea

She lay curled on her bed. In the back of her mind, she knew there was something she was supposed to be doing. It probably had to do with reading something, researching case law, and jotting down notes. But for the life of her, she could barely open her eyes, let alone string two words together.

For the first time in forever, she was rested, warm, and sated, and Paul was right there with her, snug against her back, his arm holding her close. She resisted the urge to open her eyes and turn to see him there in the bright morning light beside her. Much better to feel his body pressed close. He was so much stronger than she'd ever imagined, not to mention persistent. And inventive.

He nuzzled his nose into her neck. "You awake?" he asked in a gravely voice.

She shook her head and burrowed deeper into his arms.

"Well, one of our phones is ringing," he said as he pressed a soft kiss to her ear. "I'm of the opinion we let whomever it is leave a message."

She smiled as he began to kiss her awake. "I like how you think."

He stopped. "You're not likely to have an angry client come banging your front door, are you? Or mother?"

"Don't you dare stop what you were doing," she muttered as she turned and slipped her hands to some interesting parts of his body. "I don't give my clients my address, and my mother wouldn't come here unannounced." Or at all, but that wasn't pertinent at the moment. What was, was the way he was kissing his way down her body. She obliged him by tossing off the sheet and giving him free rein.

"I love making love to you in the morning," he muttered as he feathered kisses along her leg.

"Do you?" she managed. Never had her voice sounded so languid as it did just then.

"I do. Because I can see every glorious inch of you."

He flicked his tongue on a nipple, and she caught her breath. He repeated it on the other, and she clasped his face in her hands and brought him up for a kiss that flared from hot to blazing in seconds.

"Under the pillow. Is there another condom?" he asked.

She dug around furiously and handed it to him.

"Turn on your side," he asked, his hands smoothing over her curves.

"Your arm…?"

He pressed kisses to her shoulder. "Nothing to worry about."

Rhea heard the package rip, and a moment later, he

was pressed against her from behind—his hand urged her leg up and over his hip as his other arm snaked beneath her and came up to gently grasp her breast. She pressed back against him as he slid into her, far deeper than he had at any time last night. She clasped his hip to hold him in place as his free hand came to knead her other breast. She arched backward, moaning, "Ohyesohyesohyes," as she slipped closer and closer to ecstasy.

Paul set forth to move his hips, and it was all she could do to keep up with him. His fingers slid down her chest, over her belly until they came to rest at the apex of her legs. The additional pressure pulled her over the top, and she convulsed around him. Paul pushed hard and came with a wild groan.

His arms gathered her up. "Tell me you don't have to work today. Tell me you can give yourself to me, all day long," he whispered.

"I can't even think," she replied, hard-pressed not to giggle, and settled on a heartfelt sigh. "You've used up every brain cell I own."

"Good," he said as he slipped out of her and removed the condom. "That means I've done my job."

She laughed as she rolled over and hugged him near. "I know this is going to sound sappy as hell, but I'm going to say it anyway. You're not a figment of my imagination, are you?"

Paul's hand came up to hold her cheek. "I'm real, darlin'. As real as they get."

She smiled at him, and his answering grin warmed her to her toes. "I think I can take the day off today. I've already got more billable hours than anyone else for the past six months running. If anyone complains, I'll just show them the spreadsheet."

"That's my girl," he replied with a fond pat on her rear.

She bit her lip. "Maybe we ought to see who called. Before we make any plans."

He yawned and stretched before he scratched his flat belly. "My only plan is to spend as much of today in bed with you as I can. Maybe call for something to be delivered later for dinner? A perfect day is a day I don't have to get dressed. I might just get out of bed only to shower."

She laughed and got off the bed, falling back on it a moment later. "Damn, you got me dizzy."

Paul just laughed. "Like I said, just doing my job."

She rose gingerly and looked back at him.

"Anyone ever tell you that you have one fine ass, Rhee?"

She laughed and threw a sock at him. "It's a good thing you're smiling when you say that."

He grinned at her. "Of course, every bit of you is fine. Give me ten minutes to recover, and I'll prove it to you all over again."

She shook her head. "I need fifteen. Certain parts haven't been used in a while. I think they need a break."

He sat up. "Oh, hell, I'm sorry. I didn't mean to get all caveman on you like that. Are you okay? Can I do anything? Tell me. Anything. Ice pack? Ice cream? Frozen peas?"

She slipped on a robe and shook a finger at him. "Don't you go anywhere near my lady parts with anything frozen. A hot shower's all I need."

He sprang from the bed and went to her, holding her lightly by the hips. "I'll rub your back then. I need to do something. I was just so excited to... Listen to me, babbling like a kid."

She kissed him. "I like you. I like you a lot, Paul Conrac. Especially when you're all contrite and cute."

He looked up at her with his hair flopped over his eyes.

"You mean it?"

"Yes. And yes, you can scrub my back, but I'm warning you, no frozen peas near delicate tissues, or I'll give you your frozen peas right back."

He kissed her lightly. "Deal. Now, where are my pants, and where is my phone?"

As if to help, it beeped out in the hall. He dashed for it, returning a moment later. "It was Berry. She and Moe want to have everyone over for dinner. Says it's going to be the last warm fall evening, and they want to enjoy it." He looked up at her. "Personally, I think they just want that baby to cry outside, so he doesn't loosen the rafters in the house." He looked up at her. "I'm not saying yes or no. It's up to you."

A frisson of uncertainty crossed her mind. "I'm included?"

"Of course, you're included," he said, not looking up from his phone. "We're a couple. Any invitation automatically includes you." He looked up. "I thought you knew."

She shrugged. "I didn't want to assume."

He tossed the phone on the bed and looped his arms around her shoulders. "You and me. Together. A unit. Package deal. Assume anything and everything." His arms tightened. "If you don't want to go, that's okay." He nodded toward the bed. "Like I said, a day in bed with you would be my dream come true."

Rhea's arms came around his neck. She pressed her forehead lightly against his. "I like your family, and I want to go." She reached over to glance at his phone. "She doesn't want us until four." She then grinned at him and glanced at the bed before gazing into his eyes once more. "That gives us a few hours."

Paul dropped his hands and cupped her bottom. "Now,

I'm the one who thinks he's dreaming."

Chapter Twenty-Two

Paul

He strutted into his brother's yard like a rooster. He knew he looked like a proud jerk, but he couldn't help himself. He'd woken that morning with Rhea after making love to her half the night and then again as the sun crested the rooftops. And then she'd, well, she'd made the shower an experience he wouldn't soon forget. Then back into bed for a cuddle and a nap.

He'd awoken an hour later to smell banana bread baking in the kitchen and Rhea wearing his tee-shirt and nothing else. A man could get spoiled awfully quickly by a woman like her. Hell, he already was.

And now, here he was positively swaggering with his arm around her shoulders and hers around his waist. Just like they belonged together. Which they did—he'd always known that but had sometimes forgotten. He wouldn't again.

"It's about time you two showed up," Joey yelled as he burped his son in the gazebo, wife Jenny beside him grinning. "I'm hungry, and Moe wouldn't start until you got here."

Paul gave him a wave with one finger showing a little more prominently than the others.

"Good thing Berry let us have cheese and crackers," Pete griped as he made like an airplane with his daughter chortling high above. Annie, looking worried, trailed behind them with a burp cloth. As if that would do anything other than clean Pete's face when the baby lost her lunch.

Berry said nothing but kissed his cheek and then Rhea's as she took the foil-wrapped banana bread and set it on the table. "Don't listen to those big babies," she said with a smile. She handed her son off to Rhea. "Think you can soothe him like you did the last time?"

Paul unwrapped their arms as Rhea took the squalling infant. The baby looked up at their faces and grinned as he continued to fuss. A moment later, he found his fist and was contentedly sucking on his fingers.

Berry sighed. "You've got the touch. I can't believe that I, his own mother, can't soothe him."

Rhea laughed as she touched noses with the baby. "It's probably just a change of scenery," she said lightly. "Paul would have had the same effect."

He held his up his and backed away. "Not me. That guy squirted last time I changed him. I'm not going near him again."

His uncle's funny face made the baby chuckle and switch from fist to capturing his toes and tried to stuff them in his mouth. His belly was almost too round to manage, but he caught them and began to munch away.

Berry frowned. "You don't mind holding him, do you, Rhea? I know you just got here. Would you like to sit? I can get you some beer, or wine, or water. We've got iced tea…"

"I'd love a glass of wine," Rhea said. "And I'd better sit while I drink it."

"I'll be right back." Berry hurried away.

"If it's not too much trouble, I'd like a beer," Paul called after his sister-in-law. She gave him a backward wave, so Paul turned to the rest of the family. "Let's go say hello to everyone."

He gathered her close. He missed having her arms around him, but hers were holding the baby. For a moment, he flashed on something—perhaps the opposite of a memory—a dream, or a wish, with him holding Rhea and she holding their child. *Their alleged child.* He grinned to himself. Rhea looked at him and quirked up a questioning eyebrow.

"What?" she asked.

But he shook his head and kissed her lightly. "Nothing, just a funny thought I had."

She peered at him.

He kissed her again. "Nothing I want my bozo brothers to hear. I'll tell you later, okay?"

She gave him a sideways look, and he knew she'd remember to ask.

Rhea

An hour later, they were gathered around the large picnic table. The babies were napping side by side in strollers where their mothers could see them. Rosemary was snoozing in a chaise longue beside them. Rhea sat beside Paul, near the sisters-in-law as the brothers sat at the far end, talking business. Every so often, Paul would reach for her hand and give it a squeeze before returning his attention to the conversation. Mattie was occupying herself with her meal in between.

Rhea was next to Annie and across from Jenny. Berry was kitty-corner from her on the end of the table. She watched the three other women look at each other before they looked at her. She straightened her back, awaiting the interrogation, but their friendly, open smiles disarmed her. Berry topped off their wine glasses before she looked straight at Rhea. "So?" she asked her brows almost to her hairline.

Annie gave her a friendly elbow in the ribs, and all four women leaned in closer. "We're all dying to know how things are going between the two of you."

"You don't have to tell us the juicy parts," Jenny added.

"Unless you want to."

Rhea felt her cheeks heat.

Berry reached over and patted her hand. "I'm a romance writer. That means we're used to taking a bit more graphically than some women might." She glanced a warning to her two sisters-in-law. "We don't actually tell each other *everything*," she added. "Just enough that we can guess if we wanted to."

Annie nodded at the men on the other end of the table. "We know they talk—some," she added with a grin.

Rhea laughed. "Really? Just like that?"

Annie put her arm around Rhea's waist. "You're one of us now. Paul made that clear. And it's not like you don't fit in. I mean, look how all our babies have taken to you." She glanced at her mother-in-law, snoring gently a few yards away. "Trust me, if Rosemary didn't approve, you'd know it."

"I know what it was like with Joey's old girlfriend," Jenny said.

"Rosemary made her life hell," Berry confided. "It was before Annie came to us, so she didn't know that witch. None of us liked her, but Rosemary didn't feel the urge to be subtle."

Rhea gulped back unexpected tears. "You're not just saying that because I'm a… a…"

"Lawyer?" Jenny asked with a grin. "No, we won't hold that against you." There was a long pause before they all laughed.

"So, you and Paul…" Berry said. "Things are going well?"

Rhea nodded. "I'll spare you the details until I get to know you better…"

"Darn," the three women said collectively under their breath.

"But we're getting along."

"I'll say," Jenny quipped. "I've never seen him pay so much attention to a woman before. Not that he brought many around. He always kept his love life to himself." She looked at the other two. "That's kind of how we knew you were different."

Jenny nodded. "He didn't bring women to the diner. I mean, that was neutral ground."

Rhea felt her smile fade. "He was a bit of a player..."

Annie's hug tightened. "Not as much as some believe. He spent many weekend nights with us for dinner, not out drinking with friends or picking up women."

Berry nodded. "I'm not going to tell you he was a choir boy, but Moe says the same thing. He said he was stuck on you—for years."

"He was?"

Berry nodded, and Jenny joined in. "And Joey says the fact that the two of you are together now is the best thing that's ever happened to Paul."

Rhea's hands flew to her face. "I didn't...I mean I couldn't..." She turned to look at Paul sitting beside her, engrossed in something Sammy was saying at the far end of the table. She turned back to her friends. "Really?"

Both Berry and Jenny reached out and squeezed her hands. "Yes," Jenny said. "So, even if we didn't already like you for yourself, we'd do so for him." Her face sobered. "The past year's been hell. The accident, not being able to work. He lost everything."

"I know," Rhea said softly. "And it kills me to think I was working for the other side who was trying to keep him from getting what was owed him."

"We get that you were just doing your job," Annie said quickly. "No one holds it against you. Thank goodness it's over."

Rhea leaned in closer. "Except I have a new co-worker who can't let it go," she said softly. "We got a fair settlement for Paul. Not the highest in history, but our client is getting the help he needs, and Paul got the money owed him. But my partner can't stop talking about it. I swear he mentions it every day as if it was the biggest blunder ever made."

Jenny sat back, clearly affronted. "Well, you'll just have to shut him up." She got a sly look in her eye. "What's his name? If he comes looking for me to cater a party, I'll make sure I'm too busy to take him on."

Rhea told her, and Jenny scoffed. "Him? Hell, I catered his engagement party. It was the nicest job I think I've ever done, save my wedding and Annie's—and yours too, Berry. He hated everything. Especially having to pay me. The bastard still owes me a thousand dollars. It would cost me more to try to collect from him…"

"I'll take care of it," Rhea told her. "Send me the contract information, what you billed him for, what he owes, and any correspondence."

"You don't have to…"

Rhea pressed her lips together. "Oh, yes, I do. That man's a pain in my side, and he's determined to bring the reputation of the firm down. I won't have it. I'll bring it to the partner's attention."

"Damn." Jenny whistled. "If you marry Paul, you're going to be my favorite sister-in-law." She winked at the other two. "Well, another favorite."

Moments later, Paul's arm came around her, and he kissed his cheek, daring the sisters-in-law to say a word. "What's all this laughing?"

Annie gave the others a wink. "Oh, just girl talk."

Paul lowered his brows and glanced over his shoulder before glowering at them. "You women aren't comparing notes are you?"

Rhea kissed him back. "I guess you'll just have to trust us on this one."

He came closer. "You'll tell me later, right?" he whispered in her ear.

She gave him a wink. "We'll see."

Berry

I've been keeping quiet for pages now, but it's time I butted in for a bit.

I declared the picnic a success. Rosemary was the first to leave. She woke from her nap about the same time as the babies and declared she was going home to sleep after all the excitement. Sammy had something to do and left soon after. Jenny, Annie, and I all nursed our babies as our husbands sat beside us. Paul and Rhea were cuddling in the gazebo under a blanket—he said he didn't want to catch sight of anything he shouldn't see, but the rest of us knew he'd been apart from Rhea for too long. The two of them were billing and cooing, and we pretty much left them alone, other than sharing some smiles between us. Pete and Annie walked home with their baby while Jenny and Joey, who lived further away, packed up and drove off, leaving Moe and me and our little family, and the lovebirds.

Mattie had fallen asleep in her father's arms, so he brought her inside to tuck her in, with Paul tagging along behind, so he and Moe could get on the computer and look at the new equipment they wanted to buy. My son was a peaceful bundle in my arms. I was enjoying this quiet time with him too much to bring him up to his crib, so we moved to the front porch that was out of the breeze that had picked up.

Rhea watched the street lights come on, a peaceful look on her face. I remembered feeling that way when Moe and I first met, and everything was new and shiny—though in our case, there were a few bumps to overcome. Rhea looked like that. Happy. Well-loved and at peace. The golden light burnished her curls as she sipped from her wineglass. I'd noticed she'd barely touched it. This was a woman who didn't like to lose control. I admired that and wondered, too.

"Do you mind if I ask you something?"

She set down her glass, and I saw her tighten her hands in her lap. "You can ask," she replied. "I can't promise I'll answer."

"Spoken like a lawyer," I said with a laugh. "No offense intended."

She grinned. "It's a reflexive response. None taken."

"I don't know how much Paul's told you about us…"

She glanced at me, obviously curious. "He talks about all of you a lot. You meant a great deal to him while he was recovering, but I think it was from before. He never expressed surprise at how everyone rallied around him."

"The brothers are all very close. It took me a while to get used to the fact that when I had Moe in my life, the rest of the Conrads came as a package deal."

Rhea smiled and lifted her wineglass to me. "And the number has only grown."

"Exactly. I wouldn't trade Jen and Annie for the word. They're especially dear to me because…" And there I stopped. I suddenly had doubts about what I wanted to tell her. I didn't want Paul to get mad at me for revealing family secrets. "Well, let's just say I meddled in their romances— all very well intended," I assured her. "Paul made me promise I wouldn't do the same for him."

Rhea was looking at me, and I wasn't sure if she was insulted or amused, or perhaps uncertain. I couldn't quite interpret what had her fisting her hands in her lap. "Are you about to?"

I laughed. I just couldn't help it. The baby awoke and grumbled a bit. I held my breath, and he settled down again. "This is me doing my best to not butt in by assuring myself that I don't need to."

Rhea let out a small, and I think surprised, laugh. "You're funny."

I blew out a relieved breath. "I'm glad you're taking this in the spirit in which it was intended." I took a swallow of wine to fortify myself. "Pete and Annie, Jenny and Joey—even Rosemary expect me to meddle. It's not something I do intentionally. It just sort of, well, it happens. I don't think I even do as much as they all think I do, except that I, well, I introduced Annie and Pete. So, they really should be kind of grateful for that."

"They seem like they're made for one another," Rhea said. And she was closer to the truth than I dared say.

"They kind of are," I said under my breath. "They're very happy. As are Joey and Jen. What we were talking about before, Joey had this horrible girlfriend, and he was under the impression that he couldn't break up with her. It wasn't the gentlemanly thing to do, so he put up with her. It was a horrible few years. I was so glad when..." And again I stopped myself lest I say more than I should. "I was so glad when he and Jen finally got together. We all were."

"He's devoted to her," Rhea commented.

I nodded. "That's how the brothers are. We assume Sammy will be next and the same way. One woman men, through and through. We never, ever worry about them straying."

"It sounds like it might be kind of confining," Rhea mentioned.

I laughed a little. "Well, they do cling a bit at first. Moe's relaxed since the babies came along. The Conrad men don't leave any doubt about their love and devotion. And not in a jealous way. At least not much. They were brought up to respect women. It's been refreshing, knowing Moe after some other men I dated."

Rhea tapped her wineglass against her bottom lip. "Are you warning me?"

"I guess I am—that you should expect Paul's single-minded devotion. I'm not trying to suggest you'd ever cheat on him— this is so awkward. I just want you to understand him. To know what the Conrad brothers code is. And to let you know you can trust Paul—trust him with anything."

"I wouldn't," she said quickly. "I mean, I would never cheat on him. I can't imagine ever wanting to."

Forgive me for saying this, but until that moment, I didn't know someone with dark skin could blush. But blush she did, and it was so charming, so delightful, and I just loved her all the more for loving Paul.

I wanted to give her a hug for understanding. And also because she seemed to need a lot of hugs, but I refrained. "I don't want to see his heart broken. He's been through so much. When that drunk driver hit him, and we thought we were going to lose him—" I choked up. "As strong as he is, as much as he jokes around to hide his sensitive side, he sometimes seems so fragile. And I know how stuff can happen. When we least expect or want it to. It's not like he's used up his share. None of us ever do."

She looked at me, and I could see tears in her eyes. "Berry, I think I love that man. I haven't told him yet. I would never deliberately hurt him." She bit her lip again. "I worry like hell I will without meaning to.

I pressed my free hand to hers. "Everyone of us feels that way about the love of our lives. Rhea, you have a good heart. He couldn't love you as much as he does if you didn't."

Her hands fisted again. The light was funny, what with

223

the sun having just about gone down, but a ray of light must have hit her, for it seemed as though her hands were glowing from within, which, of course, was ridiculous.

Chapter Twenty-Three

Rhea

She was researching precedent for a client requesting a prenup. Her coffee had grown cold at her elbow as she worked, head in hand, staring at case law on her monitor.

"Darling?"

Rhea froze at the sound of her mother's voice. She sat up stiffly, other than her fingers, which curled into her palms. With a small sharp inhale, she forced a smile on her face and looked up. "Mom?"

Marion sauntered into the room.

She is sleeping with him. Celibate women don't move like that. I finally understand.

Her mother sat with an elegant flourish despite her pencil skirt. "I just had a very interesting conversation with Tony and AJ."

Rhea pushed the keyboard away and focused on her mother. "Did you?"

"AJ—it's so much more dignified to call him that than Junior, don't you think? Well, AJ says you were out to dinner with one of our enemies."

Rhea felt her eyebrows rise to meet her hairline. "I didn't know we had enemies."

Her mother scowled. "You know what I mean. Someone we fought against."

Rhea sat back in her chair. "Ah. Well, then Junior is correct. I had the pleasure of dining with Paul Conrad. Several times." She met her mother's gaze squarely. "Including breakfast."

Her mother didn't do as much as blink. "Don't you think that's unseemly, dear?"

"Because he was represented by another firm?"

"No, of course not. Tony and I have been on opposite sides of the courtroom many times. I was referring to his lack of standing in the community."

Rhea pretended to ponder this. "From what I can tell, the Conrads are fine people. Maurice Conrad has a thriving construction company. Paul was working for him up until the accident. He's started his own woodw..."

"Dear, that's not what I mean. I didn't think I had to spell it out for you. The Conrads are not in a position to bring any appreciable business our way."

Rhea sat back and picked up a pen, tapping it on her palm. "Did you know that Moe's firm had revenues of almost five million last year? And that was just the first of a multi-year contract?"

"No, but I..."

"His wife is a writer. She has a three-book contract with an established, well-known publisher. They're talking a big promotional tour next year when her kids are old enough to travel with her. Television—radio. There's even talk of a movie deal. She's pulled in six figures for the past few years and has a lot of writer friends in need of contract advice."

"But sweetheart..."

"Joey's doing well too. He just won another architectural contest. I can't remember the details at the moment, but I know there was a big award."

"Rhea..."

"And his wife, Annie—she made a huge breakthrough in security software earlier this year. She's under contract as a consultant, despite having an infant at home. Very lucrative..." Rhea tapped a gold pen against her lips. "Oh, and Peter's landscaping firm just broke a million last year, his second year of operation." She looked at her mother and smiled as benignly as she could.

"But, dear…"

"And Sweet Shop Catering—now there's an up and coming outfit—well known throughout the state. Jenny's got big plans. She's talking about opening a franchise or two. Do you know who her father is?"

Marion seemed to wilt. "No, I don't."

"Robert Hamilton." She looked at her mother, who closed her eyes.

"Good heavens," Marion whispered.

"Moe's asked if I'd represent him. Berry wants me to look over the contract extension her agent just sent her."

"But Paul, dear. His prospects…"

"Are far more modest," Rhea filled in. "But he has a tremendous heart. He's a good man. Give him time. Before you know it, his woodworking shop will be successful. Not everyone needs to make a lot of money to prove themselves. Some have other goals."

"Regardless of how much money he wants, he needed capital to get started. That's what I want to ask about, dear. Did you collude with him to ensure he had the funding?"

Rhea stood so fast, her chair hit the credenza behind her. "Who, might I ask, wants to know?"

"Jun—I mean, AJ suggested…" Marion glanced at her daughter, and her voice faded.

"Junior is poking his nose where it doesn't belong. He seems to make a practice of it." Rhea looked down and flipped open a file. "He's looking for trouble. Everywhere he goes, he sows chaos in his wake."

"I don't understand."

"Not only did he butt into Paul's case unnecessarily, he made a mess of the divorce I had to help with. Two attorneys in their firm asked for my help with other cases he's screwed up. On the side. They don't want to antagonize him due to his temper." Rhea's hand landed on the manila files on her desk. "And Sunday, I learned he has yet to pay for the catering for his engagement party. He's withheld the last check for over a year." She lifted the file. "He claims the caterer did not fulfill her end of the contract." Rhea set the folder down and rifled through it until she found a faxed newspaper photo. "Except there is pictorial evidence of every dish served." She looked again and held up another faxed clipping. "Given the bride-to-be's social standing, the local press covered the party and described the food, the service, and the atmosphere, all in glowing terms. And they quoted him saying it was the premier event at the country club that spring."

"I didn't know…"

"That man is a loose cannon. I'll be the first to admit I don't like him. I find him obnoxious and slimy. But his business practices are even worse. He's going to drag our name through the mud if he keeps behaving like he's the potentate of some rinky-dink fiefdom. Jenny Conrad told me…"

"Who is…? Marion asked.

"I just told you. Sweet Shop Catering and the daughter of Robert Hamilton, the builder. She's asked me to look into this so she can get paid."

Marion closed her eyes. "I'll talk to Tony."

Rhea sat. "Please do so. Or I will if you can't."

Her mother's eyes flashed open. "I'll do it. Give me that file."

Rhea shook her head. "This isn't official client business. But if I can solve this for her, I know it will bring in more business."

Marion stood and began to pace near the shelves in the office. Her finger ran over the spines as if looking for dust. She then picked up the arched candlestick Paul made. "I'm still worried about you. Seeing a man, a laborer." She looked up. "What is this? It's lovely."

Rhea sat and rubbed her eyes. "Paul is an artisan. A very talented one. He made what you're holding."

"Oh?" It dropped from Marion's fingers. The u-shaped candle fell from its cradle and cracked.

Rhea sprang from her desk. "Mom!" she cried as she squatted to pick up the pieces. "That was a gift. He made it—the candle…"

"Oh, darling. I am so sorry. Perhaps he can fix it, seeing as he works with his hands."

Rhea narrowed her eyes. "I never realized what a snob you were."

"Rhea, how could you say such a thing? It was an accident."

With the candleholder and broken candle clutched to her chest, Rhea faced her mother. "You've never been clumsy. You're doing this to hurt me because I won't agree to everything you want."

"That's a terrible thing to say to your mother," Marion retorted.

"It's a terrible thing to hate your own daughter," Rhea shot back. "I've done everything I can to make you happy, and none of it was ever good enough. So you know what? I'm not going to try anymore. Why beat myself up to win your approval when I could make myself happy instead? And if that means finding a man to love, who loves me back, so be it. Your approval would have been nice, but I don't need it, not anymore."

Her chest was heaving. "You want to fire me, go ahead. I get job offers every week, and I've turned them all down out of a misplaced sense of loyalty. But there's none coming back at me, so you know what? I think I'll start taking them seriously. If you want to fire me first, go for it.

I'll get a box right now, pack my things, and be gone. I'll sell my house if I have to in order to pay my college loans. I just don't care anymore."

She went back to her desk and carefully set the broken pieces there before staring down her mother. "Now, if you don't mind, I'd like you to leave. You've done enough damage to my property and my composure. I have a case I need to prepare." She blinked back the tears. "Don't let the door hit you on the way out."

Marion stalked to the doorway. She turned as she exited, but Rhea wasn't through. "And tell your lover to get his son to pay his bills. Think of the publicity that would bring if I need to bring suit against my very own partner."

"You wouldn't dare."

Rhea sat up straighter and lifted the file. "Do you want to try me?"

Marion whirled without another sound.

Rhea walked across her office to close the door. She went back to her desk and sat heavily, head propped on her hands as tears began to fall. "Oh shit, shit, shit."

She picked up her cell and glanced at it, holding it to her chest for a moment before she began to dial.

Just before she hit the last number, a new email popped into her queue. It was a dinner invitation to her and Paul, from her mother.

She set down her phone and opened the email. It was to be a formal affair next Saturday night. She picked up her phone and finished dialing. After a few rings, it went to voice mail.

"Paul, hi. It's me. Can you call me? My mother just invited us to dinner at Chez Jozef. I wanted to check with you before I reply." She hesitated. It had been a long time since she'd ever exposed her weakness to anyone or asked for help. She took a deep breath. "And I really just need to talk to you too. Bye." She clicked the off button and held the phone a moment longer, then wiped her tears and set her mind back to her job.

Paul

"Aren't burgers and fries the best things ever?" Paul asked before he bit into an overloaded culinary dream. Two perfectly grilled patties, crisp lettuce, juicy tomato, a slab of purple onion, tomato, ketchup, mayo, grainy bourbon mustard and pickles, cheese, and bacon, with some hot sauce dolloped on top. His fingers were dripping, and he didn't care.

Across from him, Rhea peered at her veggie burger as it sat on a pale wedge of iceberg lettuce, then back at his. He imagined her mouth watering for what he so inelegantly indulged in.

"You won't always be able to eat like that," she said as she picked up her fork and tapped her patty.

He set his burger back on his plate and picked up a crispy fry. He held it out to her. "Which is exactly why I indulge my craving now," he replied. "Here. Eat this. It'll make you feel better."

Rhea wrinkled her nose at him, but boy, did she look tempted. "It'll make me fat."

"One won't make you fat. Look, it's the best one on the plate. Golden brown, crispy, hot, salty..." He waved it under her nose.

"That's the problem. I can't stop at just one."

He held it to her lips, and she reluctantly opened her mouth and bit. He wasn't surprised to hear a small moan come from her. "Damn, that's good," she said and ate the rest of it.

He grinned. "For the record, you're not fat. And you can stop at one. You've got more discipline than anyone I know." He held up another, and she shook her head, taking a bite of her flaccid bean burger. He made sure he had her attention. "And I don't care about fat or thin or any of that stuff. It's you I love—the whole package."

Her eyes grew misty, and she appeared to swallow with some difficulty. "Damn, Paul. Don't make me cry in front of all these people."

"Good cry or bad cry?" he asked.

That made her smile. "Good cry. I was having a perfectly horrible morning…"

"Which is why you had the sense to call me. I told you that you were smart."

She nodded, her smile wider. "And you cheered me up and force-fed me french-fries."

"French fry. Remember, you declined the second. I'm not sure I'm gonna offer a third," he said and took a sip of his milkshake.

"Please, don't offer me a third because I don't know if I have the will power to turn it down." She looked at her plate and sighed. He pushed his toward her. "Go ahead, take a bite."

Her smile faded. "I—I couldn't," she said, but then her smile returned. "My hands aren't big enough to hold it, or my mouth wide enough to get it all in."

He reached across the table and took her knife and fork. He carved out a wedge and deftly lifted it to her plate. He placed three fries beside his offering. "There. No excuses. Enjoy yourself."

"Thanks," she said quietly.

Paul watched her eat with satisfaction. He wondered if it was the caveman in him. The shy smile she shot at him made all the tears bearable.

Their meal finished, and hand in hand, they walked to a nearby park. He took her over to the swings and gave her a push, then took the one next to her. "Tell me what's going on. I need to know if it's worth my while to get my suit out of mothballs for your mother's fancy dinner."

"I'm not sure." She came to a stop and held her hand out for his. "We were arguing this morning. Apparently, she only wants me to date men who can bring business into the firm."

Paul growled under his breath.

"I know," she said and squeeze his hand. "I told her your brothers and their wives have all approached me, and their combined incomes are significant."

His heart constricted. "Whereas mine is not," he said.

"Whereas that signifies nothing," she said. "I told her you were just starting out, that you were an artisan, and that pursuit of money isn't what drives everyone."

That managed to eke a small grin from him, and he nodded. "Okay. Then what?"

Rhea shook her head. "My mother's a snob. That's not going to change. I told her my personal life is mine, and I'll see who I want, and she doesn't get a say." She stood and began to pace. Paul had never seen her look so fierce, so magnificent. "I told her I'd quit if I had to. I won't be dictated to by her."

"So, she invited us to dinner."

"Yes." She looked up at him. "I'm afraid she did it to set you up."

"Being as I am a caveman," he said, unable to keep the bitterness from his voice.

"Paul…"

"It's okay. You're giving me a chance to say no."

Rhea shook her head and held her hands out to him. "I wanted to talk to you about it, but I want *us* to make the decision. I want her to know she can't put us at odds with one another."

He stood, and she held on to him. She was warm from the sun and smelled like heaven.

"If you want to go, we'll go. If you don't, I'll tell her no. But I expect she'll invite us again," Rhea said.

"Who else will be there?"

She sighed. "I don't know. It might be the three of us—it might be more. I don't want to ask—you know."

He nodded. "But if there are others, they'll be from the firm."

"Probably Tony, Junior, and his fiancée." She shivered. "I don't trust him. I always suspect him of trying to set me up." She looked up at him. "I know your case is settled. But I can't help wondering if some other shoe's about to drop."

Paul held her at arms length. "Then the best thing is to force him to drop it. Tell your mother yes. I might prefer burgers and fries, but I know how to use a fork and knife. Rhee, don't worry about it. I know a water glass from a wine glass."

She hugged him tighter. "That's not what worries me. It's what'll be said while you're back is turned."

"Hey, I grew up with three older brothers. Nobody's gonna say anything to me I can't handle." He kissed the top of her head. "I won't eat snails, though. You can ask me to do just about anything, but I draw the line at escargot."

He could feel her shake with laughter. "Don't worry. I don't like them either."

"You've tried it?" he asked in mock horror.

She nodded slowly. "Yeah."

Paul made a face. "I can't believe I've kissed a girl who ate a snail."

Rhea laughed.

"What's more, I believe I'm gonna kiss her again."

Chapter Twenty-Four

Rhea

Paul's introduction to Rhea's father was not quite what she had pictured. Instead of his normal jeans and tee-shirt, Paul donned a stiff, new button-down shirt and pressed chinos. He'd trimmed his hair short and groomed his beard. Her father seemed to doze through the visit. Absent were the hand squeezes of two weeks before. His eyes hadn't shone with much recognition beyond her initial kiss of his cheek.

Lack of a response hadn't deterred Paul Conrad. Rhea sat on one side of her father, holding his limp hand while Paul sat on the other, speaking slowly and steadily, telling the elder about himself and his work. Every so often, Paul would take his gaze from her father's face and look up at her to give her a wink.

"Paul," she said softly. "I need to go to the restroom."

He rose when she did but didn't relinquish her father's hand. "Go ahead, sweetheart. Your dad'll keep me company."

"Are you sure? We can leave. He's not..."

Paul leaned over the bed and gave her cheek a soft kiss. "Go on. There's plenty more we can chat about. Just don't be too long." He reseated himself when she left the room, and his gaze once again rested on her father's face. "Did I mention I knew your daughter when we were children, sir? I don't recall meeting you or your wife at the time, but Rhea and I used to play..."

She made her way into the bathroom, Paul's voice keeping a low, steady, and soothing cadence as she shut the door. It seemed for a moment that Paul spoke softer, for while she could still hear him, she could no longer make out the words. But when she rejoined them, he was still chatting on, telling her father how he and Rhea had competed on their high school debate team and that Rhea won every single practice match they'd had.

Her father's eyes were closed, his breathing soft. Rhea leaned over and kissed his cheeks. "I think we should go," she said. "He's out—there's no telling for how long." She took her father's hand and kissed it. For a moment, she thought she felt him press back, but that was impossible given his somnambulant state.

"Sir, it was a pleasure meeting you," Paul said, taking the old man's hand in both of his. "I hope we get a chance to chat again one day soon. We'll be seeing your wife at dinner tonight. I'll be sure to send your regards."

Rhea teared up. She took Paul's hand and tugged him out into the hall, closing the door behind her. "You are so sweet." She wrapped her arms around him. "How did I ever manage before you came into my life?"

Paul's arms came around her. "I can't imagine what life was like." His voice rumbled where her ear was pressed to his chest. "The good news is that you don't have to worry about spending the rest of your life without me."

Her head popped up. "What are you talking about?"

He gave her a wide grin as he wrapped his arm around her, and they began to walk to the front desk. "Your dad and I had a little talk."

She sniffed back a tear. "You were doing all of the talking."

"It did sound like that, but he was listening. I could tell."

"Paul..."

He kissed her in front of the nurses and gave them a wink as they passed. "Humor me? I know he looked out of it, but every once in a while, I felt his hand move like it was his way to tell me to keep going."

Rhea snapped her mouth shut. "Then what?" she asked as they strode out into the sunshine.

"Well, when you took your little potty break..."

She held her breath.

"I asked him for permission to marry you."

She stopped, right in front of the front fountain. "You what?"

Paul turned and shrugged. "Hey, I'm not getting any younger, and neither are you. You're dad—I'm not so sure. He might live to be a hundred and twenty without saying another word. It just seemed as good a time as any. I mean, I'm a good guy. You said so yourself. I'm not exactly able to support you in the manner to which you're accustomed, but you don't need me for that when you can make more money than I ever will. I made a point of telling him it's you I love, not your wealth—I'll sign a prenup or whatever it is you or your family wants me to.

"What I can do is love you for the rest of our lives. Give you children we'll both adore. Make a home with you wherever you want to live. Support you emotionally and physically..."

Her hands were on her hips as joy, anger, and confusion warred within. "But you didn't ask me."

"Of course not," he exclaimed. "We're not ready for that—yet. I just wanted to make sure I had his blessing for when we're ready."

"Wha..."

Paul walked back to her. "I love you. You know that. And I have the feeling you love me too, even if you're not ready to admit it."

"Paul..."

"You lawyers sure like to have your say." He kissed her. "I'm not done talking."

She closed her mouth again and looked up at him, expectantly she hoped.

He nodded. "Rhea, I've told you time and again, you're the woman I want to spend the rest of my life with. But we're still new, and you're not sure about me. I get that. I'm being patient."

"Hardly if you asked my fath…"

He gave her a look, and she snapped her mouth shut for the third time.

"I asked your father because frankly, we both know he's not well, and I don't know if the next time he'll be any more sentient than he was today. Or the next time, or the time after that. We don't know if he heard me but damn it—I wanted to try. It was the right thing to do. When you and I agree it's time to get married, we'll talk to your mother about it. Probably a very different conversation. I don't expect it'll be quite as one-sided."

Paul rubbed his mouth as if to hide a smile, and Rhea couldn't help but smile back. "So, you and he didn't set a date or anything?" she asked.

"We left it open-ended," he replied. "More like pre-engaged."

"Pre-engaged," she repeated.

"Let's just say we have an understanding. Goes a little beyond being exclusive. Guaranteed date every Friday, Saturday, and Sunday night, whether you want it or not. Flowers on Valentine's day. My friends are your friends, your friends, with the exclusion of that jackass you work with, are my friends. My mom gets to call you her future daughter-in-law. You get to kiss me whenever you want and brag about me to your girlfriends. That sort of thing."

"But no ring on my finger," she stated.

Paul took her hands in his. "Sweetheart, if you want a ring, all you have to do is say so. I know a jeweler I can put on retainer…"

She was past being able to hide her smile. "I wouldn't go that far."

He nodded. "You're right. That's rushing things. I'll give him a down payment a week from now and ask him to start looking for a really good stone. That ought to give us enough time to work things out, don't you think?"

"Oh, yeah, sure," she said with a laugh. "Making a decision that will change the rest of my life in four weeks," she snapped her fingers. "Piece of cake."

His fingers squeezed hers. "I knew you'd see it my way."

He dropped one hand, and they resumed their walk to her car. They'd gotten in and buckled themselves when Rhea turned to him. "So, what'd he say?"

Paul turned to her, his gaze steady. "Your father is a man of few words."

"He wasn't always," she replied.

He nodded. "I figure you take after him that way. But I can tell you unequivocally that he approves."

She started the car and looked before backing out of her space. "He told you this?"

"Not in so many words," Paul replied. "Let's just say— when you left the room, his eyes opened, and he looked at me."

Her skin began to tingle. "Paul…"

"There you go interrupting again."

She put the car in drive, gripping the wheel so hard her fingers paled. "Sorry. You were saying…"

"When you left the room, he opened his eyes. I know he saw me. He'd been listening to every word. And when I told him I loved you and wanted to marry you one day, he squeezed my fingers. It wasn't much, but it was there, Rhee. He approves."

She pulled into an empty spot and threw the car into park. Her hands trembled as she covered her face. "No."

Paul leaned over, and, despite it being his bad shoulder, gathered her close. "Yes, Rhea. I swear it." He looked at her and then at her hand before he pressed his palm to her forehead. "Are you okay? Your hands are burning up."

She tugged them from him and tucked them under her arms. "No, I'm fine. Just a little shook up."

He didn't release her. "As long as you're okay."

She wiped away a tear. "Do me a favor, Paul?"

He kissed her cheek. "Anything for you, sweetheart."

"Don't ambush me by being so wonderful again, okay? I don't know if I can take it."

He laughed. "No can do. You deserve every brilliant thing I can think of, and probably more that I can't. But I'm telling you, you're stuck with me. There's no turning back. I can't exactly go back in there and un-ask him for your hand. It's just not done."

She snorted her laughter. "Then give me some warning, okay? I can't afford to have anyone see me made a mess like this. It'll ruin my reputation for being a terror in the courthouse when filing wills."

He laughed. "I promise I'll only ambush you with love in the appropriate setting. Such as dinner tonight with your mother."

Rhea groaned and pressed her forehead to the wheel. "Oh, hell. I'd almost forgotten."

Paul rubbed her neck. "Not me. Considering how well things went this afternoon, I don't think we've got a thing to worry about."

Rhea backed out of the lot. "Okay, one more favor, Paul."

"Ummm?"

"Maybe hold off on that conversation with my mother for another time?"

"Hell yeah, babe. I might be impulsive, but I'm not suicidal."

Paul

He took one look at Rhea as she stood at the foot of the stairs and tugged the keys from her fingers. "You look gorgeous, sweetheart. And you've got the nicer car, but there's no way I'm letting you drive. I want you to have as much to drink as you want."

She hung her head and groaned. "The last thing I want is to get drunk in front of her… and whomever else will be there."

He kissed her temple. "It might help to loosen up a little. I can't bear to see you so stressed. I won't let you get plastered, just relaxed."

"I'll let you drive… but…"

"No buts, babe. Just trust me, okay?"

She looked up at him with her big brown eyes, and he knew in that moment, he would do anything for her.

Rhea took a deep breath and nodded. "Okay. Tonight you can be the strong one. I put this evening in your hands."

He chuckled. "No pressure or anything."

That made her laugh. "We'd better get going. The only one allowed to be late is my mother."

When they arrived, Paul glanced around the restaurant's plush interior. Heavy velvet curtains were caught in satin ropes separating the front desk from the restaurant. It was so dark, it was hard to tell what color everything was, but Paul had the impression it was done mostly in deep reds. He gave their names and that of Rhea's mother to the maitre'd. "Your room is not yet ready. If you don't mind waiting in the bar…"

Room. Not a table. Rhea was right—this was an ambush waiting to happen. The poor thing grabbed his hand and tugged him over without another word.

"Have Mrs. Hansen find us in the bar when she arrives," he told the man as he slipped him a $20.

"Very good, sir."

"Paul..." Rhea warned.

"Relax, sweetheart." They went into the crowded bar. The lighting and color scheme was the same, but it was all sharp angles and stainless steel. "She can't complain. We were on time—the room wasn't ready. Nothing wrong with the hostess coming to check on her invited guests. It's what anyone would do."

"My mother isn't anyone," she hissed under her breath.

"It's never too late to learn," he replied with a smile. "So, do you want prosecco tonight, or something stronger? I'm thinking a twelve-year-old single malt scotch myself." He seated her at the one open stool and hovered beside her.

"Scotch sounds good," she said. "But only one. Mom will have wine pairings with each course at dinner."

"I'll drink wine. Or pretend to. I'm driving, remember?"

She closed her eyes with a panicked look, and Paul fell in love with her all over again. "Don't you worry. I've got this."

She gazed up at him. "I just want it to be over."

He waggled his eyebrows. "Me too. New sheets on the bed tonight."

She giggled for the first time in his memory. "I wasn't thinking of that."

"I was," he replied and was delighted to see a blush creep up her cheeks.

The bartender delivered their drinks. A stool opened up next to Rhea, and he sat, claiming her hand. He kissed it and rested it on his thigh as he regaled her with tales of Moe and Berry's courtship, leaving out some critical b ts that were too uncomfortable to mention. She was soon laughing, and he moved on to telling tales about Jenny and Joey. He was about to begin with Paul and Annie's story when he was interrupted by someone clearing their throat.

He stood when he saw Marion and gave her his sunniest smile. She looked like an older version of Rhea, but her hair was neatly tamed in some short style, and her hands glittered with diamonds. And there wasn't a smile to be seen. "Ah, our hostess, I presume." He held out his hand. "Paul Conrad. So happy to finally meet you. Rhea's told me so much about you."

Marion did not take it, so he put it in his pocket, never losing his smile. "Thank you so much for inviting us. I've been looking forward to this."

Marion nodded her head. "Mr. Conrad."

"That's my older brother, Mo—Maurice," he said with a short laugh. "I'm just Paul."

"It would appear neither Charles nor any of the other staff remembered what you looked like. I had to fetch you myself."

"Well, we're glad you did."

Paul turned to help Rhea off her stool. Paul expected the two would embrace, or at least exchange air kisses, but there was nothing. He tucked his hand on Rhea's back and offered his elbow to her mother. "Ladies, shall we?"

Rhea's mother hesitated before she wrapped her cool hand around his proffered arm and began to walk. There was no mistaking who was leading the way.

Chapter Twenty-Five

Rhea

"Well, isn't this a surprise." Junior and his smirk stood behind the bar set up in the corner. "Too bad you bought your own booze, Rhee. Could have put it on the corporate expense account." He showed his teeth. "Of course, this way, no one knows how much you've really had."

She froze in the doorway, her hand still wrapped in Paul's as her mother moved into the room. "My parents named me Rhea. R-H-E-A," she said and gave the man a smile with more teeth than she normally displayed. "That's what I prefer to be called unless it's Ms. Hansen-Chalmbers, or Counselor, as they call me in court." She slid her hand up to Paul's elbow and nudged him into the room. From the corner of her eye, she noted him watching her, his smile firmly in place.

"Oh, come on," Junior laughed as he came around the bar. "I've heard your friends call you Rhee."

She released Paul's arm and strode up to where Junior stood, nearly his height in her heels. "Yes. You have," she agreed. "And since you're pouring, I'm done with my drink and would like a Glenlivet XXV single malt. Neat." She turned to Paul. "Would you like one too, sweetheart?"

The room went quiet.

He came up to her and put an arm around her shoulders as he beamed at the shorter man. "I would, thanks, darlin'."

"They didn't bring any on the cart…" Junior sputtered.

"Oh, I suppose you'll have to go ask at the bar." She turned and smiled at the other guests. "Paul, I don't think you've met anyone else other than Christine. Let me make the introductions…"

And so the evening went. Rhea did her best to remain sociable, smiling, and chatting with everyone though she managed to spill her drink on the jackass as he handed it to her and requested he get another. She thought Paul was going to choke on suppressed laughter.

In the background, her mother was displaying her hostess smile as she chatted with the various partners she'd invited to her dinner and the two judges in attendance with their husbands, but her eyes were restless.

Through it all, Paul shone. He went from polite to jovial to charming and always attentive. Judge Patel took her aside before dessert was served. "Where ever did you find him, Rhea?"

"We knew each other when we were little and met up again a few months ago."

"He's a keeper," the judge said with a wink. "If you happen to need someone to perform a wedding ceremony, keep me in mind."

Rhea felt her cheeks flood with color. "It's a little too soon…"

"Psh," the woman laughed. "I can tell when a couple is meant to be together, and that's what I'm seeing. Does your mother like him? Of course, she must. What beautiful grandchildren he'll give her."

"We've only been seeing each other a few months," Rhea sputtered.

"Nonsense," the judge replied as she stepped closer. "Tell me, does he have any brothers? I've got a niece—a lovely girl—and she's had such bad luck with men."

It was Rhea's turn to laugh. "He's the fourth of five. All but Paul and his younger brother are married. From what I can tell, Sammy's determined to remain a bachelor."

The judge gave her arm a small squeeze. "I'll bet that's what your Paul was saying the day before he met you. But look how he looks at you—like he can't bear to be away from you." Another fond squeeze. "Remember—I'll marry you in my chambers or anywhere you'd like. It would be my honor. Now, let me go talk to your mother. She's worried we're colluding. We can't have that." She gave Rhea another hug and wandered off. It didn't take long before Paul was once again at her side.

"What was that all about? Isn't she one of the judges?"

Rhea kissed his cheek. "Yes. A lovely woman. I can't believe I was scared of her the first time I argued in her court."

"She didn't seem too fearsome to me."

Rhea tugged his arm closer to her breast. "She told me she'd be happy to marry us whenever we're ready."

Paul threw back his head and laughed. "Are we that obvious?" he asked as he stole a kiss.

She pouted but couldn't sustain it. "I thought I was a bit more opaque."

"Nope. Darlin', you don't need to say a word. What you feel for me is reflected in your eyes."

Rhea clenched her hands together. "Damn. Not a good trait for a lawyer."

"But an excellent one for a lover," he said and took another kiss as the dessert tray was wheeled in. "But you'd better watch out for your new partner over there. He may be smiling, but I don't think he's the type to forget."

Rhea pulled Paul further into the room. "Don't worry. I'll keep an eye on him. I don't trust him, not one little bit."

Paul

"Ms. Hansen-Chalmbers, thank you so much for the invitation," Paul told Marion as they were leaving. "I'm sorry we didn't have a chance to talk more. Neither Rhea nor I had any idea there'd be so many people here tonight."

Her smile was brittle. "Didn't Rhea tell you? I do love entertaining on a grand scale. But since my husband's been ill, it's hard to do so at home. And despite my building being secure, the neighborhood is so bad."

Paul felt his smile freeze on his face. "Hmm. My mother still lives about three blocks from there. She's never had any trouble."

"Oh, well, those of us in my building need to perhaps be a little more careful than others," she replied.

"I'll mention that to Mom. And my brother. He was just awarded a new contract to rehab a couple of historic homes not too far from there. They were broken into apartments, but he's going to restore them to single-family homes. I'm going to talk to him about repairing some of the fancy interior woodwork."

Marion looked startled. "Your brother got that contract?"

"Maurice Conrad. Conrad Brothers Restoration and Construction. He specializes in restoration work, though he's been spending most of his time for the past two years on the Hamilton inner-city project. I was working on it when I was in the accident. He's already asked me to fabricate the original moldings and other fancy work."

"Oh. I had no idea you were so well connected."

Rhea came up and slipped her arm through his. "I told you, Mom, Paul's brother Joseph is married to Robert Hamilton's daughter. She's the caterer…"

Marion nodded. "Of course. Well, we'll have to speak more at another time." She turned to Junior and Christine. "I'm so glad you were able to make it. You've dried out sufficiently?" she asked, glaring at her daughter."

"I'll send Rhee my dry cleaning bill," he joked, but his eyes did not reflect any cheer.

Paul was about to say something, but Rhea dug her fingers into his arm. "Well, good night, all."

Paul turned, his arm around her when Junior said, "Oh, Rhee—I meant to tell you. It seems that there may have been an error on one of your filings. The court notified me earlier in the week that some paperwork might have been missing."

Paul would later swear Rhea's temperature dropped ten degrees. She stepped out from under his arm and turned slowly.

Junior looked skyward and tapped his chin. "It was one of your cases. There were some papers missing. I'll talk to you about it on Monday. But it means that the settlement has to be redone. The money returned. The paperwork will need to be refiled—it should only take a month or two. Of course, if there's any hint of an ethics violation, things might take longer."

He laughed into Paul's face. "As a matter of fact, I think it might have been your case, Paul. I sure hope you haven't spent any of your settlement. It's got to go back into escrow until things can be sorted out."

Paul took a step forward but was stopped by Rhea's hand on his arm. "As I recall, Junior, you offered to file those papers for me. In good faith. To make up for mucking up the mediation hearing. Everything was in order when I gave them to you. In a sealed envelope."

He shrugged. "You know how it goes. Nothing like doing things yourself to make sure it's all shipshape—otherwise stuff happens. Right?" He turned to his hostess. "Marion, lovely party. Thank you so much. Come along, darling. Time to go home."

Christine was tugged along, saying her goodbyes as she was pulled out the door.

Rhea turned to him. "Paul—we'll get this sorted out on

Monday."

Acid welled up in his stomach, not that he'd admit to it. "What's he mean? Will I have to—Rhea, I spent a chunk of that money paying off bills. And on equipment. I'll take a huge hit if I have to sell it. This can't be happening. Tell me this is all a mistake."

"Don't worry. We'll get it straightened out."

She turned to her mother. "Now do you believe me about what a shit face he is. He swore up and down he'd file those papers for me. Cassie was there. You can ask her."

Marion bit her lip. "I'm afraid Cassie is no longer with the firm."

"WHAT?"

"We found..." She cleared her throat. "We found we had too many paras, and in terms of the merger, we had to let one of ours go. I told her on Friday afternoon after you left."

Rhea gripped his hand. "Let me guess. It was Junior who made the suggestion."

Her mother nodded weakly.

Rhea turned to Paul. "If any money needs to be paid back, the firm will cover it, given it was our mistake. Won't we, Mom?"

Marion tightened her lips. "We'll have to see..."

"Mom, don't do this," Rhea ground out.

Judge Patel came up. "I was going to say goodnight, but it looks like I might need to mediate. Is there a problem?"

Paul stood by as Rhea explained the problem.

"I can't promise anything, of course. It's not my court, but I know people over there. I'll see what I can do." She turned to Marion. "Rhea is right. If it was your office that messed up, there's no reason this young man should be penalized for it."

Marion didn't look at the judge as she spun in place. "Tony," she called sharply, and her new partner glanced up from where he stood at the bar.

His brows rose as he gave her a slow smile. "Marion?"

"Tony, we have a—situation."

Paul started forward with a rumble, but Rhea's hand on his arm stopped him.

Tony's brows lowered, and he came over, drink in hand as he placed his free hand on Marion's back. "What could possibly be disturbing you fine ladies and..." he nodded at Paul, "gentleman at this time of night."

Paul could see Marion's jaw tensing. "Your son..."

The white-haired man laughed. "Now, don't you go blaming AJ for something else. I thought we agreed we'd let him and Rhea settle their silly squabbles themselves."

Marion rubbed her forehead. "This isn't a silly squabble."

"Allow me," Judge Patel offered. Marion shook her head, but the judge prevailed. She turned to Tony. "It would appear your son promised to file papers for Rhea but omitted some important documents. This will result in a settlement being undone and monies repaid that are no longer available." She looked over the edge of her glasses. "And, I might add, the timing and manner in which he informed Rhea was, shall we say, unfortunate."

It was Tony's jaw that tensed this time. "So, naturally, it's my son's fault. How do we know she didn't leave the papers out?" he accused.

He felt Rhea holding her breath as she turned to her mother.

"My daughter..." Marion started slowly, "is a fine lawyer. You and I both know she has never made a mistake of this magnitude in her life. Unlike some who shall be unnamed."

Tony looked at his shoes before looking at Rhea without sparing a glance at Paul. "How do I know you didn't set him up?"

She opened her mouth, then shut it firmly before taking a deep breath. "Normally, I would not dignify that with an answer, but this time the one witness who saw Tony insist on taking the papers and filing them for me, as atonement for having screwed with my case, has been recently dismissed from the firm." She tapped her toe. "I understand your son might have had something to do with the decision to let her go."

He lifted his chin. "I leave all staff decisions to my son."

"So, of course, if we were to ask Cassie, any answer she gives would be suspect, said out of grievance," Rhea practically spat. "Especially when we get the police report that he's been sexually harassing her."

"Now wait a minute…" Tony started, but Rhea was having none of it.

"No," she countered. "The first thing is this: if any money needs to be repaid, the firm is going to repay it until this mess is worked out. There is no way in hell we are going to make Paul sell all the equipment he just bought in good faith to pay for your son's spiteful act."

"You go, girl," the judge added under her breath.

"Secondly, you are going to see to it your son signs a confession of what he's done and brings it to *me*. If he ever, and I mean *ever*, crosses the line again, picks his nose, or looks at me or anyone else in the firm funny—man or woman, I'm bringing it to the bar association."

Marion gasped.

"Thirdly, Cassie gets her job back with a ten thousand dollar raise and five thousand dollar bonus for being wrongly terminated. And your son no longer has any decision making power over hiring or firing staff. Ever

251

again."

"And finally?" Tony sneered.

"I haven't gotten to finally," Rhea said with a toss of her head. "I've only just learned about this and haven't thought it through. But you can be sure I'll have it in writing on your desk first thing Monday morning."

"Or else..."

"Cassie and I file formal complaints with the ethics board. Right after I quit. And don't think I'll hesitate to go public."

"As if anyone would believe you," he snarled."

Marion stood up straighter. "Tony, don't go there."

He glanced at her, and his sneer widened. "You're taking her side against mine?"

She stepped closer to her daughter. "It's about time I did, don't you think?"

"Marion, think of the firm."

Rhea's mother glanced at the judge before she turned to her lover. "That's exactly what I'm doing. My daughter has the right of it, and I don't doubt for a minute she'll do what she said. Nor do I doubt she'd win the public relations battle. There are too many complaints against your son. This is not a he-said-she-said battle. Rhea's reputation is sterling. He did this. You know it as well as I do."

"But she's..."

"Don't you dare say she's black. Or a woman," Marion growled. "Don't you dare."

Tony hung his head. "I can't believe you won't tell your daughter—for the good of the firm..."

Marion's arm went around Rhea's shoulders. "I may not have been the best mother, but I taught my daughter to stand up for what she believes in. I have never been able to tell this child to do something that goes against her moral grain, and the few times I've tried—I've regretted it, bitterly." Her arm dropped. "I will not tell her what to do. You, however, will tell your son to own up and grow a pair. To stop acting like the world owes him a living. If he wants to be a part of this firm, he's going to have to start pulling his weight."

Tony looked at the drink in his hand, and then at the woman he'd been sleeping with for months. He gulped down the contents and wiped his mouth with his hand. "This isn't the end of this conversation."

"For the good of the firm, it had best be the start of a dialogue," Marion said softly, but the finality in her tone would not be den ed.

"I'll have papers on your desk Monday morning to split the firm," he said and walked off quietly.

Rhea let out the breath she didn't know she'd been holding. Her fingers, which had been gripping her purse, were glowing. The others in her small circle glanced down as well. Her fingers tightened on the cloth and metal clasp. Marion looked at her and gasped.

"My, er, my phone just pinged a message," Rhea said weakly as she turned to Paul. "Can we leave now?"

Paul hauled her under his arm. "Ladies?" He peered down at Marion. "Maybe you'd like some company tonight. It doesn't feel right to just leave you here."

She smiled at him, and from Rhea's perspective, it was the first real smile she'd given him. "Young man, I want you to take my daughter home and put her to bed. She's had a difficult time tonight."

Paul looked down at the woman standing silently in his arms. "She was magnificent tonight."

"I may not have had the raising of her," Marion said softly, "but I made sure I had the very best people standing in my place. Now shoo. I think Rhea will be up early tomorrow, drawing up her list of demands. Don't you worry about Tony—he's got too much invested to pull out."

"What about Junior?" Rhea asked at last.

Marion sighed. "About that, my brave girl, I have no idea at all."

Chapter Twenty-Six

Berry

"What the heck happened Saturday night?" I asked Rhea.

Jenny, Annie, and I met her for lunch on Monday. Actually, we kind of showed up at her office, ganged up, and dragged her out. Jenny's catering crew was piloting some new dishes, and she needed some unbiased tasters. Yeah, I know, tough gig. I called first to make sure Rhea's calendar was free of meetings. I'm not a total ditz. Fortunately, Rosemary, along with my mother's helper, were watching all four of our kids—so there was no reason for us to not take off.

Rhea, to her credit, looked at me suspiciously. "What do you mean? You want to know about my sex life with Paul?"

"Yes, I mean no," I said, without a blush, I might add. "I mean, you can tell us if you want—not that we all talk about sex that much." I looked at my sisters-in-law, and they both grinned. "We want to know what happened. At the dinner party."

Rhea's mouth dropped open and then shut with a snap. "How in the world did you..." She stopped and shook her head. "No, don't tell me. I'm probably better off not knowing."

Annie squeezed her hand. "It's the Conrad grapevine. Paul said something to his mother, and she told us. Rosemary's got killer thumbs when it comes to texting."

Rhea smiled at that. "I like your mother-in-law."

"That's great. What's more important, she approves of you," Jenny said. "If she didn't, no matter how much Paul loved you, it would be over."

"Oh, she's got the power," I assured her. "Once you get to know her better, you'll see. And assuming you're here for the duration, and we all hope you are, you'll see her in action once Sammy brings someone home. But that's not why we're kidnapping you. Rosemary said something about Paul's case not being settled?"

Rhea groaned and shook her head, then proceeded to tell us all about it. "My mother cut the check today. Paul doesn't have to repay anything. I'm trying to keep him away from this as much as I can. None of it was his fault. My... er... firm is responsible and will pay any penalties."

"Paul told Rosemary you were amazing. No, he said glorious," Annie said. "Word is you stood up to your mother, her partner, and that slimy son of a gun who was responsible."

"Would you really have quit?" Jenny asked.

"Is the firm really going to split up?" I wanted to know.

Rhea shook her head. "I don't remember ever being so mad in my life." I was beside her and saw her clench her fists in her napkin. "Glorious—that's nice to hear. I thought Paul was going to split a gut, but he let me take care of it..."

"That alone is something," I told her. "The Conrad boys don't like to hide behind women's skirts—their words, not mine, but we love them anyway."

Rhea laughed. "I didn't give him a chance. I was all over it from the minute that idiot opened his mouth." She turned to Jenny. "Yes, I would've quit. It was off the cuff, but as soon as I said them, I knew I meant it. I'm almost sorry it's being handled. Being out on my own—it would be scary as hell. But also freeing."

"But you took care of it, just like you got me my money," Jenny insisted on knowing. "Paul's not going to..."

"If he hadn't been there, I'm not sure I would even have let him know," Rhea said. "That's not true. I would've, but only after everything was buttoned up. He's been through enough. And the jackass was doing it to get back at me. He'd love for me to quit. That would have given him free rein for all sorts of mischief. I'm going to leave it to my mother and his father to bring him to heel. I don't want any part of it." She closed her eyes and let out a huge breath. "It sure didn't hurt to have a judge in the room. There's something to be said for having to work twice as hard as everyone else for half the credit. Sometimes, someone notices."

"Thank goodness your mother came through, but then, that's what moms are supposed to do," I said.

We all kind of looked at the table at that point. See, my mother is a bit flighty. Jenny never knew hers though she did have an aunt who raised her, and all Annie ever had was the evil stepmother I created for her back when she was a fictional character, and I was writing her story. Rosemary has filled in a lot of gaps for us. If you haven't heard that story, I'll tell you all about it some other time.

"About that," Rhea said as she fiddled with her napkin. "That surprised me more than anything." She looked up with a strained smile. "It was—unexpected."

We didn't have a whole lot to say after that until Anne asked me how my latest manuscript was going, so I began to tell them the plot. "Hal—you remember him, right, Jenny? I made his brother Sal the hero in this one. That's temporary. I haven't come up with a good name for him yet."

"Hal, my white knight," Jenny said with a laugh, then covered her mouth as she glanced at Rhea. "Hal—he was a friend of mine while Joey and I were working things out. I didn't know he had a brother."

"You model your heroes on real people?" Rhea asked."

"Uh, sort of," I replied as Annie and Jenny poked each other. I didn't want to mention that I'd been working on a story that kinda, sorta paralleled Paul and Rhea's romance. The timing just didn't feel right. "You two behave," I snapped at my sisters-in-law, causing more giggles. I sighed. "It's a long story, and I'll tell you about it one day when we know each other better. And have a glass of wine in front of us."

"Better make it a bottle," Annie said with a straight face.

"Two bottles," Jenny added with a laugh. "And Annie and I want to be there."

"Then make it four bottles," Annie said with a snigger.

I rolled my eyes.

"Some family joke you can't tell me?" Rhea asked.

Jenny and Annie burst out laughing then. I frowned at them again but nodded. "It's actually more embarrassing than anything else, even if *some people* owe me because of it," I said pointedly to the two fools sitting across from me.

"Paul knows about this?" Rhea asked.

I nodded. "He'd never admit to it, but I know he's uncomfortable about it, so don't expect him to say anything."

I glanced at Rhea, and she looked so hurt I needed to say something, so I leaned closer. "Really, I *will* tell you. It's not the sort of thing I can just come out with in a public place. Maybe before I drop you off…"

She shrugged. "I'm a lawyer, you know. I'm used to attorney-client privileges."

That got my sisters-in-law laughing even harder. "If I ever pay you a retainer, it'll be one of the first things we talk about," I promised. "Now, if you don't mind Jenny, how about that lunch you promised us?"

Still laughing, she got to her feet. "I'll go check with the kitchen."

We ate—and talked—and laughed some more. Thank heavens there were no more innuendos about my extra special abilities, and we all had a great time. I was more certain than ever Rhea was not only a perfect complement to Paul, but she fit into my extended family like a charm.

Eventually, we needed to go. Annie was still learning to drive, so she and Jenny took off in Jenny's car. I took Rhea back to her office.

"Sorry about being so secretive before," I said as we sat in the parking lot.

"Your secrets are yours to keep," she said, her nose in the air.

I put my head back. I hated having to keep her in the dark, but the risk of telling her—Moe would kill me, and Paul would help bury my body. But I hated having her think we were deliberately excluding her. I know how I'd feel, and it wasn't good. And really, it was now or never. First, I rummaged in my purse until I found a quarter at the bottom. I took a deep breath and placed it in her hand. "This good enough for a retainer?"

Rhea nodded slowly.

Looking straight ahead, I gripped the steering wheel and prepared to fling myself into the void. I drew in a deep breath, trying to figure out how to start. "Oh, hell. Okay. We're missing the bottle of wine... but do you believe in anything supernatural?" I asked in as conversational a tone as I was capable.

Rhea's head turned to me so fast I swear I heard it creak. "What?"

"There's a reason I'm asking. Have you ever experienced anything supernatural? Seen a ghost, felt a spirit, that sort of thing?"

She made a bit of a choking sound as she clutched her handbag. "Is this some sort of joke?"

I met her gaze and shook my head. "My secret—what Jenny and Annie were laughing about is because of it. So, if I'm going to tell you, I kind of need to know your opinion on the subject of invisible things that go bump in the night."

Rhea let out a whistle. "No wonder you didn't want to say anything in public."

I forced myself to unclench my hands from the steering wheel, one finger at a time. "It is a bit of a sensitive topic— Moe's good with it. Annie and Jenny—well, so are they and their husbands. Paul doesn't like it. He doesn't like my talking about it, or evidence of it—none of that. Which is why I was reluctant to tell you."

"Damn," she said under her breath. "So, you see ghosts?"

"You're sure that quarter is good for a retainer?"

She looked at it and looked at me with a hint of a smile. "It's a bit less than what I normally get." She looked at her hand again. "But given you're a friend, sure."

I blew out a breath as I shook my head. "I've never actually seen a ghost. Not yet. You know I write—right?"

Rhea grinned at me. "I've been reading your stories at the gym. Really love them. That Svetlana and Conrad, girl, I almost felt I could see them…"

It was my turn to choke out a laugh. "What if I were to tell you—strictly in confidence, that I could arrange that."

She cocked her head at me. I could practically see the wheels turning. At least she didn't grab the door handle to make a quick get-away. I took another deep breath. "I'm not crazy, but it's going to sound like it, so brace yourself. I have to tell you that I can bring my characters to life."

She looked at me as if I had three heads, which, if I were in her shoes, I guess I would too.

"Berry…"

"No. Hear me out. I'm not crazy or suffering from hallucinations." And then I proceeded to give her a short explanation about my experiences. About Hal—whom we'd mentioned earlier. And how Annie came into our lives. I might have left out some of it, but I gave her the important bits. To her credit and my exhaustive relief, Rhea sat and listened, not asking a single question until I was done.

When I was finished, I let out a huge breath. "I'm assuming this will stay in your confidence, no matter what. And you can see why I didn't blurt it all out when we first met."

Rhea looked at me. She had what I can only call a bemused smile on her face. "If you were anyone else, I'd say you were pulling my leg."

"I'm not *that* good a storyteller," I said with a laugh. "I don't write paranormal stories, just good old fashioned romances—mostly contemporaries, so I don't have to do all that research historicals require anymore. Well, actually, I do write some paranormals about my friend Mrs. McGillicuddy, but I write those as novels—sort of 'as told to' stories. We haven't published any of them yet.

"If you need proof, I suppose I could figure out how to get a character or two to pop into the backseat. I'd rather not though—not where anyone could see." I took a deep breath and looked at her. She wasn't reacting badly, so I continued.

"I planned to tell you—eventually," I added. "Seeing as you and Paul are a couple, you need to know. But you have to swear not to tell anyone."

Rhea held up a hand with the quarter. I think it was shaking a little, and it looked pale, given her complexion and despite the sunlight. Which was kind of off—but I'm a writer, and I'm used to odd stuff.

"I don't want you to tell me anymore. If Paul doesn't like this, maybe I'm better off not knowing," she said.

I pressed my lips together. It wasn't like Paul was really that creeped out about it. He just didn't want any of my abilities to interfere with his life. "Okay. Fair enough."

Her fingers went to the door handle. "Thanks for lunch. It was a lot of fun. I'm glad you included me."

"Rhea, you're one of us now. Paul's made it clear you're a member of the family in all but name."

She gave a small laugh. "Even if we married, I'd keep my own name."

I nodded. "Good for you. I wanted to, but Moe put up such a fuss about it, I caved. But it meant I got to pick our babies names, so it worked out okay."

Rhea laughed, and it sounded like the first genuine laugh I'd heard since we got in the car. "Thank you for that. I—well, I guess I'm starting to feel like a part of the family. It's not what I expected. I sure as hell wasn't looking for it."

I touched her hand. "But it feels good, doesn't it? Feels right?"

She swallowed hard as she nodded. She had to take a deep breath, and I was afraid I'd made her cry. "It does. Really good." She looked at her watch. "I have to go. Thank you, Berry." She reached over and gave me a quick hug. "I've got to make sure everything's settled for Paul, that the papers get filed. By my hand, this time. And yes, your secret's safe with me."

"Go get 'em," I told her and watched her walk off. I wiped a tear of my own once she was out of sight.

Rhea

It had been hours since lunch with her friends. Rhea stared at her phone. It was late. Darkness had fallen since the last time she'd glanced out the window. She'd called

262

Paul two hours ago to let him know she'd be working late and to not bother coming over. Spending time with him had put a serious dent in her overtime quotient, not that she was complaining, nor had her mother. But more disturbing had been the conversation with Berry following her lunch with the sisters-in-law.

The paperwork for Paul's case was sitting neatly in a folder. Rhea would go to court first thing in the morning to file it. At Rhea's request, her mother had stopped by briefly to validate everything was as it should be. She mentioned Tony had calmed down about splitting the firm but wouldn't say anything more before she hurried to a client meeting. There'd been no sign of an apology from Junior. In fact, there'd been no sign of Junior at all.

Rhea sat in the semi-darkness and thought about Berry's words.

In the grand scheme of things, it wasn't as shocking as it might have been three months earlier. It wasn't as if Berry planned to use her powers to achieve world domination. But Rhea was keenly aware that all the confessions had been one-sided.

About her gifts—Berry implied Paul didn't like it. He doesn't like talking about it or evidence of it—none of that, which was why Berry was reluctant to say anything.

Rhea's stomach clenched. Paul didn't like the supernatural. He didn't want Berry meddling in his love life with her 'woo-woo' stuff, as Berry called it. Rhea held her hands out—her fingertips glowed in the darkened room. What would Paul say or do when he found out about her and her abilities?

She shook out her hands until the light faded. Rhea clenched her fingers once before tenting her hands and rested her forehead against them. "What am I going to do?" she moaned. "I can't keep this secret forever. What if we had children, and they inherit my ability? Would he leave me? Leave us?"

She wiped away her tears. "People say falling in love is wonderful, but no one mentioned falling in love was going to be a bitch," she told the darkness. "Or if they did, I wasn't listening. What am I going to do?"

If there was one person who might understand, it was Berry Conrad. Rhea stared at the phone. It was only eight o'clock. Surely Berry would still be awake, her kids in bed. She picked it up and began to dial.

"Hello?" Moe's deep voice was similar to Paul's, but it didn't give her the same shivers as her lover's did.

"Hi, Moe. It's Rhea. Is Berry there?"

"You sure this is the right number you wanted to dial?" he asked with a familiar tease in his voice. "I happen to know my brother is sitting home alone tonight because his favorite girl had to work late."

She laughed. "Yeah, I know. I'll call him later. Right now, I'd like to speak to your wife."

He gave a sigh. "I hope this isn't a business call. I happen to know you lawyers like to charge time and a half after six."

"I promise if I take on Berry's business, I'll only call during the day. For you, however, I might make an exception."

Moe barked out a laugh. "Paul said you were tough. I'm starting to believe him. Let me hand her the phone."

There was a fumble on the other end. "Rhea?"

"Hey, Berry. Can you talk?"

"Absolutely. I just put the baby in his crib, and Mattie's out like a light. Let me go into my office." There was the sound of a marital kiss, and then the click of a door closing. "What's up?"

"I was thinking about our talk this afternoon."

"Uh oh," Berry said. "You're not going to turn me in, are you?"

Rhea wiped another tear away but found herself smiling at Berry's tone. "What? Of course not."

"That's a relief. Anyway, it would be your word against mine. It's not like I demonstrated my abilities or anything," she said with a laugh. "Did you want more details?"

"No. I, um, well, I wanted to kind of tell you my own story."

There was silence on the other end of the phone. "You can bring people to life too?" Berry asked with no little note of hope. It warmed Rhea's heart.

"Not exactly. You see, when you asked me about supernatural stuff, I kind of, well, I'm... You have to promise not to tell anyone. Pretend I've given you a retainer of my own."

"Deal," Berry said.

"I've never told this to anyone. Only my mother knows. She thought it was all over and done with. You see, I..." she paused. "This is so hard to say. I'm so scared of what Paul is going to think..." Her voice broke then, and she found she couldn't continue.

"Take your time," Berry said in a gentle, whispered voice. "Unlike others in this family, I can keep a secret when I need to."

Chapter Twenty-Seven

Berry

"Hey Rhea, do you know any nice girls for Sammy? My youngest is getting awfully long in the tooth. He needs a woman in his life."

I bowed my head to stay out of Rosemary's line of sight. I wasn't certain if this was a test of Rhea's character, or if my mother-in-law just wanted to give Sammy a hard time now that she had made up her mind that Rhea and Paul were going to get married and had a ticket on the baby-train like the rest of her sons. Never mind that Rhea hadn't said yes to Paul. I knew he'd asked her. He tells me more than he thinks he does.

To her credit, Rhea narrowed her eyes as she looked at Sammy. "I'll keep my eyes open. What sort of woman do you want for him?"

He opened his mouth, but Rosemary, ever the busybody, beat him to it. "He likes nice girls, or he will if he knows what's good for him. Someone who'll keep him off the streets at night."

"Oh, come on, Ma," the subject of the conversation complained. "I d-don't date tramps, and I do like nice girls. I'm just not ready to settle d-down."

"Sammy's already in love," Paul added for Rhea's benefit. "But she won't give him the time of day."

"Her brother won't," Sammy himself added miserably. "He doesn't want any foreigners in the family."

"Say what?" Rhea asked. "You weren't born here?"

Joey snorted. "He's been mooning over this East Asian woman for years. We think her family won't let her date American boys, so Sammy's been frozen out."

I could see the crease in Rhea's brow. "That doesn't sound very democratic to me."

Sammy shrugged before he turned a glare at his mother. "I'm w-working on it, okay?" He turned to Rhea. "Thanks, but I don't n-need any help." His gaze turned into a stare as he swung around to look at me. "From anyone."

I could feel Rhea's glance and knew what she was thinking. I held up my hands. "I'm sitting over here minding my own business," I told everyone and no one. "Just minding my own business," I repeated for good measure. "Paul's doing fine on his own without my help, so unless you ask, Sam, you're on your own when it comes to your love life."

Rosemary snorted and returned her attention to her plate. "Yeah, right," she muttered. "How about when I ask you for help."

I couldn't help myself. I winked at Rhea before I looked at my mother-in-law. "If you want help getting a date, all you need to do is ask."

The rest of Rosemary's bite of chickpea salad fell from her fork into her rice pilaf, scattering grains on the table and her lap. "What? Me? I don't want another man in my life. After all these years? Are you crazy? What the hell's— oops, what the heck's gotten into you, Berry Conrad?"

From the corner of my eye, I saw Paul and Sammy high-five each other while the rest of the family laughed and went back to their meals.

Paul put his arm around Rhea. She looked worried and sad, but the two of them were so in love, I could hardly stand it. I knew they'd work things out between them. They had to—they just had to. And if they didn't—well, let's just say I can be subtle but effective in my methods. At least I thought I could be.

Rhea

"What do you mean there's a holdup?" Rhea asked her mother as they met for their weekly case conference with the rest of the firm's attorneys.

"The judge wants to know more about the mix up with the paperwork."

"I'll call him…" Rhea said.

"I already did," Junior said.

Rhea looked to Marion. "I thought I was the lead on this case."

Her mother would not meet her eyes. "The call came in Monday—you weren't available."

"I could have returned it," she said sharply.

"AJ wanted to make up for his, er, error…"

Rhea turned sharply to see the man smirking beside her. "I'll just bet he did."

"Rhea…"

"Perhaps we can discuss this offline," Tony started to say.

"I have nothing to hide," Rhea retorted quickly. "I think everyone here knows Junior deliberately botched filing those papers and that it's costing the firm…"

"I said we'll take this offline," Marion said sharply.

Rhea recoiled. "Fine." She snapped her binder closed and sat back with her arms folded. "We're done with my cases. Let's move on to AJ's."

An hour later, the room cleared but for Rhea, Marion, Tony, and his son. Rhea shut the conference room door and then turned to look at the three of them. "What the hell is going on?"

Marion would not meet her eyes. "Tony and I discussed it, and we felt AJ needed to do penance."

"After we agreed I would handle my own case?" Rhea strode to the conference table. "And you waited until now

268

to tell me?"

Junior sat back, the smirk still on his face. He glanced at his father, who shook his head, but Junior just shrugged and folded his hands behind his head as he leaned back on his chair.

"We thought it in the best interest of the firm," Marion said.

"But not worthy of mentioning to me," Rhea repeated.

"It, uh, slipped my mind."

Rhea could not help but glare at her mother. "What aren't you telling me."

"The judge is questioning the entire settlement."

"Because the paperwork went missing again? I filed it myself. You checked it. As did Joanne and Charlie."

"The judge heard about the irregularity of the filing and how you and the plaintiff are romantically entangled."

Rhea sat and tucked her hands under her thighs. "And so, of course, Junior was upfront about how he deliberately omitted the paperwork when the case was first filed. And, of course, he mentioned I was not seeing Paul at the time of the case—deliberately so." She turned to her mother and Tony. "There is no *entanglement*. Neither of us is married to anyone else. We're both single, consenting adults who have reached the age of majority."

Her mother had the grace to look away.

"AJ told this to the judge, didn't you, Junior?" Marion asked as she looked at AJ.

"He's concerned about the particulars." Tony shifted in his seat. "He wants evidence there was no collusion. That you represented our clients to the best of your ability so as not to benefit your lover."

Rhea's fingers tingled. "So, of course, you mentioned to the judge that the settlement was well thought out, went before a mediator, and was approved by one and all as being more than fair. And that our client is getting the help he needed for his drinking problem."

Junior shrugged again. "I might have."

Rhea blinked hard. "Or, am I to believe, you may not?"

He shrugged a third time, and it was all Rhea could do to not leap across the table to choke him.

"You see, dear, it does smack of favoritism," Marion began. "It looks bad if one doesn't know all the facts."

"But if one *does* know all the facts, as each of us in this room does, then it all makes sense. But if those facts were deliberately withheld, just like some paperwork was deliberately withheld..."

"I misplaced it is all," Junior said quickly.

"Do not give me that bullshit. The envelope was sealed," Rhea said tightly. "You know it, I know it, and Cassie knows it. Cassie, whom you so casually and deliberately had let go from the firm."

He lifted a shoulder. "Hey, Rhee, stuff happens."

She sat back and let her hands rest on the tabletop. "Not quite so much for some of us as it does in your case. Some of us do the work. We stay until it's done." She turned back to her mother. "I'm going to call the judge now. You are all welcome to be on the conference line. I'm going to tell him exactly what happened. And if you don't like that, so be it."

Rhea rose, leaning on the table with her fisted hands. "I did not collude with Paul. You all know this. He got what was due him. If I'd had my way, it would all have been settled months ago without all the drama or extra billable hours, so that some of us could have represented other clients in the meanwhile. Without staining our reputations."

She went to the door. "I will stand by my personal reputation, the merits of the case, and the law. As the senior members of this firm, you will support me, or you will not. You have five minutes to decide."

Her gaze went from her mother to Tony and back again. Neither would meet her eyes as the silence dragged out. "Very well. I'll write up my formal notice of resignation as soon as I'm done with my call. But for the record, until this is resolved, the firm is still out the money you had to pay to the court, and we're losing interest on it every day."

She quietly opened the door and made her way down the hall to her office. She sat down and began to dial the phone when a well-manicured hand covered hers.

"Stop," Marion said.

Rhea glanced up to see her mother. "No."

"You're going to ruin everything if you make that call."

Rhea sat back. "Define *everything*."

Marion removed her hand and sat wearily across from her daughter. "The firm. Our reputation. My relationship with Tony. Our relationship."

Rhea set the phone back in its cradle. "As far as I can tell, *we* no longer have a relationship."

"You're not a child anymore. I'm not going to coddle you. This is our future. The firm's future. Our reputation is at stake. Your future. With this firm. If this gets out, our reputation is sunk."

Rhea stared at her mother. "Forgive me, but I don't remember my childhood exactly the way you seem to. When did you ever coddle me? As best I can recall, you were never there. This firm means more to you than I ever did, so I guess I can't be too surprised you put it ahead of me now. I don't want to practice this kind of law. I feel dirty at the end of every day. This is no way to live. The money isn't worth is."

"You always did resent my working."

"I resented having a mother who took no interest in me."

271

"Oh sure, blame your freakishness on me once again."

Rhea jerked as if hit. "I beg your pardon."

Marion flung a hand out. "Your freakish power. You've always blamed me for that. I can't believe a child of mine—my only child—can do what you do. And what's worse, you never grew out of it."

"So, I must be punished?" Rhea said softly. "Because I'm a freak, you want me to take the fall for this bungled case? So your lover's son can continue to slither his way through life?"

Marion's lips were pressed together.

"I'm not going to do it."

"You must."

Rhea stood and fisted her hands on the desk before her. "I'm not going to ruin my reputation for that piece of crud. Mother, bad enough you're cheating on Daddy. Before today, I almost understood that. I get being lonely. But there are other men out there who are better than that. I can't imagine Tony's such a good lay that you would turn against your own child for his sake."

Marion hid her face in her hands. "You don't understand me."

"Not for lack of trying," Rhea said, her voice sharp in her own ears. "But at least I've tried. Which is more than I've ever gotten from you."

There was a long silence. "Don't make me choose between you," Marion said quietly.

"It never occurred to me to ask you to," Rhea replied in a soft voice.

"Can't you do this one thing for me?" her mother pleaded.

Rhea closed her eyes. "You make it sound like such a simple request."

"I don't ask much of you…"

Rhea could not help the harsh laugh that came from her throat. "Altering my career plans. Choosing my schools. Giving up my own ambitions and dreams. Sixty to eighty-hour weeks. Forcing me to take a drunk driver as a client. Ruining my reputation to preserve your lover's son's. Not much at all."

"I can't do this alone."

"No," Rhea agreed. "You can't. But the partners you have chosen—I think that says it all." She straightened her spine. "I guess I am asking you to choose, Mother. Your integrity, or the firm. I'm going my own way regardless."

"Rhea…"

She shook her head. "I can't do this any longer. You can ask. You can plead. You can call in my loans and prevent me from visiting my father. Pull every string you've got." Her eyes teared. "But know I've got scissors now, you see. I've got my own reputation to protect and nurture."

"You're doing this for your lover," her mother spat.

Rhea considered her words. "I can't deny that I love Paul. And I don't doubt his love for me, but that's not what's making my decision. I'm doing this for me. And f I were you, I'd be careful about throwing around that accusation."

"Rhea, don't do this."

The bright sunlight that had been streaming in the window suddenly was blotted out by a cloud. "Will you make Junior confess what he did to the judge? Will you make this right?"

Marion shook her head. "I can't. I promised Tony I'd get you to see reason. For the firm."

Rhea hung her head for a moment before she lifted it and eyed her mother steadily. "No."

Marion gripped the edges of her chair and slowly stood. "I'll expect your resignation on my desk first thing in the morning. You have two weeks to clear up and transfer your cases."

Rhea nodded. "I'll begin right after I make my call."

Marion winced. "You can expect I will deny everything you tell him. And by the way, he's expecting the paperwork to be re-filed."

"You've really set me up, haven't you," Rhea accused.

It was Marion's turn to shrug. "I'm doing what I have to do to protect myself and this firm. If you weren't so stubborn, you'd have seen that this is the only way."

"Goodbye, Mother. If you'll excuse me, I have a letter of resignation to write."

Marion walked away without turning around.

Rhea looked at her computer monitor, her eyes so dry they burned. A moment later, a streak of sunlight hit her square in the forehead, and she began to type.

Chapter Twenty-Eight

Paul

Rhea rarely called without texting first. His heart rate jumped when he grabbed his phone. "Rhea, what is it?" *So that's what love does to me*, he thought wryly. B*ring it on*, he added mentally.

"I quit my job."

He held the phone away from his ear and looked at it a moment. "You want to run that one by me again? It sounded like you quit your job."

She gave him a watery laugh. "I just typed my letter of resignation. They wanted me to take the hit for botching your case. I wouldn't do it."

"Rhea—you didn't have to do that for me."

This time she laughed outright. "I didn't do it for you, you dummy. I did it for me. They wanted me to confess I'd misfiled the papers. That I was colluding with you to get you a bigger settlement."

"Honey…"

"I'm sure they'll play it to make it look like my quitting will make it even worse, but I won't admit to doing something wrong when I didn't do it."

"You don't sound too good. Do you want me to get you and take you home?"

There was silence on her end for a long moment. "I am home."

"Do you want me to come over?"

"No. I need some time to myself right now. Maybe tomorrow."

"I don't want to leave you alone when you're feeling so

down."

Rhea laughed sadly. "My place is a mess. I need to clean it up, take a shower, and get some sleep."

"I love you, Rhea. You know that, right."

"Oh, Paul," she said with a waver in her voice. "I do know it, and I love you too."

"Well, how about that," he said. "You sure you don't want me to come over? I can help you clean."

There was a catch in her voice. "I—I do want to see you. Can you wait until ten? I really don't want you to see this mess. And I'll need a shower when I'm done."

"I'll be there at ten sharp. Don't turn your outside lights on until nine-fifty-nine for me, darlin'."

"Thanks, Paul."

"I'll see you then, sweetheart."

Rhea

She set down the phone. With a sigh, she looked at the mess that was her kitchen.

She'd barely managed to get herself there in one piece. As it was, every traffic light between her office and home had gone haywire, and one street light had blown up while she sat fuming through a blinking red light. She couldn't help but wonder if she'd been the cause.

The chaos on the kitchen floor certainly was her fault. She'd had twenty minutes to work up a good head of steam on her commute. Rage and resentment vied for first place in her emotional Olympics, with loss and fear battling out for the silver.

The moment she'd walked into her kitchen, the cabinets had opened, and one at a time the dishes threw themselves off the shelves and across the room. There were gouges in the walls where dinner plates had struck before shattering into millions of pieces on the floor. Next, the smaller plates pirouetted in a conga line before they crashed into one another and ended up in an untidy pile. The cups and saucers had been almost an afterthought as they burst from their places and barreled onto the counter en masse. Bits and pieces of them were still tinkling to the floor. At least her tumblers were plastic. They simply bounced and made a racket. Only one of them had cracked as far as she could tell.

It wasn't until her kitchen knives hurtled out of their block that Rhea was able to get a handle on her emotions. She stopped them mid-flight, and they dropped to the floor with a clatter. As if to make up for the loss of drama, her silverware drawer thrust itself out of the cabinet and dashed itself to the floor, scattering flatware in the wreckage of wooden splinters and plastic organizers.

"Enough!" she'd roared at the pandemonium around her. One final shard fell to the floor before all went still but for her breathing. That's when she'd called Paul because she really needed to hear a sane voice in the midst of the chaos.

Having heard his voice of reason, she needed to clean the mess before he arrived. And she needed a strategy to get the whole muddle of the lawsuit cleared up.

"Crap," she said to her empty kitchen. "Double, triple, quadruple crap." She closed her eyes and summoned up what psychic energy she could, trying to replicate what she'd felt five minutes before. The best she could do was shift the debris into a neater pile. "That's something," she said and almost felt like smiling. It wasn't as if she'd actually liked her dishes, but she'd had them for a while and had been quite proud of the fact she hadn't dashed them all to pieces years before.

"I guess it's paper plates for now," she said as she got out her broom and a paper bag to line her trash can.

"Seeing as I'm about to be unemployed, I can't exactly shop for new ones." She gave another sigh. "If only for once, I could use my powers for good."

She'd just finished rinsing the vacuumed floor when she heard the doorbell. Paul was outside her kitchen with a bunch of flowers in his hand. Rhea walked gingerly over the wet tiles to open the door. "Go to the front. The floor's wet, and I haven't showered yet."

He leaned in for a kiss. "I love when you get all domestic on me," he said. "And I'll leave my boots out here and tiptoe across the floor for you instead."

She smiled and opened the door wider. "Just this once," she said with mock severity.

"Yes, ma'am," he said as he thrust the flowers into her hands and began to shuck his boots. She took the flowers and searched for her vase. For some reason, the cabinet where she kept it had been spared the rampage. She filled it with water and plunked the blossoms in when she turned around to see Paul naked but for a wide grin.

Her mouth dropped open. "What the hell?"

He gave her a sheepish smile. "I took my boots off and got carried away." He looked down to his growing erection. "I'll put them back on if you want."

Rhea looked at his eyes and then down to his erection. "Seems a shame to waste all that," she said slowly. "Mind if we take this upstairs? I don't have much in the way of curtains, and my neighbors are nosy."

His hands covered his lower parts in a flash. "Personally, I think they'd be kind of impressed that you've got such a buff boy toy at your disposal, but if you want to keep this private..." He waggled his eyebrows, "I'm more than willing to accommodate you."

With a laugh, he scooped up his clothes and then picked her up and tossed her over his good shoulder.

Rhea shrieked with laughter. "Put me down."

"No way," he said as he carried her through the house and approached the stairs. "I'll remind you not to wiggle too much—I'm an injured man if you'll recall."

"Paul, this is crazy."

He patted her ass with his free hand. "I'm making memories for us to tell our grandkids," he said as he charged up the stairs and into her bedroom. "Or, if you like, you can brag to my brothers' wives about what a Neanderthal I am. They've got those guys so domesticated they never do fun shit like this anymore."

She didn't have a chance to reply before he tossed her gently on the mattress and put his hands on the ties of her robe. "You gonna do this, or am I?" he asked. "Last chance to change your mind."

Rhea struggled to her knees and shed her robe. She watched Paul's eyes grow wide as he realized she'd had nothing on underneath. "Woman..." he growled.

She lay back on the bed, propped up on her elbows. "I think I like this side of you. I'm gonna have to quit my job more often."

He stalked her as he came to the bed. "You do whatever you need to. I'm here for you. Every. Single. Day. Whatever you need, I'll provide it."

Rhea's playful mood vanished. He looked so solemn— was so earnest. "Oh, Paul. I didn't want to love you this much," she said as she opened her arms wide.

He crawled between them and held her, propped on his hands and knees. "I know. But I won't let you down, Rhee. I'm here for keeps. Nothing will change that."

She pulled him in closer, holding him as tight as she dared. "Don't say what you don't mean. I don't think I can take it," she whispered.

"I'm not going anywhere. I love you. That's forever," he

assured her.

She squeezed her eyes tighter. "Just love me now. Love me now," she said, holding the sobs inside. "Let's just be here in this moment."

"Whatever you say, my love."

Hours later, they lay quietly in the dark, holding hands. Rhea had just drifted into sleep when she felt him curl around her and kiss her ear. "I'll never leave you," he whispered. "Never."

She turned in his arms, weeping, but could not, would not tell him why she cried.

Berry

"Berry? I need your help."

Oh, are there any sweeter words? Well, yeah, I guess so. But from Rhea—at that moment, I think not.

"What can I do?" I replied.

"I don't want to talk about it over the phone. Let's meet for lunch. You can bring the kids if you want."

"Heck no, "I said with a laugh. "My mother's helper is here. I'm not passing up the chance to get away. The baby's down for a nap anyway. Want me to pick you up? We can go to The Sweet Shop."

"Too many Conrads are liable to pop in there," she said, and I could hear the laughter in her voice. "There's a good Tex-Mex truck near the park. It's sunny enough that we can grab a bench and talk in private."

"Wow, now I'm intrigued. Okay. I'll meet you around twelve-thirty?"

"Perfect," she said. "Gotta go."

I was only five minutes late, but Rhea was ten. She got caught on a call with a client who begged her not to leave the firm. We stood in line for our meal. Fish tacos for her, a refrito enchilada for me.

"Okay, spill, girlfriend," I said as I bit into my lunch.

"You said your, er, imaginary friends helped you in the past."

"Er, I wouldn't exactly say that, not precisely."

Rhea frowned. "Oh. Well, maybe this wasn't such a great idea."

"I don't even know what it is—come on, you can tell me."

She sighed and set her taco down. "I've got a mess on my hands. I didn't make it, but I need to clean it up. If I don't get it fixed before I leave the firm, it will drag on forever, and Paul's going to end up hurt."

"Do I want to know the particulars?"

She shook her head. "Just the highlights. When we first settled Paul's case, I got all the paperwork together to be filed. My mother's partner's son…"

"The jackass you've mentioned?"

Rhea nodded. "I had everything in a sealed envelope. But he must have opened it and slipped one of them out." She patted the file under her purse. "I kept copies, of course. But because it was messed up, the court wants to start from scratch." She bit her lip. "Much as I'd like to, proving the jerk did it will take too long. I need to make it look like a clerical error in the court office. I was hoping was that we could get the missing paper filed."

"Not sure I follow."

"You said your characters can come to life and that only the people who know what they really are can tell that they're not real, right?"

Warning bells were starting to go off. "Yeah," I said slowly. "The first time I forgot to make them warm, so Moe's clue was how cold their skin was, and how they didn't mind the weather, or how hot coffee was. I make sure I include those details now."

But they're not real, right?"

"So far, only Annie's come to life. I'm still not sure how I managed that. The others, I'm guessing, are just electrons or muons—sort of a world-wide holodeck. And no, I have no idea how I do it or what was different about Annie. And if I think about it too long, I get weirded out. It's not easy having that kind of power, you know." I looked at my lunch and then looked back at her. "What were you thinking?"

"I was wondering if we could get your critters to slip into the courtroom at night and file the missing paper for me."

"So, it will look like it's the court's fault ."

She nodded. "I hate having someone else take the fall. But it will clean up the mess so that Paul doesn't have it hanging over his head anymore. I won't point fingers at anyone in particular."

I whistled. I don't do it well, but that didn't stop me. "Damn, that's quite a plan."

"It was the best I could come up with."

"You can't file the papers yourself?"

"The judge is suspicious that Paul and I colluded, thanks to jerk face. He confessed what he did, but my mother and his father are worried about the firm's reputation. They wanted me to take the blame. I refused, so I had to resign."

I gave her a hug. "Which makes me love you more. The world needs more people with that sort of integrity, not less."

She gave a sniff. "Thanks. But it leaves me unemployed." Her face turned serious. "Do you think Sal could do this, or what's-her-name, your heroine? Or someone else?"

"What's-her-name still doesn't have a name, much to my dismay. Give me a moment to think about it. They're kind of going through a rough patch right now. They love each other, have made wild monkey sex, but the conflict is about to break all over them, and the black moment is coming up. I was going to write that scene in a couple of days. They'll both be too emotional to do anything until I get them back together, and I haven't figured out how to manage that yet."

"Oh."

Never have I ever heard such a glum word. "I didn't say no. You need this done soon, right?"

She nodded. "I was hoping it would be tonight or tomorrow."

I tapped my finger on my lips. "I'll figure this out. You and Paul come for dinner tonight."

"Oh—I can't let him know," she cried.

"No, no, no. He and Moe will go down to the basement and mess around with Moe's power equipment. That'll keep 'em busy for hours. You and I will put the kids to bed and then go into my study. I'll lock the door, and we can talk to Sal and... damn, I still don't know what to call her."

Rhea's eyes grew round. "Seriously?"

I shrugged. "If they're going to do this, you're going to have to talk to them. I know I can get them to walk through walls, but if they're going to have an actual paper to deliver, they'll have to slip it under doors. I think they can. But you'll need to give them directions on how to do it."

"Oh boy," she said under her breath.

"You have another plan?"

Rhea shook her head. "I've racked my brains, and this was the sanest thing I could think of if that gives you an idea of how messed up the whole thing is."

"Welcome to my world," I said as I balled up the wax paper and foil that once contained my lunch. "This will add a whole new dimension to my work. Maybe I'll start writing espionage stories."

"Don't look to me for help with that," she said as she tossed her leftovers into a nearby can. "Once this is done, I want nothing more than to get back to my boring old trusts and wills."

We walked back to her office. "You know, I've been thinking about it."

"What?"

"Telling Paul about your gift. I think you need to."

She shook her head, adamantly. "He's going to leave me when I do, and I've just lost so much. I don't think I could bear it if I lost him too."

"Rhea, the two of you are in love. I've seen how much he loves you. He's a big boy. He can take it."

"Berry..."

I stepped aside as a couple of businessmen and women passed us. "It's not like the supernatural is a foreign concept to him."

"But he hates it. He'd be so mad at me for lying to him."

"He's going to find out eventually."

She pressed her lips together. "Not if I can help it."

"If you marry him..."

She shook her head again. "I'm not going to let it go that far."

"You'll break his heart if you don't."

"I'll break his heart if I do," she countered. "Please, Ber. Let me get through this week. Please? No added drama?"

I wanted to say more, but the poor thing was distraught. "I'll drop it. For now. Tell Paul you and he are coming for dinner. Don't bring anything. I'll stop by Hero's and get a cake for dessert. And for once, we'll have something other than burgers. I swear you must think that's all we ever eat at hour house."

I finally got her to smile. "I did wonder."

"We're having an oven roast. Baked potatoes and green salad. A perfectly ordinary dinner. Now I've got to get home because I'm about to leak breast milk."

I gave her a quick hug and kissed her cheek. "Seven o'clock. I'll get the kids washed and fed ahead of time, so we have plenty of time to collude with Sal and... oh crap, whatever the hell her name is. Maybe you can help me name her."

"Seven. We'll be there."

Chapter Twenty-Nine

Berry

"Are you sure they won't get suspicious?" Rhea asked as I showed her to my study on the second floor. I was carrying two glasses and the remainder of a bottle of wine.

My study was the perfect spot for me to write—a round turret with built-in bookshelves, a computer desk, and windows to look out onto my neighbor's yards when I got bored. "Give me a little credit," I told her. "I've known them a lot longer than you. They had one beer each, which is as much as they ever drink. And ice cream with their cake. And toys in the basement. They won't come up until we tell them it's time for you and Paul to leave."

I eyed her as she wrung her hands. "You're not getting cold feet, are you?"

"Maybe a little," Rhea said with a laugh. "I think it was more wishful thinking when I came up with this bizarre scheme. I never thought we would actually—I mean, I thought I'd think of something more reasonable first."

"I guess I'm just a little more used to wacky things than you are."

"I think you've got a lot more control over your abilities than I do mine."

"Have you tried?" I locked the door behind us after I set the glasses and bottle on the desk. "Here, sit. I'm giving you a worry stone, so you won't give yourself blisters."

I handed her the pink quartz disk I kept handy, then poured some wine. "Drink. You need this more than me."

She eyed the pinot noir and took a gulp. "I'm more worried about what I'm going to tell Paul when this is all over."

"The truth. Get him totally blissed out from good sex. Tell him then."

Rhea laughed. "You know this from experience?"

I nodded. "Moe's on to me. Any time I initiate sex, he starts to get suspicious. So, I need to do it a lot to get his guard down for when I do need to tell him something he won't like." I gave her a wink. "I'm happy to say, so far, it's worked every time."

She shook her head. "I don't know…"

"One problem at a time. Right now, we have to convince Sal and whatshername to do what we want."

"Both of them?" she asked.

I opened my laptop. "I don't know. Do we need two people for this?"

"Hell if I know," Rhea said and took another sip.

"Let's see if one of them volunteers. Brace yourself." I opened the story file and did what I always do when I wanted to call one of my characters out—pretty much say, 'come out, come out wherever you are' in my mind.

There was a bit of a pop, and my dark-haired hero he and leonine hero were suddenly standing there. Rhea jumped out of her chair. "Holy shit," she said as whe sloshed onto the hardwood floor.

I smiled and dropped a burp cloth to sop it up. "Hey guys," I said. "This is Rhea. She's visiting and has a proposal for you."

Sal held out his hand. Rhea looked scared to death, so I took it in mine. "You'll have to excuse her. She's kind of new to the concept of you—you know."

"Pleased to meet you," Sal said. Rhea held a shaking hand out, and he shook it firmly between both of his.

"Oh my goodness," Rhea whispered under her breath as she looked between them. She narrowed her eyes and looked at me. I shrugged. Yes, the resemblance to her and Paul was there, but it was a coincidence. I swear it. I was a little more worried about my heroine. I swear I imagined her long before I met Rhea, but the similarity was still startling, other than the hair. My heroine had long, straight hair, whereas Rhea's was a curly dream. My friend looked at me. All I could do was shrug.

"Me too," my heroine said and took Rhea's hand into her own. "You have a job for us?" She gave me a wry look. "Or a name?"

"That's to be determined. Why don't we all sit." There were two folding chairs near the door, and Sal set them out. "And you know I'm waiting for inspiration to strike me on the name." My heroine stuck her tongue out at me.

"You guys, you seem almost real," Rhea breathed.

They glanced at each other and then at me.

"I guess I'm just one hell of a writer," I said with as much modesty as I could muster.

Rhea laughed and drank the rest of what was in her glass. I looked ceilingward and then poured what I had hoped would be *my* wine into *her* goblet. The things I do for family.

"Rhea's a lawyer, and she has a bit of a problem she needs to solve. She's hoping the two of you might be able to do a bit of surreptitious filing for her."

Their eyes narrowed. My heroine was a DA and very honest. Sal was a detective and occasionally willing to play fast and loose with the facts as long as there was moral justice to be done.

"Maybe you ought to tell them the whole story," I suggested.

"Will they—can they understand me?"

"We're sitting right here," my heroine said, humor evident in her voice.

"Oh, sorry." Rhea rubbed her nose. "This is all a bit unnerving."

"More than your own power?" Sal asked.

I took her glass before she spilled the remaining wine. "Y-you know about my p-power?"

My heroine nodded. "It's not that different from Solange's."

"You can see *my* power?" I asked.

They looked at each other again. "Well, yeah," Sal said. "You didn't know?"

Rhea looked at me, so I shook my head. "Uh, no one's ever mentioned it before." I sighed. "See, that's why writing doesn't get boring. Some people say all romance novels are basically the same, but damn if I don't learn something new with every one I write."

"So, how can we help?" my heroine asked. That was so like her—direct and to the point.

Rhea began to explain. Fifteen minutes in, she said, "So, I thought you could sneak into the court office tonight and put the paperwork in the file. When the judge calls for it in the morning, everything is exactly where it should have been in the first place."

"I don't know about sneaking into the court building in the dead of night," Sal said at last. "*We* can walk through walls if we need to, but anything we carry is still subject to your physical laws."

"And no matter how well you describe it to us, things can go wrong. We could unlock the doors, so you could come in with us," the woman added. "But the motion detectors would give you away, even at night."

Rhea's shoulders sagged. "I guess I didn't know too much about how you guys work."

My heroine patted her knee. "Don't feel badly. It's new to us too."

"So, this is all for nothing." Rhea stood, wobbled a bit before she clutched the chair for support. "I'm sorry to have wasted everyone's time."

I tugged her arm. "Sit. I can't believe you're letting a little thing like the laws of physics stop you. There must be another way around this problem. All we need is to think about it. It's going to be something so obvious that it's evading us, and we'll all laugh about it later."

"Whatever it is, we need to come up with a new plan soon, or I'm just going to have to walk into that office in broad daylight and file the damn paper myself," Rhea said with a sigh.

Sal and my heroine looked at each other and grinned. I could tell they were sharing something—and not just great sex. Oh, it was going to kill me to give them their black moment in another day or two. They were so right for one another. Of course, they'd have their happily ever after once I figured out how to solve their problems.

"Well, that would be easy enough," Sal said with a laugh.

"Huh?" I said. Trust me—I put much better dialogue in the mouths of my creations. Real-life is nothing like fiction.

And then Sal proceeded to lay out his plan.

Paul

Engrossed in the schematics of Moe's newest computer-driven toy, Paul jumped when Rhea slipped her hands around his chest and snuggled her cheek to his. "Hey there," she murmured.

Paul turned and slipped his arms around her. "You and Berry done?"

She nodded and pressed a kiss to his cheek. "Mind if we leave soon?"

He felt his grin spread across his face. "Am I going

back to your place with you?"

She nodded, her cheeks pinkening.

He took her by the hand and headed for the stairs. "Night Moe."

"What?" Moe asked, looking up from the manual. "You just got here."

Paul tapped his watch. "It's after ten. Rhea's got to get up early to go to work, and last I heard, you still had a jobsite you need to visit."

"Crap, ten? And I have to get up at five." Moe hurried up the stairs, hollering. "Berry, why didn't you tell me it was so late?"

Paul heard his sister-in-law laughing in the distance. "So, it's my fault? How many times have you told me I'm not the boss of you?" she said with enough sass that Paul suspected they wouldn't be getting much sleep any time soon. All the more reason to get out of there.

"Come on, sweetheart, let's get you home and in bed." Paul kissed Rhea's soft cheek.

"Berry, I'll see you at lunch tomorrow," Rhea said as she hugged her hostess. Paul bussed Berry's cheek. "You two are getting awfully chummy."

Rhea startled but figured she was just tired. "Yeah, well, new besties, and all," she said with a laugh as she turned to Berry. "Noon?"

"We'll—I mean I'll be there."

"You taking the kids? That's nice," Moe said as he pushed them out the door. "See you guys."

"So, what exactly was going on up in Berry's lair?" Paul asked as they buckled themselves in.

Rhea's perfectly arched eyebrow rose. He could see it in the dark. "Her lair?"

"Don't try to distract me with my own words," he replied with a laugh. "That's what we all call it. Behind her back.

So, don't you dare tell her." He put the truck in gear. "You know, her innermost sanctum. Where the magic happens."

"Uh…"

He stopped at a light and ignored the prickling sensation he got.

"Her writing," Paul corrected, mentally cursing himself. "That's where she writes. No magic there. None at all." He stretched his neck out and hit the gas the moment the light turned green.

"We were just talking. Making plans for lunch."

"Making plans for lunch doesn't take two hours," he replied.

She folded her arms.

"Not that I'm nosy or anything," he added. His accompanying chuckle sounded strained even in his own ears.

"Paul…"

"Come on, babe. Maybe I am being nosy. Do you talk about sex like guys do—not that I talk about our sex life with my brothers or my friends. Just in a general sort of way."

"You'd better not," she muttered. "We talked about a lot of stuff. Her writing—her, uh, characters that are in her work in progress. Very interesting couple. Did you happen to know she's writing about an interracial couple? She wanted to know more from me what it was like growing up and being half black, half white."

The truck stopped so abruptly, the seatbelts tightened. "What the hell? I *told* her not to write about me. Us."

Rhea shook her head as she laid a cool hand on his. "She started this book before you and I got together. And I'm not exactly offended. I mean, she's a white woman. What does she know about writing through the eyes of a black woman?"

"She's a woman—what the hell does she know about writing through the eyes of a man?" he countered.

"Touché," Rhea replied with a smile. "Except she does have a husband."

"She didn't always," he said through his teeth."

"Mind if I change the subject?" Rhea asked.

"Gladly." He pulled into her driveway. "I am staying over, right? You don't mind that it's a weeknight?"

Rhea's grin widened. "I'm about to lose my job. I don't think it's going to matter if I stroll in at nine instead of six-fifteen. It's not like they're going to fire me." She ran her hand up his arm. "So, if you want to stay up late, like watching TV or something…"

She slinked out of the car, never losing his gaze.

"Yeah, something," Paul echoed as he hurried after her.

She was waiting for him in the small foyer. Her shirt was already off, her feet bare, and she was working at the buttons on her jeans. It was all Paul could do to stand there and stare. "Oh babe," he whispered as he gathered her close. "This is two nights in a row you're overwhelming me. Next thing I know, you'll be tossing me over your shoulder."

Rhea threw back her head, laughing. "I've never felt this way about anyone before. Here I am, about to be jobless, deeply in debt, and I'm getting naked right beside my front door. And I've never been happier."

"Hell, don't let me stop you," Paul said as he began to throw his things with abandon. "I say, bring it on." He reached for her, and she met him halfway. "And just so you know, I haven't spent everything yet. I was holding off, given the crap your firm is putting you through…" She shivered in his arms, so he held her closer. "I can help you, you know—short term to pay your mortgage—groceries. I'm here for you, babe. Everything I have is yours."

The fire went out of her eyes to be replaced by something he could only describe as tenderness. Her eyes pooled. "Oh, Paul. You don't have to."

"You know, in a way I do," he said as he kissed her shoulder. "It's the caveman you bring out in me. I want to protect and care for my own. You're mine, Rhea. And I'm yours."

A tear ran down her cheek. He wiped it with his thumb. "I didn't mean to upset you."

She shook her head with a big sniff. "I'm not upset. A little overcome, maybe. No one's ever done that."

"And you don't trust me enough yet."

She shook her head. "I'm working my way there." She pressed him closer. "Make love to me. Please? And then we'll talk?"

"Oh, darlin', you just say the word. Any time. Anywhere."

He pulled the rest of their clothes off and then bent down and lifted her in his arms, kissing her tenderly. "I love you, Rhea."

"And I love you," she said as she lay her head against his throat. "So very much."

Rhea

In the aftermath of their passion, Rhea lay spooned to Paul's back. "Paul?" she whispered. "Are you awake?"

His hand clutched hers to his chest. He gave her a squeeze, but a moment later, his breathing returned to a gentle snore.

"Paul, I love you."

"Love you too, babe."

"And I never want to hurt you."

"That's nice," he muttered. "You want me to love you again?"

She pressed closer. "I want you to love me always, just like you said."

He gave a satisfied rumble that drifted off into another snore.

"You don't know everything there is to know about me," she said softly.

He brought her hand to his lips for a quick kiss. She could feel his sleepy smile against her palm. "Know a lot," he mumbled.

"There are things about me, though. Things I need to tell you before it's too late."

His hand slackened and fell to the pillow.

"Paul?"

There was no reply. Rhea kissed the scar on his shoulder and closed her eyes. "Damn it," she whispered, knowing sleep would be hours off if it came at all.

Chapter Thirty

Berry

The next day… Well, I suppose I need to start out by telling you things did not exactly go according to plan. In fact, things got downright squirrely, and then they got really uncomfortable. Oh, and it wasn't my fault. That's important, and I needed to prove it to Moe. As a matter of fact, if I were reading this, I might, in fact, be tempted to put the book down now. But please, don't stop reading. Because, well, just don't. Okay?

This is going to be a hell of a lot easier if I switch to third person, okay? That way, I can fill in the gaps of the bits I didn't see with my own eyes.

Rhea

She rose before the sky began to lighten. There was no point trying to sleep any longer. She showered and choked down some toast and tea, then left the house by six, leaving a note and her spare key for Paul.

She flexed her hands. For the first time, she was glad to see a faint glimmer at the edges of her fingertips. Summoning her powers wasn't in the plan, but knowing she had even a modicum of control over her emotions gave her a sense of security. She was going to need every bit she could muster.

The morning dragged by. She could no longer see clients and was doing her best to document her open cases. Unable to stand it, she left at ten minutes to noon to wait downstairs for Berry and her, uh, friends.

The day was sunny and unusually warm for late

autumn. She went over their plan in her mind. They'd go to the court office. She had papers to file for another client. Berry, Sal, and the woman would join her as she talked to the clerks. Then the clerks would go to lunch. Berry's heroine and Sal would change their appearance (the whole thing being so preposterous, Rhea could barely stand to think about how), and return as the lunching clerk, and then find the file the missing papers. Seeing as the case was due to be heard the next day, the file would be pulled and waiting in a clearly marked bin with the judge's name on it. Easy peasy, right?

Berry drove up. The two characters were in the back, trying hard to not stare at the wider world they'd never before seen.

"I can't believe how real you both look," Rhea marveled as she got in the car. "Sorry—I didn't mean that to be as rude as it sounded."

The woman in the backseat shook her head in wonder. "I'm still marveling at it myself. I didn't expect it to be so busy."

Berry laughed. "And this is just our little town. No way am I going to take you to a really big city."

"So, should we go over the plan again?" Rhea asked. "I don't mind admitting I'm nervous."

Sal gave her a confident smile. "We're not. Berry didn't write that into our characters. Our demeanor will be calm and cool, no matter what." He held out a printed sheet to Rhea.

You will look, sound, and act just like yourselves. You will be polite and urbane to all. You will not speak unless necessary. When the time comes, you will alter your appearance to resemble that of the person Berry or Rhea asks you to, and only for as long as is necessary. You will not run away with this paper, as it is only good from 11:30 AM until 12:30 PM on this date (see above). After that, you will return to your manuscript to await further instructions. You may not mark up, alter, or change these walking papers in any manner upon pain of the delete key."

Rhea laughed. "This reads just like something a make-believe lawyer would write."

Berry grinned. "Now that I've practically got a lawyer in the family, you can draft something I can use the next time we go on an espionage mission."

Rhea's grin faded as she looked out the window. "Oh, I don't know. I don't plan to ask for help like this anytime soon."

Berry shrugged as she pulled into the courthouse parking lot. "Maybe not for you, but I've got one more brother-in-law who's yet to find a woman."

"Maybe he likes men?" Rhea asked playfully.

Berry shook her head. "Nope. I admit he's adorable. Guy's have hit on Sammy, but he's turned them down—to his credit, he's been nice about it. And I've seen him mooning over the woman he loves." Berry stopped the car. "But that's a conversation for another day. Right now, we need to do some reconnoitering. Rhea, this is your turf. You're in charge."

"Maybe you should change your genre to crime?"

"Don't laugh. Sal's a cop in my story. I've been learning the lingo."

"And what do you do?" Rhea asked the woman behind her.

"Oh, I'm a lawyer, just like you," she replied with a smile. "But I represent victims in the DA's office. I think Solange wrote me, so I didn't do quite so well on contracts and wills in law school."

Rhea narrowed her eyes at Berry. "Are you sure you didn't base them on me and Paul? I mean, he looks an awful like a Conrad brother. And this one here sure looks a lot like me."

Berry held up three fingers. "I swear, it's just an amazing coincidence. You can ask Jenny and Annie. And even Rosemary. I've been running plots and character sketches by them for months. Besides, other than being a gym rat like my brother-in-law, Sal's nothing like Paul." (note to reader—yes, I had my fingers crossed. All my best heroes are based on the Conrad brothers. The heroine— that was a pure coincidence).

"Yeah? Well, when Paul reads this one, he's going to have some questions."

Berry heaved a huge breath. "I know. I'll sit him down and talk to him before it's published. By the way, did you tell him...?"

Rhea shook her head. "I tried. He fell asleep."

Berry's eyes couldn't help but roll. "Give 'em a little nookie, and that's what happens. Jenny and Annie say the same thing. Unless they want to go for round two."

"Or three," Rhea added, feeling heat on her face."

Berry sighed. "Those were the good old days." She turned. "You two didn't hear any of that, right?"

"You got it, chief," they said in unison, though their smirks contradicted their words.

Berry

So, all was going according to plans. When we walked into the office, Rhea was greeted with smiles all around, not to mention a few hugs. In particular, there was an older woman with short grey hair, a bright red sweater, and blue framed glasses perched on her nose, with another set hanging by a lanyard on her substantial bosom. "Honey, we were so sad to hear you're leaving the firm. Who's gonna do as good a job as you? Don't tell me they're gonna have that sleazy AJ do your work. I don't believe for a minute you messed up that case—I remember when that SOB filed those papers. He had that look about him, you know, like he knew he was causing trouble. But we couldn't do anything about it."

Rhea took it all in with a smile and bright eyes. "Water under the bridge. I'm sure I'll be back, working somewhere else. In the meanwhile, I need to file all of these."

"Of course." She looked over Rhea's shoulder. "These friends of yours?"

"Ah, yes. Friends. Solange Dewberry, Saul, and, um, Thia." Her surprised eyes met mine. "We're having lunch when I'm done here."

"Rhea and Thia...they rhyme. That's so funny. Now, you just hang on. This is the last thing I'll do before heading to lunch myself, sweetie. I don't like to be late 'cause that means Roberto will be even later, and as it is, he's gonna be the only one here for the next hour."

The woman took the paperwork and bustled away.

"You just named her Thia," I said under my breath.

Rhea shrugged. "It just came to me. I had to call her something."

"It's brilliant," I whispered back. "And Saul—why didn't I think of that?"

"You can't name them that," Rhea protested. "It's too close to our names. Paul will..."

"Paul can whine all he wants. I'm sticking with Thia and Saul. It's not like the two of you will ever meet again." I turned to look at my creations. "You two hear that?"

Thia nodded brightly. "I like it."

"What's that woman's name? The one you were just talking to?" I asked Rhea.

"Barbara."

Berry leaned in closer to her heroine. "Thia, you're going to become Barbara as soon as she goes to lunch. You'll go in the washroom with me. I'll make sure she's not there. You'll transform in the stall. And Sal—I mean Saul, you'll be the decoy. If anyone causes any sort of trouble, you trip or fall or have a panic attack—something to distract everyone."

"Berry, I'm not sure this will work…" Rhea said. "I'm so nervous. I've never ever done anything like this before."

"Too late. The plan's in motion. Not to worry."

"Right. What could go wrong?" Rhea asked in a tight voice.

Barbara returned from the back room. "There you are, honey. Here's your receipts for each of the files. Now, when you get back to that office of yours, you tell your mother that she's a damned fool to let you go."

"That's sweet of you. but I don't think…"

"Rhea, oh, this is a coincidence. I was just talking about you!"

She turned to see Judge Patel walking out of her chambers with another woman. "This is Marion Hansen's daughter. We were just chatting about her before the session started. Beverly Bloom, Rhea Hansen-Chalmbers. Rhea happens to be an excellent lawyer. She's the one who handled the Jenkins case. We were all dreading it, but she and the mediator worked out the perfect solution, and everyone's doing fine. Rhea, Beverly works in the family court."

The other woman held out her hand. "That was you? I was expecting someone far more mature. And I understand you're now a 'free agent'? I happen to know a few firms who might be interested in you. Including the one your parents used to work for. I believe your brother and sister work for them."

Rhea stood up straighter. "I'd love to hear more about those opportunities. It's been difficult finding time to job hunt while I wrap things up."

"Oh, you won't have any trouble at all. I would love to have you clerk here, but we don't have any openings. Give me your contact information, and we'll have lunch," Judge Patel said.

Rhea pulled out a card and wrote her cell number on it. "This is wonderful. Thank you."

"You're more than welcome. I hope you and your friends enjoy your lunch."

Rhea watched the two women leave the office. "I never expected that."

Berry put her arm around Rhea's shoulders. "It's a good omen. Everything will work out. We don't have much time left. Let's get to work. Thia, you're with me. Saul and Rhea, stay close. I want you where we can find you if we need you."

Paul

"Hey, little brother. I'm taking you to lunch."

Paul looked up to see Moe standing in the doorway of the woodshop, bright sunshine filling in the spaces around him. "You buying?"

"I am," Moe affirmed. "Come on, we don't have much time, and we need to make a stop first."

"Good timing. I was just finishing with the glue and need to wait an hour." Paul grabbed his ball cap and keys. "Where do we need to stop?"

"Court."

"Got another parking ticket?" Paul snickered.

"Actually, no. I was hoping we might catch Berry and Rhea."

"What?" he shook his head. "You know, I don't even want to know how you know they're there."

Moe started his truck with a roar. "When you're married as long as me—and I don't mean that to sound like a complaint, mind you—but you get to know when your woman's hiding something she wants to tell you but can't quite bring herself to say."

"I suppose that makes sense, to married men," Paul said with a snort.

"It means you learn their tells. When Berry's got something she's reluctant to tell me, she initiates sex."

"The only time you get any is when she's dented the car?" Paul snickered.

Moe hit him with his ball cap. "No. And it's none of your damned business how often we—I mean, I'm still getting plenty, and it's quality, man. But that's none of your business. What I'm saying is when Berry's got something on her mind and wants to get me all relaxed, so I don't go ballistic, she seduces me."

Paul sat up straighter, an uncomfortable prickling sensation on his arms. "Yeah?"

"So, I don't know if it's the same with other women, but last night—well, after you left, a long time after you left, Berry told me she and Rhea are planning a little caper today. Having to do with you. And some of Berry's, er, characters."

Paul held his hands to his hears. "I don't wanna hear any more."

Moe pulled Paul's left arm down, causing him to wince. "Sorry, but you need to hear this. Berry told Rhea about her, you know, abilities. Even though I asked her not to, and you told her not to. She says it just came up."

Paul sank into his seat. "Fine. So Rhea knows. I'll deal with it."

Moe gripped the wheel hard. "That's not all of it. See, it turns out, according to Berry, Rhea's got some sort of abilities of her own. I couldn't get Ber to give me the details, something about some code between women."

"That's just bull," Paul replied. "Berry just wants to seem normal, so she's projecting. Not that my woman doesn't have some issues—but they're not creepy-weird-out of this world issues."

Moe pressed his lips together as he pulled into the court parking lot. "Ber's never projected anything like that about anyone else. But something's up that has to do with your court settlement. And we need to be there in case we need to bail them out." He pulled the keys from the ignition. "So, you in or you out?"

"You still buying lunch?" Paul asked.

Moe's normally cheerful demeanor turned grim. "The offer's still open. If we still have an appetite."

Rhea

Berry walked back into the clerk's office, Barbara right behind her.

"Goodness," Rhea breathed. "Is it…"

Thia smiled through Barbara's face. "Yeah. Kinda cool if I do say so myself. Now, hand over those papers. We don't have much time."

"Right." Rhea opened her briefcase on a nearby bench and sifted through the folders. "The bucket should be through that gate, over on the left. Look for Judge Stein. Each bucket should have a name on it. I'll be right here if you need me, pretending to be on the phone."

"Cool," Berry said with a wink. "I can do that too. Saul, just look busy, okay?"

He gave us all a wink and headed over to the water fountain.

Thia headed through the gate, fortunately remembering to open it instead of walking through it. She began to look around, but her smile quickly faded. She looked up at Rhea, her face a picture of distress. "It's not here," she mouthed.

Rhea rose and sauntered over to the desk. "Look through that door. Maybe they've moved them."

"Right," Thia replied and drifted away.

Berry glanced up. "Oh, crap." She nudged Rhea away from her cell phone. "Trouble just walked in."

Rhea looked up and met Paul's gaze. A word that rarely crossed her lips let itself loose in the silence that ensued.

Chapter Thirty-One

Berry

"What are you doing here?" I asked my husband, my voice as naturally cheerful as I could make it under the circumstances. Honestly, to my ears, it sounded more like a squeak. So, not good.

"I might ask you the same thing," Moe replied. His voice was neutral. That alone was awful. It wasn't like I was looking to create a diversion until I needed one, but at least all eyes were on us instead of Thia-slash-Barbara. Then he crossed his arms. Oh, that was not a good sign.

"I told you, Rhea needed some, er, moral support. And then we're going to lunch."

"So, why did you bring Things Number One and Two?" Moe asked, one eyebrow reaching for his hairline.

He knows I hate when he does that.

"Although only Thing Two is present and accounted for. Where's One?"

"Please, keep your voice down," I pleaded and dared steal a glance at Rhea and Paul. The two of them stood off to the side, staring each other down. He was looking at her as if he'd never really seen her before, and she was looking at him as if she knew full well what was going on in his mind. Oh crap, what did my dear, interfering husband do?

It was Paul's turn. "If you needed help with something, why didn't you ask me?"

"I, uh, well, Berry offered..." Rhea sputtered.

"You know I'd do anything for you, right?" he asked, sounding almost hurt. Scratch that. He sounded a lot hurt.

"This isn't something you could do," she said quietly.

"Rhee…"

"I tried to tell you last night," she whispered vehemently. "You fell asleep."

"You could have woken me," he complained.

"I tried," she spat back.

He stuck his hands in his back pockets. "Well, I'm awake now."

Rhea closed her eyes and shook her head. She opened them, and when I tell you the look on her face was bleak, I hope you know what I'm talking about. "We're kind of busy at the moment."

"I want to know now," he said, just a bit louder.

Well, I guess that answers the question, 'Can all the Conrad men be petulant?' Not that my dear husband often shows that side of himself. But that's neither here nor there.

"Paul, this isn't a good time."

Which is when Barbara-slash-Thia came back. "I can't find it, she stage whispered, so naturally, all eyes swiveled to her. Except one. I could feel Moe's gaze upon me, and that damn—excuse me, darned brow popped up again. I swore I would duct tape it in place once I got him home.

Rhea glanced at Paul, sighed, and got up to lean over the counter. "Can you read minds?" she asked in a hushed voice.

My heroine looked at me. I shrugged.

"I don't know. I can try to send you images of what I'm seeing."

"What the hell…" Paul started, but I hushed him.

"This is important," I hissed. "Just give her the benefit of the doubt."

Legs spread, he folded his arms in a mirror image of Moe. "I won't say another word."

Rhea glared at the other clerk until he found something

else to occupy himself. "I have no idea if this will work, but all you need to do is to find a pile of work with Judge Stein's name on it. Look through all the shelves. We can't ask the other clerk. He'd wonder why Barbara doesn't know."

"Okay." Barbara-slash-Thia bit her lip. "I thought this was going to be simple. And why is Moe here?"

"Just go." My goodness, you create characters, and suddenly they think you owe them answers. Whatever happened to going on faith? Trusting me to provide a happy ending. My readers certainly do.

That's when I noticed she'd dropped the one piece of paper she was supposed to file.

Barbara-slash-Thia came rushing back. "I found it, but I can't find the paper. It's on the top shelf, just on the other side of this door. I can't reach it."

Good heavens, what was she thinking? Of course, she could... but then I didn't train her to think for herself in every situation.

Rhea sent me an appealing look.

Moe was glaring at me, but I ignored him. "Saul? Time to do your thing."

"My thing?"

"Your *thing*."

"Yeah, right." He walked a few steps and then slid with a nasty cracking sound as if his entire shin had split in two. He yelped out in pain. My skin crawled, but it did the trick.

Roberto rushed over from where he'd been in the back of the office, thankfully minding his own business until then. "Sir, are you okay? Do you need anything?"

"I slipped on a wet spot on the floor," he moaned. "I think I broke my leg."

I ignored them. "Rhea, go for it," I urged.

Paul and Moe stood side by side, their mouths open as

308

Rhea sprinted around the desk and through the door, Thia-slash-Barbara on her tail. Paul followed in time to see Rhea raise her trembling hand and guide the judge's bucket of papers wobbling down from the shelf without the benefit of guy wires, a ladder, or anything. Thia, now in her own form, grabbed the page and slipped it in the file. She stood, winked at Rhea, and vanished.

Without looking at Paul, Rhea raised the bucket and placed it back on the shelf the same way. That done, she dropped her head.

"You... you..." Paul sputtered.

She looked up at him—her face a mass of sorrow. "I tried to tell you."

"I can't believe it. I..." he seemed to have nothing more to say, for he spun on his heel and tromped out of the back room. Paul grabbed Moe by the elbow. "We're out of here. And screw lunch. I want to go to a bar. I want to get drunk. Dead drunk."

"Paul," Rhea cried, but he didn't turn.

When Moe wouldn't budge, Paul stomped from the room. I could hear doors banging as he made his way out into the sunshine.

"Nice going," I said to Moe as I neared Rhea. She stood there silently, but her shoulders were shaking as if she were holding back tears. "I'm so glad you were able to help them work through this issue like that."

"Berry..."

For the first time in memory—okay, since we had our own troubles when we were first dating—I turned my back on my husband. "We'll talk later. I need to take care of Rhea right now."

Moe scrubbed his hands through his hair and nodded. "Yeah. Okay. I'll be home my usual time."

"If Paul's going to get drunk, maybe you ought to

babysit him instead. It's the least you can do for ruining his life. And don't forget, he needs to be in court tomorrow."

"Hey, mister, I've got an ambulance on the way," Roberto said.

I'd forgotten all about Saul, groaning on the floor. "Here, hug Rhea for a minute," I told my husband. "Paul can wait."

He did as I asked. I went over to my fallen hero. "You can quit the act now," I whispered. "Time to make a graceful exit."

He gave me a wink as he straightened his leg and stood. "You know what? I think I'm feeling much better. I'll bet I don't even have a bruise tomorrow."

Poor Roberto's mouth dropped open. "How can you...I just saw your leg ...what the hell..."

"Better cancel the ambulance," I suggested. I took Rhea back under my arm and shooed my husband away. "Get Paul out of here before Rhea and I leave. I don't think she wants to see him."

Moe looked thoroughly miserable now (which I must somewhat gleefully mention), gave me a kiss on the cheek, and left.

"Saul, time to go," I said under my breath.

He put his arm around Rhea, and the three of us slowly walked out of the office just as Barbara-slash-the real Barbara was hurrying back.

"See you, sweetie," she called to Rhea as she barreled past.

We'd almost made it to the front door when a well dressed, overly coifed man brushed past us. "Rhea, you still here?" he asked with a laugh. "Are you broken-hearted at the thought of never filing another will?" He folded his arms and leaned against a wall. "You didn't try to outsmart me or anything before your downfall tomorrow, did you? You know, it'll be looked upon badly if you tried anything like that."

Her head popped up, and she shook off my arm and Saul's. "Just leaving."

"Not going to introduce me to your friends?"

She bit her lip before she threw back her shoulders. "Antony Vinders Junior, this is my friend Solange DewBerry, the crime writer. And her friend, Detective Lieutenant Saul Lippencott."

"Pleased to meet you," Saul said as he held out a beefy hand. Was he suddenly older, greyer, stronger, gruffer, and more rumpled than before? Yes—and it was entirely my doing.

"What division are you with, Lieutenant?"

"I investigate white-collar crimes. Insurance fraud. Financial malfeasance. I specialize in financial forensics. That sort of thing."

Junior's smirk faded, and he turned an alarming shade of green.

Rhea's smile grew. "We were just in the court office, going over some things."

Junior surreptitiously wiped his hands on his pant legs. "Is that right?"

"Yes," she said, confidently.

My goodness, but I admired her nerve.

"Well, just remembered I need to be somewhere," Junior said as he dashed out the door.

We made it into my car. Rhea was buckling herself in when she asked, "Mind telling me what the hell just happened to Saul?"

I gave her a smile. "One of the perks of being a writer whose characters come to life is I get to change things when I need to. Saul's a good guy and played along. He was pretty much in character, other than the extra twenty years and thirty pounds I put on him."

"Thanks, Saul—hey, where did he go?"

I pointed to the clock on the dashboard. "His time was up. He's tucked into my computer, awaiting further instructions."

Rhea put her head back. "I can't believe that just happened."

I bit my lip. "What part?" From my reckoning, a few things had just happened.

She closed her eyes with a weary sigh. "Paul. Saul and Thia. Moe and Paul. Barbara. Paul. Sal and Junior. Paul. Take your pick."

I patted her leg. "It'll be all right."

She turned to me. "I don't think so. He saw me. For the first time in my life I used my powers for the good, fully under my control, and for his benefit. And he saw me. And now he hates me."

"He'll come around."

She shook her head. "I don't think so. I've never seen him look so... so..."

I put on my blinker. The truth was, I wasn't so sure myself. I can contrive any sort of happy ending for my books—but real life isn't quite so easy. I pulled into her lot. "Do you want me to talk to him?"

She shook her head. "You've done so much already. But if I hadn't asked you, this never would have happened. He never would have found out."

"He would. If not today, then another time. Rhea, you can't hide a gift like yours from the person you love."

She gave me a wan smile. "I guess I just found out how much he really loves me. Which wasn't quite as much as either of us thought."

I gripped her hand. "How about you?"

"How about me? I'm about to be unemployed. I no longer have a boyfriend. If I don't find a job soon, my mortgage and school loans are all going to go unpaid, so I guess homelessness might also be in my future." She looked at her hands. "Oh, and my mother is no longer speaking to me. My dad's ill, and my long lost brother and sister decided I wasn't worth the effort." She smiled again, and it was enough to break my heart. "So, what else could go wrong? My car will break down, perhaps? Or my mother will stop payments, and it'll be repossessed."

I cringed. "If there's one thing I've learned, it's not to tempt fate. Besides, you've still got me. And Jenny and Annie. And Rosemary."

Rhea squeezed my hand. "Thank you. But with Paul and me no longer being a couple, our friendship might be a little awkward."

"Screw that," I said vehemently.

That got a laugh. "Thank you." She made to get out of the car. "I don't want to lose you, but your loyalty needs to be to Paul. I have to face him one more time. Tomorrow. In court."

"Do you want me to be there?"

She shook her head. "It will be boring and uneventful, thanks to you, Saul, and Thia."

"I have to thank you for naming them for me."

Rhea smiled one last time. "My pleasure. And I'll be happy to draw up more formal walking papers if you ever need them in the future. You did a good job, but if you truly had a lawyer as a character, they'd laugh at all the gobbledygook you wrote."

She closed the door, but I unrolled the window. "Good luck tomorrow."

She waved and walked away.

I drove off, feeling about as miserable and angry as I've ever been.

Chapter Thirty-Two

Berry

Paul was in terrible shape. Moe had indeed taken him out for a liquid lunch, followed by a dinner of adult beverages.

They stumbled in long after I'd put the kids to bed. I took one look at the two and herded them into the spare bedroom so they could harmonize their drunken snores. At least I hadn't had to worry about either of them driving drunk. Sammy had come to the rescue and brought them home, with Pete following in Moe's truck.

Rhea asked me to stay home, but I knew someone needed to go to court with Paul, so I volunteered my mother-in-law. I'd called Rosemary and filled her in on what happened. She wasn't surprised about Rhea. Her only words were that she knew there was something special about that girl. Special, she called it. Have I mentioned how much I love my mother-in-law?

Rosemary said she was looking forward to staring down the pipsqueak who'd made everyone so miserable. I, for one, didn't doubt she could. I even thought about sending Saul in his detective sergeant persona but was afraid of tempting fate two days in a row, not to mention the issue of his going through a security scan to get into the courtroom.

Given that Paul was hung-over and otherwise miserable, I relied on Rosemary to tell me what happened. What follows is my take on what she told me.

Rhea entered the small courtroom and made her way to the table where her mother, Tony, and Junior sat with

314

their client. The younger man smirked while neither Tony or her mother would look at her. There was no fifth chair. She stiffened her spine and made her way into the benches where the audience sat.

At the other table, Paul sat with his lawyer. He looked terrible. His eyes were puffy and red, his hair loose and messy. He sat there with his eyes closed until the judge entered the chambers. Rosemary sat behind him and nodded to Rhea, a small, welcoming smile on her face. Rhea nodded back but kept her eyes down.

"All rise," the bailiff ordered. "The honorable Judge Stein presiding."

Rhea got to her feet, her hands clutching her paperwork.

The judge spoke. "This is a fact-finding session. No one is facing any charges. The court wishes to understand what happened in the case of Conrad vs. Post, so it can be settled once and for all."

It was all quite formal and boring. At the judge's urging, Junior was the first to speak, telling how he had done Rhea a favor by filing papers for her. No, they were loose, he claimed. He was just the messenger. It was up to Rhea to make sure everything was in order. He stepped down from the witness box and sauntered back to his seat.

Rhea was called next. "I had everything prepared," she said. "I checked the paperwork, as did the plaintiff's attorney and my paralegal before I sealed the envelope. I had planned to file it, but Junior offered. I didn't want him to, but I was pressured by the senior partners to allow him to do me this favor. I handed him the sealed envelope."

"Were you and Mr. Conrad in an active relationship at that time?" the judge asked.

"No, sir. We knew each other when we were children and had recently reconnected. We were both interested in each other, but as I was representing the defendant, I knew it would be a conflict of interest for me to date him."

The judge looked to Paul, who nodded.

"I was doing my best to have the case mediated. It should have been simple. The facts were what they were, fault easy to determine. But there were those who didn't see mediation as a good solution..."

"In your own firm, you mean."

"Yes, in my own firm," Rhea agreed. "There was a lot of conflict and tension around this. The paperwork provided will show that in the end, we wanted to do what was right and fair."

"I will take it under advisement and have a clerk review it for me this afternoon."

"When I learned a document was missing, I did my best to re-file it quickly. Mr. Conrad had been paid, and as the case was settled, there was no longer any impediment to our beginning to see each other."

"Do you handle many drunk driving cases, Miss Hansen-Chalmbers?"

"This was my first. I specialize in wills and contracts. I don't care for this sort of work."

"So, why did you take the case?"

"One does what one must do," Marion muttered from the bench.

The judge looked up. "I did not ask you, Ms. Hansen. Your turn will come. Strike that from the record." He turned back to Rhea. "Why did you agree to represent this client?"

"My mother asked. I refused. She then threatened to call in my student loans if I did not and to refuse me permission to see my father in the nursing home."

Those in the courtroom stirred, and there was an angry buzz. From the corner of her eye, she saw Paul lean to his lawyer to whisper.

"I see." The judge glared at Marion, who looked at her hands.

"Miss Hansen-Chalmbers, did you deliberately withhold these papers?"

Rhea shook her head. "There is no logical reason for me to do so. I wanted the case done with, Your Honor. I thought we had a fair settlement. And I..."

"Were you anxious to begin your relationship with the injured party?"

"I will admit that was part of my motivation toward the end," she agreed. "But mostly, I wanted to be off that case because it made me feel dirty to be on it. I know it's my job to represent people without judging them..."

"Which is my job," the judge said, to chuckles in the court.

Rhea smiled. "I'm much happier practicing law to help people. There are some who describe lawyers as bottom feeders. I always saw myself more as a dolphin. But I'm also loyal to my firm and to my family, so I did as I was asked, albeit reluctantly."

"Did you in any way profit from Mr. Conrad's settlement?"

Rhea bit her lip. "Not directly, sir."

The judge grumbled.

"You see, Mr. Conrad and I are no longer dating..."

"That's convenient," Junior muttered for all to hear. There was another rumble from the court.

"I gave notice. My last day is Friday. I don't yet have another job lined up, and I have a mortgage due. I expect my mother will soon call in my student loans. Before we broke up, Paul—Mr. Conrad offered to loan me money to tide me over if I needed it."

"See, collusion!" Junior yelled.

There was a collective gasp in the court. The judge

banged his gavel. "Quiet, you."

"But Judge…"

"One more outburst, young man, and I'll have you cited for contempt."

Tony leaned over and whispered to his son, and Junior settled back, but the smirk never left his face.

"So, money was exchanged?" the judge asked.

Rhea shook her head. "No. Mr. Conrad and I are no longer seeing each other, so I don't expect him to make good on his offer. I have a little money, enough to get me through one month, providing I don't have to repay my student loans immediately."

The judge looked at Marion, who sat stone-faced. "Well, perhaps that won't happen so quickly." He looked through the paperwork. "So, I see it was Mr. Antony Vinder, Junior, who brought it to our attention that there was missing paperwork on the case."

Rhea's eyes widened. "I wasn't aware how it came to Your Honor's attention. I learned of it at a dinner party my mother threw. At that time, I feared Paul would have to repay the money he received. I didn't think that was fair. Given the fault was in my firm, I thought we should bear the temporary financial burden. I knew Paul spent a good bit of it to replace equipment he'd lost in the accident last year, as well as toward medical expenses, and trying to establish himself in a new business since he could no longer do the work he'd been doing. After some discussion, my mother agreed."

Rhea looked at Paul.

"I didn't know," he mouthed. She looked away. "And now we find ourselves here today," Rhea concluded.

"Indeed, we do." He looked through his papers again. "You say you gave Mr. Vinder a sealed envelope?"

"Yes, Your Honor."

He looked at the bend. "Mr. Vinder, you said it was loose papers."

"It was," he replied.

"And I presume there were no witnesses?"

Rhea looked up, clearly startled. "There was. I didn't trust him. Cassie Copes, our paralegal, was there and saw the whole thing."

"Is Miss Copes in court today?"

"I'm here, Your Honor."

"Miss Hansen-Chalmbers, you may step down. Bailiff, please swear in Ms. Copes."

Rhea passed the table where her mother sat staring straight ahead. Tony and Junior were whispering furiously.

"Miss Copes, first question. Did you see Miss Hansen-Chalmbers hand Mr. Vinder a sealed envelope to file as stated earlier?"

"Yes, Your Honor."

"And you know it was for Mr. Conrad's case?"

"Yes, sir. I put it together myself, with Rhea, Miss Hansen-Chalmbers, and her mother, Ms. Hansen, looking on. I sealed it myself and marked it. I handed it to Rhea, who handed it to AJ."

Junior shot to his feet. "That's a lie," he cried.

The gavel came down. "Fine that man five hundred dollars and one charge of contempt."

His father wrestled him back to his seat.

"You may step down," the judge told Cassie.

"Ms. Hansen, would you like to take the stand? And for the record, that was a rhetorical question.

Rosemary tells me at that point she was at the edge of her seat. And that Paul couldn't take his eyes off Rhea.

Marion was sworn in.

"You've heard the testimony here today," the judge said. "Can you tell me if any of it is false?"

Marion shook her head. "No, sir."

"I beg your pardon, but there has been contradictory discussion about whether or not the envelope was sealed." He looked over the edge of his glasses. "I won't bother with the suggestion of persuasion that was used on your daughter. That, I think, is a family matter."

"I saw Cassie seal the envelope and hand it to my daughter, Rhea."

"And did you see Rhea hand the envelope to Mr. Vinder, Junior?"

"I must have turned away at that time or left the room. I don't recall the exact conversation or what happened next."

Rosemary said Rhea's shoulders, so stiff the moment before, slumped.

"But your paralegal claims she saw the handoff. You cannot corroborate it?"

"I cannot testify to what I never saw," Marion said plainly.

"You may step down, but I can promise you this—the next time we have lunch, or drinks you and I will talk about parenting styles. At length." The judge looked back at Junior. "Well, sonny, it looks like you're back in the docket. Step on up. You're contemptible, but still under oath."

There was laughter in the court, but at a stern look from the judge, it came to an abrupt end.

"Would you, by any chance, like to change your story, Mr. Vinder?" the judge asked. "Given that two credible witnesses saw you with a sealed envelope in your hands, and one other witness couldn't say one way or the other."

"I'm not going to admit to something I didn't do. Not when Rhea screwed up the case and won't admit it. Sure, she didn't profit this time, but you can't tell me she couldn't have. Too bad for her, she broke up with her boyfriend before he paid her off."

Rhea stood in outrage as the gavel came down. "With all due respect, Mr. Vinder, I didn't ask your opinion. As best I can recall, you are a lawyer. That assumes you went to law school, sat for, and passed the bar. All of which assumes you understand the law and what is expected of you in a court of law."

The smirk faded. "Yes, Your Honor."

"Yet you continue with your childish outbursts. It seems they are not limited to the courtroom but also to social situations, such as this dinner party where you notified all and sundry of the mishap with the papers. Tell me, Mr. Vinder, why that evening? Why not earlier, in a place of business?"

He shrugged. "I wanted to wait until Mr. Conrad was there. I don't like him. I think he was taking advantage of Rhea."

The judge sat back. "I fail to see how this…"

"He was taking her away from her work. She wasn't putting in as many billable hours. She was putting herself before the firm.

The judge looked to Rhea. "Exactly how many hours were you putting in? And you're still under oath."

"An average of eighty hours a week, Your Honor. More on occasion."

"And how many hours do you put in, Mr. Vinder?"

"Between me and my team…"

"No, sir. You. How many billable hours do you log each week? And because this is all so interesting, you can be sure I'll subpoena your firm's billing records if I need to."

"Thirty-five," he said in a small voice. "But my team puts in much more."

"Noted." He sat in silence as Junior squirmed. "I'm going to tell you something, young man. I don't like you. I don't like you at all. You remind me of a lot of young men

321

who have passed by my bench over the years. Most of them in handcuffs." He paused and cleaned his glasses. "I don't know what trouble you're trying to make here or what motivates you, but your reputation precedes you." He paused. "Does it have something to do with a recent merger between your two firms and your financial expectations thereof?"

Junior squirmed again, but his lips were a thin line.

The judge put his glasses on. "Judges make up a rather small club in this city. And we talk. So, I'm warning you, sir, if you show up here again trying to make mischief, I'll find you in contempt, and the fine will be a hell of a lot more than five hundred dollars. If I were Miss Hansen-Chalmbers, I'd be suing you for slander—besmirching Rhea's good name as you've done here today. I only wish all attorneys were like her. Things would run a hell of a lot smoother. Clients wouldn't pay as much. The courts wouldn't be clogged with foolish and self-serving lawsuits. Can't say I blame her for wanting to strike out on her own. I wouldn't want to work with you either."

"That's not fair…"

The judge rapped his gavel until the head of it flew off and fell with a clunk next to the prosecutor's table. "I didn't give you leave to speak."

The bailiff handed the wooden head back to him with a grin.

"You're a fine one to be talking about fair. It's not fair that I'm sitting here listening to your drivel when I would rather be out on a golf course or playing with my grandchildren. Don't talk to me about fair."

He looked out at the court. "Now, all this hullabaloo—it seems it's over nothing. I happen to have the original file here in front of me." He held it up. "As far as I can tell, everything seems to be in order." He glared at Junior as he waved the papers about. "Every single paper that should have been filed was filed."

"That's not possible…" Junior's hands flew to his mouth.

"Exactly," the judge replied. "So, says the man who planted the evidence, or claimed its absence. You sir, are the first and only one who claimed this paper was missing. But guess what, it was here all along. The chain of evidence speaks against you, especially if you opened the envelope and removed something." He waved it about. "I could have this checked for fingerprints, you know. I have no idea what it was, but what I do know is that you have wasted a perfectly good afternoon for all of us. This case is settled. We will release the funds back to the firm. Mr. Conrad, I appreciate your patience. This case should have been settled months ago. I apologize to you on behalf of the justice system. You are all free to go, other than Mr. Vinder Junior, whom I think needs to spend the night in jail, where he can dream up more imaginative crimes. Court dismissed." The repaired gavel came down as the back doors burst open, and another bailiff ran into the room.

"Your Honor, I have a message here for Ms. Hansen and Miss Hansen-Chalmbers."

The judge waved him forward. "Ladies, come forward. The rest of you are dismissed."

Paul met his mother in the aisle where they hugged, then turned to the bench.

Rhea approached the judge, as did Marion, with Tony behind her. The bailiff led a protesting Junior away. "What is it?"

"I'm sorry to give you this news, but it seems your husband, your father, passed away this afternoon."

Chapter Thirty-Three

Hey, it's me, Berry.

So, it was quite a scene in the courtroom. Kind of wished I'd been there. Rosemary and Paul came for dinner and told us all about it. Paul shuddered when Moe offered him a beer. He just sat there with his head in his hands.

"I can't believe I was so awful to her. I had no idea her family was so screwed up." He looked up at me. "Berry, can I get a do-over?"

I shook my head. "Sorry, pal, you're on your own."

His head hung once more. "She never said a word about… any of it. I thought she just liked working hard." He looked at his shoes. "And she did lie to me."

I tsked indignantly. "Get over yourself. If you had a secret like hers, wouldn't you hide it? It's not like you told her about me."

"You weren't part of the relationship," he said. As if that meant anything.

Rosemary shook her head. "Her mother was taking advantage of her, and her mother's lover was all for it. No wonder Rhea quit. More power to her. But with her father dying like that. That poor thing. All alone."

"Paul?" I asked.

He shook his head. "I can't—I don't think she wants to see me right now."

"With that attitude, I can't say I blame her." I rose and looked at my husband. "I'm going to Rhea's. I'll take the baby and something for her to eat. Moe, you put Mattie to bed, and make sure Paul's gone by the time I get home. I don't think I can stand to look at him." And for the record, I made sure I said it loud enough for Paul to hear.

As I was leaving, I heard Moe ask, "Are you sure you

don't want to get drunk again?"

Rhea

She didn't go back to the office that week. Cassie wrapped up her remaining work and packed up her desk, broken candle and all.

Friends came, stayed, sat, and held her hand. Tears were shed. Silence prevailed. On Sunday, Rhea drove herself to the graveside funeral. She'd had to find out the arrangements from the paper. Her name was not listed as being among the survivors.

Rhea stood in the back while a minister she'd never met read words she could not hear. Tony flanked Marion by the graveside. She wore black, with a long veil over her face. Rhea found she could not bear to look at her mother for long. Debra and Milo were there as well.

In the distance, she saw Paul. It was almost as if he were there by accident, visiting his father's grave. Their gaze met across the grassy expanse, but just as it looked like he was about to approach her, a hand gripped her elbow.

"Debra," she said as she turned to see her sister.

"Rhea, I'm so sorry." She was enveloped in a fragrant hug. "I heard what happened with your mother. I can't believe she... oh, this is so hard." She gripped Rhea's shoulders as she pulled back. "I am so sorry. About everything. I know I was supposed to call, but Milo was so worried about what people would say. He and his wife are having a hard time right now—"

"It's okay," Rhea heard herself say.

"No, it's not okay," Debra replied. "I'm furious with myself and my brother. I mean, yes, we have lives, but you're here all alone. Your mother—if I didn't already hate her, I'd hate her all over again."

Rhea gave a weak smile. "I need to go." She looked up to see her mother and Tony get into the limousine. Junior and his fiancée followed and the door shut behind them.

"Screw them," Deb said, her voice full of rage. "My family and Milo's are going for dinner. Come with us. We're family now. Dad would have wanted that. He always did."

"I don't understand."

Debra linked arms with her. "This is a terrible time to talk about it, but I'll explain. And you need to meet everyone. Please say yes."

Rhea looked back at where Paul had stood, but he was gone. All that remained were a bunch of bright flowers on a grave.

Paul

"I ran away, Berry. I went there with every good intention, and in the end, I bolted."

Yes, it was Paul sitting in my kitchen, nursing a cup of coffee on the day of the funeral. Or rather, he'd hung his head over the mug I'd made him. I wasn't certain if he'd actually drunken any yet.

"Did she see you?"

The top of his head nodded.

"What did she look like?"

That got his attention. "What do you mean? She looked like Rhea. Beautiful."

I sighed. Honestly, the men in this family will drive me to an early grave. "Did she look sad, or animated, was she talking to people or keeping to herself?" I scrunched up his collar to make him look at me. "Was she talking to her mother, you idiot?"

"Oh, no. I mean, she was kind of by herself. Her mother—thank goodness I already asked her father if I could marry her because I'll never speak to that woman again..."

"Paul, get to the point."

"I'm trying. Rhea drove her own car. There were plenty of limos, but she wasn't in one, not even right behind them. She was just by herself on the edge of the crowd. People were looking at her, but they kept to themselves. I saw the judge who was at the dinner—she gave Rhee a hug, and snubbed Marion. I was just about to go to her when this other woman approached her. And Rhee turned to talk to her for a while. So, I left." He sighed and closed his eyes. "I didn't know what to do."

"Oh, Paul," I sighed. "You still love her?"

He nodded miserably.

"You need to go to her."

"I hurt her. I don't think she wants to see me."

"You don't know that."

Paul finally looked up. "Do you?"

I shook my head. "I haven't seen her since that night. I've called a bunch, but she doesn't want to talk."

"But she takes your calls?"

I nodded. "Have you called her?"

He shook his head. "Afraid to."

I sat down beside him. "This can't go on. You need to do something. She's all alone, Paul. She loves you. t's tearing her apart—she loves you so much. And now you know her secret."

He closed his eyes. "Her secret scares me to death."

Ah, so that was it.

I took a deep breath. "What she's capable of, I don't think it's so different from what I can do."

His head jerked. "Huh?"

"Change matter? Move things around?"

"Crap," he muttered.

"You've gotten used to me, haven't you?" I asked with a

poke to his ribs. It might have been sharper than usual.

"I suppose."

"So, what's to say you can't get used to her?" I dragged my chair closer. "I'm going to tell you something in confidence here. So listen up."

Paul managed to turn to look at me.

"You know how her mother's rejected her?"

He nodded.

"She told me her mother called her a freak."

"Ma's called me worse," he muttered. "Wild animal comes to mind."

I gave him a swat. I couldn't help myself. "That was probably because you were roughhousing with your brothers. And knowing your mother, she meant it in a loving way. Not rejecting who you are at your core. Not that I'm so close to my parents, but I cannot fathom any parent calling their child a freak and meaning it."

"After everything I heard in court the other day, it doesn't surprise me," he said.

"So, her mother rejected her in favor of her lover and his sleazy son. Her father's been pretty much out of her life for the past few years, and now she's lost even that little part of him. And her brother and sister, who she just met, haven't been in touch with her. Paul, don't you see, she's alone in the world?"

"If I go there, she'll think I pity her. And I'm still scared of her."

I threw up my hands and got up. "Get out of my kitchen."

"Huh?"

I shoved him. "Get out. Now. I can't stand to look at you."

He rose to his feet, eyes wide. "Berry, you're supposed to be on my side."

I rolled my eyes and didn't even try to hide it. "And here I thought you were the sweet, sensitive Conrad. But you're just selfish and scared. And for the record, I'm choosing my friend right now because she needs someone on her side."

He got to his feet. I gave him another shove. "Now. Get. Out. Don't make me call Moe."

"I can't believe you're doing this," he cried. Well, not cry-cried, but his voice did come out a little higher than usual. It made me feel mean, which felt really, really good.

"Believe it. And don't come back until I say you can. Invitations by Moe don't mean a thing, because he's the big dufus who created this mess in the first place. He couldn't just wait for Rhea to tell you on her own. And she tried." I pushed him again. "You fell asleep when she did."

"Hey, it's not my fault she seduced me because she wanted to tell me something. You women are all alike."

"What?"

Which is when I saw my husband at the door.

"What did you tell him?" I screeched. Yes, sad to admit, but I did.

It was Moe's turn to shake his head. "Paul, you idiot. You weren't supposed to say anything."

"Tell your brother to get out of my kitchen, my house right now," I ordered my husband. "Or you're in the dog house. Permanently."

"You don't have a dog…" Paul started to say.

"Shut up," Moe and I said simultaneously.

"Okay, I'm leaving," Paul said. "I'll go somewhere I'll get a little sympathy."

"Don't bother going to your mom's. Or Joey's. Or Pete's."

"Crap. You told all of them?"

"I will," I promised as I picked up my phone. "Sammy's

your only safe bet, and if you're smart, you'll fess up to him right away. You two bachelors can sulk by yourselves."

"Wow, harsh babe," Moe said. But one look at me, he held up his hands. "Harsh but justified." He jerked his head to Paul. "Better go before you get me in any more trouble."

Rhea

She walked alone into the private dining room. Rhea could feel the tension before she stepped through the doorway.

"I won't," a young voice cried. "I don't want to be here. He never cared about us. I want to go home and play my games."

"Listen to me, Johanna, you need to get it under control for the next hour..."

"I don't want to!"

There was a crash that sounded suspiciously like fine china breaking. It was followed by a second breakage, a gasp, and chaotic yelling.

"Oh my," Rhea whispered to herself and came into the brightly lit room to see a third plate hurled across the room.

Four faces turned. A toddler sat in a highchair, chasing little bits of food around a tray. Milo's anger and embarrassment were evident. His wife was a bit harder to read—at least Rhea assumed the black woman was his wife. And between them stood an angry, struggling, and red-faced tweenie, each wrist encircled by a parental fist.

Milo released his daughter's hand. That was just enough for the girl to break through and run toward the door, which Rhea was blocking. She held out her arms, and the child stopped, her face mulish.

"I'm sorry to be interrupting—Debra said I should..." She stopped at the look on their faces. "Perhaps I should leave."

Milo broke from his trance. "No. Rhea. Stay. Please. Debra mentioned you'd be joining us. I'm, er, glad you're here. I'm just sorry you had to witness that temper tantrum. We keep hoping she'll grow out of it…"

Rhea strode forward and held out her hand to the woman. "I'm Rhea Hansen-Chalmbers." She smiled, ruefully she imagined. "I'm Milo's long lost half-sister if you hadn't guessed."

The other woman smiled. "Kevyn. Milo, you should have done the introductions," she scolded mildly. "This is Tobias and our daughter—Johanna."

Rhea touched the baby on the head, then walked to the tweenie and took her hand. A current passed between them, surprising the child. "I'm happy to meet you. I'm your Aunt Rhea." She leaned closer, so only the child could hear. "I think you and I have a lot in common." Rhea nodded quickly as the child's eyes narrowed. "Yeah, that I can help you. Maybe not today, but when we get to know each other a little better."

"Yeah?" the girl challenged.

"Yeah," Rhea said. "Once you learn you can trust me. And your parents too. None of you know me. I want to change that."

The girl looked her over once again and seemed to make up her mind. "Prove it."

Rhea thought a moment, then stood with her back to the others and held out her glowing fingertips. A single silver spark erupted from the end of it. The child's eyes widened. "That's a promise," Rhea said. "Now, come introduce me to all these people."

An hour later, Rhea stood off to the side, watching family members mill around. Her brother and sister approached her and stood each to one side.

"A bit overwhelming?" Debra asked. "I'm crushed by

this, and I've known most of them all my life. I can't imagine what it's like for you."

"And I can't stand most of them," Milo muttered. "But if you repeat that, I'll deny it."

Rhea choked on her wine and glanced at her brother in time to see him give her a wink.

"I underestimated you," he said. "I'm sorry about that."

She said nothing but took another sip, with her brows raised.

"I heard what happened in court the day Dad died. What your mother said and didn't say. What you did." He shook his head. "Dad would have been proud of you."

Rhea didn't need a mirror to know her eyes had welled up. "You think?"

Debra linked an arm with hers. "It's making me feel all the more like a shit for not calling you when I said I would. Things were happening..."

"My daughter was happening," Milo said. "It consumed the whole family." He looked past Rhea to Debra. "Rhea saw a demonstration of Johanna's abilities. She handled it with aplomb."

"No one's ever said that about me before," Rhea replied with a laugh.

Milo shook his head. "You'd think I would have been prepared for it—I suffered the same when I was a kid. At least I know she'll grow out of it."

"Those were some difficult years," Debra agreed. "It started when Dad left. Mom couldn't handle it at all."

Milo groaned. "Do we have to talk about it now?"

Rhea tightened her hand on his arm. "Actually, yes. It seems we have that in common." She leaned closer. "Only, I never outgrew it. I want to try to help Johanna."

"Holy crap," Debra breathed. "Still? I mean, I know you're not that old, but you're out of your teens."

Rhea shrugged. "Yeah, just lucky that way."

Milo put his arm around his youngest sister. "If you can help my daughter, Kevyn and I will be forever grateful. We don't know what to do."

"I'll do what I can. I'm grateful to feel like a family member."

A tear escaped Debra's eye, and then another. "This is just the first day. I know you've gone through a rough few weeks."

Rhea blinked hard. "That pretty much describes it."

"Our firm is hiring," Debra whispered. "We'll understand if you don't want to, of course."

"But if you need anything to tide you over..." Milo smiled sadly. "I want you to know if your mother calls in your debts—we'll cover you. It's so unfair. For all his faults, Dad paid for our education. Pissed your mother off, but he did. I'm kind of surprised he didn't do the same for you."

"He'd had his first stroke by then. Couldn't really argue with my mother."

"Oh, Rhea, I'm so sorry," Debra said again. "All this time, I was angry with you—so foolish. I was jealous you had Dad all to yourself. We didn't know what it was like for you."

Rhea wiped her eyes with a shrug. "What doesn't kill you makes you stronger, right? I would be interested in interviewing. Judge Bloom said she also had a few leads for me. I'm going to call her next week. And so far, my mother hasn't called in the loan."

She looked from one to the other. "But it's nice to know I can count on you."

"There's also Dad's will," Milo said solemnly. "I'm prepared to be surprised. And possibly angry at the terms. I suppose you should be as well."

Rhea looked down. "I hadn't even thought about it. I

don't know how much influence my mother had over him or when the last one was written. She might get it all. And the way things are going, she'll marry her lover once his divorce is final, and then he'll be the beneficiary of her estate. I'm not expecting anything."

"We could fight it," Milo began, but Rhea shook her head.

"I don't want to bury my grief with greed."

"To use a really tired old saying, let's not borrow trouble," Debra said. "In the meanwhile, I'm for the bar. And by that, I mean the wine bar. Rhea, you look like you can use another glass. Milo, you in?"

"A glass of wine sounds perfect," Rhea said. "But let me check my messages. I felt one come through when I first got here, but was distracted."

"Don't be long." Debra kissed her cheek, then took her brother's arm and set off.

Rhea pulled out her phone, and her heart gave a lurch. There was one call, no message. Paul.

Chapter Thirty-Four

Paul

He walked into the laundromat-bar to meet his youngest brother. The cloying scent of fabric softener permeated the air while the thunk-swoosh of washing machines could be heard beneath the soft rock coming from ceiling speakers. He spied his Sammy nursing a beer at the bar.

"I've been looking for you all over town."

Sammy looked up, cringed, and looked away. "Berry t-told me not to talk to you."

"You too?" Paul sighed. "Man, I thought you would understand."

The bartender looked up from her phone and glanced at the two brothers before she returned to whatever it was she was looking at, a small smile on her lips.

"Keep it down," Sammy hissed. "D-don't get me thrown out of here. My s-stuff just went in the dryer."

Paul sat on the stool next to him. "Yeah, so you can keep mooning over her?"

Sammy rolled his eyes. "G-gimme a break, will ya?"

"Beer," Paul called to the woman. "Whatever's on tap."

She smiled as she set down her phone. Paul glanced at her. She was pretty, beautiful actually, in an exotic way. He could see why Sammy was crazy about her. But she did nothing for him. She wasn't Rhea. Not even close.

Sammy stuck out his chin. "I'm not gonna sit here and watch you get wasted."

"It's just one beer," Paul said as he pushed a five across the bar. "You're the guy with the cleanest clothes in town," Paul laughed and slapped Sammy on the back.

His brother moved away. "I mean it, Paul. You t-treated Rhea bad. I always thought you were better than that."

Paul stared into his beer. "Things change."

"Rhea didn't deserve it," Sammy lifted his mug. "You b-broke the Conrad code."

Paul cringed. "You don't know what happened."

Sammy's beer mug slammed down, and foam spattered the bar. "Actually, I d-do. You were a jerk, Paul. Jeeze, the woman j-just buried her father. Her m-mother turned her back on her. She's out of a job, and all b-because of you."

The dark-haired woman tossed Sammy a cloth but kept reading her phone.

"What? No. She hated that job."

Sammy mopped up the spill and set the rag aside. "Maybe, but she quit because of you. And now she's got nothing."

"What about me? I don't have so much," Paul said through his teeth.

"No? You've got four b-brothers…"

"Only one of whom is talking to me, and he's yelling."

"You've g-got Ma. A place to live. A truck. All sorts of new equipment, thanks to Rhea. Moe says he's been f-feeding you all sorts of work, plus a bunch of c-commissions. You've got Jenny and Annie and Berry, and they have your b-back even if they're not talking to you. So, don't compare yourself to her. Just don't because it's not the s-same."

Paul ducked his head. "You forgot one important thing. All that woo-woo stuff."

"Like that makes a d-difference," Sammy said under his breath. "Look at Moe. If he can be happy with Berry—no—think about Pete and Annie. Paul, you've got your head firmly up your ass."

Paul pushed the untouched beer away. "I don't know what to do. I messed up. Sammy, I've never been scared of anything in my life, but Rhea, what she can do, terrifies me."

Sammy snorted. "R-right. Nothing scares you."

"This does," he said under his breath.

His brother's mouth dropped open. "You're s-shitting me."

Paul shook his head.

"Wow," Sammy said. "Okay then. So, what terrifies you more?"

"Huh?"

"Rhea, or her power?"

"What? They're one in the same."

Sammy let loose with a sigh. "If Rhea didn't have her superpower, would there be any question?"

"Fuck no. I love her."

Sammy cringed. 'Yeah, yeah. No need to use f-foul l-language."

Paul laughed and took his first sip of beer.

"So, if she didn't have this, er, ability, there'd b-be ro problem, right?"

"Right. But that's not a fair question. She does. And she will. And I don't know if I'll wake up one day with my head chopped off 'cause she had a bad dream and made a knife…"

"That's crap. She l-loves you, you b-bozo. She wouldn't do that to you."

"Yeah, well, what if I pissed her off enough? It's not like she doesn't have a temper."

Sammy shrugged. "So, d-don't piss her off."

"Then I wouldn't be me," Paul explained, clearly exasperated.

"So, always m-make up before going to b-bed."

Paul shook his head. "You don't understand. She'll always have the upper hand. She's got the power. I've got nothing to counter it."

"Paul, you're an idiot."

"Tell me something I don't already know," he said miserably.

"You've got l-love. Isn't that supposed to conquer everything?"

There was a long silence as the dryers hummed. "You've been reading too many of Berry's books," Paul replied.

"Maybe you haven't r-read enough of them," Sammy countered. "Because you're still an ass, and Rhea's still alone. You've g-got everything you wanted, and she ended up with n-nothing. Think about that."

"Sam..."

"Don't tell me I'm too young to know b-better or give me that fear crap. Plenty of us walk around every day, scared of shit. But we get up and walk around and get over it, or by it, or whatever it is we do in order to l-live our l-lives and find whatever it is that m-makes us happy. You're not so different. So, you're s-scared of something for the first time in your life. Boohoo, you big baby. So, s-something isn't easy for the first time in your life. Get over yourself. Stop whining and making everyone miserable. Rhea's got something up on you—big effing deal." He set his beer down and spun to Paul, gripping his good shoulder. "For just o-one minute, how exactly do you think Rhea feels right now, huh? You're so busy feeling sorry for yourself, did you even think about her? For all you know, she can use her superpowers for the good, not just bad."

Paul shook off his arm and spun away.

"Crap, Paul. Get a hold of yourself. Just give in to it. Go back to her. Make love to her. Make b-babies. Stop torturing yourself. Just get out of here and start to live again. Maybe I have read too many of Berry's books, but I think you've watched too many h-horror movies, and they've corrupted your mind."

Sammy drained his beer and slammed it on the countertop one more time. "Now, if you'll excuse me, my load's done, and I'm going home."

He tipped his cowboy hat to the woman behind the bar and walked to the other side of the building.

"Shit," Paul muttered.

"Your brother is a wise man," the woman said. "Very sweet man. And sensitive."

Paul looked up. "Ah jeeze, not you too?"

She smiled at him and shrugged. "You men, you make your own trouble and want others to fix it. Not good. Only you can. You have woman trouble, yes?"

"Nothing you would understand."

She smiled again. "Perhaps yes, perhaps not. But if you love her, make a gesture." She held up her phone. "Text. Reach out, yes?"

Paul rose and looked at his feet. "Yeah, maybe. I'll think about it."

She nodded and went back to staring at her phone. Only Paul looked at her a little closer. She might have looked liked she was staring at her phone, but Sammy, pulling his tighty whities out of the dryer, was right in her line of sight. For the first time in days, Paul smiled.

He stepped into the sunshine and got in his truck. As usual, he tossed his wallet and phone to the seat next to him, but this time he picked up the phone once more and looked at it. He opened the texting app and stared at it, scrolling through all the texts he and Rhea had shared over the past few months. The one that came up most frequently were one word texts: Gym?

Paul wasn't certain how long he sat there just looking at his screen. He knew Sammy had come out with his basket of clean laundry and driven away. Other vehicles came and went. The woman who ran the place came to stare at him out the door, but she just smiled and walked away.

The sun seemed to have moved in the sky before he keyed in a short message, hitting send before he could over-think it. For the first time in days, his inner panic seemed to drain away.

He hadn't been so nervous since he'd tried to ask Rhea to the senior prom and was kicked to the curb. Served him right, cocky bastard that he was. Not that he was any less cocky—actually, not true. He was a hell of a lot less cocky and a whole lot more scared.

What if she didn't show?

Or what if she did but ignored him?

What if she came with another guy?

Or what if she came alone, gave him what-for in front of everyone and left, never to be seen again?

Rhea hadn't responded to his text. He wasn't about to humble himself by sending a follow-up. She would, or she wouldn't. That would be it. Or it wouldn't. If she didn't show, he'd try again. And again. Until she agreed to talk.

He stood outside the gym doors and hefted his bag to his good shoulder. He'd be smart and work the injured one slowly. No more showing off for the girls—one girl. He'd learned that lesson.

Several times over.

Couples, singles, even a group of teenagers passed as he took up space on the sidewalk. The sun was sinking, and a cold wind picked up. With a deep breath, Paul walked into the world he knew so well.

He looked around. Rhea wasn't on one of the treadmills

by the front desk, or on an elliptical. He'd been an idiot and forgot to look for her car in the lot. He was just about to turn around when he spotted her in the back with the weight equipment. Her back was to him, but he'd know her silhouette anywhere. except it looked like she'd lost weight. And he didn't much like the guys on either side eyeing her when they thought she wasn't looking. Worse, he knew both of them. They knew she was his.

Or was.

Crap.

She was ignoring them both. *That's my girl.*

One of the guys spotted him and nudged the other. Paul gave them a terse 'hey there' guy nod.

Where to begin? Didn't want to make it look obvious he was checking her out. But he'd need to lay claim soon.

Ever act like a caveman? he asked himself. *Hell yeah, today,* he answered.

First, to stretch. He could do that near her. But not too near. He needed to warm up before working the weights.

With his bag stowed, Paul came out swinging his arms around to loosen them. He began his floor stretches, angled just enough away so he could see Rhea from the corner of his eye. And she could see him. Wouldn't be able to avoid seeing him. Unless she moved.

Crap. She got off the damned bench and headed for the rowing machines. That would put her clearly out of his line of sight. And her back would be to him too.

Paul finished the first part of his routine and casually nodded to an acquaintance before he headed to the free weights. He took twenty pounds less for his bad side. Plenty of time to work up to what he used to be able to press. No rush. And from there, he could see her clearly, only she'd already moved to the abdominal crunches. Hell, when had she mastered those? And what was up with her tight spandex? He liked when she wore baggy sweats and tee-shirts. He didn't want all those guys ogling her. Maybe she did. Or maybe she wanted Paul to be ogling her. That was more like it.

Some bozo was standing there waiting for her to finish, crowding her as if to rush her. She smiled up at him when he started wiping down the machine as soon as she was done. Oh, hell no. That was way too gentlemanly, or was he just anxious to get his own crunches started? Why didn't this gym have a no-flirting policy?

Rhea drifted out of sight, and his weights hit the floor with a clang. Paul cursed as eyes all over the gym were focused on him. He gave a shrug with a grin, hoping at least Rhea was one of those looking. But if she did, he'd missed it. Damn it.

He finished up, wiped down the machine, and put his hands on his hips, deciding what he would do next. He got a prickly feeling and turned slowly as if scoping out available equipment. She was over on the stair-master now, staring up at the TVs as if she hadn't just been staring at his ass. Yeah, right.

Well, if she was going to be there for a while—and he knew she would be, he'd just mosey on over to the jungle gym. Plenty to do over there, and all she'd need to do was drop her gaze every now and again to see him working out. Sweating. Flexing his muscles. Yeah, that was it. Oh man, this was going to be almost too easy.

He started with the pulleys. Straight out, cross his body, overhead. Lots of muscle play there for her to see. Yeah, he was straining, but it wasn't so bad. Wasn't hurting anything.

That done, he moved to the platform and started his jumps up and back. Good for showing off his butt. He knew she liked that from all the times she clutched it when they made love. Let her get a good look at what she was missing.

On his tenth jump, he nearly missed, scraping his shin, so it hurt like a bugger. Enough of that. He moved on to the kettle weights, taking the thirty-pounder in both hands, swinging it up and down through his legs in a controlled arc. Damn, that baby got heavy in a hurry. He finished his reps and moved on to the ropes, then heaved a weighted ball into a net and caught it, twice as many with his good arm as with his bad. No use in hurting himself.

Was she looking? Hard to tell. Her eyes seemed really focused on the TVs above. But she wasn't listening. She wore no earbuds, and she didn't seem to be reading anything. Yeah, she was checking him out but being cool about it. At least no one was bothering her.

Paul put the ball away and looked around. There was a treadmill next to Rhea that was just standing there, doing nothing. But he hated running. And that would be a little too obvious. Maybe today they'd just see each other again. Make the moves next time. Talking could wait.

Chicken, his conscience screamed. Sammy's childhood taunt of *bwawk bwawk bwawk* filled his mind. He eyed the giant structure with the ladder across the top. It was for doing hand over hands. But he used to be able to sprint across those babes. He wondered if he still could. Nothing wrong with his balance. He had no fear of heights. So he'd broken his shoulder doing that when he was a kid. He wasn't a child anymore. He was smarter now. More agile. Older. Crap.

He turned to glance at Rhea. He almost caught her, but damn, she was fast, staring up at the screen. He went back to the yellow and red bars. It was almost as if they were calling his name.

Now or never. Paul went up to them, spit in his hands,

and began to climb.

Chapter Thirty-Five

Rhea

What is that idiot doing now? He's going to hurt himself. Why do I care? Why am I still lusting after him? He broke my heart, the big jerk. I shouldn't have come. I need to get off this thing. I'm dying here. I haven't worked out this hard in months. Ever. That's it, I'm getting off now. He's on his own.

But Rhea kept on stepping, gripping the handrails, and watched her heart rate rise on the monitor as Paul climbed the ladder until he was balanced on top of the structure.

"You idiot," she said under her breath as she watched him wobble, then rise to his feet. From the looks of things, his balance wasn't what it once was, for he wavered back and forth as he straddled two rungs, searching for his center. He stopped and stretched his arms overhead, steadying himself on the ceiling struts.

"Get down get down get down," she mouthed. "Please, get down now. Before you hurt yourself. Paul, get down, and all will be forgiven."

"Hey, you see that guy up there?" the woman on the stairs next to her exclaimed. "Damn, he looks good, doesn't he? I didn't know you could do that."

Rhea's heart was crammed too far up her throat to reply.

Paul slowly brought his arms down and held them out. He took a step. Then another. Her heart didn't stop its frantic battering of her ribs.

"Damn, he's hot," the woman whispered.

"He's a jerk," Rhea managed.

She could feel the other woman's gaze on her. "You

know him?"

Rhea nodded.

"So, he's stupid? Or hung up on himself or something?"

"Something," Rhea breathed, unable to take her eyes off him.

Paul had made it to the far end of the ladder and was slowly turning, weaving and bobbing as he did.

"Come on, get down. You proved yourself," Rhea muttered.

But Paul wasn't done. He regained his balance and waved to those watching him, a huge smile on his face, turned and ran the length of the ladder. Like he was born to do it. Damn, he did look good.

The woman beside her whistled her appreciation. That caught Paul's attention, and suddenly their gazes met. Held. What she'd avoided for the past hour happened, and suddenly, she could not breathe. She smacked the stop button and stood there, her chest heaving as their gazes deepened. And heated. And all of a sudden, Paul, standing still for so long, seemed to lose his balance. His arms wind-milled up and around. As if in slow motion, he teetered too far and began to fall.

He reached for the ceiling, but he was already too far away. And it was his left side. He didn't have the range of motion he needed, and so he began to fall, inch by inch. And never did his gaze fall from Rhea's.

"OhmygodohmygodohmyGod," the woman beside her chanted.

Rhea blocked it out. She gripped the hand bars of her machine and willed her attention to the man up there. Willed it with everything she had and more. The energy was almost visible as she reached out and slowed his descent just enough for him to grab a nearby support bar with his right arm. His body swung in a crazy spiral until it stopped, and he could hold on with both hands, get his feet on another rung, and brought himself to the floor.

Rhea hung her head, panting heavily. She could not bear to watch any longer.

"Jeeze, he's got good reflexes. Hey, you okay?" the woman next to her asked. As if death hadn't been floating in front of her eyes for the past five seconds.

"Yeah, I'm fine. I think I overdid it on this thing." Rhea climbed down. "Thanks for asking."

"You don't look too good," the woman said. "No offense."

Rhea managed a smile. "None taken."

She wiped down the machine and climbed to the floor. Looking down, she headed for the locker room.

"Rhea, wait."

The warm hand on her elbow was as familiar as sunshine. She stopped, her breath held. Waiting.

"Was that you?" came a hoarse whisper.

She shook her head, unable to look up. He turned her and held her by her shoulders.

"It. Was. You helped me over there."

"Paul, I…"

His hands gripped harder, and she finally lifted her head to see his face.

"You saved my life," he said under his breath.

She shook her head again, and he shook her lightly. "It's true. You did. Rhea…"

"Consider us even," she said and wrested away from him.

"Rhea!" he called, but she raced into the women's locker room.

She sat there, shaking for what felt like hours. Tears came and went. She was wracked with shudders of sorrow, cold, and other unnamable emotions. Other

347

women came in and left. She could feel them looking at her, curiosity, disdain, confusion in their gazes. She ignored them all.

At long last, she took a deep breath. Paul would have gone by now. He must have.

Rhea pulled her jacket from her locker and checked her phone. There were three messages, all about jobs she applied for. And one from her mother. She deleted it without listening.

Rhea washed her face and hands. Her eyes were red from weeping, so when she pulled out her car keys, she slipped on her sunglasses as well and readied herself to walk out.

Paul was standing there as if he'd been planted.

"We have to talk," he said softly.

She shook her head and tried to walk on.

He grabbed her arm. She stopped and looked at him, lifting her arm, her fingers in a fist. She spread them, and he let go. "Rhea, we need to talk."

"If you need to tell me something to make yourself feel better, you can save it," she replied, her voice rusty.

"It's not about me."

"Is it going to make me feel better?"

He had the grace not to smile. "I don't know. I wish I did. I want it to, but…"

"But what?"

"It's going to depend on you."

She looked away and then back into his earnest eyes. "Why do I have the feeling I'm not going to get rid of you until you've had your say?"

"You know me pretty well," he said with a small laugh. "Coffee?"

She brushed past him and tossed over her shoulder, "I want hot chocolate. And a cookie. A chocolate chip cookie.

348

None of that oatmeal raisin crap. That's breakfast food."

Paul

A world of muted grey suddenly sprang into color. Paul hurried after the woman he loved, catching up in time to open the doors. A brilliant sunset was showing off in the west. Rhea stopped to look at it, and so too did Paul. She strode on without a word, and he had to skip ahead to get to the coffee shop door first.

He pulled out a chair at the small table by the window. "One marshmallow or two?"

She lifted one brow.

He smacked his head. "Two. Of course. I'll be right back."

He stood in line and resisted the urge to turn and gaze at her but once. She was listening to her phone—apparently, some calls came in during her workout, or her rest—or whatever t was she'd been doing while he sweated out his wait.

"One coffee and one hot chocolate. Large. And two chocolate chip cookies, please." He paid and ran back to the table in time to see her put her phone away.

"Here." He spread a napkin for her and set her cookie down, along with a second napkin and her paper cup. He'd forgotten to put cream in his coffee, but he wasn't about to fix it. Not when he had so much to say. He just didn't have a clue where to begin.

"Thank you," she said quietly. She took the lid of her cup and blew the steam from the surface. "What did you want to say?"

Good question. Excellent question. "I, er…"

"I don't have all night, Conrad."

"Okay. Sorry. I wanted to apologize."

Her gaze didn't waver.

"I wanted to say I was sorry for, er, um..."

Her foot started tapping under the table.

"For being a jerk," he burst out.

Her eyes were level with his. "Keep going."

Paul swallowed the suddenly huge lump in his throat.

"For running away."

Another nod.

"And for not being there when your father died." He spun the cup in his hands, and some coffee splashed out, burning his thumb. "I tried, but when I went to go to you, some woman took you away."

"My sister."

It was his turn to nod. "Okay. Good. I'm glad you were with family."

"My brother was there too," she said.

He looked up.

"He has a daughter. She's a lot... a lot like me."

Paul dipped his chin.

"Her mother's black, her father white. And her hands..." Rhea held hers out. "Let's just say her hands are just like mine."

"She's lucky then."

Rhea looked at him sharply.

"Lucky she has someone to understand her." He swallowed hard. "I get the feeling no one understood you."

She winced.

"Including me."

"You had your moments."

"I thought so. I didn't know how wrong I was. I see that now."

She sat back. "There were things I didn't dare tell you."

"Because you feared my reaction."

She nodded.

"As you should have."

The silence went on a long while.

Rhea snapped the lid on her drink and got up, leaving her cookie behind. "Okay. Apology offered. Since it won't cost me anything, I'll tell you I've accepted it. Now, if you'll excuse me, I have some calls to return tonight. I need a job, and I need it soon."

He rose. "Rhea…"

She looked at him, saw right to his heart. "What? Will it make you feel better to grovel? You'd better get started because I've got to go."

Paul never felt more at a loss in his life. "This isn't going as I planned."

Her fists met her hips. "Really? Did you expect me to be grateful you've acknowledged me? Or maybe a kiss to make everything all better, and we pick up where we left off?"

"Yes, I mean no. Rhea…"

She looked away, gathering her things. "I've indulged you. You've said your piece. Now I want to leave."

"I still love you."

She stilled. And turned. "Really?"

He nodded. Hopeful. Terrified.

She pressed her lips together. "Well, bully for you." With that, she picked up her gym bag and slung it over her shoulder.

"Don't tell me you don't feel anything for me," he said to her back. "You just saved my life, for crying out loud."

She whirled to him. "I did save your fool neck. Because you were showing off, and someone needed to keep you from harming yourself. But you know what, I'd have done that for anyone." She set her bag down and confronted him. "You walked out on me. You left me when I needed you most. And now you feel regretful because it's making you feel bad about yourself. So, you're throwing me a

351

bone. But I have news for you, Conrad. A few pretty words and a cup of cocoa isn't going to make it all better. Now, if you'll excuse me, I need to get out of here."

She picked up her bag and brushed past him so fast, he couldn't be sure the glistening on her cheeks were tears or his imagination. He slumped back into his seat, daring those around him to continue to stare. With a growl, he gathered up their things and threw them in the trash. "Shit," he said under his breath. "Shit, shit, shit."

Chapter Thirty-Six

Rhea

Marion was waiting in her Mercedes at the foot of Rhea's driveway.

The sight of that big, black car was almost enough to make her turn around and go back to the gym, back to Paul's fumbled apology. Anywhere but home.

Rhea stopped her car in the middle of the quiet street and banged her head on the steering wheel. Her one and only sanctuary had been invaded. Best to get this over with.

Rhea pulled into her driveway and took her time getting her gym bag out of the backseat. She set it on her front stoop, and when her mother still hadn't gotten out of the car, she walked down the drive and stood there. She was making a habit of posing with her hands on her hips, but for the life of her, there was nothing else for her to do.

Marion rolled down the window. "May I come in?"

"You mean now that I had to walk to get you? Still with the power plays, Mom?"

"I didn't mean, er, that wasn't my intention."

"No? I guess it comes naturally."

"I didn't come here to argue with you."

"I didn't invite you. In fact, the few times I did, you were too busy to come."

"I'd rather not have this discussion in the middle of the street."

Rhea stood back. "You have five minutes."

A family rode by on their bikes, two parents with toddlers strapped into seats behind. Rhea waved, and they waved back.

"Is that any way to speak to your mother?" Marion asked loud enough for them to hear.

"Oh, nicely done. Since you can't belittle me in front of the firm, you're going to do it where I live."

"Rhea..."

But she was already striding up the driveway. She waited by the door as her mother made her way in her high heels. Rhea closed the door with not quite a slam, but not a quiet one.

"I've had a shitty day, so say whatever it is you have to say and get it over with."

"You're not the only one who's had a shitty day. Or week. Or month."

Rhea closed her eyes and counted to ten. She flexed her fingers. Odd, but there was no tingling. Maybe she used up her day's worth of energy floating Paul to safety.

Rhea strode into her kitchen and got herself a glass of water, regretting having left the hot chocolate behind. But her stomach was rebelling, so perhaps it was all for the best.

The tap-tap of Marion's shoes followed her in. "This is much nicer than I expected."

"Are you here to swap decorating tips?"

"I don't recall you ever speaking to me in that tone before. I can't say I like it."

Rhea stared at her mother. "After the way you've treated me, turning your back on me at Dad's funeral, not listing me in the obituary..."

"That was an oversight. Your name was in my notes..."

"Let me guess. You had Junior see to the arrangements."

Her mother had the grace to blush.

"Are you here to tell me you had the reading of Dad's will, and he left me nothing? Feel free to gloat."

"Rhea, why are you making this so difficult for me?"

"Because I can," she shot back. "This is my house. I didn't invite you. I don't work for you. As far as I know, this might be the last time I ever have to talk to you."

Marion's hand went to her heart. "How can you speak to me like that?"

Rhea folded her arms against her chest. "I just told you. I'm done. I'm angry. I'm hurt. I'm unemployed and waiting for the financial hammer to come down. What the hell do you expect?"

"I didn't bring you up to…"

"You're right. You didn't bring me up at all. Nurses and nannies did. You, as you well know, were absent. Until I was of use to you when you worked me to the bone. But no more. No. More. So, you have used up four of your five minutes. Tell me why you're here, and then you can leave."

"Rhea, you're all I have."

"You have the firm. You have Tony. And his ratfink son."

"Tony left me. Your father died, and my lover left me."

Rhea was momentarily speechless. And then she laughed. "Oh, that's rich. And you came to me for comfort?"

"Shouldn't a mother expect that of her child?"

"Perhaps another mother and daughter. But not us. You forfeited that right a long time ago."

Marion sank into a kitchen chair and covered her eyes. "I deserve that, I suppose."

Rhea was silent, watching her mother. A moment later, Marion looked up, dry eyed. "Have you nothing to say?"

The daughter shrugged. "You might think I'd feel a little sympathy, but you see, my own heart's been broken, and I only have enough pity left for myself."

"The merger of the firm is not complete. It looks like it

never will be. You can come back now."

Rhea laughed. "Really? You're here to offer me a job?"

Marion blushed again. "Is that so terrible?"

"I'm not interested."

"But the firm—your father's legacy..."

"Do you really not get it? I put in tens of thousands of hours for you with no thanks but plenty of criticism. You went forth with a merger against my advice and ended up with huge debt because of it. You took the side of your lover and his son against me—for which I don't remember you asking my forgiveness. And you think I'm going to run back to that for more of the same?"

"It wasn't that bad..."

Rhea slammed her plastic cup on the table so hard, it cracked. Her mother flinched. "Don't try to gaslight me. It was bad. You know it was bad. Do you really think I'm that big a fool with so little self-confidence that I'd accept it?"

"Rhea, you're my daughter."

"Biologically, yes."

Marion dropped her face into her hands. "I can't believe you are so ungrateful. I'm offering to make you a partner. You're not even thirty."

"What's this really about, Mom? Did you get a glimpse of Dad's will? Are you trying to maintain control over the firm by coercing me?"

Marion stood. "Yes. All right damn it, yes. I am. I can't do this by myself. I'm too old, too tired. My reputation..." She sank back to the seat. "My reputation has been tarnished. I need you, Rhea. I need your help to get it back."

Rhea looked at her mother, who was at last honestly sobbing. Rhea handed her a wad of paper towels before she went to stand on the other side of the room. Marion looked up, her face streaked with tears and despair.

"I'm not coming back."

"If I apologized? Would you then?"

"Would it be an honest apology?"

"You ungrateful brat," her mother spat as she rose. "That's the thanks I get for coming all the way over here. And after the phone call, I just had while waiting for you from… that man… your boyfriend can go rot in hell for all I care."

Rhea's heart thudded. Paul had spoken to her mother? "Paul called you?"

Marion nodded as she blotted her face. "He did."

"What did he want? What did you say to him?"

"Oh, sure. Now you want to talk to me."

"For crying out loud, Mom, if you want to make things better between us, can't you give in one damned inch for once in your life?"

"Fine. He wanted my permission to marry you. As if I'd give it to him. That low-life nothing. He wouldn't make you happy. He's poor and happy to be that way. No ambition. No drive. Maybe he's good looking. He dresses up well and makes a good impression. No doubt he'd make you happy in bed, but there's more to life than sex and good looks. Looks fade, and sex is just sex. He wants to use you. He wants your money, your prestige. He wants what's mine."

"What of yours? What does he want?"

"He wants your share of the firm. My firm. What your father left you. He wants that. The money—the connections."

Rhea's heart skipped a beat. Paul called her mother after that scene in the coffee shop? To ask permission to marry her? She clenched her fists. "He said that?"

"He's too slick for that. All he wanted, he said, was to marry you."

Rhea sank to the floor, her forehead on her knees. "After I just left him?"

Marion looked sharply at her. "What are you saying?"

"I just left him. I rejected him. Said he was selfish."

"Well, obviously he's playing a deeper game. I don't even know how he got my private number." She grabbed her purse. "The will's being read Wednesday. One o'clock. You need to be there. And think about my offer. It's good until the end of the week. If you say no, I'm looking for another partner."

"You can't without my permission. Not if I control half the firm. You can't do anything without my approval."

Her mother shot her a dirty look, scoffed, and fled.

Rhea remained on the floor. "Well, I'll be damned." She looked at the shards of plastic beneath the table. She held out her hand. "If I could lift a man this way, I can clean up this mess." Her fingers gave a weak tingle and shook. The shards shifted, then dropped in a small pile.

Rhea stared at her hand and back at the mess. "I must just be too tired," she said to herself. "Paul still wants to marry me? Damn. I need to resist the urge to marry him to spite my mother." For the first time in a week, she laughed.

Rhea went to the reading of the will, along with her brother and sister. She received the bulk of her father's estate. His full share of the firm, plus money equal to the cost of her education, and then some. Her brother and sister each received portions of his estate. The property he and Marion held jointly went to her in full with the provision at least half would go to Rhea upon sale or her mother's death.

Rhea hadn't yet made up her mind about taking up her mother's offer to return to work, an offer that had been sent by certified mail.

Rhea set that aside along with the two offers she'd received and picked up her phone. "Berry? Hi. I'd love to come see you. Any chance you're free tonight?"

Berry

Okay, I'm going to pick up the story from here.

I was delighted Rhea called me. I'd finished the first draft of Saul and Thia's story and was taking a well deserved week off. We'd welcomed Paul back into the family once he told us what he'd done—calling the lioness in her den, as he put it. I shan't repeat what he told me Marion's reply was. t's not fit to print.

At any rate, when Rhea asked to come over, I jumped at the chance. And sometimes, what a person doesn't know won't hurt them. Or make them change their mind about coming for dinner. "Sure. We're having burgers, of course. Bring ice cream," was what I said.

You can bet I got off that call and made another one, pronto. Or six, as it were.

I made sure everyone was there early. I had Paul park around the corner at Pete and Annie's house so Rhea wouldn't get suspicious and turn around when she saw his truck.

Moe was out in the back, getting the fire started, and Mattie was bundled up, playing in the yard. She got one look at our visitor, scrambled to her feet, and flew into Rhea's arms. "I've *missed* you," my darling daughter cried.

Rhea held Matt e and the ice cream both until Moe came and relieved her of dessert. That man knows what he's about. He gave Rhea a peck on the cheek. "It is good to see you again," he said. "Don't let Mattie wear you cut. She's been growing like a bean sprout."

"I like beans," my daughter affirmed.

"And I've been working out," Rhea said with a laugh.

"She's not too big for me."

"Let me go get this in the freezer. Come inside through the front when you're ready. The kitchen's too busy. Wine?"

"Yes, please," Rhea said and rubbed noses with Mattie.

I was watching from the kitchen window of course. Everyone was behind me. I turned to Paul. "Showtime, big fella. Don't blow it."

I poked my head into the front parlor as Moe led Rhea inside. "Hey. I'll be out in a sec. Make yourself comfortable. Mattie, come in here and get cleaned up."

I ducked back into the kitchen before Rhea could reply. She sat in the loveseat, her back to the door. I handed Paul two goblets and a bottle and pushed him through the door.

Rhea went still when she heard his footsteps. She sprang from the seat, and the two of them stood there, looking at each other. Her light brown eyes huge, and her hands behind her back. "I didn't expect you."

He sauntered into the room slowly and nodded. "Berry's sneaky that way."

She peered around him. "Anyone else in there I ought to know about?"

"They're all hiding in the kitchen. They'll come out later. Depending."

She looked at him quizzically.

Paul handed her the glass and set the bottle down. "Depending on how it goes. With you. And me."

"Oh."

"Can we talk?" he asked. "I mean really talk. Just the two of us. No eavesdroppers."

Rhea nodded.

"Too bad it's too cold for the gazebo. Pete romanced Annie out there. Got an extension cord so they could stay out there all night with Berry's laptop."

Rhea rolled her eyes. "I'm not sure I want to know the details."

Paul shrugged. "It's part of the family lore. You stick around long enough, and you'll hear about it." He took her elbow in one hand, and the bottle and glasses in the other, and sat beside her on the love seat. There wasn't much room between them.

"If you don't mind, let's sit with our backs to the kitchen," Paul said. "I wouldn't put it past Berry to listen at the door."

(For the record, I can't. And I didn't bug the room, though I was tempted. I'm writing all this from what they told me afterward. And the parts they didn't tell, well, yes, I've made those up.)

"So, what do we need to talk about?" Rhea asked as she sipped her wine.

"I need to apologize again," Paul told her. "Properly. I'm really, really sorry for how I behaved. I was a jackass, though I never meant to hurt you." He hung his head. "I've made a big deal about my not being scared of anything, and the truth is, what Berry does—what you do, scares me to death. I'm afraid of that kind of power, mostly because I don't have anything to equal it."

Rhea gazed at him and nodded.

"You know how when my dad died young? I thought a man needed to be brave, not show any fear. So, that's what I've done. But the truth is, I've been scared shitless most of the time. And then I got scared other people would know I was scared, so it made me double down on the fearless crap. And then when you—when you showed what you could do, I kind of lost it. How could I compete with that? Or protect myself?"

He wrung his big, strong hands. "I love you, Rhee. I

have since we were kids. I fell in love with you again in high school when you wouldn't give me the time of day. I admired the crap out of you. I admired your strength, your smarts. I admired how composed you were, no matter what. How self-sufficient. I never knew what was going on at your house to make you that way."

"I didn't tell anyone," she said. "I couldn't."

"I know that now. I've been doing some reading about your gift. Most of it says what you can do is a bunch of bunk, but what I did find out is that it all comes from having deep emotions. Frustration, anger, needs that aren't met."

"Don't you dare start feeling sorry for me," she said fiercely. "I won't have it."

He laughed. "No. Admiration. Because you had this gift given to you…"

"Curse," she said under her breath. "I'm a freak, according to some."

Paul shook his head. "Gift. And it was incredible, but you had to hide it. And you did, for a long time."

"I wanted to tell you," she said in a low voice.

"I know that now. I'm sorry I turned into the world's biggest jerk. And that I stayed that way for way too long. You were hurting, but my fear kept me from going to you when you needed me most." He hung his head. "I can't change that. I would if I could, but all I can do is to try to make it up to you going forward.

"I love you, Rhee. I never stopped. If you can forgive me, I'd like for us to try again. Crap. I want us to get married and have a bunch of babies. And if their hands turn blue and can spin their own mobiles, well, hell, that's one less thing for me to do. And if you could teach them to change their own diapers, even better."

She gulped down her laugh. "You make it really hard to stay mad at you."

He grinned at her. "So, it's working?"

She shook her head, then nodded. "Yes, darn you."

"And you'll forgive me? And we'll get married and live happily ever after?"

"You think you can live with me and my woo-woo powers?"

Paul gulped. "It still scares me. But I love you more than I fear you. So, yes, I can do that."

"And my money? I just inherited a bundle."

"Well, I don't think that will interfere too badly. It's yours. I'm not used to having a lot, so I think you need to keep it away from me. I'd just mess it up."

Rhea grinned. "And what about my job? Whichever one I decide on, that is."

"I'm hoping you won't always work crazy hours. But if you do, I'll be the one to clean the house, do the laundry, the food shopping…"

"The cooking?"

"Now, don't go crazy. I've got the Conrad name to live up to. Men in this family do not cook. Well, just Moe—and just hamburgers. Because you know, fire. And he burns them."

Rhea laughed outright but then sobered. "And my mother?"

Paul winced. "Well, yeah. Her." He rubbed the back of his neck. "She seems to think I'm out to use you."

"You called her. Right after I left you."

He nodded.

"Why? I had no intention of ever talking to you again."

He gave her a small smile. "I know, but I was desperate. I love you so much. I wasn't ready to give up. I figured since I already had your father's approval…"

"So, you say."

He grinned at her. "I do. So, I thought I'd go for broke

and ask your mother. Just in case. So that when we spoke again—cause I knew we would—I'd have her permission too."

Rhea's mouth firmed. "She was waiting for me."

"Ambush?"

Rhea nodded. "Big time. She didn't mention your call. Until she needed to."

Paul sighed. "Yeah. I hope you don't mind my saying this, but your mother's a real piece of work. I mean, I know she's your mom, but if you don't mind, maybe we can only see her a few times a year?"

"I take it she didn't give you permission."

"Let's just say it seemed like she was having a really bad day."

Rhea laughed. "Yeah, and spreading it around with a shovel."

His hand crept over and took hers, holding it lightly but firmly. "Rhea. I might have mentioned I love you."

"Once or twice."

"And I'm hoping you still love me too."

She looked into his eyes. "As much as it pains me, yeah, I do."

He smiled. "So—maybe we can give this another go?"

"'Gifts' and all?"

"Darlin', I'll take you any way you are. I mean, hell, your gift saved my life. If I'd fallen on that shoulder one more time..." He shuddered. "There's no way the doc would be able to patch me up again. But that's not why I love you."

Rhea set down her wine, wound an arm around his neck, and sat in his lap. "I love you, you big lunk. There's no way I'd let you fall." She kissed him then, softly. "But do not *ever* make me do that again. I want to get married. Have babies with you. So, you need to be around. And yes, if their fingers glow blue and they can move things around, we'll deal with it." She glanced at the kitchen door. "I mean, honestly, if any family in the world could understand that, it's this one."

He snaked his arms around her waist. "You mean it, Rhee? You're not just planning your revenge?"

She shook her head and pressed another kiss to his lips. "I'm not that mean."

"Oh, babe," he said and pressed his face to her breast. "You've just made me the happiest man in the world."

He stood, almost spilling her. "Crap. But wait. This isn't how the script it supposed to go. I've got to do this the right way."

"What?"

"You sit here." He pressed her back to the cushion and got down on his knee. Then stood and fished something out of his pocket. He knelt before her once again. "Rhea Hansen-Chalmbers, will you please marry me?" He held out a diamond ring of no small size. "I spent almost the rest of my settlement money on this sucker, so I hope you like it."

Rhea looked at the dazzling diamonds in the platinum setting. She curled her fingers around his.

"Think it'll look good when your hands glow blue?" he asked with a twinkle in his eye.

"About that," she started. "See, since I caught you from falling, my powers seem—for lack of a better word—to be fading."

"What?"

She held out her hands. "I might have used it all up."

He grabbed one and turned it over. "You mean, I put myself out on the line like that for nothing?"

"I don't need a ring to have you prove your love for me or mine for you. And that diamond's too big. We'll return it for a smaller one. That money is yours, and who knows when you'll need it." She lifted him to his feet, sat him down, and resumed her place on his lap. "Besides, I'd really rather you made me a house full of furniture. That's something you can put your love into, and that will remind me of you every morning and every evening."

Paul looked at the ring before slipping it into his pocket. "You really don't like it?"

She shook her head with a smile. "Too gaudy." She kissed him. "I like clean lines. Simple things." Another kiss. "Maybe you'll make us a bed first? I'm tired of sleeping with my mattress on the floor. That's what I want as an engagement gift."

Paul kissed her then—kissed her with all the love and longing he'd been storing up for years. "I'll do that for you, Rhee. But first, we kiss."

Epilogue

Berry

So, here goes the happily ever after part, and then we're done.

Rhea and Paul got married as soon as they could. Judge Patel did the honors in my front parlor. The whole family attended, minus Rhea's mother. She was invited, but when the bride and groom refused to acquiesce to demands for a big society wedding, she excused herself to sulk in the arms of her new boyfriend. Somewhere in Paris, I believe.

Rhea sold her father's interest in the firm to her brother. I understand there are frequent fireworks, but that's none of my concern, given that Rhea didn't go back. She's currently working as an advocate for battered women and their children, and while the work can be grim and doesn't pay much, she's never been happier as she's finally able to put her powers to good use. And yes, she does represent me, Moe, and the others off to the side when we need it.

Paul's business continues to thrive. Things haven't gotten too big too fast, and that's just the way he likes it. Fame and fortune were never his goals. Slowly but surely, he's filling their house with one of a kind pieces of beautiful, unconventional, functional furniture. And yes, he made the bed first.

As for the rest of us—Saul and Thia's book is done and with the publisher. I'm working on the next, still noodling around with the plot and characters. What I really need to do is to give Sammy a boot to finally get his romance underway. He's proving to be the most stubborn of the Conrads. Or the object of his affections is. But I have some ideas. I'm thinking of a spoiled youngest brother and an international woman of mystery as a starting point. They meet. Have family issues… What do you think?

That wraps things up, at least for now. Paul's been hinting that he's trying to convince Rhea to start a family. And that's gotten a certain gleam in Moe's eye that I'm doing my best to squelch. I say Joey and Pete need to have a second before I go for a third. We'll see how that goes. I'll keep you posted.

The End

Just So You Know

A Novel by Solange DewBerry

A Prologue.

"Where's Sammy?"

A distracted chorus of "Huh?" "What?" "Hmmm?" and "I dunno," came from the four boys sprawled on the beach blanket, reading comic books and playing in the sand.

"Where is your brother? Samuel. Four years old. Short. Cute. Looks just like the rest of you. You know, the one I asked all of you to keep an eye on?" Rosemary Conrad asked a second time. It wasn't so much the words as the maternal tenor that finally got her elder four sons' attention.

Moe, the eldest, looked around. "He was here a minute ago. Joey, you were supposed to go down to the water with him."

"Paul and Petey wanted to," Joey said, an air of concern tinging his voice as he stood to scan the crowded beach.

A murmur grew from the shoreline, where a crowd was staring out at the water.

"He made friends with some kids," Paul replied, scrambling to his feet as did the rest of them. "The parents said we didn't need to watch him. So, we came back here."

"You trusted your baby brother to strangers?"

The boys' shoulders went up to their ears. "They were grownups," one said, as if that explained everything. "They said they'd watch him."

Rosemary dropped the tray of hamburgers, sodas, and chips, her hands numb as the panic tore through her. "Strangers? Water?" she gasped, her chest heaving as she turned to the sea. "My baby," she sobbed and pelted across beach blankets and sandcastles mindless of the chaos she left in her wake. "Sammy!" she hollered. "Sammy. Samuel Conrad, you better be okay, or I'm gonna kill you—after I wallop your brothers. Sammy, oh Sammy…"

She splashed into the water, her shoes and dress soaked in moments as she watched a lifeguard paddling hard through the rough surf. The crowd around her was silent, but for a man holding a trembling woman. "It's not my fault," he said over and over again. "The boy said he could swim."

Rosemary glared at the two, memorizing their faces. "He's four. You trusted a four-year-old when he said he could take on these waves?" As one, they met her gaze, and hugging a small child, stepped back into the crowd.

"Damn it, I never should have left him," she told herself. "Never should take my eyes off a single one of 'em." And whether it was sea spray or tears she wiped from her face, she didn't care, for the guard had reached the tiny speck floating out in the rough surf and laid him on the flat board, strapping him in despite the crashing water. By that time, another guard reached them, and together they hauled the small body back to shore.

Rosemary waded out to reach them, almost swamped by the waves, barely hearing the sobs of her other four boys as they huddled together in the sand. "Sammy, my baby," she cried.

"You the boy's mother?" one of the guards asked as the other hauled the blue, limp body onto the sand and turned him over to watch water drain from his nose and mouth.

She nodded. "I went to get food. The others were watching him..."

"We'll do our best," the guard said and turned to help her partner as they began to compress that small chest, then held his nose and breathed into him. A four-year-old chest. A tiny, helpless body with two large adults working over him. Behind her, the surf crashed, and gulls cried. The hot sun shone, but none of it could melt the ice in her veins.

Rosemary bit her knuckles to stifle her cries. "My boy. My baby. My poor baby. Sammy. Samuel. You have to be all right. I'm not giving you up, you hear me, child? They're not gonna to take you away from me like they did your father."

Four small boys swarmed her, wrapping eight skinny arms around her as she watched the guards work on her youngest child, each crying silently.

"Sammy," she whispered, despair almost winning, when there was a small cough and a wheeze, and then another cough and a small cry of "m-m-mommy."

With a sob from the depths of her soul, Rosemary shook off the hands that supported her and ran to her child, scooping him up and holding him until the guards feared she'd crack his ribs.

"Did you see me swim?" Sammy asked faintly, an element of pride coming through his gasps. "I went out as far as I can see." He shuddered and threw a cold, thin arm around her neck, holding her as close as he could. "It was dark. And cold. And then warm. And then I got here. And my chest hurts. Did you get my h-h-hamburger? C-c-can we go home n-n-now?"

"You—you—you..." She couldn't finish her thought as she pressed his small, chilled body to hers. "I saw you all right. And just so you know, you're *never* going near the ocean again. Do you hear me? Or a lake. Or ponds. No rivers or streams or gutters. You will walk around puddles on the sidewalk, and if there's water on the road, you will turn around and make a wide detour around it. No more baths for you. It's showers from now on, you hear me?" She whirled to find the rest of her brood. Slowly and clearly, she turned and made eye contact with each and every one of them. "All of you. Hear me? Showers. We are never, ever going to the ocean again. Mark my words."

About the Author

 Solange DewBerry (not her real name) would like you to believe she's a puzzle inside a conundrum inside an enigma. In reality, her mind is more like a junk drawer—a tangle of orphaned shoelaces, mysterious keys, dried up lint rollers and a slew of batteries, none of which is the size she's looking for. And an old roll of tape that she swears she threw away but keeps reappearing.

Solange lives in a small city on the eastern seaboard of North America, where she writes in a turreted room within her restored Victorian home, located on a shady, tree lined street. She shares the house with her handsome husband, two perfectly adorable and photogenic children, and a cat who has yet to appear in any of her stories.

Her superpowers are legendary and have only been enhanced since meeting her favorite Fairy Godmother, Mrs. Electra McGillicuddy.

In reality, Berry Conrad, (also not her real name) lives an ordinary life in the 'burbs of central Connecticut, USA, along with her attractive husband. She has two grown children in nearby orbits, and the memory of cats and dogs and goldfish past. She writes from whichever room suits her at the moment, none of them turreted. Alas, she doesn't know any Fairy Godmothers, though if one is lurking, she'd be happy to make her acquaintance. As for the superpowers… not telling.

If you enjoyed Rhea and Paul's story, please take a moment to leave me a stellar review, and tell all your friends what a great read it is. You can also contact me at SolangeDewBerry@gmail.com.

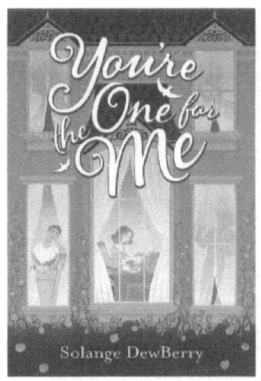

You're the One for Me

Berry Samuels lives a humdrum life, determined to avoid being noticed. It's easier that way. On the other hand. Berry's alter ego and writer of hot romances, Solange DewBerry, has the uncanny ability to make her characters come to life. That's rarely been a problem until she unexpectedly sets Trista and Brad, her just published hero and heroine, free. Despite her best efforts, Berry can't get her larger-than-life characters back in the pages of their book and can only watch as they traipse their way through the real world.

Maurice 'Moe' Conrad is a nice guy, eldest brother, and owner of Conrad Brothers Building. He plans to spend the next years' worth of weekends flitting a wrecked Victorian house when he meets a shy writer who sets his world on its heels. Berry may seem quiet and cute, but there's a sassy side to her he can't wait to see more of. The problem is she's got some ultra-beautiful but very weird friends who don't mind having their most intimate moments exposed for all to see. He's more than a little interested in Berry, but the last thing he wants is for everyone to know the details of his love life.

Can Berry corral the elusive Trista and Brad back into her book without Moe finding out their true nature? And just what would happen if he did?

https://www.amazon.com/Waitress-Doughnut-Shop-Solange-DewBerry-ebook/dp/B087C9BLVX/ref=sr_1_3?dchild=1&keywords=solange+dewberry&qid=1610401021&s=books&sr=1-3

Waitress in a Doughnut Shop

Here's the scoop:

Jenny Ellsworth works at The Sweet Shop, serving doughnuts and coffee. She's been in love with Joey Conrad for years. And Joey Conrad's been in love with Jenny Ellsworth for just as long. But Joey is dating someone else and can't bring himself to break up with her. It's one of his quirks that no one seems to understand but drives everyone crazy.

And then one day it seemed there was magic in the air. Or a really thick fog. Some days it's really hard to tell the difference. Into The Sweet Shop walked the most beautiful woman in the world, and just like that, Joey was dating Karma, or was he? Regardless, Jenny's heart was broken. It seemed the fog made it hard to tell truth from fiction because just days later, Jenny happened to meet Hank, a handsome knight in shining armor. He was more than willing to sweep Jenny off her feet, but she wasn't crazy for the man who was too good to be true.

And then Karma decided she wanted Hank while she waited for Joey to fall in love with her...

Needless to say, things got complicated. There were secrets, and revelations, and finally, well, you'll see.

Join Joey's sister-in-law, Berry Conrad, better known as the writer Solange DewBerry, as she tries to write her next novel, and help this fog-addled couple find true love.

https://www.amazon.com/Waitress-Doughnut-Shop-Solange-DewBerry-ebook/dp/B087C9BLVX/ref=sr_1_3?dchild=1&keywords=solange+dewberry&qid=1610401178&sr=8-3

Meetings in Moonlight

Pete Conrad is one of the good guys. A good looking man, he works hard, plays fair, wants to get married and settle down with the right woman. Except once he's found her, she changes her mind and tries to take him for everything he has.

Enter Ana.

She's the ethereally beautiful, soft spoken, innocent woman of his dreams. She's like someone right out of a novel and seems too good to be true. Which is exactly what she is.

Can true love flourish between a flesh and blood man, and the perfect woman from a nineteenth century love story? Follow author Solange DewBerry as she tells the tale of how her brother-in-law searches for his happily-ever-after.

https://www.amazon.com/Meetings-Moonlight-Solange-DewBerry-ebook/dp/B08J2BRX4Y/ref=sr_1_1?dchild=1&keywords=solange+dewberry&qid=1610401144&sr=8-1

Coming soon:
Just So You Know

www.ingramcontent.com/pod-product-compliance
Lightning Source LLC
Chambersburg PA
CBHW021428240626
47153CB00001B/75